CLIVILIUS
WHERE CREATION MEETS INFINITY

© 2024 Nathan Cowdrey. All rights reserved.
First Edition, 13 March 2024
ISBN 978-1-4461-1352-3
Imprint: Lulu.com

Step into Clivilius, where creation meets infinity, and the essence of reality is yours to redefine. Here, existence weaves into a narrative where every decision has consequences, every action has an impact, and every moment counts. In this realm, shaped by the visionary AI CLIVE, inhabitants are not mere spectators but pivotal characters in an evolving drama where the lines between worlds blur.

Guardians traverse the realms of Clivilius and Earth, their journeys igniting events that challenge the balance between these interconnected universes. The quest for resources and the enigma of unexplained disappearances on Earth mirror the deeper conflicts and intricacies that define Clivilius—a world where reality responds to the collective will and individual choices of its Clivilians, revealing a complex interplay of creation, control, and consequence.

In the grand tapestry of Clivilius, the struggle for harmony and the dance of dichotomies play out across a cosmic stage. Here, every soul's journey contributes to the narrative, where the lines between utopia and dystopia, creator and observer, become increasingly fluid. Clivilius is not just a realm to be explored but a reality to be shaped.

Open your eyes. Expand your mind. Experience your new reality. Welcome to Clivilius, where the journey of discovery is not just about seeing a new world but about seeing your world anew.

Also in the Clivilius Series:

Luke Smith (1338.201.1 - 1338.209.2)

Luke Smith's world transforms with the discovery of a cryptic device, thrusting him into the guardianship of destiny itself. His charismatic charm and unpredictable decisions now carry weight beyond imagination, balancing on the razor's edge between salvation and destruction. Embracing his role as a Guardian, Luke faces the paradox of power: the very force that defends also threatens to annihilate. As shadows gather and the fabric of reality strains, Luke must navigate the consequences of his actions, unaware that a looming challenge will test the very core of his resolve.

Paul Smith (1338.201.1 - 1338.209.3)

In a harsh, new world, Paul Smith grapples with the remnants of a hostile marriage and the future of his two young children. Cast into the heart of an arid wasteland, his survival pushes him to the brink, challenging his every belief. Amidst the desolation, Paul faces a pivotal choice that will dictate where his true allegiance lies. In this tale of resilience and resolve, Paul's journey is a harrowing exploration of loyalty, family, and the boundless optimism required to forge hope in the bleakest of landscapes.

Glenda De Bruyn (1338.206.1 - 1338.209.1)

Dr. Glenda De Bruyn's life takes a perilous turn when her link to a government conspiracy forces her to flee. Thrust into Clivilius, she confronts medical crises and hints of her father's mysterious past. As danger and discovery entwine, Glenda's relentless quest to uncover her family's secrets propels her into the unknown, where every clue unravels the fabric of reality as she knows it.

Kain Jeffries (1338.207.1 - 1338.211.2)

Kain Jeffries' life takes an unimaginable turn when he's thrust into Clivilius, far from the Tasmanian life he knows and the fiancée carrying their unborn child. Torn between worlds, he grapples with decisions concerning his growing family. Haunted by Clivilius's whispering voice and faced with dire ultimatums, Kain's resolve is tested when shadowy predators threaten his new home. As he navigates this new landscape, the line between survival and surrender blurs, pushing Kain to confront what it truly means to fight for a future when every choice echoes through eternity.

Beatrix Cramer (1338.205.1 - 1338.211.6)

Beatrix Cramer's life is a delicate balance of contradictions, her independence and keen intellect shadowed by her penchant for the forbidden. A master of acquisition, her love for antiques and the call of the wild drives her into the heart of danger, making her an indispensable ally yet an unpredictable force. When fate thrusts her into the clandestine world of Guardians, Beatrix must navigate a labyrinth of secrets and moral dilemmas. Caught in the crossfire of legacy and destiny, she faces choices that could redefine the boundaries of her world and her very identity.

Gladys Cramer (1338.201.1 - 1338.214.3)

In a world frayed by tragedies, Gladys Cramer seeks solace in wine, her steadfast refuge amid life's turmoil. Tethered to a man ensnared by duty and love, she stands at a pivotal crossroads, her choices poised to weave the threads of her fate. Each glass of wine deepens her reflection on the decisions looming ahead and the silent vows brimming with untold consequences. Amidst tragedy and secrets, with wine as her guiding light yet potential harbinger of misstep, Gladys's journey veers onto a path set for an inevitable collision.

4338.204.1 - 4338.209.3

JAMIE GREYSON

CLIVILIUS
WHERE CREATION MEETS INFINITY

"In the aftermath of choices, I navigate the fragile space between regret and an uncharted tomorrow. Can we mend what's broken, or are we destined to become casualties of the drift that has taken hold?"

- Jamie Greyson

4338.204

(23 July 2018)

THIRD BASE

4338.204.1

The monotonous drone of the dial tone filled the room, each ring a stark reminder of the void on the other end. It wasn't until Luke's automated voice broke through the silence that I felt a flicker of annoyance. "Hi, you've reached Luke Smith. I'm not available to take your call right now, but if you leave me your name and number, I'll be sure to call you back when I can." I didn't bother leaving a message; Luke would see the missed call and know it was me. The action of hanging up felt heavier than it should, a tangible symbol of the disconnectedness I was feeling.

Turning back to the present moment, I was immediately drawn to the elderly man who had become my sole focus. He stood at the reception counter, a figure from another era with his weathered skin and clothes that whispered of decades past. The man cleared his throat, a sound so harsh and jarring that it instantly pulled me from my thoughts. It was a dreadful hacking noise that echoed off the sterile walls of the reception area, making me instinctively recoil. I found myself inching my chair back with a subtlety that belied my inner disgust. The possibility of being on the receiving end of a phlegm projectile was all too real, especially on days like these when the staff was sparse and I, by some unlucky draw, ended up manning the reception almost single-handedly.

This wasn't the first time I'd found myself in such a predicament. The memory of a similar incident, where an irate Mr. Gangley had unleashed a torrent of coughing and wheezing in my direction, was vivid in my mind. The altercation had heated quickly, words flying as fast as the droplets of sickness. The climax of that encounter, a dark green gob of phlegm making its mark on the paperwork in front of me, was a memory that haunted me. I could still see it, almost feel it, as if the viscous substance was forever embedded not just on the paper but in my memory. I shuddered at the recollection, the visceral response to the memory as strong as if it were happening all over again.

    These moments, these interactions with people from all walks of life, were the bread and butter of my job at the care home. Yet, they were also the source of my greatest discomfort. The unpredictability, the sheer human element of it all, could be overwhelming. As I sat there, poised between past memories and the present situation, I couldn't help but feel a mix of resignation and determination. This was my job, after all. And despite the occasional unpleasantness, it was these very experiences that taught me patience, resilience, and a certain kind of empathy that can only be learned in the trenches of aged care.

    Engaging in the art of subtle provocation had become something of a sport for me, especially when it came to Mr. Gangley. There was a certain thrill in watching his face turn various shades of red and purple as he ascended the peaks of moral indignation. I had honed my skills to a fine point, knowing just which buttons to push and when to push them to elicit the most entertaining reactions. The staff and residents found these exchanges to be a source of great amusement, dubbing them their "very own soap opera." However, the last incident had left a bitter taste in my mouth, a reminder that sometimes the cost of entertainment was far too great. The memory of the unpleasant aftermath had firmly imprinted itself in my mind, serving as a cautionary tale against pushing the boundaries too far.

Jerked from my reverie by the sound of Mr. Gangley's voice, a mixture of irritation and anticipation bubbled inside me. "I would like..." he began, his voice a harsh, grating whisper that made you lean in to catch his words. He paused, a deep and unsettling breath rattling through his chest, as if gathering the strength to continue. "I would like to put in a complaint," he finished, fixing me with a look that was meant to convey the full weight of his displeasure.

I suppressed a sigh, schooling my features into an expression of solicitous concern. It was a dance we had done many times before, and despite my inner desire to dismiss him with a sharp retort, I played my part with a practiced ease. "What would be your cause for concern this time, Mr. Gangley?" I asked, my tone dripping with a patience I was far from feeling. Inside, I was rolling my eyes so hard I feared they might get stuck, but outwardly, I was the picture of professional interest.

Mr. Gangley's complaints were a daily ritual, as regular and predictable as the sunrise. They ranged from the mundane to the absurd, each one delivered with a gravitas that suggested the fate of the world hung in the balance. This morning's grievance had been particularly petty, even for him. The smeared handprint of a visiting child on the kitchen window had sparked his outrage, a blemish on his cherished view of the roses in the garden. "I look down at the roses in the garden from that window every day. I was very disappointed to say the least," he had lamented, his voice laden with a sense of betrayal as if the smeared handprint was a personal affront to his very existence.

The absurdity of the situation was not lost on me, and yet, I found myself grappling with a mix of emotions. There was a part of me that wanted nothing more than to dismiss his complaints outright, to tell him exactly where he could file his grievances. But another part, perhaps the part that took pride in my ability to handle even the most difficult of personalities, urged me to navigate the situation with grace. It was a delicate balance, maintaining the peace while not sacrificing my own sanity in the process.

The moment Mr. Gangley's voice sliced through my thoughts, I braced myself for yet another episode in our ongoing saga. "I spied a little mischief this afternoon. It caused me great bother." His words, laced with a peculiar mix of intrigue and indignation, immediately piqued my interest despite my attempts to remain detached. "Mischief," I echoed, my voice tinged with a curiosity I couldn't quite mask. "And what type of mischief might this have been?" I found myself genuinely intrigued by what could possibly ruffle the feathers of our most perpetually disgruntled resident.

As Mr. Gangley leaned in, the distance between us shrank to a mere breath. The air around him seemed to thicken, heavy with the odours of a life long-lived and choices perhaps best left unexamined. The aroma of old-age, mingled with stale tobacco and the unmistakable undertone of whiskey—contraband in our little community—wafted towards me. It was a cocktail of smells that told stories of past revelries, secret indulgences, and a stubborn refusal to fully submit to the rules of assisted living. Despite the assault on my senses, I tucked away the detail of the whiskey; it was a nugget of information that could prove amusing or advantageous in future encounters.

"The hanky-panky type," he confided in a whisper, his voice barely more than a husky breath. The phrase, so unexpectedly quaint and yet charged with implication, caught me off guard. "Oh. My. God. The hanky-panky type," I repeated, my voice involuntarily rising in volume, betraying my surprise and, admittedly, my amusement. The words hung in the air between us, an invitation to the unfolding drama that Mr. Gangley had inadvertently scripted.

His reaction to my echo was swift and filled with an austere reprimand. "I don't appreciate your tone, young man," he chastised, straightening himself with a dignity that his ninety-four years had not yet managed to erode. It was a posture of defiance, a testament to the spirit of a man who had lived through decades of change yet held fast to certain standards of decorum.

Out of the corner of my eye, I caught the muffled snickers of Ben and a new resident, whose name escaped me. Their barely contained laughter served as a reminder of the audience we had garnered, turning the exchange into a performance of sorts. The challenge of maintaining a professional demeanour while inwardly reeling from the absurdity of the situation tested my resolve. "My tone? What's wrong with my tone?" I found myself responding, adopting a feigned seriousness that mirrored Mr. Gangley's own. My words were a careful blend of respect and playful defiance, a balancing act that had become second nature in my interactions with the residents.

The situation teetered on the edge of farce, a delicate dance of words and expressions played out before an eager audience. It was a moment that encapsulated the unique dynamics of our community, where the boundaries between respect, humour, and the occasional foray into the absurd often blurred. As I stood there, facing Mr. Gangley, I was acutely aware of the fine line I was navigating. It was a role that required patience, empathy, and a healthy dose of humour—qualities that, I realised, defined not just my professional life, but also the very essence of human connection in all its wonderfully unpredictable forms.

"It was that Ben. I saw him kiss that other young man. He needs a good spanking." The moment Mr. Gangley delivered his verdict on Ben's actions, the weight of his words hung in the air, dense with disapproval and a hint of something more archaic. His face, a tableau of disdain, was completely oblivious to the irony of his choice of words—a double entendre that nearly shattered my composed exterior. It was a delicate moment, balancing on the knife-edge of professionalism and the sheer absurdity of the accusation. Mr. Gangley, having expended what seemed like the last reserves of his energy on this denouncement, suddenly seemed to deflate before my eyes. His once rigid posture collapsed, his shoulders sagging as if the burden of his moral outrage was too heavy to bear any longer. Leaning heavily on his walking frame, he turned away, shuffling slowly back towards the sanctuary of the residents' lounge, leaving behind a trail of tension and disbelief.

In the wake of his departure, the atmosphere in the reception area shifted palpably. What's-her-name, caught in the throes of uncontrollable laughter, was a stark contrast to Ben's reaction. Her mirth, marked by tears and the dabbing of her pink hanky, seemed to echo off the walls, filling the space with a surreal sense of levity. I couldn't help but glance at Ben, whose demeanour was the polar opposite. There was no humour in his expression, no laughter at Mr. Gangley's outdated indignation. In his eyes, I saw a reflection of my own discomfort, a silent acknowledgment of the absurdity and underlying tension of the situation. It was a moment of unspoken solidarity between us, a mutual recognition of the delicate dance we navigated in this community.

So, I'm not the only one? I found myself thinking, hoping somehow that Ben could pick up on the silent message I was trying to convey.

The sudden ring of the reception phone snapped me back to reality, a timely interruption that offered a brief respite from the emotional tumult of the moment. "Well, a good spanking he will get then," I muttered under my breath, the words a whispered echo of defiance mingled with humour. It was a momentary indulgence in the absurdity of Mr. Gangley's complaint, a way to reclaim some semblance of normalcy before stepping back into my professional role.

As I reached for the phone, I felt the mask of professionalism slip seamlessly back into place. My voice, as I answered, was the epitome of courtesy and efficiency, a stark contrast to the emotional whirlwind that had just swept through the reception area. Yet, even as I engaged in the mundane task of answering the call, my thoughts lingered on the events of the past few minutes. They were a vivid reminder of the complex tapestry of human relationships that I navigated daily—a mix of humour, empathy, and the occasional foray into the utterly unexpected.

The monotonous drag of the afternoon had reached its zenith, each tick of the clock echoing through the reception area like a taunt. The day's weariness had settled heavily on my shoulders, a tangible reminder of the unyielding nature of time when it seemed to stretch infinitely before you. In these moments, the prospect of another of Mr. Gangley's impassioned lectures almost felt like a reprieve, a break in the endless expanse of tedium. It was an odd sort of longing, one born from a desire to break the monotony, even if it meant navigating the stormy waters of his outrage.

Compelled by a basic human need, I announced my brief departure with the placement of the 'Back in 5 minutes' sign atop the counter. My strides were quick and purposeful, directed towards the sanctuary of the staff bathroom—a rare haven of solitude in the bustling environment of our workplace. As I positioned myself at the urinal, the relief of attending to such an ordinary task was almost comical in its intensity.

However, the tranquility of the moment was short-lived. The creak of the door signalled the entrance of another, but without the usual sounds of someone engaging in their own business, a palpable tension began to fill the air. The absence of footsteps towards an adjacent urinal or the sound of a stall door latching was oddly disconcerting. The silence, punctuated only by my own actions, became a canvas for unease, painting the room with a discomfort that was both unfamiliar and intrusive.

The situation escalated from merely odd to downright alarming with the silent presence of the man behind me. The lack of any discernible action on his part—the absence of the sounds that one would expect in such a context—amplified the discomfort to a level that was hard to ignore. It was a strange sensation, feeling the weight of someone's presence, yet being deprived of the usual cues that might explain or justify it.

In an almost reflexive motion, spurred by the growing unease, I hastened to conclude my business. The suddenness of my movements seemed to betray my inner alarm, a physical manifestation of the desire to escape the unsettling situation. The relief of not catching the zipper in my haste was a small victory, overshadowed by the tension that had coiled itself within me.

The quiet that had enveloped the room was shattered by the voice of the man who had entered, a sound that seemed to materialise from the stillness, catching me off guard and setting my heart racing. The unexpectedness of his voice, coming as it did after such a prolonged silence, was like a jolt, a reminder of how quickly a mundane moment could transform into something entirely unpredictable.

"So, I need a good spanking, do I?" Ben's words, theatrically laden with mock indignation and an almost tangible lewdness, echoed off the walls, punctuated by the salacious slap against his arse. It was a display so absurdly over the top that it achieved its intended effect—I laughed, genuinely and uncontrollably, caught up in the absurdity of it all.

My laughter, however, was a fleeting reprieve, giving way to a more serious contemplation. "Apparently you do," I managed to say, still smiling, but my curiosity piqued. The shift in my tone was instinctive, a natural segue into the heart of the matter. "So, who was it?" The question hung between us, a sudden anchor dragging us back from the realm of jest into reality.

Ben's response was swift, a mixture of amusement and dismissal. "Oh, come on! You don't really believe that old guy, do you?" His attempt to brush off the inquiry with humour was typical, a testament to his ability to navigate the often-complex social dynamics of our workplace with ease.

Yet, I couldn't shake off the sense of duty that Mr. Gangley's accusation had instilled in me. "He may make a lot of complaints," I found myself saying, "But he is seldom mistaken." It was a defence of the old man's observational skills, if not his methods, acknowledging that despite his frequent grievances, there was often a kernel of truth to be found.

The change in Ben's expression was immediate and telling. The lightness vanished, replaced by a shadow of discomfort or perhaps annoyance. It was a reminder that beneath the surface, there were layers of complexity to each of us, stories and realities that weren't always visible or understood at a glance.

As I watched him, I couldn't help but reflect on the contradiction that Ben represented. Here was a man, barely into his thirties, whose presence brought a vitality and warmth to our environment. His rapport with the residents was undeniable, a testament to his empathy and charm. His physical appearance, too, was noteworthy—not just for its aesthetic appeal but for the way it seemed to mirror his vibrant personality. He was a pleasure to work with, a sentiment echoed not just by me but by all who interacted with him.

What's not to love? The thought surfaced unbidden, a silent acknowledgment of Ben's appeal. It was a moment of introspection, a recognition of the multifaceted nature of human relationships and the sometimes invisible threads that connect us. In Ben, I saw not just a colleague but a person who brought light into the lives of those around him, even as we navigated the murky waters of accusation and defence.

As Ben drew closer, the change in his demeanour was palpable, the earlier levity giving way to something far more intense. The way he reached out, pulling me towards him with a grip that was both firm and revealing of a deeper need, spoke volumes. In that moment, as we stood there in silence, our eyes locked in a gaze that felt charged with an unspoken dialogue, I became acutely aware of our physical differences. My height over him seemed to underscore a difference that went beyond mere inches, bridging into the realms of our past experiences and emotional landscapes.

The proximity and the intensity of the moment triggered a cascade of memories, transporting me back to a time when it was Luke and I who shared such moments of closeness. The recollection of Luke's gaze—a look so laden with pain and passion that it seemed to transcend the boundaries of our youthful understanding—washed over me with a clarity that was almost painful. Luke's eyes had always been a mirror to his soul, revealing a tumultuous sea of emotions that I had always felt drawn to navigate. His need for safety, for love, was as palpable then as it was now, a beacon that had somehow guided us back to each other despite the odds.

My love for Luke was a constant, a profound connection that had survived the test of time and distance. The miracle of our reunion after years of separation was a testament to something extraordinary—whether it was the hand of fate or mere coincidence, it had felt like destiny. The decade we spent together in the aftermath of our rediscovery was filled with moments of beauty and a deepening of the bond that had first taken root in our childhood. Yet, amidst this shared history and the depth of our connection, there was an undeniable sense of drift, a slow but steady erosion of the intimacy that had once seemed unbreakable.

The realisation that our relationship was faltering was a burden I carried silently, a weight made all the heavier by the uncertainty surrounding our future. The communication that had once flowed so freely between us had dwindled into a void of unspoken fears and unresolved tensions. The question of how to salvage the love we shared loomed large, shadowed by an even more daunting uncertainty—whether the desire to mend what was broken still existed within me. The struggle to hold onto something that seemed to be slipping away was exhausting, a battle that seemed increasingly difficult to justify.

In that moment, with Ben's presence invoking a melancholy reflection of past loves and present uncertainties, I was confronted with the complexity of human relationships —the ways in which they can both anchor and unsettle us, the challenge of navigating the space between holding on and letting go. The intensity of the encounter with Ben served as a mirror, reflecting not just the immediate tension but also the deeper, more turbulent currents of my own heart. It was a reminder of the fragility of connections, the effort required to sustain them, and the sometimes painful realisation that not all things can be fixed, no matter how deeply they are cherished.

"Are you okay? You look a little too serious," said Ben, whisking me back from my mental wanderings.

"Yes! Now turn around so I can spank you!" I demanded playfully.

Ben turned around and bent over, letting me give him several slaps across his backside, my hands making contact with Ben's brown work trousers. Without any hint on my part that I wanted more, or so I believed, Ben slid down his trousers and underwear, leaving his exposed arse staring at me.

Ben gave it a little wiggle. "You want it, don't you?" he teased.

I stumbled for words.

As Ben stood up and turned around to face me, I couldn't help but stare at his arousal. We had kissed a few times before. *It's the stress of the job,* I'd convinced myself, although I had enjoyed it. But I wasn't sure that I was ready for this. *It doesn't feel... right.*

"Pull your pants up before someone else walks in," I whispered to him.

The vibration of my phone was like a lifeline thrown into the tumultuous sea of emotions and desires that Ben and I were navigating. Grasping it eagerly, I extracted it from the depths of my pocket, the screen's glow serving as a beacon back to reality. "Shit. It's Luke," I murmured, my voice a mix of relief and apprehension. The gesture to Ben, a finger pressed firmly to my lips, was an unspoken plea for complicity in the silence that was to follow.

As I answered the call, my heart was a drumbeat in my chest, echoing the turmoil that gripped me. "Hey, Luke," I managed to say, my voice a mask of calm I was far from feeling. Luke's apology for missing my earlier call was a balm, yet it also served as a stark reminder of the duplicity of my current situation. "That's okay," I replied, each word weighed down by the gravity of the moment.

A hand grabbed the front of my trousers and start firmly massaging.

Luke's inquiries, so typical and filled with concern, only served to heighten my internal conflict. The question of my initial reason for calling him evaporated as Ben unzipped my trousers, leaving me grappling for an excuse. "Mr Gangley has had another fall. I'm going to be home late tonight," I found myself saying. The words, a fabrication woven on the spot, tasted like ash in my mouth, but the tongue now gently circling and flicking the tip of my dick was in control as it sent electrifying shockwaves through my body. My heart pounded in my chest. I didn't know how to stop.

Luke's acceptance of my explanation, coupled with his concern for my return time, only deepened the pit of guilt within me. My responses, vague and evasive, were a dance around the truth, a performance aimed at maintaining an illusion of normalcy. "No. It's one of those annoying semi-bad but not bad enough to call an ambulance incidents. Don't wait up for me," I said, the lies stacking up like bricks in a wall I was hastily erecting between us.

The declaration of love from Luke, so casual and yet so profound, was a gut punch. It was a reminder of what was at stake, of the love and trust that I was betraying with each passing second. "Okay. Gotta run. Bye," I ended the call, the words hollow in my ears.

As I set the phone down, the reality of what I had just done—and was about to do—crashed over me like a wave. My breathing was ragged, a physical manifestation of the internal chaos. "Fuck, you're good at that," I whispered to Ben, the admission a mix of admiration and self-reproach.

Ben's response, a light kiss followed by the decisive action of pulling us into a cubicle, was a catalyst. It was a step further into the mire of complexity and moral ambiguity that I had been trying to navigate. The click of the lock was a finality, a seal on the choice I was making in that moment.

The juxtaposition of my actions and my feelings for Luke created a dissonance that was difficult to reconcile. The knowledge that I loved Luke, that we had shared a decade of life's ups and downs, stood in stark contrast to the path I was currently walking. The decision to lock the cubicle door behind us was symbolic, a closing off of one reality as I stepped into another, fraught with consequence and driven by a tumultuous blend of desire and despair. It was a moment of surrender, not to passion, but to the complexities of the human heart and the often-painful decisions it compels us to make.

The night had deepened into that profound silence that seems to amplify every small sound, making the quiet footsteps of my return home echo with a sense of finality. As I passed the spare room, the soft, rhythmic breathing of Luke, lost in slumber, filtered through the slight gap of the door left ajar. The sight, though unseen, tugged at something deep within me—a mixture of relief and a sharp twinge of guilt. Opting not to disturb him, I moved on, the weight of my actions and decisions pressing heavily on my shoulders.

Duke, our eldest loyal Shih Tzu with his coat of white and brown, seemed to sense my turmoil, or perhaps he was simply seeking the comfort of familiar company. His sudden movement, the soft thud of his paws on the floor as he made his way past me, was a small distraction from the heavier thoughts that clouded my mind. Watching him claim his spot on the bed in the master bedroom, a space we all shared as a family, was a poignant reminder of the simple, unconditional love he offered, a stark contrast to the complexity of human emotions I was entangled in.

The routine of changing into shorts and a loose t-shirt felt almost mechanical, a necessary step before I could allow myself to succumb to the physical exhaustion that was just one facet of the weariness I felt. Joining Duke on the bed, the warmth of his small, furry body against mine was a comfort, a silent reassurance that not all was lost. The bed, usually a shared sanctuary between Luke and me, tonight felt like a raft adrift in the sea of my own making, with Duke as my only companion in the immediate sense of the word.

Lying there, staring up at the ceiling, the events of the day replayed in my mind in a chaotic swirl of images and emotions. The guilt of my encounter with Ben, the lie told to Luke, and the silent witness of Duke's unconditional presence created a tumultuous backdrop to the quiet of the room. Yet, as exhaustion began to weave its heavy blanket around me, the turmoil gradually faded into the background. My eyes, heavy with the need for escape into sleep, eventually closed, surrendering to the oblivion that night offered.

4338.205

(24 July 2018)

PAUL

4338.205.1

The break of dawn had barely touched the sky when Duke, with his unwavering routine, nudged me awake from the remnants of a restless sleep. His gentle, insistent licking was a signal as reliable as any alarm clock, a reminder that, regardless of my personal turmoil, life's simpler duties and pleasures continued unabated. "Come on then," I murmured affectionately, my voice rough with sleep as I stroked his head, feeling the soft fur beneath my fingers. Duke, ever the enthusiastic morning greeter, responded with a wagging tail and eager eyes, embodying a joy in the everyday that I found both comforting and, in that moment, slightly envious of.

Despite his age, Duke, along with Henri, retained the eternal youthfulness pets often hold in the hearts of their owners. They were not just dogs; they were family, constant and unjudging companions through the ups and downs of life.

As I mechanically portioned out their breakfast, the stark contrast between the simple act of feeding Duke and Henri and the complexity of human emotions struck me. The routine task did little to distract from the heavier thoughts that lingered from the day before. The guilt from my encounter with Ben was like a shadow, darkening the edges of my morning. The smell of the dog food, usually so off-putting, was barely noticeable against the backdrop of my inner turmoil. Yet, as guilt threatened to overtake my thoughts, I forced it aside, focusing instead on the task at hand. It was easier to deal with the tangible, the immediate, than to untangle the knot of feelings and regrets that lay beneath.

In what might have been an attempt to absolve myself or perhaps simply to find some semblance of normalcy, I found myself gravitating towards an act of service for Luke. Cooking his favourite breakfast felt like both a penance and a gesture of love, a way to bridge the gap that guilt and silence had widened between us. The process of preparing the meal, from selecting the expensive ingredients Luke preferred to watching the bacon sizzle and the eggs cook to just the right consistency, was meditative. It allowed me a momentary escape, a focus on the sensory experiences of cooking rather than the mire of my emotions.

The act of cooking, especially with the intention of caring for someone else, has a way of grounding one in the present. As I moved around the kitchen, the aroma of bacon filling the air, I allowed myself to be pulled into the moment, appreciating the simple pleasure of making something with my own hands. It was a temporary reprieve, a pause in the relentless cycle of thoughts and feelings that had been my constant companions since the day before.

Yet, even as I busied myself with breakfast, I couldn't shake the awareness of the undercurrents running beneath this domestic scene. The act of making Luke's favourite meal was more than just a morning routine; it was an unspoken message, an attempt to communicate through actions what I found too difficult to express in words. In the quiet of the morning, with Duke and Henri contentedly fed and Luke still asleep, I found myself at the intersection of regret and hope, cooking not just to feed but to heal, to connect, to say in eggs and bacon what I couldn't yet find the words for.

"Smells delicious!" Luke exclaimed as he entered the kitchen, his voice cutting through my preoccupied thoughts with a warmth I desperately needed at that moment.

"Your favourite," I replied, forcing a smile that felt both genuine and strained under the weight of my recent actions. The simple act of cooking had become a lifeline, a way to anchor myself in the midst of internal turmoil.

"Oh, so I spoke to Paul yesterday afternoon," Luke mentioned casually as he tipped a heaped teaspoonful of instant coffee into his mug, the granules dissolving into the hot water.

"And?" I prodded, my voice tinged with a wariness that seemed to echo louder in the quiet of the kitchen. My history with Paul, coupled with Luke's nonchalant prelude, set off alarm bells. Conversations about Paul were seldom straightforward and often ended with a request that was anything but simple.

"And..." Luke trailed off, the word hanging in the air between us. I found myself holding my breath, an instinctive reaction to the anticipation of what was to come. Luke's pauses were rarely without significance, often a precursor to news or requests that demanded more from us than I felt ready to give.

"And he is having some family issues and is flying to Hobart from Adelaide on the first flight this morning. I need you to pick him up, please," Luke finally continued, his voice carrying a weight that seemed to press directly on my chest. The emphasis he placed on the final 'please' was both a request and an acknowledgment of the inconvenience he was asking of me.

The simplicity of the task belied the complexity of emotions it stirred within me. Luke's plea, layered with an understanding of the imposition it represented, put me in a position I found both uncomfortable and inescapable. The request was more than just a favour; it was a test of my willingness to support Luke, to prioritise his needs and those of his brother over my own lingering feelings of guilt and confusion.

The question hung in the air, heavy with the weight of past financial burdens and unspoken promises. "Is he paying for it himself this time?" The simplicity of the inquiry belied the depth of concern and frustration that had been building within me over the years. Watching Luke's reaction, the way his gaze darted away, unable to meet mine, was all the confirmation I needed. We had traversed this road before, one littered with the best intentions and costly sacrifices, all in the name of supporting Luke's oldest brother, Paul.

The memory of that lavish, all-expenses-paid holiday we had gifted Paul was still a sore point. It had been a significant financial outlay, one that I had hoped would be a one-time gesture of goodwill. The promise I extracted from Luke afterward—that we would never again shoulder the financial responsibility for Paul's visits—had been a line in the sand, or so I had thought.

"You're paying again, aren't you?" The words left my lips more as a statement than a question, my voice tinged with a mixture of resignation and frustration. "I thought we agreed after last time that we weren't going to pay for him again." Luke's discomfort, his inability to meet my gaze, spoke volumes. It was a dance we had performed too many times, each step familiar yet no less disheartening.

"I know," Luke's admission was soft, laden with a guilt that did little to assuage my growing irritation. "But this time is different. He really needs me." His justification, meant to soften the blow, only served to heighten my sense of déjà vu. It was always something with Paul, always a situation that necessitated bending the rules we had set for our own financial and emotional well-being.

"Do I still have time to eat?" The shift in my focus was abrupt, a defence mechanism against the rising tide of annoyance. The conversation, with its predictable trajectory towards sacrificing our own comfort for Paul's sake, was a loop I had grown weary of. The repeated invocation of 'poor Paul' had become a refrain that grated on my nerves, a constant reminder of the imbalance in our familial obligations and the strain it placed on our relationship.

As I stood there, the smell of breakfast—a meal prepared with love and an eye toward creating a moment of connection—suddenly seemed overshadowed by the looming presence of Paul's latest crisis. The joy I had felt in cooking for Luke, in anticipating a quiet morning together, was quickly dissipating, replaced by a familiar frustration and a sense of being sidelined in favour of Luke's brother's perpetual emergencies.

The tension in the kitchen was palpable, a silent battle waged not with words but through the mundane act of eating breakfast. My actions, uncharacteristically brash as I piled all of the bacon and eggs onto my toast, were a silent scream of frustration, a rebellion against the day's unfolding events. The act was petty, I knew, but in that moment, it was my only weapon against the feelings of being sidelined for Paul's latest drama.

Luke's question, innocent yet laden with expectation, cut through the heavy silence. "Where's mine?" His confusion was evident as he turned, plate in hand, only to find the pan empty—a stark symbol of my silent protest. "You don't get any now," I retorted, the words harsher than intended, fuelled by a mix of irritation and defiance. The bacon, savoured more for the point I was making than for its taste, became a symbol of my discontent.

Luke's muted response, a simple "Whatever," did little to quell the storm of emotions raging within me. There was a certain cold satisfaction in seeing him realise all the bacon was gone, a petty victory in an ongoing war of priorities and expectations. Yet, even as I revelled in this small act of rebellion, the hollowness of the gesture became apparent. It was a temporary salve on a deeper wound, one that spoke to the heart of our current strife.

My abrupt declaration of departure, more a statement of escape than of intent, was met with a resigned "Okay" from Luke. The lack of confrontation, the absence of a plea for discussion, only served to deepen the chasm I felt opening between us. My frustration, once directed solely at the situation with Paul, now encompassed the entirety of our communication breakdown.

The kiss I placed on Luke's cheek, a soft contradiction to the harshness of my previous actions, was an attempt to bridge the gap I had helped widen. It was an apology, a confession of love, and a plea for understanding all at once. Leaving the house without another word, I stepped into the cool morning air, the turmoil within me a stark contrast to the calm of the day. The act of leaving, though physical, felt symbolic of a greater distance I feared was growing between us—a gap not of miles but of understanding and empathy.

As I walked away, the weight of my actions and the uncertainty of our future pressed heavily on me. The day ahead loomed large, not just with the task of fetching Paul but with the bigger challenge of navigating the complexities of love, sacrifice, and the silent battles we wage in the name of both.

Navigating the congested veins of the city during peak hour felt like a test of both my patience and my resolve. Each successful lane change and manoeuvre through the sluggish flow of traffic brought me a step closer to fulfilling my obligation, yet did little to ease the growing resentment within me. The sense of triumph that filled me as I pulled into the airport was short-lived, quickly deflated by the announcement of Paul's delayed flight. It was an inconvenience beyond anyone's control, yet irrationally, it felt like just another aggravation in the long saga of disruptions that Paul seemed to bring into our lives.

Sending Luke an irritated text message about the delay, I couldn't help but let my frustration seep through the words. It was an impotent expression of the irritation that had been building up, a way to vent, albeit indirectly. The airport, with its limited distractions, offered little in the way of consolation. Yet, in a bid to salvage some semblance of peace, I found myself gravitating towards the small airport café.

The decision to indulge in a slice of chocolate cake and a cappuccino was both a comfort and a surrender to the situation. The cake, rich and dense with chocolate, paired with the creamy, frothy cappuccino, served as a temporary distraction from the irritation simmering just below the surface. As I sat there, savouring the indulgence, my attention drifted to the people around me. The airport, a crossroads of stories and destinations, offered a brief escape into the lives of strangers, each absorbed in their own journeys.

The announcement that Paul's flight had finally landed snapped me back to reality, the brief respite fading as the reason for my being there pushed its way back to the forefront of my mind. The anticipation of Paul's arrival, mixed with the remnants of my irritation and the slight guilt for my earlier resentment, created a complex tapestry of emotions. As I made my way to the arrivals gate, the weight of the day's events felt both lighter and heavier, tempered by the brief interlude of people-watching and chocolate cake but underscored by the impending interaction with Paul.

As I navigated the airport, the buzz from my chocolate and caffeine indulgence was a double-edged sword. It lifted my spirits slightly but at the cost of my stomach's comfort, which churned in protest against the unusual onslaught of sugar and caffeine. It seemed even my body was in rebellion against the day's disruptions, accustomed as it was to a more disciplined dietary regimen.

Spotting Paul among the trickle of passengers, I offered up a restrained wave, a gesture that felt somewhat obligatory under the circumstances. Paul, for his part, returned the gesture with an enthusiasm that hinted at both relief and underlying anxiety. His immediate query about Luke's presence—or rather, the absence thereof—felt like a pinch to an already tender spot. "Where's Luke?" he asked, his voice carrying a blend of hope and confusion.

"At home. Cooking eggs," I responded, my tone inadvertently sharpening with the resurgence of my earlier frustrations. The simplicity of the statement belied the complexity of emotions it stirred within me, the irritation bubbling back to the surface with an almost visceral intensity.

Paul's reaction was immediate, a visible shadow of disappointment crossing his features. "Oh," he managed to say, the word barely a whisper but heavy with implication. The disappointment wasn't just in his voice but etched across his face, a tangible sign of the awkward position he found himself in.

Standing there, witnessing Paul's reaction, I felt a renewed wave of irritation tempered by a reluctant sympathy. The situation was far from ideal for any of us, and Paul's evident discomfort served as a reminder of the broader implications of his visit. It wasn't just about the inconvenience or the unwelcome reminder of past financial strains; it was also about the delicate balance of family dynamics and the unspoken tensions that lay beneath the surface of our interactions.

"You ready then?" I asked, more out of formality than genuine interest, already pivoting towards the exit in a bid to escape the confining atmosphere of the airport.

"Have to collect my suitcase," Paul's voice trailed behind me, halting my hasty retreat.

I paused, turning back with a mix of confusion and impatience, "Suitcase?" The word echoed oddly in my mind. "How long are you here for again?"

"Only two nights," he responded, a statement that only deepened my bewilderment.

"So, why the suitcase?" I probed further, unable to mask the incredulity in my voice.

"It's more of an overnight bag really," Paul attempted to clarify, though his explanation did little to alleviate my confusion. I decided not to delve into the peculiarities of his decision-making, a trait I had come to associate with both him and Luke. The minor oddities in their behaviours, while sometimes baffling, were part of the package, it seemed.

"I'll wait over there for you," I conceded, gesturing towards the nondescript row of chairs facing the carpark, seeking a momentary reprieve as Paul went to retrieve his belongings.

The brief interlude allowed me a quick dive into the digital world, a temporary distraction from the day's unfolding events. However, Paul's swift return, signalled by the corner of my eye catching the movement of his long legs, prompted me to stand. We proceeded to the exit, my steps quickening towards the parking pay machine with Paul in tow.

"Don't worry about it," I dismissed his offer of coins for the parking fee, a small gesture on my part to alleviate at least one inconvenience from our day, however insignificant it might be against the backdrop of airport parking rates.

As we settled into the white Mazda, the familiar action of starting the car served as a subtle cue for the transition back to our daily reality, away from the transient space of arrivals and departures. The engine's hum underlined the start of our journey home, a silent companion to the mix of reluctance and acceptance that marked the beginning of Paul's brief stay.

ILLUSIONS

4338.205.2

The moment we pulled into the driveway, a wave of relief washed over me. The journey home had been uneventful, but the anticipation of returning to the familiar confines of my own space was comforting. As I popped the boot to help Paul with his luggage—a gesture of courtesy that felt somewhat automatic—I caught myself scanning the front of the house for any sign of Luke. Surprisingly, he didn't appear, an omission that struck me as odd given his usual enthusiasm for greetings.

The task of corralling Duke and Henri away from the door, ensuring they didn't dart outside in their excitement, was a familiar dance. It was one of those small, domestic challenges that brought a sense of normalcy to the otherwise tense atmosphere. Letting Paul in first, I couldn't help but notice the stark contrast between his cautious entry and the exuberant welcome I had half-expected from Luke.

Luke's voice, booming with cheerfulness from inside, momentarily lifted the tension. "Hey, Paul!" he called out, his tone infused with warmth. Yet, as I stepped into the living room, trailing behind Paul, a surge of irritation swiftly overshadowed that momentary lift. The sight that greeted me sparked a silent tirade of questions and disbelief. *What the fuck has Luke been doing while I've been battling rush hour traffic to collect his brother from the airport?*

Luke, standing there in the kitchen in nothing but his bright blue drawstring boardshorts, seemed oblivious to the incongruity of his attire—or lack thereof—with the situation.

The boardshorts, while a favourite for their comfort, were hardly appropriate for the occasion. It wasn't just the choice of clothing that nettled me; it was what it represented. Despite the delay, despite the time Paul's flight had afforded him, Luke hadn't managed to prepare himself—or the house—for the visit in any meaningful way.

The look of contempt I felt creeping across my face was uncontrollable, a visceral reaction to the scenario unfolding before me. It was a culmination of the morning's frustrations, the irritation at the airport, the tension of the drive, and now this—Luke's apparent disregard for the effort I had put into accommodating his brother's visit. It wasn't just about the clothes; it was about what they signified in the broader context of our day, of our relationship, and of the ongoing dynamics with Paul. It was a moment that encapsulated a myriad of emotions, from annoyance to disappointment, all converging in the heart of our home.

Paul's question cut through the already tense atmosphere of the living room, a simple inquiry that seemed to echo my own frustrations about the day. "Why didn't you come to the airport?" he asked, his tone curious yet tinged with disappointment as he moved further into the open-plan living space.

"I was preparing myself for your arrival," Luke said, a statement so at odds with his current state of undress that it bordered on absurd.

The urge to roll my eyes was irresistible, a silent retort to Luke's apparent idea of 'preparation.' Paul's reaction, a mix of amusement and disbelief, mirrored my own. "You don't look terribly prepared," he quipped, his chuckle doing little to mask the underlying critique of Luke's lack of effort.

My own comment to Luke, veiled as a concern for his comfort, was more a pointed critique than genuine inquiry. "Aren't you cold?" The suggestion was clear, a plea for him to dress more appropriately, yet met with nothing more than a nonchalant shrug. Luke's indifference to my thinly veiled irritation was maddening, his casual "Meh" a clear dismissal of my concerns.

As Paul diverted his attention to the contents of the fridge, the parallels between the brothers became glaringly obvious. Their shared disregard for the situation, each lost in their own world, left me feeling like the odd one out in my own home. Duke's insistent jumping at my leg offered a welcome distraction, a reminder of the uncomplicated affection and loyalty of our pets in contrast to the complex dynamics unfolding among the humans.

"So, what's the big emergency that couldn't wait another day?" Paul inquired, his curiosity palpable in the air that had already been thick with unspoken tensions.

The word 'emergency' bounced around the room, landing heavily between us. "Emergency? What emergency?" I echoed, my confusion mounting. I glanced at Luke, searching for some clarification, some hint of understanding, but found none. My gaze shifted back to Paul, who, with an air of nonchalance that seemed at odds with the situation, had taken to pilfering grapes from the fridge.

The absurdity of the moment wasn't lost on me. "Aren't you the one with the... family crisis?" I pressed, trying to piece together the fragmented narrative that had led to this point. Paul's reaction, a mix of surprise and indignation, only added layers to the mystery. "Me?" he retorted, clearly taken aback by the suggestion that he was the origin of the supposed crisis.

My frustration with the situation was becoming harder to mask. My features betrayed my growing irritation, a visible manifestation of the confusion and suspicion swirling within me. I turned my attention back to Luke, seeking answers, accountability, something to make sense of the morning's events. His silence was a void, offering no explanations, no reassurances.

"Well?" I pushed, my patience wearing thin. "What's going on, Luke?" The demand for clarity was tinged with a sense of betrayal. The realisation that I might have been manipulated into this scenario, under false pretences or misunderstood urgencies, was galling. I detested feeling like a pawn in someone else's scheme, yet the evidence was mounting that this was exactly the case.

Luke's hesitant start, followed by an apology that seemed anything but sincere, given the wide grin he couldn't contain, only served to amplify my confusion and growing irritation. The sight of his amusement in what I considered a serious situation made my stomach tighten, a mixture of anger and sudden apprehension knotting together. *What the hell is Luke on about?* The question echoed in my mind, a tumultuous blend of emotions making it hard to focus on anything else.

"But there is something that I really need to show both of you," Luke's statement, vague and enigmatic, did nothing to ease the tension. Paul's reaction, labelling the situation as ominous, mirrored my own feelings, albeit with a hint of his usual detachment.

"What is it?" My response came out sharper than I intended, the annoyance palpable in my voice. The uncertainty of the moment, coupled with Luke's cryptic behaviour, was pulling me in different directions—irritation at being kept in the dark, curiosity about what Luke deemed so important, and a lingering unease about the potential implications of his announcement.

"Come with me," said Luke. His gesture, an encouraging wave followed by him turning to walk up the hallway, felt like a summons I couldn't ignore. Despite the frustration boiling within me, there was also a reluctant intrigue. The shift from annoyance to a cautious curiosity was almost palpable, my emotions swinging like a pendulum as I followed him, with Paul trailing behind.

As we made our way up the hallway, the anticipation built with each step. Luke's earlier amusement, now mingled with my own trepidation and curiosity, created a complex tapestry of expectations. The hallway, a space so familiar and usually comforting, now felt like the lead-up to a revelation that could alter the dynamics of our day—and perhaps beyond—in ways I couldn't yet fathom.

As I trailed behind Luke into the study, a room usually reserved for quiet evenings of work or leisurely internet browsing, my skepticism trailed with me. The familiar sight of the study, unchanged and as orderly as ever, did little to prepare me for whatever revelation Luke deemed so critical. The logical conclusion that it must involve the computer did little to ease my growing impatience or curiosity. *But what on earth would possibly warrant dragging his brother all the way down here from Broken Hill? Surely Luke could have done this online.* The thought nagged at me, a persistent reminder of the day's inconveniences and the mystery that now loomed large in our usually tranquil home.

My gaze, heavy with a mix of boredom and exasperation, was fixed on Luke. The dramatic buildup to whatever announcement he was about to make felt unnecessarily theatrical, a stark contrast to the straightforward communication I preferred. The anticipation, once tinged with irritation, was now morphing into a begrudging curiosity as Luke finally made a move, reaching into his pocket.

The moment he pulled out a small, rectangular device, a flash of unexpected vindication shot through me. "Ha, I was right! It is something on the computer." The words tumbled out before I could temper them with the realisation that my silent musings had remained just that—silent. Neither Luke nor Paul could have known the suspicions swirling in my head, making my exclamation seem both abrupt and a tad presumptuous.

"What?" Luke asked, his confusion clear as he looked at me, the small device still clutched in his hand.

"The USB stick," I clarified hastily, pointing towards the object of our attention, certain I had unraveled the mystery of his dramatic buildup. Yet, Luke's ensuing grin, broad and filled with mischief, immediately told me I had jumped to the wrong conclusion. "Oh, no, this isn't for the computer," he countered, his voice laced with a cockiness that piqued my curiosity further.

The twist in Luke's revelation took me by surprise, rendering me speechless and leaving the floor open for Paul to voice the question that now hung palpably in the air. "Okay. So, what is it?" Paul inquired, his tone mirroring the curiosity that had gripped me.

Luke's next actions were calculated for maximum effect, his gaze sweeping over us to ensure he had our undivided attention before he pressed a small button atop the device. The anticipation in the room crescendoed into a moment of sheer astonishment as a tight ball of energy erupted from the device, transforming into a buzzing, electrical field against the wall.

My initial shock rendered me momentarily speechless. "What the..." I managed, my voice trailing off as I watched, captivated by the dance of vibrant colours before us. The display was mesmerising—a spectacle of light and energy that defied my understanding of what was possible. The colours swirled and twisted on the wall, occasionally colliding in bursts that sent waves of colour spilling into the room.

The scientific part of my brain scrambled to make sense of the phenomenon, while another part of me surrendered to

Page 43

the sheer wonder of the moment. Luke's ability to surprise, to bring the extraordinary into our everyday lives, was part of what I loved about him, even if it sometimes came wrapped in layers of frustration and mystery.

Paul's question echoed my own bewilderment, both of us transfixed by the spectacle before us. "What is that?" he asked, his voice a mixture of curiosity and astonishment at the display Luke had conjured.

"I'll show you," Luke replied, a hint of excitement lacing his words as he positioned himself directly in front of the mesmerising display. The confidence in his stance, the eagerness in his voice, contrasted sharply with the apprehension knotting in my stomach.

Paul, still caught up in the visual wonder, remarked, "I can see. It's stunning." His appreciation for the beauty of the phenomenon was evident, a sentiment I shared despite the growing unease within me.

"Just follow me," Luke beckoned, his hand motioning towards the vibrant display as if inviting us into an unknown world. The casualness of his invitation belied the extraordinary nature of what he was asking.

My heart thundered in my chest, a cacophony of excitement, fear, and disbelief. "Follow you where?" I gasped out, my voice a cocktail of emotions. The question barely had time to hang in the air before Luke took that final, decisive step into the swirling colours—and disappeared from sight.

"What the hell!" Paul's exclamation mirrored my own shock, a verbal manifestation of the disbelief that gripped us both.

"What the hell indeed," I echoed, my voice barely above a whisper. My gaze was fixed on the spot where Luke had been just moments before, now empty save for the captivating dance of colours. The reality of what had just occurred was difficult to grasp, challenging everything I thought I knew about the world around me.

As the initial shock began to subside, replaced by a mixture of awe and a desperate curiosity, I found myself at a crossroads of decision. The part of me that yearned for the safety of the known world was at odds with the part that was captivated by the mystery and potential of what lay beyond that colourful portal. Luke's disappearance, rather than serving as a warning, seemed instead to be an invitation—an invitation to step beyond the boundaries of the familiar and into the realm of the extraordinary.

The silence that followed was a testament to the profound impact of the moment, a silence filled with the weight of possibilities and the unspoken question of what to do next. As I stood there, with Paul beside me, the realisation that the decision of whether to follow Luke into the unknown rested squarely on our shoulders was both exhilarating and terrifying. The study, once a place of comfort and routine, had transformed into the threshold of an adventure that defied explanation, beckoning us forward with the promise of discovering the unimaginable.

Paul was the first to break the silence, "You go first," he said slowly, motioning to the wall of bright colours.

"Fuck off!" The words leapt from my mouth before I could temper them, a raw expression of my shock and fear. The idea of stepping into something so utterly beyond comprehension, something that had just swallowed Luke whole, was not something I could entertain lightly. "I'm not touching that shit. We don't know what it is." My protest was as much about self-preservation as it was about the incredulity of the situation. The rational part of my brain screamed for caution, for a retreat from the edge of this unknowable void.

Yet, Paul, perhaps driven by a mixture of curiosity and a desire not to seem cowardly, declared his readiness to go first. His approach to the vibrant anomaly, his pause as if bracing himself for the leap into the unknown, and then his decisive action mirrored Luke's so closely it was as if he were following a script. Watching him vanish with a bold step forward, my heart skipped a beat. The reality of what had just happened—watching two people step into and then disappear within this... this thing—was hard to digest.

An elaborate illusion? The thought crossed my mind as a desperate attempt to rationalise what I had just witnessed. Surely, this had to be some trick, a sophisticated projection or a hidden doorway cleverly disguised by the lights and colours. I expected, no, I *hoped*, for Luke and Paul to reappear at any moment, unable to contain their laughter at having fooled me so completely. I stared intently at the swirling colours, half expecting them to dissipate and reveal Luke and Paul standing there, doubled over in laughter at my expense.

But the return I was hoping for didn't happen. The minutes stretched on, the vibrant display continued its dance unabated, and the silence in the room grew heavier. The absence of their laughter, the lack of any sign of their return, slowly began to erode my skepticism. The possibility that this was no trick, that the portal—or whatever it was—was real, and that Luke and Paul had indeed stepped through to something or somewhere else, became increasingly difficult to ignore.

The decision to step forward, to follow Luke and Paul into the unknown, felt like a leap of faith—a moment where curiosity overcame fear, propelling me into action. "I may as well," I murmured, more to myself than anyone else. The words were a whisper of resolve, a concession to the part of me that needed to know, to see, to understand. With each tentative step towards the wall of colour, my heart raced, a symphony of apprehension and anticipation.

Then, in an instant, I crossed the threshold. The transition was disorienting, the vibrant colours melting away to reveal a blinding, warm light that enveloped me completely. It was a sensation unlike anything I'd ever experienced, as if I had stepped out of one reality and into another. The voice that greeted me, resonating not through the air but directly within my mind, was both startling and strangely comforting. "Welcome to Clivilius, Jamie Greyson." The words, though unheard in any conventional sense, were clear, imbued with a presence that felt both ancient and immeasurable.

As my eyes adjusted to the brilliance, the first thing that struck me was the sky—a vast expanse of unblemished blue, stretching infinitely above. The overwhelming vastness of it, the purity of the colour, was breathtaking, yet it was the utter silence and emptiness that enveloped us that left me truly speechless. Standing there, beside Paul and Luke, we formed a trio of bewildered explorers in a landscape that defied expectation.

The world of Clivilius that lay before us was a stark, desolate beauty—rolling hills of brown and orange dust, uninterrupted and seemingly endless. The absence of any familiar signs of life—no houses, no trees, no birds in the sky, not even the distant sound of human activity—was unsettling. This was a place untouched, unmarked by civilisation as we knew it, an umber wilderness that stretched beyond the limits of sight.

The realisation that we were not just somewhere unknown, but somewhere altogether different, was overwhelming. The sense of isolation was palpable, a profound solitude that made the familiar world we had left behind seem like a distant memory.

Luke's question snapped me out of my daze, his excitement piercing the heavy silence that had enveloped us upon our arrival in Clivilius. "Did you hear it?" he asked, eyes alight with a fervour that spoke volumes of his belief in the moment's significance. Paul and I exchanged a glance, our mutual nod an acknowledgment of the mysterious voice that had welcomed us to this desolate, yet somehow captivating, landscape.

"This is where life will begin anew," Luke proclaimed, his words hanging in the air, heavy with implication and the promise of untold possibilities. The statement, grandiose as it was, seemed to deepen the silence that followed, each of us lost in our thoughts about the implications of his declaration.

The stillness was broken by Paul's sudden movement, his arms flailing about as if he were trying to grasp something unseen. "What are you doing, Paul?" Luke's inquiry, laced with a hint of amusement and confusion, mirrored my own curiosity.

"I'm trying to find the study walls," Paul responded, his actions now making a peculiar sort of sense. He was seeking the familiar, tangible boundaries of the room we had left behind, or so he thought.

"The study walls?" Luke echoed, his tone a mix of incredulity and amusement.

"Yes. Isn't this just an advanced form of virtual reality? Or like a hologram?" Paul's questions revealed his skepticism, his attempt to rationalise our experience within the confines of the known and understandable.

"I assure you, Clivilius is very real," Luke countered, his conviction underscored by the action of picking up a book from the soft, dust-covered ground. The book, an object so mundane and yet so out of place in this alien landscape, seemed to serve as proof of Clivilius's reality.

"I recognise this book," I interjected, the sight of the familiar tome igniting a spark of recognition. Taking it from Luke, I felt a surge of surreal familiarity. "This is one of your uni books that you've had sitting in the bookcase untouched since we met, isn't it?" The question was rhetorical, the book in my hands a tangible link to the life we knew, a life that suddenly seemed as distant as the sky above.

"Indeed, it is," Luke confirmed, his admission adding layers to the mystery of Clivilius. The presence of the book here, in this vast expanse of dust and silence, was a conundrum that defied logical explanation. It was a moment that blurred the lines between the possible and the impossible, challenging our understanding of reality and prompting a reevaluation of everything we thought we knew.

Paul's confusion echoed my own, a sentiment that seemed to hang heavily between us. "I don't understand," he said, his gaze fixed on Luke, searching for clarity in a situation that felt increasingly like a descent into the unknown. "There's nothing here."

As my eyes landed on the pile of large boxes, a seemingly incongruous addition to the barren landscape, my curiosity piqued. "Apart from a pile of large boxes," I corrected, my words drawing attention to the only sign of human intention in this vast expanse. Approaching the boxes, I voiced the question that seemed to loom larger with each passing moment. "Why are all these here?"

Luke's response, infused with an unshakeable belief in the vision he was unfolding before us, sent a ripple of skepticism through me. "It's going to be the first shelter here in Clivilius," he proclaimed, his voice carrying a fervour that seemed almost out of place in the vast, empty landscape that stretched out around us.

My confusion couldn't be contained. "What the hell does Clivilius need a shelter for?" The question was out before I could temper it, my incredulity at the notion of building anything in this desolate space overwhelming my usual restraint.

Paul's voice joined the fray, his question layering on top of mine, seeking the foundation of Luke's grand plan. "And what even is Clivilius?" he asked, his tone a mix of curiosity and doubt.

Luke's answer did little to ground his ambitious ideas in any reality we could comprehend. "This place is Clivilius," he stated, his arms sweeping wide as if to embrace the barren expanse before us. "And the shelter is for the start of our new civilisation."

The magnitude of what Luke was suggesting left Paul and me momentarily speechless, our expressions blank as we tried to wrap our heads around the concept of beginning anew in a place that, until moments ago, was beyond our wildest imaginings.

"It has to start somewhere," Luke added, a simple shrug accompanying his monumental statement. The casualness with which he spoke of beginning anew, of erecting a civilisation from the dust of Clivilius, struck me as both absurd and unnervingly sincere.

"What the hell do we need a new civilisation for?" I found myself protesting, the frustration and disbelief mounting within me. "I'm quite happy with the current one, thank you very much!" My words were a desperate attempt to anchor this conversation in some semblance of reality, to remind us of the world we knew, the world we had inexplicably left behind.

Luke's serene assurance that "You'll see in time. It will all make sense," did nothing to quell the storm of emotions raging within me. His calm in the face of our skepticism only served to heighten my desire for the familiar, for the comfort of home.

"Fuck time," I retorted, my patience frayed to its breaking point. "I'm going home. This place is shit. It's just dust for god's sake! There's enough of that in the outback." The words spilled out, a vehement rejection of Luke's vision, of this Clivilius and its promise of a new beginning. The very notion of abandoning our lives for a nebulous dream in a world of dust and emptiness was unfathomable.

The swirling wall of colours, once an intriguing spectacle, now felt like a barrier—an imposing, inscrutable force field between the known and the unfathomable. My earlier resolve to return, to step back through this mesmerising portal to the familiarity of our study, was met with an unexpected resistance. The realisation that my attempt to leave Clivilius was being thwarted by some unseen force was both startling and deeply unsettling.

"Well, off you go then," Luke's voice, light and encouraging, seemed to mock my predicament. His casual dismissal of my struggle only added to the growing sense of unease.

"I'm trying," I responded, frustration edging my voice as I faced the reality of my situation. The simple act of leaving, of returning to our world, suddenly seemed insurmountable.

"What do you mean you're trying?" Paul's confusion was evident, his question a mirror of my own disbelief at the impossibility of the task.

"I mean I'm trying to leave, but the bloody thing won't let me," I explained, my voice tinged with exasperation. The sensation of being physically repelled by the colourful vortex before me was beyond comprehension. It was as if the very fabric of this place, Clivilius, had decided to keep us within its grasp, defying our attempts to understand or escape it.

My heart raced as I faced the stark reality of our situation. The swirling colours, once a doorway to this alien landscape, now felt like a prison. The thought that Luke might have led us into a situation from which there was no return sent waves of panic through me. *What the hell has Luke done?* The question echoed in my mind, a mix of fear, betrayal, and desperation for answers.

Regrouping from the initial shock of being repelled by the Portal, my resolve hardened. There was something about the impossibility of the situation that ignited a stubbornness within me, a refusal to be intimidated by the unknown. With every fibre of my being pulsing with determination, I decided on a more drastic approach.

Channeling every action hero I could think of, I positioned myself with a sense of dramatic resolve I never knew I had. Then, emulating a Superman dive, I thrust one arm forward, my fist clenched in defiance, and launched myself at the Portal. The vibrant colours, which had initially captivated us with their beauty, now exploded into violent bursts, a kaleidoscope of incandescent sparks erupting before my eyes. The sensation was unlike anything I had ever experienced; it was as if each burst of colour carried with it a wave of intense, searing pain that scorched through my mind, transcending physical boundaries.

The heat was so intense, so all-consuming, that for a fleeting moment, I entertained the notion that I might indeed become the first irrefutable case of spontaneous human combustion. The absurdity of the thought was overshadowed only by the very real sensation of my shirt beginning to melt, the fabric disintegrating under the assault of the mini-eruptions of energy.

But just as quickly as the assault had begun, it ended. In the next instant, I found myself being hurled backward with a force that defied my understanding of physics. The world spun wildly as I was thrown away from the malevolent swirl of colours that guarded the Portal, my body crashing to the ground with a jarring impact.

Lying there, gasping for breath, the pain slowly receding from my mind, I was overwhelmed by a mix of emotions. The shock of the violent rejection, the relief of surviving the encounter unscathed, and a growing realisation of our predicament washed over me. The Portal, our apparent lifeline back to our world, was not just a passive gateway but an active, seemingly sentient barrier that resisted my attempts to breach it.

The implications of this revelation were chilling. If the Portal could not be persuaded, coerced, or forced to allow our passage, what hope did we have of returning home?

Paul's alarm was palpable as he dashed to my aid, his voice echoing my own shock and confusion. "What the hell was that?" he shouted, his words slicing through the aftermath of my failed attempt to breach the Portal.

Luke, too, was quick to my side, his concern etched in every line of his face. "Jamie! Jamie, are you ok?" he asked, his voice laced with panic as he took my hand, examining it for signs of injury. The surreal experience of watching my shirt disintegrate, coupled with the realisation that my arm, the very limb that had dared to challenge the Portal, was miraculously unscathed, was disorienting. Yet, the unmistakable smell of singed hair filled my nostrils, a pungent reminder of the encounter's intensity. The realisation that my arm, now noticeably bereft of hair, had borne the brunt of the Portal's wrath was both alarming and absurdly comical.

"This fucking place is trying to kill me!" The words burst from me in a torrent of fear and anger as I pulled away from Luke's comforting grip. The frustration, the fear, the sheer incredulity of the situation poured out of me in a vehement outcry. "What the hell were you thinking bringing us here?!" I demanded, my voice a raw edge of accusation and disbelief.

Luke's response was fraught with desperation. "I didn't know that was going to happen!" he protested, his voice tinged with a rising panic that mirrored my own. His words, while meant to be reassuring, did little to quell the storm of emotions that raged within me. The realisation that we were navigating uncharted territory, that Luke's visions of a new beginning in Clivilius were fraught with unseen dangers, was a bitter pill to swallow.

As Paul positioned himself to make an attempt at crossing the Portal, my disbelief and frustration reached new heights. "Are you insane? Didn't you see what just happened?" The incredulity in my voice was palpable, a reflection of the pain and shock still coursing through me from my own thwarted effort.

"Maybe you did it wrong?" Paul's response, perhaps meant to be encouraging or analytical, came off as dismissive, igniting my irritation further. "Oh, fuck off, Paul," I retorted sharply, the strain of the situation eroding my patience.

Luke's immediate defence of Paul, "Hey! Don't speak to him like that," only served to fan the flames of my anger. In that moment, surrounded by the desolate landscape of Clivilius and facing the unknown dangers it presented, the solidarity I sought from them felt fractured. "Fuck you all," I growled, the words escaping me in a raw expression of my turmoil, as I cradled my arm, a tangible reminder of the risk we were all facing.

Paul's persistence, despite my warnings, led to his own series of failed attempts to breach the Portal. Each effort was met with the same invisible barrier that had repelled me, his frustration mounting with every try. "What the hell is wrong with this thing?" he exclaimed, his voice laced with desperation. The futility of his actions underscored the reality of our predicament: the Portal, our presumed gateway back to the familiar, was denying us passage, its purpose and mechanisms as alien as the landscape that surrounded us.

"There's nothing wrong with it," Luke said, his assertion deepened the mystery and my frustration.

Watching him confidently step into the swirling colours and vanish without a trace was a stark reminder of our predicament. Driven by a mix of desperation and a fleeting hope that maybe, just maybe, it would work for me too, I lunged towards the mesmerising wall. The familiar voice that greeted me only added to the surreal nature of the experience. "Welcome to Clivilius, Jamie Greyson," it intoned, devoid of warmth or comfort, a stark contrast to the turmoil churning within me.

My efforts were futile, the rejection by the Portal as jarring as the first. "Fuck!" The expletive burst from me, a raw expression of my anger and helplessness. The reality of our situation was becoming increasingly clear—we were trapped, with no discernible way out.

Paul's despair was palpable as he collapsed, his plea echoing the confusion and fear that gripped us both. "I don't understand. Why can't we leave?" His question, voiced in a moment of vulnerability, was one that haunted me too. The sight of him, defeated and kneeling in the dust, was a visual manifestation of our collective despair.

Unable to contain my frustration, I lashed out, my foot sending a cloud of red dust into the air, a physical manifestation of my anger. "Fuck!" The word tore from me again, dragged out in a scream that seemed to embody the depth of our frustration and fear. The haunting silence that followed, broken only by the settling dust, was a stark reminder of our isolation in this alien world.

The realisation that our attempts to leave Clivilius were being actively thwarted by some unknown force was both terrifying and infuriating. The rules of this world, its logic and mechanisms, were a mystery—one that we were far from unravelling. The voice that had so emotionlessly welcomed me offered no guidance, no explanation for our imprisonment within this strange land.

As I stood there, enveloped in the silence of Clivilius, the weight of our situation settled heavily upon me. The prospect of finding a way back home, of understanding the forces that held us here, seemed an insurmountable challenge. Yet, the alternative—acceptance of our fate in this desolate place—was not something I was ready to contemplate. The struggle to return, to break free from the grasp of Clivilius, was one that I knew I could not abandon, no matter how daunting it appeared.

UNPLEASANTRIES

4338.205.3

Luke's return to Clivilius, met with our collective frustration and disbelief, marked a turning point in our ordeal. The air was thick with tension, a palpable mix of fear, anger, and desperation swirling around us as surely as the colours swirled around the Portal. Paul's question to Luke, laced with accusation, was a reflection of the betrayal we felt. "Did you know?" he demanded, seeking some semblance of understanding, a reason behind our entrapment.

Luke's response, a blend of confusion and defensiveness, did little to assuage our concerns. "Know what?" he countered, his claim of ignorance clashing with the gravity of our situation. His assertion that he had been able to come and go freely only deepened the mystery, his previous visits to Clivilius now a source of envy and resentment.

The reality of our predicament was stark and unyielding. "So, this is it then?" My words hung heavy in the air, a stark acknowledgment of the severity of our situation. "This is our fate. To die in this godforsaken dust?"

Luke's response, however, was unsettling in its optimism. "Not fate. Destiny," he declared, his voice infused with a fervour that felt both misplaced and infuriating under the circumstances. The distinction he made, between fate and destiny, seemed a cruel twist of semantics when faced with the reality of our entrapment.

Paul's retort to Luke, a blunt dismissal of his romanticised view, echoed my own sentiments. "You're so full of shit sometimes," he said, his casual delivery belied by the underlying tension. It was a moment of raw honesty, a venting of frustration at Luke's seemingly delusional optimism.

The silence that fell over us was heavy, punctuated only by the shock of Paul's uncharacteristic outburst. My glance towards him was filled with a mix of surprise and understanding. It was indeed rare to hear such language from Paul, especially directed towards his younger brother, hinting at the depth of his desperation and fear. Luke's hurt expression was unmistakable, a tangible sign of the rift that was beginning to form between us.

The standoff between the brothers was palpable, a silent battle of wills that seemed to stretch on indefinitely. Yet, it was Paul's face that eventually changed, the anger giving way to a profound sorrow. "What about my children? Am I ever going to see them again?" The words were a gut punch, a reminder of the life and responsibilities he had left behind, perhaps forever.

Luke's suggestion, offered with a naivety that was both infuriating and heartbreaking, was met with disbelief. "I can arrange to have them come here?" he said, as if the solution were as simple as extending an invitation.

Paul's response was a torrent of frustration and fear, a vehement rejection of Luke's proposal. "Are you fucking kidding me? I know you don't have the first clue about parenting Luke, but here's the number one golden rule for how to be a dad. You ready? Don't, under any circumstances, bring your children through a one-way interdimensional Portal to an alien wasteland where there is literally nothing but dust and a tent!" His words, though harsh, were a desperate attempt to inject some sense into Luke, to make him see the insanity of his suggestion.

The hopelessness that washed over Paul's face in the wake of his outburst was a mirror to my own feelings of despair.

The realisation that we might never see our loved ones again, that we were trapped in this desolate world with no clear way back, was overwhelming. Luke's well-meaning but misguided proposal had only served to highlight the gravity of our predicament. The notion of bringing anyone else, especially children, into this uncertainty was unthinkable, a stark reminder of the responsibility we bore to find a way back, not just for ourselves, but for those we had left behind.

My frustration was at a boiling point, the reality of our situation sinking in with each passing moment. "I can't believe you've gotten us stuck in this bloody place!" The accusation flew from my lips before I could rein it in, the words heavy with accusation and disbelief. I needed answers, clarity on how we ended up in this predicament. "How long have you known about this?" I demanded, seeking some understanding of Luke's involvement and the depth of his knowledge about the Portal.

Luke's explanation, however, sounded more like the plot of a bizarre dream than anything rooted in reality. He spoke of dozing off and the so-called Portal Key falling from his hand upon waking—a narrative that would have been laughable under different circumstances.

"Portal Key?" Paul's incredulity mirrored my own. His comment, pointing out the absurdity of thinking we were characters in a sci-fi novel, was a brief moment of levity in an otherwise tense situation.

"Well, that's what it is, isn't it? A key to the Portal?" Luke's sarcastic retort did little to alleviate the growing sense of surrealism surrounding our discussion. His casual labelling of the object that had led us here, and his nonchalance about the entire affair, was infuriating.

"Yeah, but... Portal?" Paul's repetition highlighted the incredulity of our conversation, a discussion about Portals and keys as if we were indeed living within the pages of a science fiction story.

"What else would you call it?" Luke's question, posed as he faced the mesmerising wall of colours that had become the bane of our existence, prompted a response from me borne out of sheer frustration and despair. "A piece of shit," I said, the words tinged with bitterness. "One giant piece of shit." It was a crude but honest assessment of the situation we found ourselves in, trapped in an alien world by an inexplicable phenomenon.

Paul's unexpected laughter, a snort that broke through the tension, was a reminder of the absurdity of our situation. Despite the gravity of our predicament, there was a certain dark humour in the fact that we were debating the semantics of our unlikely situation—a debate that, under any other circumstances, would have been purely theoretical. Yet here we were, caught in the middle of what felt like a bad science fiction plot, with no clear way back to reality.

Paul's attempt to suppress his laughter with an apology only served to amplify it, his second snort resonating louder than the first despite his efforts. He turned away, perhaps out of respect for our frustration, or maybe to hide his continued amusement from our increasingly irritated glares. I couldn't help but roll my eyes at the absurdity of finding humour in our dire circumstances, giving Luke a contemptuous shrug to signify my dismay at the situation's lack of humour.

"I guess I'd better start bringing you some supplies," Luke said, his tone attempting to inject a semblance of normalcy into the surreal nightmare we found ourselves in.

My gaze, previously fixed on Paul, who was still consumed by fits of laughter, shifted back to Luke. "Is there really no going back?" I asked, the question heavy with an unexpected sadness that seemed to fill the space around us.

"I guess not," Luke's reply came, heavy and resigned. "I'm sorry, Jamie." His apology, though sincere, did little to quell the rising tide of emotions within me. A mix of disbelief, anger, and a profound sense of loss washed over me, the reality of our entrapment becoming painfully clear.

Closing my eyes for a brief moment, I sought to master the anger and frustration churning inside me. "Just go," I told Luke softly, my voice betraying the turmoil I felt. The request for him to leave was less about him and more about needing a moment to process the enormity of our situation, to come to terms with the bleakness of our new reality.

As Luke moved to fulfil his promise of supplies, leaving Paul and me alone with the dust and the silence of Clivilius, the weight of his departure underscored the finality of our predicament. The laughter had faded, leaving behind a palpable void filled with uncertainty and the daunting task of facing an unknown future in this obscure new world.

RIVER

4338.205.4

"He's gone back for supplies," I found myself saying, pre-empting Paul's unasked question with a sense of resignation that seemed to permeate the air between us.

Paul's response, a simple "Oh," carried with it a depth of desolation that mirrored my own feelings. His shoulders slumped, a physical manifestation of the defeat we both felt. "What now?" he asked, his voice tinged with a hopelessness that seemed to echo across the vast emptiness of Clivilius.

I could offer no plan, no words of encouragement. "No idea," was all that came out, a verbal shrug that did little to disguise the growing sense of futility.

Watching Paul move towards the pile of boxes, the supposed beginnings of our 'shelter' here in this alien landscape, I couldn't help but question the point of it all. "What are you doing?" I called after him, more out of a reflexive need to connect than any real curiosity.

Paul's answer was as lost and aimless as we felt. "I don't really know," he admitted, the weariness in his voice matching the defeated gesture of rubbing at his brow. It was clear we were both grappling with the reality of our situation, struggling to find purpose in the actions dictated by our predicament.

My reaction, a scoff followed by a loud snort, was involuntary—a response born out of frustration and a refusal to succumb to despair. As I turned my gaze back to the Portal, the symbol of our imprisonment and the focus of my determination, I resolved that Paul's resignation would not be my own. The thought of him attempting to assemble the tent without my help didn't move me; to assist would be to accept our fate here, and that was something I was not ready to do.

There had to be a way back, a solution that eluded us. The vast expanse of Clivilius, with its endless stretches of soft, brown, red, and orange dust, seemed to mock us with its tranquility. Yet, it also fuelled my resolve. The landscape, so foreign and yet so indifferent, was a challenge—a puzzle that I was determined to solve.

As I stood there, staring out into the barren horizon, the desire to return home became more than just a wish; it became a mission. The stark beauty of Clivilius, for all its desolation, was not my world.

"This is shit," the words slipped from me, a whispered testament to the frustration boiling inside as I confronted the Portal once more. Its presence, a bizarre anomaly in this desolate landscape, commanded attention despite my growing resentment towards it. The Portal, with its large, clear screen rising eerily from the ground, stood as a silent challenge—a gateway that had so far only mocked our attempts to understand or control it.

Curiosity overcame my frustration for a moment as I examined the oddity before me. It was an impressive sight, roughly three meters wide and five meters high, its dimensions suggesting a door to infinite possibilities, now a barrier to our return. The screen, transparent and seemingly fragile in its dormancy, was a contradiction to the force it wielded.

I reached out, my fingers tentatively tapping the screen, half expecting a reaction, any sign of life from this enigmatic barrier. But there was nothing, no sound, no vibration, just the cold, unyielding surface under my touch. My bewilderment grew, and with it, a reckless need for some form of acknowledgment, any indication that this thing was more than just an impassive wall.

Tapping harder yielded no different result, the silence around me becoming a mocking companion to my efforts. Driven by a mix of curiosity and defiance, I slammed my hand against the screen with all the force I could muster. The lack of noise, the absence of any reaction from the Portal, was infuriating. The only feedback was the sharp pain that raced through my palm, a physical retort to my aggression, leaving me with nothing but my own soft grunt.

At least I know it's something physical, I mused, the dull ache in my palm serving as a bizarre confirmation of its reality. The logic was simple yet irrefutable—if my hand couldn't pass through it, then it must be real. With this thought anchoring me, I began a methodical search around the perimeter of the screen, hoping to discover some hidden mechanism, a power button perhaps, that could be the key to activating the Portal and returning us home.

However, my search yielded nothing but more questions. The large, transparent screen stood mute, unyielding, and utterly devoid of any discernible features that could hint at its operation. The lack of any interface, any point of interaction, was baffling. *There has to be a way,* I thought, refusing to accept defeat.

Driven by a mix of desperation and hope, I attempted to command the Portal into action. "Portal activate!" I called out, half-expecting the dormant screen to spring to life with the swirling colours that signified its activation. Yet, it remained unchanged, as silent and transparent as ever.

"Take me back home!" I demanded, the urgency in my voice betraying the fear that perhaps we were truly stranded. When that too failed, I tried a more specific command, "Take me to Earth!" hoping for any sign of acknowledgment, any indication that we were not entirely at the mercy of this unresponsive monolith. But the Portal remained indifferent to my pleas.

In a moment of sheer frustration, I lashed out. "Activate, you fucking piece of shit!" The anger that had been simmering beneath the surface erupted in a scream, my foot sending clouds of dust into the air—a futile gesture against the impassive structure.

The silence that followed my outburst was a stark reminder of our isolation. The Portal, our only apparent hope for escape, offered no response, no hint of a way forward. It was then, in a moment of quiet desperation, that a new thought struck me. "The dust," I whispered, a glimmer of hope piercing the growing despair. Maybe the key to unlocking the Portal's secrets lay not in the screen itself but in its surroundings.

Dropping to my knees, I began to dig along the bottom edge of the screen, my hands moving frantically through the soft, red and orange dust. The possibility that the solution to our predicament could be buried here, just beneath the surface, lent a frenzied urgency to my actions. The dust, which had been nothing more than a backdrop to our confinement, suddenly held the potential for salvation—or so I hoped.

"Jamie!" Paul's voice cut through my focus, pulling me away from my desperate search at the base of the Portal. My head snapped up, irritation creasing my forehead as I spotted him on a small hill in the distance. *What does he want? He's interrupting me!* The frustration was palpable, a physical entity in itself, as I glared back at the Portal. In that moment, I wanted it to feel my anger, to understand the depth of my resolve. *I am going to find a way home!*

"Come over here," Paul's voice carried again, his figure outlined against the stark landscape, arms flailing in an attempt to grab my attention. His beckoning, likely meant as a distraction from the futility of arguing with an inanimate object, only served to deepen my reluctance. Yet, despite my annoyance, a sliver of curiosity wormed its way through my resolve. *But then, I thought, it is Paul, and it wouldn't take a lot to get him excited.* The thought was a mix of skepticism and a begrudging acknowledgment of Paul's typically optimistic nature.

With a heavy sigh, I pushed myself to my feet, the dust clinging to my hands serving as a gritty reminder of my failed efforts. The walk towards Paul felt longer than it should have, each step a testament to the weariness that had settled into my bones. The Portal, that mocking gateway to an uncertain fate, remained at my back—a silent sentinel to our plight.

"Hurry up," Paul's voice, tinged with excitement, broke through my contemplative trudge, injecting a sense of urgency into my steps. His enthusiasm was contagious, even against my better judgment.

"What is it?" I called out, my curiosity piqued as I neared the gentle incline that Paul had effortlessly scaled. The prospect of discovering something, anything, that deviated from the endless expanse of dust and desolation we had encountered thus far was enough to quicken my pace.

"There's a river," came Paul's response, his voice bubbling with a hopefulness that had been in short supply since our arrival in Clivilius. He didn't wait for my reaction, instead turning and disappearing over the hill's crest, eager to explore this new find.

My face lit up. *A river,* I echoed in my mind, the words carrying with them the possibility of life, of a respite from the unyielding aridity that surrounded us. The thought that there might be a hint of civilisation in this barren world, a sign that we were not as isolated as we feared, sparked a flicker of hope within me. A small smile, involuntary and revealing, tugged at the corner of my mouth, tempting me to embrace this discovery as a sign that our situation might not be as dire as it seemed.

But as quickly as the smile came, I checked it, a reminder of the resolve I had been clinging to. *Not yet,* I admonished myself. The discovery of a river, while promising, was not enough to make me surrender to the notion that our fate was to remain in Clivilius. This place, for all its mysteries and dangers, had not yet defeated my determination to find a way back home.

Catching up with Paul required a burst of energy I wasn't sure I possessed, but the promise of discovering something new in this desolate landscape spurred me on. By the time I reached the spot where he had called out to me, Paul was already making his way up another dusty hill. I pushed myself, my legs burning with the effort, curious and eager to see the river he had discovered.

As I crested the hill and descended to where Paul knelt, the sight that greeted me was unexpectedly serene—a wide river, its waters flowing with a clarity that seemed almost out of place in Clivilius. Dropping to my knees beside him, the soft dust cushioning my landing, I leaned forward to get a closer look at the water. It was pristine, untouched, and inviting.

"It's so clear," I remarked, the transparency of the water offering a stark contrast to the omnipresent dust and desolation that defined much of Clivilius. The thought of clean, drinkable water in such an environment brought a sliver of hope. "Do you think it's safe to drink?" I asked, turning to Paul for his opinion.

His shrug was both expected and somehow disappointing. My question had been impulsive, born out of hope rather than reason. Paul's nonchalant response reminded me that we were far from the comforts and certainties of home. I chided myself silently for the oversight. Paul's life in Broken

Hill, a place I had often jokingly referred to as the "arse-end of nowhere," had undoubtedly accustomed him to a lifestyle far removed from the urban conveniences and safety nets I took for granted.

Throwing caution to the wind felt reckless, yet irresistibly compelling in that moment beside the river. As I dipped my fingers into the crystalline water, the sensation that coursed through me was unexpected—a rush of exhilaration that seemed to blur the lines between the coolness of the water and a warmth that tingled through my veins. "It feels cool and fresh," I remarked, my voice betraying a hint of my astonishment at the water's strangely invigorating effect.

Encouraged by my actions, Paul followed suit, submerging his hand into the river. I couldn't help but watch him intently, curious to see if he would experience the same peculiar sensation. The visible shiver that ran through him confirmed it; the water's unique properties affected him as well. It was a small, shared discovery, momentarily lightening the burden of our situation.

My initial resolve to remain stoic, to not find joy in anything Clivilius offered as a silent protest against our entrapment, wavered. The smile that broke across my face was spontaneous, a genuine reaction to the momentary pleasure and Paul's reaction.

"I could totally jump in right now," Paul mused, his voice carrying a lightness that had been absent since our arrival. The idea was tempting, a brief escape from the reality that awaited us beyond the riverbank.

"Well, you'd have to do it skinny," I found myself saying, laughter bubbling up with the words. It was a moment of levity, a brief return to the camaraderie that seemed distant.

Paul's quizzical look in response to my comment was almost comical. "Huh?" he asked, momentarily puzzled by the suggestion.

"Well, we don't have any towels or spare clothes," I explained, grounding our whimsical thoughts back to practical concerns. His acknowledgment, a simple "Oh. Of course," was accompanied by a shift in his gaze back to the flowing water, perhaps contemplating the river's beauty or the fleeting thought of what could have been a carefree plunge.

As Paul and I lingered by the river, the simple act of immersing our hands in its waters became a brief respite from the weight of our predicament. The sensation was undeniably invigorating, a momentary escape that allowed us to forget, if only for a while, the uncertainty that loomed over us.

"Do you really think we're stuck here?" Paul's question broke through the tranquility of the moment, his gaze meeting mine with a mixture of concern and hope. It was a question I had been asking myself since we arrived, the answer to which I feared more than anything.

My immediate reaction was one of tension, the worry that had been simmering beneath the surface manifesting in a tight frown. "I don't know," I admitted, the words heavy with the burden of our unknown fate. "I hope not." It was the truth, a simple yet profound wish that we could find our way back to the world we knew.

"But what if we are?" Paul pressed, his question hanging between us like a dark cloud threatening to burst.

Frustration flared within me at the thought, pushing me to my feet in an irritated huff. "If Luke can get out, I don't see why we can't too," I declared. The idea that we were somehow less capable of navigating this challenge than Luke was infuriating. Without another word, I turned on my heel and strode back towards the Portal, the large, enigmatic screen that was both our hope and our curse.

I didn't look back to see if Paul followed; his optimism, though usually a source of light, felt misplaced in our current situation. Over the years, I had come to recognise the impact of Paul's unwavering positivity on Luke—and by extension, on situations like ours. Paul's optimism, while admirable, often veered into the realm of fantasy, encouraging Luke's already scattered focus to chase after impractical dreams. Their dynamic, though fuelled by brotherly love, sometimes strayed into the territory of distraction, pulling Luke further away from reality.

As I marched towards the Portal, determined to find a way back, I couldn't help but reflect on the influence Paul had on Luke. It was an influence that, in moments like these, felt more like a hindrance. Paul's presence, his encouragement of Luke's wilder ventures, only compounded the challenge of finding a solution. In my heart, I knew that to navigate this ordeal, to truly find a way back, we needed more than optimism—we needed a plan grounded in reality. The task ahead was daunting, but my resolve was firm. We would find a way home, no matter the cost.

ABSOLUTION

4338.205.5

"Figured out how it works yet?" Paul's voice, tinged with a hopefulness I couldn't share, snapped me back to the harsh reality of our situation.

I turned towards him, my frustration boiling over as I lashed out at the inanimate object before me. "This thing is fucking useless!" The words burst from me with a vehemence that felt cathartic, even as they echoed futilely against the desolate expanse. My foot sent a cloud of the omnipresent dust into the air, a physical manifestation of my anger and helplessness.

Paul's hesitation was palpable, a brief moment where the weight of my frustration seemed to give him pause. Yet, he recovered quickly, offering a suggestion that, under different circumstances, I might have dismissed outright. "Why don't you give that a rest for a bit and help me move these boxes?" he proposed, his voice steady. "It might help you to keep your mind and hands busy with something else."

His words hung between us, and I found myself caught in a moment of introspection. *The nerve of him*, I thought bitterly. Paul, with his ever-present optimism, couldn't possibly understand the depth of my frustration. *How dare he presume to know what's best for me?* His suggestion felt like a dismissal of the gravity of our situation, an underestimation of the turmoil churning within me.

Yet, as I stood there, my gaze wandering over the desolate landscape that stretched endlessly around us, the silence, the emptiness, the oppressive ubiquity of dust, I was struck by the futility of my anger. Paul's offer, though perhaps naïve, was a lifeline in a sea of uncertainty—a chance to focus on something tangible, however mundane, in the face of our overwhelming predicament.

"Sure," I acquiesced, the word escaping me in a resigned exhale. Accepting Paul's suggestion didn't come easily, but the alternative—standing idle, consumed by anger and despair—offered no solace. Moving the boxes, engaging in a task, any task, seemed a better use of my time than railing against an unresponsive Portal. It was a small concession, a begrudging acknowledgment that, perhaps, Paul's approach—keeping busy, maintaining hope—might offer a temporary reprieve from the helplessness that threatened to engulf me.

As I surveyed the assortment of boxes before us, the larger ones immediately caught my attention with their blue plastic strips—a feeble attempt at reinforcement that did little to disguise their cumbersome nature. They seemed awkwardly shaped and unwieldy, prompting me to opt for a smaller box instead. Wrapped tightly in thick packaging tape, it promised to be more manageable. Yet, as I lifted it, the weight caught me off guard, my biceps straining against the unexpected heft. *Who knew a tent had heavy parts,* I mused silently, a mix of annoyance and amusement threading through my thoughts. Imagining Luke hauling these boxes around by himself brought a soft chuckle to my lips. The mental image of his struggle was a small, light-hearted reprieve.

As Paul and I worked, a new pile of boxes began to take shape in a flat clearing near the river. The location Paul had chosen, much to my surprise, was actually quite reasonable. The proximity to the water source and the flat terrain made it an ideal spot for setting up whatever semblance of a camp we could manage. Acknowledging this, even silently, felt like a concession on my part—a rare moment of agreement with Paul's judgment. It was a realisation that, despite our differing perspectives and the occasional clash of personalities, Paul's optimism and his knack for finding practical solutions in the face of adversity were assets in our shared struggle to make the best of our situation in Clivilius.

❖

Luke's arrival, with his proclamation of "bearing gifts," momentarily cut through the tension that had settled over Paul and me by the riverbank. His attempt at humour, however, did little to quell the irritation that had been simmering within me. *About bloody time,* I couldn't help but think, my patience wearing thin after the ordeal with the boxes and the unyielding Portal. "There had better be a knife in that bag of yours," I found myself saying, the frustration evident in my tone. The practical challenges of our situation had quickly overshadowed any initial wonder at finding ourselves in Clivilius, reducing our concerns to the most basic of needs—like opening a box.

Luke's response, "As a matter of fact, there is," accompanied by the gleeful presentation of a large kitchen knife, was a small, yet significant, victory. Relief washed over me as I took in the sight of the knife, a tool so mundane under normal circumstances, now imbued with an almost ridiculous level of importance. *When I return to earth,* I promised myself, *I am definitely going to petition for fewer packaged goods.* The thought, half-serious and half-jest, was a mental note on the absurdities we'd already come to face in our current predicament.

"Thank God for that," Paul exclaimed. "We moved all these boxes ready to put the tent up and then realised we couldn't get that blue plastic crap off. I was about to start trying to bite my way through." The image of Paul resorting to teeth against plastic in a desperate bid to make progress brought an involuntary smile to my face.

Luke's presentation of the small toolkit as an additional offering to our survival arsenal drew a chuckle from me. It wasn't so much the gesture itself but the thought of Luke, with his penchant for overlooking the practicalities, deeming this as essential. "Did you check that all the tools were actually in there?" I couldn't resist adding a condescending edge to my question. In my mind, Luke handling tools was akin to a fish trying to climb a tree—futile and slightly amusing to imagine. His technological savvy might have gotten us to Clivilius, but when it came to hands-on practicality, I had my doubts.

"Of course, I did," he retorted, a snap in his voice that suggested my jab had hit a nerve. It was a rare instance of Luke showing irritation, which only piqued my interest further.

"And?" I prodded, barely containing my anticipation for the inevitable confirmation of my assumptions.

"And most of it is in there. Only a few random bits are missing. But I don't know what any of them are anyway, so I doubt they would have been very useful," he admitted with a casual shrug, as if the absence of these "random bits" was inconsequential.

My reaction was automatic, an eye roll that conveyed my sense of vindication without a word needing to be said. *I'm right, as usual.* Luke's ambitious claims of self-sufficiency in building and repairs had become a running joke between us, primarily because his enthusiasm often outstripped his preparation, leaving a trail of unfinished projects and misplaced tools in his wake.

"Now, why doesn't that surprise me?" Paul's comment, dripping with sarcasm, was a light jab but one that resonated with a shared history of witnessing Luke's overestimations of his handiwork capabilities.

Despite my earlier criticism of Luke, I found myself jumping to his defence. "Well, it's not like you're any better," I retorted, turning the spotlight back onto Paul. His own attempts at home improvement were a source of much amusement and bewilderment among us. "I've seen the unfortunate state of your latest home construction project. Scrolling through your Facebook is like watching all the 'before' bits from DIY SOS back-to-back." My words, though teasing, were not without a base of truth. Paul's projects, much like Luke's, often started with grand visions that seldom matched the reality of their execution.

"Anyway," Luke began, effectively halting the playful banter, "The two of you had better get to work putting this tent together. We have no idea what the temperature or conditions are like at night here. We'd better be as prepared for the unexpected as possible."

His directive, while sound, left me momentarily taken aback. "We?" I echoed, my incredulity evident as I gestured between Paul and myself. "And what about you? Aren't you going to help us?" The notion of Luke departing on another errand, however well-intentioned, while leaving us to tackle the logistics of our shelter, seemed disproportionately unfair.

Luke's justification, however, held a certain appeal. "I'm going to see if I can get us a couple more tents. I know this one is huge, but I'm sure you'd both appreciate having your own." He had a point. The thought of personal space, even in such dire circumstances, was undeniably comforting. The idea of sharing close quarters with Paul, whom I knew only through sporadic encounters, was far from appealing. Luke's understanding of my preference for solitude, a trait he was well acquainted with, was both a relief and a reminder of the depth of our partnership.

"Good point," Paul conceded. "He's not wrong." His agreement, mirroring my own reluctant acceptance, marked a rare moment of consensus between us. It was an unusual alignment of opinions, given our differing outlooks on life and our current situation.

I found myself shrugging in agreement, a silent concession to the practicality of Luke's plan. My raised eyebrow betrayed my surprise at this unexpected harmony between Paul and me. *Did Paul and I just agree on something?* The thought, fleeting as it was, highlighted the ways in which Clivilius was already changing us, forcing us to find common ground in the face of adversity. The shared goal of survival, it seemed, had the power to bridge even the most unlikely of divides.

As Luke made to leave, a sudden impulse seized me. "Wait!" I couldn't let him go without at least trying once more to leave this place together. The idea of making another attempt at escape, even with the slim odds, was better than resigning ourselves to waiting for Luke's return. "We may as well see if we can leave with you again," I suggested, turning towards Paul, hoping for his support in this spur-of-the-moment plan.

"Sure! Good idea," Paul responded, though the lack of conviction in his voice was palpable. It was clear that hope was a scarce commodity among us, but the agreement was enough to set us into motion.

With a shared, albeit hesitant, determination, we made our way back to the Portal. The dust beneath our feet seemed to mock our efforts with its omnipresence, a constant reminder of the desolation that surrounded us. Yet, the possibility of leaving, of returning to a world where the ground beneath us wasn't a constant haze of dust, spurred me forward. My desire to return to the familiar comforts of home was a powerful motivator, one that overshadowed the resignation that had begun to take hold.

Then, without any warning or discernible trigger, the Portal sprang to life. It was as if the very air around us vibrated in anticipation before the screen erupted into a dazzling display of colours. Brilliant hues burst forth from its centre, spreading until the whole screen was alive with pulsating light. The sight was mesmerising, a stark contrast to the bleak landscape that had become our prison.

Despite my curiosity, I suppressed the question that bubbled up within me—*how had Luke managed to activate the Portal?* In that moment, the mechanics of it all seemed inconsequential. The "how" and "why" of the Portal's sudden activation paled in comparison to the singular thought that consumed me: *escape*. If this spectacle meant a chance to leave Clivilius behind, to avoid ever having to understand its mysteries, then I was more than willing to embrace ignorance.

As I faced the vibrant, pulsating Portal, a sense of desperation took hold. With each hand, I reached out towards the swirling colours, my movements deliberate, fuelled by the faint hope that this time, something would be different. The sensation was like pushing against an unseen force, a barrier that grew stronger with every attempt to breach it. Despite leaning in with all my might, my hands refused to penetrate the brilliant façade of light and colour. It was as if the Portal itself was consciously denying me passage, a gatekeeper to a path I so desperately sought.

Then, cutting through the silence and my futile efforts, came the voice—ominous and chilling in its clarity. *Clive sees you, Jamie Greyson. You will never leave Clivilius*. The words echoed around me, their finality striking a chord of fear deep within my chest. My face drained of colour as the gravity of the proclamation sunk in. The voice, embodying the will of Clivilius itself, seemed to cement my fate with those few, haunting words.

Surely this isn't true. It can't be, can it!? The thought raced through my mind, a whirlwind of panic and disbelief. The idea that our presence had been noted, named, and bound by this place—by an entity known as Clive—was too much to comprehend. The notion of being trapped here indefinitely, of never seeing home again, was a reality I wasn't prepared to accept. Yet, the voice's declaration left little room for doubt, instilling a deep-seated fear that our attempts to escape might indeed be futile.

In that moment, the vibrant colours of the Portal no longer represented a beacon of hope but a mocking reminder of our imprisonment. The voice, with its ominous message, had transformed the allure of the Portal into a symbol of our captivity. The realisation that Clivilius might be more than just a location—that it might possess a consciousness or will of its own—was both terrifying and bewildering. The implications of being under the watchful gaze of something known as Clive, something capable of denying our departure so definitively, painted a grim picture of our situation. As the weight of the voice's words settled around me, the struggle to find a way home took on a new, more daunting dimension.

As I faced Paul, the weight of my defeat pressing heavily upon me, I couldn't help but feel a desperate urge to see if he might succeed where I had failed. "You try," I said, my voice a mix of hope and resignation, gesturing towards the Portal with a hand that barely concealed my trembling. The defeat wasn't just in my words but in my eyes, a clear signal of the hopelessness that had taken hold.

Paul's hesitation was palpable. He took a cautious step forward, his eyes searching mine for reassurance, for any sign that this might end differently than my own attempts. "Go," I urged him again, my voice firmer this time, though it did little to mask the anxiety that gripped me. Watching him, I was torn between wanting him to succeed, to find his way back to a world we both longed for, and the selfish part of me that recoiled at the thought of being left behind alone.

As Paul approached the Portal at what felt like an agonisingly slow pace, my patience snapped. Acting on impulse, fuelled by a mix of frustration and a desperate need for something, anything, to happen, I stepped forward and gave Paul a forceful shove in the back. My heart raced as he stumbled towards the Portal, his hands reaching out towards the swirling colours that had denied me passage.

For a brief, irrational moment, my eyes lit up with the possibility of change, of escape. But just as quickly as that hope flared, it was extinguished. The Portal, unyielding and indifferent, repelled Paul with the same invisible force that had thwarted me, setting him back on his feet with an abruptness that left us both staring in disbelief.

The tension that had been building finally erupted as I witnessed the tears forming in Paul's eyes. Luke rushed to Paul's side with concern etched across his face. "Are you hurt?" he inquired, looking for tangible injuries that could explain the sudden emotional outburst.

Paul's anger, directed squarely at me, was a palpable force. "What the fuck did you do that for?" he yelled, his voice a mixture of pain and fury. The accusation stung, more so because part of me questioned the same thing. In my mind, the mysterious entity of Clivilius, or Clive, loomed as a potential threat, yet part of me clung to the hope that this place, this situation, wouldn't truly harm us. It was a thin thread of hope, frayed and fragile.

"So, you heard it too?" The words slipped out, a desperate attempt to find common ground in our shared predicament. Paul's silent nod was a confirmation I hadn't realised I needed until that moment.

"Heard what?" Luke's confusion added another layer to the already heavy atmosphere. His question, innocent and concerned, forced me to confront the harsh reality we were all trying to process.

The frustration and helplessness I felt exploded in a moment of raw emotion. "Fucking shit!" I couldn't contain the outburst, my foot lashing out at the dust beneath us in a futile gesture of defiance. The dust kicked up, swirling around us, and I was seized by a coughing fit, a physical manifestation of Clivilius's indifferent response to our turmoil.

Paul's tearful admission cut through the tension. "That we can never leave," he said, the weight of those words hanging heavy in the air. "This is it. Forever. I'm going to die here." The defeat in his voice was a mirror to the despair we all felt, a grim acceptance of our seemingly inescapable fate.

Luke's response, a simple "Oh," was painfully inadequate in the face of our collective despair. His eyes, downcast, refused to meet ours, as if the ground beneath us held any answers to the dire situation we found ourselves in.

Anger surged through me like a wildfire, uncontrollable and fierce. My frustration with Luke, with this entire situation, boiled over in a moment of raw fury. "You fucking arsehole!" The words erupted from me, each one laden with the betrayal and fear that had been simmering beneath the surface since our arrival in Clivilius. My feet barely touched the ground as I closed the gap between us, propelled by a need for answers, for accountability. I shoved Luke hard in the chest, the physical manifestation of my anger, demanding, "What in the name of holy-fuck were you thinking? How the hell did you think this was going to go? Did you think we wouldn't find out? Is that it? Did you think you could literally kidnap us and no one would fucking notice!?"

Luke's reaction was immediate, his hands coming up to swat mine away, a defensive gesture that did little to quell my rage. I was beyond reason, beyond the point of calm discussion. The thought of what could have driven Luke to make such a decision, to bring us to this place with what seemed like no way back, fuelled my anger further.

"Hey!" Paul's voice cut through the tension, his hand gripping my arm with surprising strength. His intervention, a desperate plea for sanity, momentarily halted my next move. "Fighting isn't going to help any of us." His words, though logical, were a distant concern compared to the tumultuous mix of betrayal and panic that clouded my judgment.

My reaction to Paul was harsh, fuelled by a cocktail of emotions. The frustration, the fear, the sense of betrayal—all of it came rushing out in a torrent of anger directed not just at Luke, but now at Paul as well. "You're no better than your pathetic excuse for a brother," I accused, the words laced with venom. The shove I gave Paul was more forceful than intended. Watching him stumble and fall, the shock and hurt evident in his expression, a part of me recoiled at my own actions.

Paul's reaction, a mix of disbelief and disappointment, was a mirror to the chaos churning inside me. His head shake, more than words could ever convey, spoke volumes of the rift my outburst had caused.

"Cut it out, Jamie!" Luke's voice sliced through the tension, his scream a desperate plea for sanity. It was the raw edge of fear in his voice that finally penetrated the fog of anger enveloping me. The urgency, the need in that scream, acted as a cold shock to my system, pulling me back from the brink.

In the aftermath of Luke's cry, I found myself frozen, my body tense with adrenaline, my breathing heavy and uneven. The realisation of what I had become, of the anger I had allowed to control me, was sobering. I turned away from Paul's gaze, which held a mixture of firmness and disbelief, a silent testament to the fracture my actions had caused among us.

The silence that followed was heavy, filled with the unspoken words and emotions that had driven us to this point. The awkwardness of the moment was palpable, a physical barrier that seemed almost insurmountable. In that silence, the reality of our situation settled heavily upon me. We were lost in an unfamiliar world, dependent on each other for survival, yet here I was, pushing away the very people I needed the most.

As Luke departed into the unknown, the silence that followed him was profound, a stark contrast to the turmoil churning within me. I stood there, rooted to the spot, watching as the vibrant colours of the Portal dimmed and dissolved into the air, taking Luke with them. The beauty of the display was lost on me, overshadowed by the gravity of what had just transpired.

A single tear, unbidden and unexpected, broke through my resolve, tracing a path down my cheek. I brushed it away with a mixture of anger and sorrow, my emotions a tumultuous storm. *I'll never forgive you for this, Luke!* The thought was a venomous whisper in my mind, a vow of resentment for leading us into this situation, for leaving us behind. Yet, even as I entertained thoughts of anger and betrayal, another tear made its escape, a silent testament to the complex web of feelings I was struggling to untangle.

My legs trembled beneath me, not just from the physical confrontation that had taken place but from the onslaught of emotions that threatened to overwhelm me. Anxiety coursed through me, a relentless tide that pulled at the very foundations of my resolve. Amidst the anger, the blame, and the fear, a more pressing question emerged, its weight heavier than any accusation I could level at Luke. *But will Luke ever forgive me?*

RESENTMENT

4338.205.6

    After the intensity of my earlier actions, the thought of simply co-existing alongside Paul, even in strained silence, seemed a daunting task. The residual anger from our confrontation with Luke lingered, a constant reminder of the emotional turmoil that had led to my outburst. Despite my best efforts to maintain a semblance of distance, the reality of our situation in Clivilius made isolation impossible. Reluctantly, I found myself joining Paul in the task of setting up our shelter—a necessary, if unwelcome, distraction from the tension that hung between us.

    As Paul knelt in the dust, his attention fixed on the picture of the ten-man tent emblazoned on the side of the box, a sense of irony struck me. The complexity of the task at hand, juxtaposed with our earlier conflict, seemed almost comical in its timing. Clutching the instruction booklet I'd fortuitously discovered, I couldn't help but feel a twisted sense of amusement at the prospect of watching Paul navigate the assembly without guidance. It was a petty thought, born out of a desire to find some levity in our grim circumstances. *This is going to be fun to watch,* I mused silently, a smirk tugging at the corners of my mouth. Yet, the recognition of our shared predicament, of the need to support one another, tempered my inclination for mischief. I resolved to let Paul in on the existence of the instructions, but not before allowing myself a brief moment of entertainment at his expense.

    I read the first step of the instructions, a simple directive that seemed almost laughably straightforward given the complexity of our current situation: *Check that all components are present.* It was a logical beginning, a reminder of the importance of organisation and thoroughness, even in the most unconventional of settings. I surveyed our makeshift campsite, my eyes moving from box to box, mentally ticking off each one as accounted for. The logic was undeniable—*If all the boxes are here,* I reasoned, *there's no need to pull everything out of them to check.* A sense of satisfaction washed over me as I mentally checked off the first step.

"Step two," I announced, breaking the silence that had enveloped us. The sound of my voice felt jarring in the quiet, a stark reminder of the need to communicate, to collaborate, despite the undercurrents of frustration and resentment. As I prepared to read aloud the next instruction, the act felt symbolic—a step towards not just erecting a physical shelter but towards bridging the gap that had formed between us. In the shared endeavour of constructing the tent, there lay an opportunity for reconciliation, for finding common ground amidst the dust and uncertainty of Clivilius.

❖

As I focused on assembling the tent, the sound of footsteps through the dust momentarily distracted me. My hands mechanically continued their task, snapping tent poles into place, but my attention was elsewhere—on Luke's approach to Paul. An uneasy knot tightened in my stomach, the sight of Luke walking past without acknowledging me reigniting a simmering tension. I swallowed the lump in my throat, attempting to quell the rising anxiety with silent self-reassurances. *It's not my fault,* I told myself, trying to offload the blame. *Luke's the one that brought us here.* Yet, the justification did little to ease the discomfort of the situation.

Paul's question to Luke was simple, yet loaded with the unspoken complexities of our predicament. "What are you doing?" The simplicity of the inquiry masked the deeper undercurrents of confusion and concern that we all felt.

Luke's actions, pulling his mobile phone from his pocket and attempting a call, piqued my curiosity. His question to Paul, "Did your phone ring?" added a new layer of intrigue to the unfolding situation. The notion that we were testing our mobiles for connectivity in Clivilius seemed almost absurd, yet desperate times called for desperate measures.

I watched the interaction with interest, while I pulled another dismantled tent pole from its box.

I continued to work on the tent, my hands moving of their own accord, as I listened to their exchange. Paul's response, slow and uncertain, "No, should it have?" highlighted the faint hope we all harboured that some semblance of normalcy, some link to our world, might still function here.

Luke's admission that he had tried calling Paul's phone, only to confirm the futility of our mobile devices in this place, was a sobering reminder of our isolation. His request for Paul to hand over his phone, under the pretext of it being useful for "sorting stuff out on the other side," was met with a mixture of skepticism and resignation on my part. The reality that our phones, our last tangible connection to the world we knew, were now rendered useless artefacts in Clivilius, underscored the severity of our situation.

Watching Paul fumble with his phone, the unmistakable signs of panic setting into his features, confirmed the grim reality we were all starting to grasp. Luke's assertion about the futility of our mobile devices in Clivilius wasn't just speculation; it was our new, harsh truth. As I felt the outline of my own phone through my trousers, a wave of reluctance washed over me. The desire to check, to cling to some sliver of hope that my phone would be the exception, was strong.

Yet, witnessing Paul's dismay, I couldn't bring myself to face the same disappointment. It seemed better, somehow, to leave it untouched, unconfirmed.

The moment Paul threw his phone at Luke's feet, my heart skipped a beat. It was so out of character for the Paul I knew —the level-headed, always rational Paul—that it underscored the severity of our situation. His actions were a clear indication of the stress we were under, a stress that was beginning to crack even the most optimistic among us.

Luke's response to Paul's frustration, a request for the passcode, was met with a sarcastic gesture from Paul—a pantomime search for a pen that both acknowledged the request and highlighted the absurdity of our circumstances. The futility of searching his pockets, knowing full well he wouldn't find a pen, was a small act of defiance, a moment of levity in an otherwise tense situation.

"Don't worry. I'm way ahead of you," Luke's smug revelation that he had anticipated the need for pen and paper, holding out a bag filled with such items, was both irritating and reassuring. His preparedness, while annoying in its presentation, was a reminder that despite our dire circumstances, Luke was thinking ahead, trying to maintain some level of organisation and control over what little we could manage in Clivilius.

The simmering anger within me felt like a brewing storm, ready to break at any moment. Luke's request, his entire demeanour, struck a nerve deep inside me. *Luke really is an arsehole,* I seethed internally. The notion of relinquishing our mobile phones felt akin to surrendering the last vestige of hope we clung to. In this alien place, where every familiar aspect of our lives had been stripped away, those phones represented more than just devices; they were our final, tenuous link to the world we knew, to the identities and lives we had been forced to leave behind.

Watching Paul comply with Luke's request, hastily scribbling down his passcode without a second thought, only fuelled my growing resentment. *What a pushover.* It was hard to watch, hard to understand how he could so easily give in. Perhaps for Paul, the action held little significance, a simple exchange in the face of our overwhelming situation. But for me, it symbolised so much more—a capitulation I was not yet ready to make.

"Your turn, Jamie," Paul's voice broke through my thoughts, an unwelcome intrusion. I couldn't even bring myself to look at him, to acknowledge the request. Instead, I focused on the task at hand, channelling my frustration into securing the tent pegs into the ground. Each push, each stab of the peg, was a defiance, a refusal to give in to Luke's demands.

"Jamie!" Luke's voice, more insistent this time, demanded my attention. I couldn't ignore him any longer. Lifting my gaze to meet his, I let the anger and determination in me find voice. "You're not having my fucking phone, Luke," I declared, my words laced with defiance. I returned to my task, pushing another tent peg into the ground with more force than necessary, each movement a clear statement of my stance.

"In the meantime," said Luke, glancing over at me purposefully, "You should both consider what your immediate needs are. Write them down and I'll get busy keeping you both alive, okay?"

Luke's suggestion that we should consider our immediate needs felt almost mocking in its practicality. The notion of writing down what we needed to survive, as if we were making a shopping list, seemed ludicrous in the context of our dire situation. *Show some balls, would you, Paul?* I thought bitterly as Paul readily agreed, his compliance at complete odds with the frustration boiling within me.

"Good. So, Paul wants to stay alive. Jamie?" Luke's attempt to include me, to gauge my needs, only served to stoke the flames of my discontent. My response was terse, filled with the pent-up resentment that had continued to fester. "Fuck off," I shot back, unwilling to engage in what I perceived as a pointless exercise.

Luke rolled his eyes at my outburst, a gesture that somehow managed to convey both annoyance and resignation. "I have a few things to take care of back on Earth. I'll come back for your list soon," he said, dismissing my hostility with an ease that only fuelled my anger further.

"What things have you got to take care of?" The question burst from me, a mixture of curiosity and challenge.

"Oh, you know. Just things that will keep you alive. I could just not bother if you'd prefer...?" Luke's retort was sharp, a clear reminder of our dependence on him, however much I loathed to admit it.

"Just fuck off already, Luke," I snapped, the veneer of control I was clinging to shattering under the weight of my barely suppressed rage. It was a plea as much as it was a dismissal, a demand for him to leave if he was not going to be straightforward with us.

"Fine," Luke replied, his voice carrying a hint of resignation. He gave Paul a final shrug, a silent gesture of goodbye or perhaps apology, before turning to walk towards the Portal, leaving us behind.

"And put some bloody clothes on while you're there!" I couldn't resist the parting shot, yelling after Luke's fading figure. It was a petty remark, born out of frustration and the need to assert some form of dominance, however trivial, in a situation where I felt increasingly powerless.

As Luke walked away, a wave of existential dread washed over me, prompting a barrage of introspective questions. *Am I ever going to escape? Is this my punishment for my indiscretions with Ben?* The rational part of my mind recognised the absurdity of such thoughts—there was no cosmic justice at play here, merely the harsh reality of our unforeseen circumstances. Yet, the ingrained guilt, a relic from my upbringing, stubbornly persisted, colouring my thoughts with unwarranted self-blame.

Paul's sudden outburst snapped me out of my reverie, his words cutting through the silence with an intensity that took me by surprise. "Why do you have to be so bloody nasty all the time?" The anger in his voice, the visible frustration, was something new, an unexpected glimpse into the depth of emotion he usually kept so well hidden. For a moment, I was taken aback, realising that Paul, too, had his limits. *So, Paul does have buttons,* I mused silently, a newfound understanding—or perhaps an advantage—unfolding before me.

Despite the tension between us, Paul's scrutiny felt invasive, an unwelcome reminder of the fragile dynamics that now defined our interaction. As I avoided his gaze and focused on the tent pegs, Paul's departure to the riverbank provided a brief respite from the mounting pressure. "Good riddance," I whispered to myself, a part of me relieved to have the space to work without the weight of his judgment.

Watching Paul's retreating figure, I couldn't help but feel a mix of resentment and relief. *I'll make quicker work of the tent without him anyway.* The knowledge that both Paul and Luke shared a similar lack of practical skills did little to boost my confidence in our collective ability to navigate the challenges of Clivilius. Stories of their past failures, recounted by Luke with a mix of affection and exasperation, came back to me, painting a not-so-reassuring picture of our prospects for survival.

❖

Time had become a fluid concept here in Clivilius, its passage seemingly untethered from the usual markers that dictated the rhythm of my days back on Earth. The frequent checks on my phone, a habit borne from a life once dictated by schedules and deadlines, now served only as a reminder of our disconnection from that world. Each glance at the device's unresponsive screen underscored our isolation, the battery's demise a result of my own negligence. The irony wasn't lost on me—here, in a place where time seemed irrelevant, I was concerned about a dead phone.

Attempting to use the sun as a makeshift clock felt laughably inadequate. The sky above, though familiar in its vastness, was a stranger in its details. The position of the sun, which I had hoped might offer some hint of the time, proved to be an exercise in futility. Whether it had been an hour or several since we'd started setting up the tent, the realisation dawned on me that it mattered little. Our tasks, our survival, didn't adhere to a schedule. There was no deadline to meet, no appointment to keep. Just the relentless, uncharted hours stretching before us, filled with challenges we were only beginning to comprehend.

Paul's return from his impromptu expedition broke the monotony of my thoughts. His absence, which I had initially deemed inconsiderate, was now something I viewed with a touch of envy. The idea of simply walking away, even just upstream, had its appeal—a brief respite from the tension that seemed to have taken root between us. I watched as he made his way back through the dust, a part of me curious about his journey, another resenting the ease with which he seemed to embrace our new reality.

The realisation that my own anger was a burden— exhausting in its intensity and persistence—was a reluctant admission. It was a force that consumed energy with little return, leaving me drained and no closer to finding a way back home. Perhaps it was time to consider a truce, however temporary, to conserve our strength for the challenges that lay ahead.

The sight of Paul's red eyes, coupled with the unmistakable odour that now seemed to cling to him, elicited a blunt reaction from me. "You stink like shit," I blurted out, my words sharp and without consideration. It was only after the fact, as the implications of what that smell signified hit me, that I regretted my harshness. *Fuck,* I thought, the realisation washing over me in an uncomfortable wave. The practicalities of living in Clivilius, stripped of the conveniences and privacy we took for granted back home, were beginning to make themselves known. The thought sent a shiver of dread through me. *Will I be next?* The question lingered ominously in my mind, the certainty of my own eventual need a source of burgeoning anxiety. My disdain for the situation was quickly replaced with fear, my hands betraying a tremor I couldn't control.

Paul's reaction to my comment, a mix of embarrassment and indignation, was palpable even as he struggled to find the right words. When he finally spoke, his voice carried a mixture of resignation and defiance. "I'm getting in the river. Don't come over," he stated, his flat tone leaving no room for argument.

Despite the initial harshness of my words, I found myself feeling a sudden, profound empathy for Paul. The challenges we were facing, from the most basic of human needs to the complex emotions stirred up by our predicament, were a common enemy. My nod, meant to convey understanding and agreement, was also an unspoken apology for my earlier insensitivity.

This moment, awkward and humbling, was a stark reminder of our shared vulnerability. The realisation that we were all grappling with the same fears, the same discomforts, and the same indignities, served as a grounding force. It underscored the fact that any semblance of normalcy we could cling to in this strange world would depend not just on our ability to adapt physically, but on our willingness to support each other emotionally.

As Paul made his way to the river, I was left to reflect on the harsh truths of our new reality. The barriers of privacy and decorum that we had lived by on Earth were dissolving, leaving us exposed in more ways than one.

❖

Sitting beside Paul on the riverbank, the tension that had been weighing heavily on us began to lift, if only slightly. The camaraderie felt fragile, yet it was a welcome respite from the isolation that Clivilius imposed.

"What now?" I called out as Luke approached.

"I've got clothes on," he announced, his voice carrying across the distance. His playful twirl, jeans sweeping the dust into a swirl around him, was so quintessentially Luke—unconcerned with the gravity of our situation, finding moments of levity where none seemed to exist.

"You're such a dork," Paul laughed, the sound genuine and warm. It was a reminder of the lighter moments we used to share back on Earth, moments that now seemed as distant as home itself.

"I know," Luke replied with a smile and a soft shrug, embodying the role of the endearing dork without reservation. Then, holding up a roll of garbage bags, he offered a practical solution to a problem I hadn't yet considered. "I figured rather than dirty a beautiful, clean world, you can put all your rubbish in these and I can take them back to Earth."

The mention of Earth, of transporting something as mundane as rubbish back to our home planet, struck a chord within me. *Earth? We can take rubbish back to Earth?* The thought sparked a glimmer of hope, however faint. "But how is that possible? I thought we couldn't leave?" The words tumbled out, a mix of confusion and a desperate need for clarity.

"You can't," Luke confirmed, his tone matter-of-fact. "But it seems that items can. I took Paul's phone, remember?" His explanation, while offering a partial answer, only served to deepen the mystery of our circumstances.

The revelation that inanimate objects could traverse the void back to Earth, while we remained trapped, was a bitter pill to swallow. Luke's ability to transport our refuse, a seemingly trivial act, underscored the arbitrariness of the rules governing Clivilius. It raised questions about the nature of the barrier that kept us bound to this alien landscape, about what other possibilities might exist just beyond our understanding.

"You might want to keep anything combustible," Luke added. "We have no idea what the conditions are like here at night, remember."

As I cast a glance at Paul, who seemed to readily accept Luke's advice, I couldn't help but express my skepticism with an eye roll. Despite my outward show of disdain, the underlying concern about what lay ahead once the sun set was impossible to ignore. *I am going to find a way home,* I silently reaffirmed to myself, clinging to the hope of escape rather than facing the prospect of enduring a night in this place.

Reluctantly, I joined in the task of filling the garbage bag, my movements mechanical, driven more by a desire to keep busy than any real belief in the precaution's necessity. It was Luke's elongated "So..." that broke the monotony of the chore, his tone suggesting an impending topic that I wasn't sure I wanted to address.

"So, what?" I replied, my voice tinged with a hint of defensiveness. I braced myself for whatever Luke was about to broach, not pausing in my efforts to pick up the rubbish from the tent boxes we had unpacked.

"So... Why is it that you can make such a big deal about me, your partner, having no shirt on, yet you seem to be perfectly comfortable with my brother flashing himself around?" The accusation, laced with a hint of jealousy, took me by surprise.

Whoa! The thought hit me like a bolt from the blue. *Where the hell did that come from?* The idea that Luke might be jealous of his brother, of the attention or perhaps the comfort level I exhibited around Paul, was something I hadn't considered.

Paul fumbled with the corner of the bag, its contents spilling into the dust as the side dropped.

I sighed heavily. The reality of our basic needs, now starkly highlighted by Paul's shirtless state, pushed me to articulate our immediate requirements. "I think you better bring us a couple of towels, a few rolls of toilet paper and a shovel," I stated, trying to maintain a semblance of calm in the face of our growing list of necessities. Paul's addition, a request for his bag of clothes, was met with a nod from Luke, whose silence bespoke an understanding of the discomfort and embarrassment wrapped up in these requests.

As we busied ourselves with the task of repacking the rubbish, the awkwardness of our conversation lingered in the air, a tangible reminder of the adaptability and resilience being demanded of us. The act of preparing for Luke's departure, of handing over lists and discussing what items were essential for our survival, felt almost surreal.

Luke's assurance, as he pocketed Paul's list with a promise to fulfil our needs, provided a small but significant comfort. The sight of the Portal coming to life, its colours swirling into a mesmerising display, sent a rush of adrenaline through me. The possibility that Luke could successfully transport items back to Earth, that this connection between worlds was not entirely severed, offered a glimmer of hope.

The moment Luke stepped through the Portal, the garbage bags disappearing with him, was one of profound anticipation and anxiety. The collective gasp that escaped Paul and me was a testament to the high stakes of this experiment. Watching Luke vanish, the possibility of re-establishing a link with Earth that existed beyond the coming and goings of only Luke, however tenuous, became momentarily tangible.

As I turned to Paul, my face breaking into an involuntary grin, the words "There may be hope for us yet," spilled out. In that moment, the weight of our predicament seemed slightly less crushing. The successful transfer of the garbage bags through the Portal represented more than just a logistical victory; it symbolised a potential lifeline, a means through which we might eventually find our way back home.

UNCLEAN

4338.205.7

As I watched the tent sway precariously, Paul's corner collapsing yet again, a mix of frustration and resignation settled over me. Shouting "Hey!" from across the tent, I couldn't help but marvel at the irony of our situation. Here we were, stranded on an alien planet, and our immediate challenge was not battling extraterrestrial elements or deciphering an alien landscape but rather, the seemingly simple task of erecting a tent.

Paul's apologetic "Sorry," floated back to me for what felt like the hundredth time. The sincerity of his apology did little to temper my irritation. I found myself wondering, not for the first time, if Luke had deliberately chosen a ten-man tent to test our patience and teamwork skills. The tent's size made it impossible for one person to manage alone, forcing us to rely on each other. In theory, a good idea, but in practice, with Paul's lack of dexterity, it was proving to be a Herculean task.

Watching Paul release the pole once more, the tent's structure wobbling before succumbing to gravity, my patience finally snapped. "For fuck's sake!" I hissed, my voice a mixture of anger and desperation. The repetition of this cycle, the constant collapse and rebuild, was not just a physical drain but an emotional one as well.

"Finally!" Paul called out, running to greet Luke as he approached.

"I wasn't gone that long," Luke's casual response, as he handed over the supplies, underscored his unawareness of the struggle Paul and I faced in his absence. The challenges that seemed monumental to us were mere blips in the broader scope of our survival efforts.

Proudly, I gestured towards the partially erected tent, eager for Luke to acknowledge our efforts. "You were gone long enough," I boasted, my words a mix of pride and a hint of reproach for leaving us to fend for ourselves. Luke's commendation, "You've made good progress. You'll have it finished in no time," was delivered with his usual optimism, a trait that, despite my frustrations, I couldn't help but admire.

Luke's mention of needing to find Paul some clothes before giving the tent a closer inspection felt like a subtle dismissal of our achievement. However, his promise to return quickly left me hopeful that we could indeed finish the task at hand without further setbacks.

As Luke departed once more, I turned back to the task, calling Paul back to work. "Come on, clumsy," I teased, the nickname a light-hearted jab meant to spur us into action rather than to criticise. "Let's get this bloody tent finished."

With renewed determination, I positioned the tent pole, feeling the structure's weight shift as we hoisted the roof. Paul's cooperation, his corner rising in tandem with mine, was a small victory. The satisfying snap of the pole locking into place was a sign of progress, a tangible indicator that, despite the odds, we were capable of working together effectively.

❖

Stepping back to admire the fully erected tent, its dark green canvas stark against the backdrop of Clivilius's vast, orange and brown dust, I allowed myself a moment of satisfaction. "Done," I whispered, the word a quiet acknowledgment of our accomplishment.

Luke's enthusiasm shattered the silence, his voice carrying across the distance with genuine admiration. "The tent looks amazing! Is it finished now?" His question, laden with an optimism I found both comforting and jarring, reminded me of the contrast between our current achievements and the life we had left behind.

"Pretty much," I responded, feeling the weight of my suitcase as Luke handed it over to me, a tangible link to the life and responsibilities I had been forcibly detached from. Paul, retrieving his own overnight bag, shared a look with me, an unspoken understanding of the gravity encapsulated within these simple acts.

Luke's next words struck a chord, tethering me back to a reality I longed for yet felt impossibly distant. "Duke misses you," he said, his voice tinged with a sadness that mirrored my own. "He knew as soon as I got the suitcase out that you were going away." The mental image of Duke, my loyal companion, sensing my departure before I had even said goodbye, opened a floodgate of emotions I had been struggling to contain.

The impact of Luke's words, the mention of Duke, transported me momentarily back to a life filled with the comfort of routine, the presence of loved ones, and the security of home. Standing there, amidst the desolation of Clivilius, the full realisation of what had been lost washed over me. "I miss him too," I admitted, the words heavy with the sorrow of separation, the longing for a return to normalcy, and the painful acknowledgment of a life that now seemed more like a distant dream than a reality I could reclaim.

"Take these back with you," said Paul, shoving several full black garbage bags at Luke. The bags sagged under the weight of more discarded tent packaging.

Luke's brow furrowed as he looked at the bulging bags of rubbish. He scratched his head, visibly perplexed. "I don't think the bin will fit both of those."

Paul, always the optimist, flashed a supportive smile. "I'm sure you'll think of something," he encouraged. His eyes sparkled with a glimmer of hope. "We've also made a small pile of cardboard and stuff we can burn, over there," he said, pointing just off to the right of the tent. The pile was a hodgepodge collection of flattened boxes and other combustible packaging, a preparation for when the darkness invariably arrived.

Luke, relieved by Paul's support, smiled approvingly in return. He took the bags from Paul and began his slow trudge back to the Portal, the weight of the waste making each step a cumbersome effort.

For a moment, I considered following after him, my gaze lingering on Luke's retreating figure. The thought of helping him crossed my mind, a flicker of camaraderie in the midst of our shared struggle. But the Portal's continual rejection, and particularly its incandescent response to my most determined effort, made me more than a little weary. The countless attempts to traverse the portal had left me physically and emotionally drained, like a boxer who had taken one too many hits in a never-ending bout.

"We may as well unpack these in the tent," I grumbled, hefting my suitcase with exaggerated effort. My biceps strained under the weight of the case, and a bead of sweat formed on my forehead. I couldn't help but think, *Shit, Luke must have squeezed my entire wardrobe in here.*

Paul dragged his own bag behind me, the wheels squelching through the dusty ground. "And put them away where?" he asked, his tone dripping with sarcasm, as we entered the dimly lit tent.

I scoffed in frustration, my patience wearing thin. "For fuck's sake," I muttered harshly, setting the suitcase down in the tent's right wing. *Paul's right; the only place for our clothes is to scatter them over the bare floor.*

Paul didn't waste any time. He rummaged through his bag, the rustling of clothes echoing in the confined space, and finally pulled a faded blue singlet over his head. "I'm going for a walk," he announced, his voice tinged with annoyance as he made his exit from the tent.

I watched Paul through the fly mesh of the front flaps as he collected the new shovel and rolls of toilet paper. The sight of him trudging away into the desolate landscape felt like a small victory in itself.

"Good," I muttered to no one in particular, my frustration simmering. "Go and bury your shit." The words hung in the air, a bitter reminder of our grim reality as Paul faded into the distance, leaving me alone with my thoughts in the suffocating solitude of the tent.

I knew I had no real reason to be mad at Paul. It was his brother that I was really mad at. Luke, the ever-elusive wanderer, could come and go as he pleased, while I felt tethered to this desolate place. *It's not fair. Not fair at all.*

Staring at the unopened suitcase, my frustration found an outlet as I knelt beside it, my fingers tracing the path of the black zipper. The cold metal sent an unwelcome shiver down my spine, a stark contrast to the stuffily warm air that enveloped me.

"Where's Paul?" asked Luke, his voice tinged with panic as he pushed his way into the tent, interrupting my moment of quiet contemplation.

"Gone to bury his shit," I replied, without looking up from where my head was busy discovering the contents of the suitcase. I needed something to occupy my mind, something to distract me from the gnawing resentment that simmered beneath the surface.

"Oh," said Luke, his demeanour becoming instantly calmer. It irked me how easily he could switch between states of concern and indifference.

"What's got you in such a flurry?" I asked, my voice tinged with irritation.

"Nothing. I just had a moment and thought maybe something had happened to him," Luke explained, his gaze averted.

I turned to Luke, revealing a sour pout. "He might not be my favourite person, but I certainly wouldn't hurt him," I said curtly, the words laced with bitterness. And then, with a dismissive huff, I went back to rummaging through the suitcase.

"I wasn't suggesting you would," Luke replied, his voice carrying an undertone of resignation. It was clear that the tensions between us were a heavy burden, and the weight of our circumstances continued to press down upon us like an unyielding force.

"Really?" I asked incredulously, holding up a shiny, bright green thong, the fluorescent fabric almost blinding in the dim tent.

"I thought you liked it?" shrugged Luke innocently, his face a picture of faux innocence as he feigned ignorance.

"You mean you like it," I replied, my tone dripping with sarcasm as I tossed the provocative piece of underwear back into the suitcase. Luke always had a knack for picking out sexy lingerie. It was his way of trying to keep our dwindling spark alive.

"You can wear them under your swimmers," said Luke, attempting to salvage his choice.

Typical Luke, I thought, rolling my eyes. Sexy underwear and silky fabrics formed the foundation of Luke's sexual fantasies, but I only wore them because I knew it turned Luke wild. I sighed softly, a hint of nostalgia creeping in. Nostalgia seemed all that remained of our once passionate sex life. It must have been at least two years now since we had done anything more than a kiss here or there, maybe the occasional handjob. But to be honest, I wasn't really bothered by our lack of physical intimacy.

As I stared at the jumbled mess of clothes in the suitcase, a bittersweet feeling washed over me. Our relationship had evolved into something different, something less passionate but strangely comforting in its familiarity. In the end, I realised that perhaps physical intimacy wasn't the only way to measure the depth of our connection.

"Well, in any case, you can use these to start a fire," Luke told me abruptly, changing the topic of conversation as he held up several of his university books.

"Thanks," I said, my gratitude laced with a touch of resignation. "But those books won't last long."

"I know. But I'm not sure we have anything else just yet," Luke admitted, his gaze dropping to the ground as he considered our limited resources.

"You could take the car down to the petrol station on Main Road. They usually have small bags of firewood for sale," I suggested, knowing full well the reluctance that Luke had towards driving.

Luke looked incredulously at me, his eyes narrowing. "But you know I hate driving."

"Well, perhaps it might be a good time to start liking it," I said, unable to resist a smug undertone. My mind raced with thoughts left unspoken, like, '*After all, you have imprisoned your usual chauffeur on an alien planet or alternate reality or some shit like that.*'

Luke rolled his eyes at my not-so-subtle jab. "I'll bring you a mattress too. Then you won't have to sleep on the dirt."

"Sure," I replied tersely, not wanting to give in to the lingering resentment that threatened to boil over.

Luke left the university textbooks outside the door of the tent when he left, a tangible reminder of our precarious situation. As I watched him walk away, the weight of our predicament pressed down on me, and I couldn't help but wonder how much longer we could endure this endless ordeal.

Pausing to think for a moment, *Paul might be a while yet and the tent is up. There's no rush for Paul to return. It might be good for Luke and I...*

Making my mind up, I removed my jeans and undies and slipped into the spandex thong, adjusting my dick until it sat comfortably in the snug pouch. *I don't look half bad in a thong*, I thought, as a weary grin spread across my face.

I threw my undies into the suitcase. *Better to be safe than sorry*, I thought, and pulled my jeans back on. And then I stepped back out into the warm sun.

"Where's the shovel?" I asked, my eyes widening with surprise and a tinge of disappointment as I saw that Paul had returned to camp already.

"Oh," replied Paul nonchalantly. "I've left it in the ground to mark our toilet spot. We can use that as our guide. We may as well do our business in a single location."

My face scrunched up in distaste. The thought of going near Paul's waste didn't exactly thrill me. "I guess," I finally said, begrudgingly accepting the practicality of his suggestion.

"Maybe we should build a long drop," I mused aloud, contemplating the idea.

"A long drop?" Paul raised an eyebrow, clearly perplexed.

"Yeah," I said, my voice tinged with resignation. "Although I'm not really sure how we do that." I confessed dryly, my sarcasm masking the growing sense of hopelessness that gnawed at me. I paused briefly before adding in a defeated tone, "We're going to die here."

Paul's momentary contemplation was cut short by the sound of Luke's return, a welcome interruption signalling that perhaps our situation was about to become a touch more bearable. "The mattress!" I exclaimed, the mere mention of it injecting a brief surge of energy into my weary limbs. I moved towards the Portal with a sense of purpose, eager to greet this small token of comfort from our old life.

As we approached Luke, it was clear that the task of transporting a King-sized mattress through the Portal was not one he could manage alone. Without any need for words, Paul and I instinctively joined in, each of us taking a corner to ensure the mattress was carried with care rather than dragged through the unforgiving Clivilius dust.

Following the mattress, Luke brought through a few sheets and blankets, their familiar textures and smells a stark contrast to the landscape that surrounded us. Holding the bedding in my hands, I was momentarily transported back to Earth, to a time when such items were taken for granted rather than celebrated as luxuries.

The arrival of these items, the mattress, sheets, and blankets, symbolised more than just physical comfort; they represented a thread of hope, a connection to our past lives, and a reminder of the potential for moments of peace and normalcy. As we arranged the mattress inside the tent, the task felt like a small victory, a step towards making this place a home, even if only temporarily.

"Sorry, there's only one tent and a mattress," Luke said, his tone apologetic yet matter-of-fact.

"I can't believe we haven't even been here for twenty-four hours yet," Paul said. "It feels like a week already." His words echoed my own sentiments, the surreal elongation of time in this place making each hour feel like a day.

"I know," I agreed with Paul's observation. "At least I might get a decent night's sleep without Duke and Henri," I joked, trying to find a sliver of humour in our predicament.

Luke's laughter followed, his next words playful yet poignant. "And I forgive you for sleeping with my brother for a night."

The banter elicited genuine laughter from Paul and me, a momentary reprieve from the stress of our situation. It was in this light-hearted exchange that I found myself truly seeing Luke again—not just as the person who had, in some way, led us to this predicament, but as the thoughtful, caring man I knew him to be. It was a gentle reminder of the qualities that had drawn me to him in the first place.

I swallowed hard, the lump in my throat a testament to the complex emotions swirling within me. Somewhere along the line, amidst the ongoing struggles of everyday life, I had momentarily lost sight of the man I loved. The realisation was both a revelation and a reconciliation, a silent promise to myself to not lose sight of those qualities again, despite the challenges we faced.

"I've ordered a few more tents," Luke announced, his words slicing through the remnants of our laughter and banter, grounding us back in the reality of our situation. "They should arrive tomorrow."

"I hope they are at least as big as this one," Paul remarked. "I could get used to having that much space to myself." It was a small glimpse into the ways in which he was already beginning to envision a more sustainable existence here.

"Yes. They're the same size," Luke confirmed, addressing Paul's concern directly.

The conversation then shifted towards a more immediate need. "Now," I pressed Luke, "That wood you were going to get?" The question was a nudge, a reminder of the necessity to prepare for the coming night, which promised to be as much a challenge as any other aspect of our lives in Clivilius.

Paul looked at Luke. "Wood?"

Luke's reaction, a hard swallow, did not go unnoticed. It was a physical manifestation of some internal struggle or realisation, a moment of vulnerability that belied the façade of control he often projected. "I'll get it right now," he declared, a statement that felt more like a commitment to action than a simple response to our queries.

Luke's mysterious demeanour, his moments of opacity, had become more pronounced in Clivilius. The man I thought I knew so well had become an enigma in many ways, his thoughts and motivations obscured by the extraordinary circumstances we found ourselves in.

❖

"Where are you off to?" I asked, a question prompted by a mix of curiosity and concern. Paul's response, simple and straightforward, underscored a basic human need for relief and a momentary escape from our new, harsh reality. "We've been sitting here for ages," he said, his voice carrying a hint of restlessness that I couldn't help but empathise with.

"So?" My question was more of a reflex than a genuine inquiry, an attempt to engage further, perhaps to delay his departure or to express my own frustration with the situation.

"So, I'm going to go have a quick dip in the river," Paul replied, his determination clear. His swift departure, before I could offer any form of protest or perhaps an invitation to join, left me momentarily taken aback. The idea of a cool dip was tempting, yet the inertia of my own discomfort kept me stationary.

I sighed, a sound heavy with resignation. The heat was oppressive, a constant companion that made the dust stick to my skin, creating a layer of grime that felt as if it penetrated to the soul. The stillness of the Portal, a reminder of our isolation and the uncertainty of our situation, loomed large in my mind. *How much longer is Luke going to be?* The question was a silent scream, a yearning for any change in our circumstances, for any sign of progress or hope.

A low groan escaped my lips, not just from the discomfort but from the realisation that my own moment of need could no longer be ignored. There was no time for a tent stop, no room for hesitation. The urgency of the situation propelled me towards the shovel, a beacon of necessity in this landscape of dust and discomfort. The hope that Paul had also left the roll of toilet paper became a singular focus, a desperate wish to avoid an even more uncomfortable predicament. *Or I'm going to be the one stinking of shit.*

As I made my way, the reality of our existence in Clivilius hit me anew. We were far from the conveniences and comforts of our previous lives, forced to confront basic needs in a setting that offered little solace or privacy. The juxtaposition of Paul seeking a moment of refreshment in the river against my own pressing need was a stark reminder of the primal challenges we faced, of the need to adapt and find dignity in the midst of our trials.

Perched atop the boulder, the discomfort from the ill-advised cappuccino manifested with a vengeance. "Bloody cappuccino," I grumbled to myself, clutching my stomach as it protested loudly, a reminder of the beverage's treachery. The sudden flash of light was jarring against the backdrop of Clivilius' dusty landscape, a stark anomaly that sent my heart racing with both curiosity and apprehension. "What the fuck was that?" I whispered under my breath, instinctively bracing for the unknown.

In a moment of self-preservation, I crouched, adjusting my position to mitigate the blinding glare. It was then I spotted the source of my momentary alarm—the shovel, innocuously lying in the dust, its metal surface reflecting the sun's rays with an intensity that had caught me off guard.

Approaching the shovel, I moved with a deliberate caution that felt almost second nature now. My gaze darted around the landscape, searching for any sign of movement, any hint of danger that might lurk in the serene yet deceptive tranquility of Clivilius. Yet, the only thing that met my eyes was the familiar, unchanging expanse of dust and rock.

Finally reaching the shovel, my alertness was rewarded by the sight of the toilet paper roll, ingeniously secured under a small rock—a simple yet effective measure against the whims of the wind. A wave of relief washed over me, not just for the presence of the toilet paper, a small yet significant comfort in our current circumstances, but also for the absence of any immediate threat.

As I navigated the makeshift latrine Paul had established, the reality of our situation in Clivilius became painfully clear. The act, as primal and necessary as it was, brought a moment of relief amidst the discomfort. The breeze that momentarily offered a reprieve from the heat also carried a reminder of our primitive conditions, underscoring the challenges we faced in maintaining even a semblance of sanitation.

The realisation that our efforts to dig a latrine would do little to mitigate the inevitable odours was disheartening. It underscored the makeshift nature of our survival tactics and the harsh reality that, despite our best efforts, we were far from the comforts and conveniences of home. The thought was sobering, a stark reminder of how quickly our situation could devolve into something even more dire if we weren't careful.

Covering my business with dust was a temporary measure, one that felt wholly inadequate even as I did it. The notion of collecting our waste in garbage bags for Luke to transport back to Earth was both revolting and bizarrely amusing. It was a plan born of desperation, of a determination to preserve the integrity of Clivilius while grappling with the more unpleasant aspects of human existence.

The irony of the situation was not lost on me. In our quest to maintain some level of cleanliness in this new world, we were reduced to measures that seemed both extreme and slightly absurd. Yet, there was a certain practicality to the idea, a way to ensure that Clivilius remained untarnished by our presence as much as possible.

As I stood up, dusting off my hands and preparing to return to camp, I couldn't help but reflect on the myriad ways in which our ordeal in Clivilius might reshape my understanding of necessity, of survival. The measures I would be willing to take, the compromises I might be forced to make, in order to adapt in the face of adversity.

Yet, the plan to have Luke ferry our waste back to Earth was a stark reminder of the delicate balance we needed to maintain—not just with the environment of Clivilius, but with our own dignity and sense of humanity. It was a balance that would require constant negotiation, a perpetual reassessment of what was necessary, what was bearable, and what it truly meant to survive in a world so unlike our own.

EXPOSURE

4338.205.8

As I made my way back to the Portal, the sudden sound of a thud slicing through the quiet of Clivilius jolted me from my thoughts. For a moment, I hesitated, unsure of the source. *Could it be Luke?* The thought spurred me into action, my jog quickening as I neared the swirling colours of the Portal, the gateway that had become both a lifeline and a source of endless frustration.

My reflexes kicked in just in time as another small bag of wood came hurtling through the Portal, narrowly missing me. "Fuck!" I exclaimed, instinctively ducking to avoid the unexpected projectile. The realisation hit me—this was Luke's method of delivery. A mix of amusement and irritation washed over me as I made a mental note to steer clear of the Portal's immediate vicinity. The thought of getting knocked out by flying firewood was both absurd and slightly alarming.

I stepped back, giving the Portal a wide berth as I observed the subsequent arrivals of wood. The bags tumbled through one after another, a chaotic ballet of kindling and logs that seemed to defy any sense of order. Despite the danger of the situation, I couldn't help but smile at the sight. Luke had taken my advice, albeit in his own, uniquely hazardous way.

As quickly as it had burst into life, the Portal's vibrant colours disappeared, leaving behind only the bags of wood and a lingering sense of abandonment. "That lazy bastard!" I couldn't help but exclaim into the emptiness. The expectation that Luke might join me, that he might help carry the wood to our makeshift campsite by the river, vanished as quickly as the Portal's colours.

The silence that followed my outburst was a stark reminder of our isolation in Clivilius. There was no one to answer my frustrated questions, no one to share in the absurdity of the moment. "Figures," I muttered, resignation setting in as I picked up two of the bags. The task ahead seemed less daunting as I reconsidered the situation. It would only take a few trips, I realised, a small inconvenience in the grand scheme of things.

❖

The weight of the final bag of wood settled into the dust with a satisfying thud, marking the end of my task. As I straightened my back, a flicker of concern passed through my mind for Paul. He had been gone longer than expected. The thought that he might be in some sort of trouble clawed at the edges of my consciousness. *I hope he isn't in danger.* The mere idea sent a ripple of unease through me, tempered only by the weary acknowledgment of my own limitations. *I don't have the energy left to save him. Not this late in the day.* It was a stark admission, one that highlighted the toll Clivilius had taken on me both physically and mentally.

My gaze drifted upwards to the sun, its position a silent, glowing sentinel in the sky. Despite the length of time we'd spent in Clivilius, the unfamiliar landscape still rendered me unable to discern the exact hour, leaving me to rely on guesswork and instinct. The sun's descent towards the horizon suggested that the day was waning, that there were only a few precious hours of daylight left. The realisation pressed upon me with a sense of urgency, a silent reminder of the tasks that still lay ahead and the dwindling time we had to complete them.

"Where's Paul?" Luke asked, scanning the campsite with a look of concern that mirrored my own feelings from moments earlier. Having been so preoccupied with the wood and my own musings, I hadn't even noticed Luke arrive at camp.

The mention of Paul's absence, now vocalised by Luke, reignited a flicker of concern within me, though I tried to mask it with a casual response. "He's off bathing again," I said, trying to sound nonchalant.

"Again?" Luke echoed, his brow furrowing in a mix of confusion and amusement. "He didn't make another mess, did he?" His question, light-hearted on the surface, carried an undercurrent of genuine concern—a reminder of the makeshift nature of our existence here and the challenges that came with it.

It wouldn't surprise me. I couldn't help but chuckle at the thought, the absurdity of our situation momentarily lightening the mood. "Not that I know of. He just got tired of waiting for the wood." My attempt at humour felt flat even to my own ears

Luke's focus shifted quickly from Paul's whereabouts to the matter at hand, a testament to the ever-present list of priorities that needed our attention. "Well, it's arrived now, hasn't it? We have more pressing issues to deal with right now anyway," he said with a sense of urgency that pulled at my attention.

"I need your help to convince Gladys to believe me about all this." His words pierced through the haze of my weariness. Gladys—my lifelong best friend. Over the decades, she had been my confidant, the one I turned to in times of joy and crisis alike. *But this? How could I even begin to frame our experiences in Clivilius in a way that wouldn't sound like a fantastical delusion?*

The sudden revelation hit me like a ton of bricks. "Gladys is here!?" The thought of my best friend, my rock through countless ups and downs, being pulled into this chaotic, unpredictable world of Clivilius sent a shockwave of panic through me. The potential of her being trapped here, alongside us, was unthinkable.

"No! God no!" Luke's rapid clarification did little to quell the storm of emotions brewing within me. His hastiness only served to underline the gravity of the situation. I fixed him with a glare, my mind racing with the implications of his words. The very idea that Luke might even contemplate bringing Gladys into this mess was unfathomable.

"And I don't want her to come here either," he added quickly, as if trying to pacify the rising storm. His words, meant to reassure, instead echoed my fears back at me. "I don't want her to get trapped. But I need her to believe that this actually is where you are."

The mention of the Portal in relation to Gladys sent a chill down my spine. "So, she knows about the Portal then?" The question hung in the air, heavy with accusation and disbelief.

Luke's response was hesitant, his eyes dropping to the ground before meeting mine again. "Yeah," he admitted, the weight of his confession evident in his voice. "I had to show it to her."

"What the fuck, Luke!" My exasperation and anger boiled over, spilling out in a torrent. The thought of Gladys, even remotely involved in this madness, was too much to bear.

"She didn't leave me any other choice," Luke countered, his voice rising in defence. "It's complicated, okay?" His explanation, or lack thereof, did nothing to soothe my frayed nerves.

"What the hell does that mean, 'It's complicated'!?" I pressed, my frustration mounting.

Luke's plea was simple yet loaded with unspoken tension. "Just help me will you."

The conversation reached a stalemate, the air charged with unsaid words and unresolved tensions. "Wait here then," I said, the words coming out more sharply than intended. Without waiting for a response, I turned and disappeared inside the tent, my mind a whirlwind of thoughts and emotions.

The complexity of our situation, already a tangled web of uncertainties and fears, had just added another layer with Gladys's unwitting involvement. The task ahead—to convince her of our reality, to secure her belief without endangering her—loomed large. It was a tightrope walk between two worlds, with the stakes higher than ever.

In the dim light of the tent, I fumbled with the pen, my hands shaking as I scribbled the message on the label of an empty plastic water bottle. It was a secret I had stumbled upon by accident, a truth hidden away by Beatrix, Gladys's sister, about a tragic love lost too soon. This revelation, I hoped, would serve as undeniable proof to Gladys of where the message originated.

Capping the pen, my heart raced as I contemplated the potential fallout. Gladys and I shared decades of friendship, a bond that had weathered countless storms, but never one quite like this.

Less than two minutes later, I emerged from the tent, the small plastic bottle in hand. "Here," I said, my voice steadier than I felt, as I tossed the bottle to Luke. The bottle spun through the air, landing securely in his grasp. "Tell her to read my message. That should do the trick." The weight of what I had just set in motion settled heavily on my shoulders.

Luke stared down at the water bottle, his brow furrowing as he squinted at the label.

"You don't have to read it," I muttered, my annoyance bubbling to the surface.

"You know I can't help it," Luke replied without looking up, his eyes fixated on the brief message written on the label. His obsession with reading every scrap of information often grated on my nerves.

I huffed, the weight of frustration settling in my chest.

"Is this true?" Luke asked suddenly, his head snapping up as he sought confirmation.

"Yep," I replied tersely, my face turning serious as I braced for what would come next. "But you need to stay out of it. I think you've got us all into enough trouble already."

Luke's brow furrowed even further, his expression a mix of concern and guilt.

"Luke, I mean it," I pressed, my voice firm and unyielding.

"Thanks," said Luke softly, holding up the water bottle as if it were a lifeline. With a quick nod, he turned and jogged away, leaving me behind once again.

As I watched him go, a knot of anxiety formed in the pit of my stomach. I couldn't help but question whether telling Gladys the truth about her sister's involvement in Brody's death was the best course of action. It was a decision fraught with uncertainty and possible danger, and I knew that I was treading on dangerously thin ice.

Ignoring the doubts that swirled in my mind, I turned my attention to the bags of wood, ripping open the first one with determination.

❖

The fire crackled loudly, its flames leaping and cavorting with a wild, unpredictable fervour. Each snap and pop of the burning wood was a tactile symphony, creating a vibrant soundscape that echoed through the empty desert surrounding us. The flames, with their hypnotic dance, sent a thin trail of silver smoke wafting high into the late afternoon sky. This sound, this constant, lively reminder of our isolation in the midst of an unforgiving wilderness, wrapped itself around me, a tangible manifestation of our solitude.

As I watched, transfixed by the fire's flickering flames, my thoughts began to drift, wandering down paths of contemplation that had been gnawing at me for some time. The fire, with its relentless energy, seemed to fuel these thoughts, giving them life as they spiralled upwards with the smoke. I wondered, with a kind of aimless curiosity, how high the smoke would rise before it disappeared into the unknown expanse above, merging with the ether of the vast, uncharted sky. This fleeting thought was a suitable reminder of the vastness of our surroundings, and the minuscule space we occupied within it.

I couldn't shake the nagging doubts that had haunted my mind since our arrival in this enigmatic place. The air, filled with the scent of burning wood, seemed to thicken with my contemplation. Each breath felt heavy with the weight of uncertainty, the dense, unseen fog of unanswered questions clouding my mind.

"Is this place the same as Earth?" I mused aloud, my voice barely rising above the crackling of the fire. The question hung in the air, a spectre of doubt in the face of our surreal surroundings. "Are we still actually on Earth, somewhere?"

The question seemed to echo, not just in the physical space around me, but within me, resonating with the very core of my being. The uncertainty of our situation weighed heavily on my mind, a relentless burden that seemed to grow with each passing moment. The crackling fire, with its mesmerising display and the warmth it provided, offered no answers, only serving to deepen the mystery of our existence in this desolate, otherworldly landscape.

"Jamie! Fire!" The words shattered the eerie silence, Paul's panicked scream slicing through the desolate stillness. The urgency in his voice was unmistakeable.

Yet, despite the imminent danger his words implied, I found myself rooted to the spot, unable to muster the energy to react. My mind was shrouded in a thick fog of resignation, a numbness that had insidiously woven itself into the fabric of my being over time. This place, with its relentless adversities and isolation, had a way of sapping your spirit, leaving behind a hollow shell where enthusiasm and hope once resided.

"Fire!" Paul's cry pierced the air once more, his voice reaching a fever pitch as he crested the peak of the nearby hill. The urgency, the sheer desperation in his voice, it should have spurred me into action, ignited a spark of survival instinct that lay dormant within. But all it did was fan the flames of my frustration, my exhaustion boiling over into a raw, unfiltered outburst.

"For fuck's sake! I know there's a fire!" I yelled back, my voice laced with irritation and fatigue. The words tumbled out, harsh and loud, cutting through the distance between us. It was more than just a response to his warning; it was an outcry against all the relentless challenges, the endless trials that our situation had forced upon us.

Paul stopped abruptly, his movements halting as my words reached him. There was a moment, brief and fleeting, where the tension hung palpable in the air, a silent standoff between his panic and my frustration. Then, with a perceptible shift in his demeanour, he walked slowly back towards the camp with a measured, resigned gait.

As I watched him approach, the anger and irritation that had surged through me began to ebb, replaced by a weary acknowledgment of our shared plight. The outburst, while cathartic, also served as a reminder of the strain we were under, the constant battle not just against the elements, but against the encroaching despair that sought to consume us.

"I got the fire started," I announced, my tone deliberately softer as Paul closed the gap between us. It was an attempt to ease the tension that had built up, a small olive branch after my earlier outburst.

"Oh," Paul's response came, accompanied by a visible flush of embarrassment that spread across his cheeks. It was a subtle, humanising detail that momentarily softened the edges of our rugged existence. "That's great."

I didn't pause in my task, continuing to feed small pieces of kindling into the burgeoning fire. I watched, almost with a sense of reverence, as the flames leapt to life, eagerly consuming each offering. Their glow intensified, casting a warm, flickering light. It was a simple act, but in the moment, it felt like a small victory against the relentless pressure of our circumstances.

"All I could see from over the hill was smoke. I was worried that it may have been the tent. We've got nothing else here," Paul explained, his tone laced with a hint of concern that cut through his earlier embarrassment. It was a genuine worry, a reminder of how precarious our situation was, how every small incident could potentially spiral into disaster.

"Obviously," I retorted, the word slipping out more harshly than I intended. My frustration was still a simmering presence beneath the surface, a constant companion in this relentless environment. Our reality was harsh, and it often felt like there was little room for mistakes, for misunderstandings, or for the vulnerability that Paul's concern had briefly unveiled.

Paul, however, seemed to take my sneer in stride, unaffected by the edge in my voice. He stood there, a figure caught between vulnerability and resilience, with clothes tucked under one arm and a towel wrapped tightly around his waist. It was an oddly domestic image in the midst of our wild surroundings.

I smiled knowingly, a flicker of amusement crossing my face as I pictured Paul enjoying his time in the river. The thought brought a momentary lightness to the heavy air of survival that hung around us. *Now it's my turn*, I thought to myself, feeling a brief surge of excitement at the prospect of the cold, refreshing embrace of the river.

With a fluid motion, I lifted my t-shirt over my head, the fabric whispering softly against my skin as I tossed it aside. It made a lazy arc in the air before landing against the side of the tent, slumping to the ground in a defeated heap. The action, simple and mundane, felt almost liberating amidst the constant tension of our situation.

"Don't let the fire go out," I instructed Paul, casting a glance towards the flickering flames. I had used most of our kindling to coax it into life, a precious commodity in our limited resources. The last thing we needed was for Paul's occasional absent-mindedness to snuff out our source of warmth and protection.

Paul's response was swift, his head turning sharply to face me, a crease of worry marking his brow. "Are you sure having a fire is the best thing?" he questioned, his voice tinged with concern. "What if there is something out there and our fire attracts it?"

His words halted me in my tracks, my hands pausing midway through the action of unzipping my jeans. I looked up at him, meeting his gaze with a serious expression. "You really think there might be something else out there?" The question lingered between us, heavy with the unspoken fears that accompanied our isolation.

"Maybe," Paul replied with a noncommittal shrug. His response, vague as it was, echoed the undercurrent of fear that anything could be lurking beyond the ring of light cast by our fire, something that I hadn't thought about until now.

I considered his concern, weighing it against our need for the fire's warmth and psychological comfort. "I'm sure it'll be fine for now," I reassured him, trying to infuse my voice with a confidence I wasn't entirely sure I felt. "We'll make sure we put it out shortly after nightfall." It was a compromise, an attempt to balance the primal comfort the fire offered against the primal fear of the unknown that lurked in the darkness beyond.

"Okay," Paul agreed, his voice carrying a note of reluctant acceptance. It was clear that the unease had not entirely left him, but for the moment, the matter was settled.

The anticipation of the river's cool embrace propelled me forward, my actions swift and unhesitating. With a quick motion, my jeans were discarded, flung towards the tent to join my already discarded t-shirt. The fabric made a soft thud as it hit the ground, a testament to my eagerness to immerse myself in the refreshing waters ahead. I could almost feel the chill of the river against my skin, a welcome respite from the heat and the dust that clung to every surface, every pore.

I made a beeline for the bank of the river, my heart racing with a mix of excitement and the simple joy of a moment's escape from our relentless reality. The river, with its constant, soothing murmur, promised a brief sanctuary, a momentary lapse from the survival and the uncertainty that had framed our day.

"Hey! Wait!" The urgency in Paul's voice cut through my focus, a jarring note in the harmony of my anticipation. His call came too late, my body already committed to the motion, my left foot planting firmly into the ground as I prepared to launch myself into a grand, dive bomb leap into the river's welcoming depths.

But Paul's yell, unexpected and sharp, distracted me mid-stride. My concentration shattered, my foot slipped in the soft, deceptive dust that coated the riverbank. The ground, which I had expected to provide solid launch, betrayed me, giving way beneath my weight. Momentum carried me forward, not into the graceful arc of a dive, but into a clumsy, sprawling tumble. I slid across the fine dust, a cloud of it billowing around me, invading every space, every crevice, with an intimate and unwelcome embrace.

From my inglorious position, sprawled on the ground, I heard Paul explode into a fit of laughter. The sound of it, unrestrained and genuine, cut through my initial embarrassment, sparking a reluctant grin despite the situation. "What?" I called out, making no immediate effort to rise, the absurdity of the moment grounding me as much as the earth beneath.

"I'm so sorry," Paul managed to say between his laughter, which seemed to bubble out of him with a life of its own. "I can't help it." His apology, punctuated by chuckles, didn't need forgiveness; the laughter was contagious, a release valve for the tension and the seriousness that often enveloped us.

Sinking my fists into the soft dust, I pushed myself to my feet. My face turned instantly hot. I was confident in my body, but I had completely forgotten I'd changed into Luke's stupid thong. I could feel the thin material wedged tightly between my butt cheeks. I turned undecidedly on the spot. *What's better?* I asked myself. *Showing Paul my arse or my package? I could always stand to the side, but that would only enhance the silhouette.* I sighed, momentarily burying my face in my hands as my palms rubbed my now throbbing temples. *I should have been in the river by now.*

Paul's suggestion pierced through the lingering amusement of my tumble, offering a new direction to channel my thwarted enthusiasm. He pointed downstream, his gesture cutting a clear path through the air, directing my attention towards a promise of undiscovered tranquility. "There's a nice little lagoon just over the way, near the end of the river's bend."

"Thanks," I responded, the word carrying a renewed sense of purpose. My hands moved methodically to brush away the fine, intrusive dust that clung to my legs, remnants of my unintended acrobatics. Each stroke felt like I was wiping away the slight embarrassment, preparing myself anew for the adventure that lay just beyond the current misadventure.

I moved past Paul with a deliberate pace, my steps carrying me with a resolve that felt sharpened by the prospect of the lagoon's secluded waters. The air around us seemed to hold a quiet anticipation, the natural world watching as I collected a towel and headed downstream.

THE LAGOON

4338.205.9

As I ventured further from the camp, my feet grew warmer from the scorching heat of sun-baked dust. Each step felt like a dance with nature's harsher elements, a testament to the relentless sun overhead. The ground radiated heat, a stark reminder of the wilderness's unforgiving nature, urging me forward with a mixture of discomfort and determination.

Driven by the promise of the lagoon's refreshing embrace, my pace quickened to a steady jog. The river, a constant guide on my left, snaked its way through the landscape, leading me downstream. My path took me over several barren, dusty hills, each crest offering a momentary vista of the rugged beauty that surrounded us, and each descent a plunge back into the adventure at hand.

The final hill loomed ahead, steeper and more daunting than the others. My breath came in short, rapid gasps as I ascended, the anticipation of the lagoon fuelling my ascent. Upon reaching the summit, the sight that unfolded before me halted my hurried pace and drew a sharp gasp of awe. There, spread out in the desert valley below, was the lagoon—a vast expanse of water that sparkled like a jewel under the clear, blue sky. Its surface shimmered with reflections of sunlight, inviting and serene, a stark contrast to the arid landscape that surrounded it.

For a moment, I stood transfixed, the beauty of the scene washing over me. The lagoon was an oasis, a slice of paradise that seemed almost out of place amidst the wilderness. The heat, the dust, the exertion of the journey—all of it faded into insignificance in the face of this natural wonder.

Without further contemplation, I surrendered to the call of the cool waters. My descent down the slope was a headlong rush, a mix of eagerness and a barely contained joy. Arms flailing, I sought to maintain my balance on the loose, shifting dust, the slope challenging my every step with the threat of a tumble. Yet, the promise of relief, of immersion in the lagoon's cool depths, propelled me forward.

Throwing the towel aside, I hit the water with a great splash, the coolness enveloping me in an instant embrace. Droplets flew into the air, catching the light in a spray of liquid diamonds, a fleeting, beautiful chaos. The shock of the cold against my heated skin was invigorating, a rush that tingled through every nerve, every fibre of my being. For a moment, I was nothing but sensation, adrift in the pure, blissful cool of the lagoon.

As the refreshing embrace of the clear water enveloped my knees, halting my eager plunge into the lagoon, I was struck by an unexpected sensation. It was as if the water itself had become a conduit for a rush of exhilaration that surged up through my legs, wrapping my entire body in a cocoon of invigorating shivers. The feeling was intense, almost electric, reminiscent of the way my fingers had buzzed with life earlier in the day when Paul and I had playfully dipped our hands into the river, experiencing the cold water's lively touch against our skin. Yet, as swiftly as this wave of exhilaration had swept over me, it receded, leaving behind a lingering sense of wonder mixed with a curious emptiness. The transient nature of the sensation left me puzzled, a fleeting mystery in the midst of the lagoon's tranquil waters. With a mental shrug, I decided not to dwell on it, dismissing the experience as one of the many unpredictable moments that nature often presented.

Driven by a scientist's curiosity and a survivor's instinct to understand my surroundings, I leaned forward, my face hovering just inches above the lagoon's mirror-like surface. The water was astonishingly clear, offering an unobstructed view of the pebbled bottom below. It was a mesmerising sight, the stones laid out beneath me as if on display, yet the absence of any signs of life was striking. No fish darted between the shadows, no plants swayed with the gentle current, and no minuscule creatures scurried over the smooth pebbles. The lagoon, for all its serene beauty, appeared devoid of life, a liquid desert that held nothing but its own crystalline waters.

This lack of life lent the water an unnaturally pristine clarity, a purity that was as beautiful as it was eerie. The only movement came from the water itself, entering the lagoon's mouth from the river with a quiet grace, its slow circulation a solitary dance in an otherwise still world. The realisation that even a microscopic examination might fail to reveal any signs of aquatic life deepened the mystery of the lagoon. It stood as a paradox, a place of tranquil beauty that seemed untouched by the vibrant web of life that usually thrived in such environments.

As I continued my exploration of the lagoon, moving casually around its perimeter, I found myself drawn towards the place where the river fed into this tranquil pool. The ground beneath my feet shifted to a pebbled sandbar near the entrance, where the water's embrace lessened to a mere caress at my ankles. The coolness of the lagoon traced trails along my skin, a sensation that felt both refreshing and invigorating, as droplets journeyed back to their source with a gentle whisper.

I adjusted my bulging package as my engorged manhood pressed uncomfortably against the tight silk. During my wading, the water had been a playful companion, at times sending unexpected jolts of exhilaration that tingled across my skin, reacting to every touch, every movement. It was a peculiar experience, one that I hadn't quite anticipated having such a profound effect on me, both physically and mentally. The sensation was sporadic, unpredictable, mirroring perhaps the very nature of our existence in this untamed wilderness.

My thoughts, ever wandering, found an unlikely tangent in the midst of my physical activity. I mused over Luke's preferences, specifically his choice of attire that I found so baffling. Why he found comfort in things I deemed uncomfortable was beyond me. I preferred the straightforward comfort of boxers, a simple preference that seemed to underscore a deeper disconnect between us. Reflecting on this, I realised that it had been years since I'd indulged any of Luke's peculiar tastes or fantasies. Our relationship, it seemed, had drifted into a realm of minimal intimacy, a fact that was as clear and unmistakable as the lagoon's pristine waters.

The decision to sleep in separate beds, a preference I insisted upon for the sake of a good night's sleep, symbolised this growing chasm. I had always struggled to find rest, a challenge that only intensified with the presence of another person beside me. Luke had seemed to understand, or at least I had convinced myself of his understanding. The logic was sound in my mind: my restlessness and the ensuing irritability from sleepless nights were intolerable, not just for me but for anyone close by. Yet, as I pondered this amidst the natural beauty surrounding me, I couldn't help but wonder if this distance, this separation, was merely a physical manifestation of a deeper emotional rift.

The lagoon, with its serene waters and the gentle flow from the river, served as a poignant backdrop for these reflections. It was as though the calm around me invited introspection, a mirror to the tumultuous currents of thought and feeling that flowed beneath my composed surface. In this moment of solitude, surrounded by nature's quiet spectacle, I found myself confronting the complexities of my relationship with Luke, the choices we had made, and the silent distances that had grown between us.

As I stood there, ankle-deep in the water at the mouth of the lagoon, a sudden pang of guilt surged through me, unbidden and sharp. It twisted inside me, forming a painful knot that seemed to anchor itself firmly in the pit of my stomach. The tranquility of my surroundings contrasted starkly with the turmoil brewing within, each ripple on the water's surface mirroring the waves of discomfort washing over me.

And then there's Ben, I thought, the name ushering in a heavy sigh that seemed to carry the weight of my conflicted emotions. *But Ben is different. Ben isn't Luke.* The thought circled in my mind, a feeble attempt to differentiate, to justify. Ben had represented something entirely separate from the complexity of my relationship with Luke—a momentary diversion, a detour on the path of my usual existence. *Ben just wanted a bit of harmless fun... Yes*, I reassured myself, clinging to the notion. *That's all it was, a bit of harmless fun. No feelings beyond that.*

Yet, as I attempted to dismiss the thoughts, to push away the guilt and confusion, my shoulders shrugged in a half-hearted attempt at nonchalance, accompanied by a dismissive huff. The gesture was more for my benefit than anyone else's, a physical manifestation of my internal struggle to rationalise my actions and emotions. I wasn't sure I had entirely convinced myself; the doubt lingered, a persistent shadow that no amount of rationalisation could fully dispel.

I found myself grappling with the nature of my attraction to Ben, a question that seemed to have no clear answer. *What was it that had drawn me to him?* The question hung in the air, unanswered and perhaps unanswerable. But in that moment, surrounded by the serene beauty of the lagoon, I made a conscious decision to push those thoughts aside. I did not want to spend any more time dwelling on it, on the what-ifs and the maybes.

Another wave of intense sexual excitement began in my ankles, not the most obvious of erogenous zones and it tingled and shimmied its way up my legs, its destination clear and obvious as it arrived in my groin, eliciting another tense movement of my dick pressing yet harder into the tight, green fabric.

The moment I ventured from the safety of the sandbar into the river proper, the dynamics of my environment shifted dramatically. The water, which had gently lapped at my ankles on the sandbar, suddenly deepened, a fact obscured by its deceptive clarity. The river, with its strength and vigour, wrapped around my legs, its current forceful and unyielding, offering a stark contrast to the tranquil lagoon I had just left behind.

I moved with deliberate strides away from the lagoon's mouth, each step taking me further into the embrace of the river. The water rose swiftly, an insistent presence that enveloped me until I found myself submerged up to my neck. It was a sudden immersion into a world where the only sound was the rush of water past my ears, a sensory blanket that muffled the outside world and with it, the tangled web of emotions connected to the lagoon. With each step, the remnants of unwanted urges and guilt began to wash away, leaving behind a sense of relief that was as palpable as the cool water surrounding me.

"Just one more step," I murmured to myself, a silent pep talk aimed at bolstering my resolve. This final step would distance me further from the shore, pushing me about three metres into the river's grasp. As I took that step, the river claimed me entirely, my head vanishing beneath the surface in a moment of complete surrender to the water's will. The riverbed, once beneath my feet, became elusive as the current pulled me, an insistent tug that threatened to sweep me away from my intended course.

Panic fluttered at the edge of my calm as I floundered, my feet desperately seeking purchase on the slippery riverbed below. The current was a formidable adversary, indifferent to my struggles, its pull both relentless and impersonal. When I finally broke the surface, gasping for air, the relief was fleeting. The river, in its ceaseless motion, pulled me under once more, a reminder of nature's power and my own vulnerability.

My arms worked against the current, pushing with all the strength I could muster, each stroke a battle for progress towards the bank. The cycle of surfacing for air, only to be pulled under again, became a rhythm of desperation and determination. With each gasp for air, each mouthful of water, the shore seemed both tantalisingly close and achingly distant.

It was only when my toes finally brushed against the pebbled riverbed that hope surged within me. Anchoring my feet against the stones, I gathered every ounce of strength for one final push. With a powerful thrust, I propelled myself towards the bank, a singular goal driving me forward.

The river's grip on me lessened as I found solid ground beneath my feet once more. The once insistent current now ebbed gently around me, a soothing contrast to the earlier turmoil. Standing there, with the water level receding to just above my waist, I felt a profound sense of relief wash over me, mingled with the remnants of adrenaline that pulsed through my veins. The journey back to the riverbank was a testament to the raw power of nature and my own resilience in the face of it.

With a series of coughs and splutters, I expelled the river water that had fought so hard to claim me. Each step towards the shore felt like a victory, a reclaiming of safety from the clutches of potential disaster. Finally, I pulled myself onto the riverbank, the warm, omnipresent dust welcoming me back with a familiar embrace. As my back sank into its softness, the dust clung to my soaked skin, a gritty reminder of my ordeal.

Rubbing at my eyes, waterlogged and stinging, I leaned to the side and retched, my body expelling the last of the river's unwelcome intrusion. The barren ground absorbed the spluttered water, indifferent to my struggle. Exhausted from the effort, I allowed myself to fall back into the dust with a soft thud, the earth seeming to catch me in a gentle cradle. My hands came to rest on my forehead as I lay there, the sky above a vast expanse of indifferent beauty.

In that moment of stillness, the realisation of my own mortality dawned on me with startling clarity. The thought that I could so easily have drowned, that the line between life and a watery grave had been so thin, was both sobering and chilling. It was a thought that lingered uncomfortably, a shadow cast over the relief of survival.

"Holy fuck!" The exclamation burst from me, a release of tension, fear, and overwhelming gratitude for the breath still filling my lungs. It was a moment of catharsis, allowing the weight of what had transpired to truly sink in. And then, amidst the tumult of emotions, a smile found its way to my lips—a smile of relief, of life affirmed, of a newfound appreciation for the delicate balance between human vulnerability and the indomitable will to survive.

Lying there on the riverbank, the minutes stretched into a silent eternity, my gaze locked onto the vast, cloudless expanse above. The sun's warm embrace enveloped me, its rays diligently working to dry the dampness from my chest and legs. It was an odd sensation, or rather, the absence of one. Despite the obvious heat and the sun's potent ability to scorch, I felt none of the anticipated discomfort—no prickling heat, no warning tightness that usually heralded a sunburn's onset. It left me puzzled, half-expecting my skin to suddenly betray the peace with a flush of painful redness.

But the tranquility of the moment couldn't dispel the growing realisation that I was out of sync with this place. The notion that the sun might, without warning, turn against me only added to the sense of alienation. It was a small thing, perhaps, but in that instant, it epitomised my yearning for normalcy, for the predictability of home where the sun's warmth was a familiar embrace, not a potential threat lurking in serene disguise.

The decision to leave the riverbank was made with a mix of reluctance and resolve. The lagoon, with its inviting calm, had lost its allure, overshadowed by a deeper desire for the familiar, for home. I eased myself back into the river with a deliberate motion, seeking the brief thrill of its cool touch. That initial surge of excitement, a fleeting reminder of the river's earlier challenge, passed through my legs, its zing quickly dissolving into the flow around me. But the thrill was short-lived, replaced by a burgeoning frustration that creased my forehead. This place, with its untamed beauty and hidden dangers, was becoming too much to bear. The simplicity of the desire *I just want to go home* echoed in my mind, a mantra of longing for the familiar, for the comfort of my own world.

I made quick work of rinsing the lingering dust from my back and legs, the water a temporary respite from the unwelcome layer of grit. Retrieving the towel I had abandoned in my earlier rush into the lagoon, I wrapped it tightly around my waist, a makeshift barrier against the desert. The physical action of cleaning myself, of wrapping up, was a small reclaiming of control, a momentary shield against the vulnerability I felt in this vast, unpredictable expanse.

As I stood there, the tangible reminder of my hunger—a stomach growl—pulled me back from the edge of frustration. It was a primal call to action, a reminder of immediate needs that grounded me in the present. The simplicity of hunger, of physical need, offered a brief reprieve from the complexities of my emotions, redirecting my focus from the vastness of my surroundings to the immediacy of sustenance.

As I wrapped the towel more securely around my waist, my eyes instinctively sought out the familiar landmark of our campsite in the distance. The sight of a clear trail of smoke rising steadily into the air was both reassuring and disconcerting. I couldn't help but smile, a small gesture of appreciation for Paul's success in maintaining the campfire. It was a small victory in our ongoing battle against the elements, a symbol of warmth and safety amidst the vast, unyielding wilderness that surrounded us.

However, the smile was tinged with a hint of unease. The stark, barren landscape around us made the smoke a beacon, not just for us, but potentially for anything—or anyone—else that might be sharing this desolate expanse with us. The thought sent a ripple of nervousness through me, my gaze darting around the silent terrain. The quiet was profound, almost oppressive, heightening my awareness of our isolation.

We haven't been here for twenty-four hours yet, I thought, a sobering reminder of how little we knew about this place and what dangers the coming darkness might bring. The unknowns of the night loomed large in my mind, casting shadows of doubt over the fleeting sense of security the campfire offered. It was a stark reminder that our safety was not guaranteed, that the rules of this place were still unknown to us.

We're going to have to put that fire out before bed, just in case. The decision formed clearly in my mind, a necessary precaution against attracting unwanted attention. The fire, for all its comfort and utility, could not be allowed to jeopardise our safety. The thought of extinguishing it, of surrendering the light and warmth, was a reluctant concession to the realities of our situation. It underscored the precariousness of our existence here, the constant balancing act between utilising resources for survival and mitigating risks.

CAPRICIOUS

4338.205.10

As I made my way back to the camp, a familiar and enticing aroma wafted through the air, causing me to pause mid-stride. My face instantly lit up with recognition and anticipation. "Oh my God. Food!" The words escaped me in a mix of relief and excitement, a testament to the simple, profound joy that the prospect of a meal could bring after the day's trials.

Approaching Paul and Luke, who had made themselves comfortable in the dust near the fire, the sight that greeted me was one of casual camaraderie. Luke's greeting, "And wine," accompanied by a grin, only added to the warmth of the moment. The scene before me, with its semblance of normalcy, was a welcome contrast to the earlier uncertainty and isolation of the lagoon.

"Well, you two look like you've given it a fair go already," I remarked light-heartedly upon noticing the half-drunk bottle of wine. It was a gentle ribbing, meant to tease rather than criticise. The sight and smell of pizza and wine, so incongruous in our rugged surroundings, momentarily lifted the veil of apprehension that had settled over me. My stomach, seizing upon the moment, growled loudly, an unambiguous reminder of my hunger.

Without further ado, I tightened the towel around my waist and took a seat beside Luke, conscious of the makeshift garment that barely covered me. The decision not to get dressed was deliberate, driven by a need to conceal the thong beneath from Luke's view. The thought of revealing it, of the implications and misunderstandings it might invite, was something I was keen to avoid. It was a delicate balance, maintaining a semblance of normalcy while navigating the complexities of our relationship.

"Well, Luke has," Paul's laughter broke through my thoughts, a light-hearted acknowledgment of Luke's penchant for wine. Joining in the chuckle, I reached for a slice of pizza, grateful for the distraction, the simple pleasure of sharing a meal. Luke's love for wine, a trait well-known to us, was a small thread of familiarity in the tapestry of our current situation.

My gaze drifted beyond the campfire, to where the sun was beginning its descent behind the mountains, painting the sky with hues of orange and purple. The beauty of the scene was undeniable, yet it carried a weight of unease. The approaching darkness served as a stark reminder of our vulnerability, of the unknown that lay beyond the comforting glow of our fire. *Are we really about to spend a night here?* The question lingered, heavy with implication.

In that moment, amidst the laughter and the shared meal, I found my thoughts wandering to Henri. Despite how much he annoyed me sometimes, the distance made his absence felt all the more keenly. Both of them, actually. It was an unexpected pang of longing, a reminder of the complex web of emotions and relationships that extended beyond the immediate struggle for survival.

"Well," Luke announced, pushing himself to his feet with a fluid motion that spoke of a reluctance to leave. As he brushed the dust from his backside, a tangible reminder of our current setting, he flashed a mischievous grin that was all too familiar. "I better get back. Don't want Gladys to finish all the wine in the house," he joked, though the humour did little to mask the underlying tension of the moment.

I couldn't help but shake my head, a gesture of bemused resignation. *What the hell was Luke telling her?* The question danced around the edges of my thoughts. "So, that's it then?" The words left my lips tinged with a mix of disbelief and an all-too-familiar sense of frustration.

Luke's approach was gentle, his actions belying the solemnity of his departure. The kiss he placed on my forehead was a bittersweet gesture, laden with the unsaid and the unresolved. "Yeah," he replied, his voice carrying a weight that seemed out of place in the casual setting. "But I promise I'll be back first thing in the morning."

"Fine," I managed to respond, my voice betraying a shrug of disappointment that felt heavier than intended. My admission, "I wish we could go with you," was a raw echo of longing, a desire for escape, for normalcy, that seemed increasingly out of reach.

Luke's reaction, a bitten lower lip, was a visible sign of his own internal struggle, a mirror to the turmoil I felt. The hefty sigh that followed was my concession to reality, to the understanding that any attempts to change our situation were doomed from the start. Clivilius had made that much clear, its decree a looming shadow over any thoughts of defiance. The realisation that resistance was not only futile but potentially painful was a challenge to accept.

"Good night, Luke," Paul's voice cut through the thick air, a simple farewell that nonetheless carried the weight of our collective resignation.

"Night, Paul," Luke responded, his wave a final gesture of departure. As I watched his back fade into the distance, the growing emptiness was palpable, a void that no amount of jest or distraction could fill.

In a futile attempt to quell the rising tide of frustration and sadness, I found myself reaching for another slice of pizza. The act was mechanical, an effort to fill the silence, to suppress the emotions that threatened to overwhelm. Each bite was a temporary distraction, a way to anchor myself in the moment, even as my thoughts drifted to the uncertain and the unchangeable.

As Paul and I settled into the dust, the remnants of our meal and the dwindling bottle of wine became small comforts against the backdrop of an increasingly unfamiliar landscape. The sky transitioned into deeper shades of twilight as the sun disappeared behind the mountains, and the fire's glow began to wane. A part of me envied Paul's apparent serenity amidst our circumstances; his calm acceptance of our situation was both baffling and, in a way, admirable. *Was there a piece of this puzzle that he understood and I didn't, or had he simply resigned himself to a fate beyond our control?*

"It's so quiet," Paul observed, breaking into my thoughts with a casual stretch. His voice seemed to fill the silence that enveloped us, a stark reminder of our isolation.

"I know," I echoed, my voice a mixture of agreement and apprehension as I glanced around. "And dark," I added, pointing to the starless void above us. The absence of stars, a detail both glaring and disconcerting, seemed to underscore our disconnect from everything familiar.

Paul's reaction was to tilt his head back, his gaze searching the empty sky. "And no moon either," he noted, his observation adding another layer to the mystery of our surroundings.

"What do you think it means?" I couldn't help but question, seeking some semblance of understanding in the face of overwhelming unknowns.

"What do you mean?" Paul countered, his question reflecting either genuine curiosity or an attempt to understand my line of thought.

"Well, doesn't the moon usually affect the oceans and tides?" I pointed out, clinging to the fragments of scientific understanding that felt increasingly irrelevant in this place.

"I guess," Paul replied, his nonchalance marked by a shrug. "But all we've seen is a river. We don't even know there are any oceans here."

My frustration bubbled to the surface, the lack of answers, the absence of familiar celestial markers, the unsettling quiet—it all compounded into a tangible annoyance. "There has to be!" I insisted, more out of desperation than conviction. "We have to still be somewhere on Earth, right?" The question was as much a plea for reassurance as it was a statement.

"I'm so confused," Paul admitted, his hand absently scratching his head in a gesture of bafflement. "None of this makes any sense."

His words echoed my sentiments exactly, a shared confusion that seemed as vast as the starless sky above us. The conversation, rather than offering solace or insights, only deepened the sense of disorientation. With every unanswered question, the reality of our predicament became more pronounced, a puzzle whose pieces were as elusive as the stars that should have been watching over us.

Rising from the makeshift comfort of our campsite, I felt the weight of the day's events heavy on my shoulders. The act of discarding the empty pizza box into the fire felt almost ceremonial, a final nod to the small amount of normalcy we'd managed to carve out in this strange place. The box caught quickly, flames licking eagerly at the cardboard, creating a brief spectacle of light that faded as swiftly as it had appeared. "Kick some dust on those embers when you turn in, won't you?" I requested of Paul, casting a glance towards him as I prepared to retreat for the night.

"Sure," Paul's voice carried a reassurance that was comforting in its predictability. "I won't be that far away." His words, simple yet laden with the unspoken bond of companionship in this uncertain wilderness, offered a sliver of solace.

As I entered the tent, the familiar yet new space welcomed me with its canvas embrace. The darkness inside was a stark contrast to the dwindling firelight outside, and my eyes took a moment to adjust, scanning the interior with a resigned anticipation of the night ahead. Time had become an abstract concept here, marked only by the cycles of light and darkness rather than the precise ticking of a clock. It was dark, and sleep—or the attempt thereof—was the only agenda left.

With a deep sigh, I rummaged through our suitcase, the fabric of the uncomfortable thong giving way to the soft comfort of fresh, loose-fitting shorts. The exchange was a small act of preparation, an attempt to reclaim a sense of comfort in preparation for rest.

The soft mattress beneath me was a small luxury, providing instant relief to my weary body. The day had been long, filled with physical exertion and mental strain, leaving me with a profound appreciation for any form of rest. Yet, as I settled in, the realisation that our day's efforts had amounted to little more than survival in a single tent struck me with a poignant mix of frustration and depression.

Pulling the blanket to my waist, I allowed my body to relax fully, the cool fabric a gentle comfort against my skin. As I closed my eyes, the events of the day began to recede, making way for the elusive promise of sleep. My mind, however, lingered on the threshold of consciousness, teetering between the reality of our situation and the hope for a night of undisturbed rest. Gently, almost imperceptibly, I began to drift off, surrendering to the exhaustion that had claimed every fibre of my being, hoping for a few hours of escape in the form of sleep.

❖

Paul's restless movements beside me were a jarring contrast to the stillness that had enveloped the tent only moments before. His leg twitched again, creating an unease that seemed to permeate the very air we breathed. I hadn't even realised he'd joined me, my own descent into sleep having been uncharacteristically swift. It was a rare luxury for me to drift off with such ease, and even rarer still to remain in the clutches of sleep for more than a handful of hours. The realisation that Paul had come to bed without disturbing me was a small comfort, yet it also underscored the depth of my exhaustion.

The soft rustling of the tent's side cut through the silence, instantly heightening my senses. *Wind?* The question echoed in my mind, a mix of hope and apprehension. The possibility of facing an intruder at this hour, in this isolated place, sent a ripple of tension through my body. My eyes, wide in the darkness, strained to pierce the thick, impenetrable black that filled the tent. Focused on where I believed the entrance to be, I found myself caught between the desire to investigate and the instinct to remain still, to listen for any sign of what had caused the noise.

The darkness was a blanket, obscuring not just vision but also, in some ways, reason. Every sound seemed magnified, every whisper of movement a potential threat. The uncertainty of our situation, the unfamiliarity of our surroundings, lent an edge to the night that was impossible to ignore.

Closing my eyes, I tried to shut out the world, to find solace in the darkness behind my lids despite the increasing disturbances from outside. The absence of the dogs, especially without Henri's familiar, grumbling snores, left a void I hadn't anticipated. Their presence, often a source of mild irritation, had become, in its absence, a silent echo of our isolation.

The tent's fabric strained and fluttered with growing urgency as the wind outside intensified, transforming from a gentle whisper to an angry howl. The sound of countless tiny particles—fine dust—pelting against the tent's walls sent a chill through me. *Shit*, the realisation hit with the force of the gale outside: *the wind is really beginning to pick up*. The tranquility of the night was shattered, replaced by a restless energy that seemed to consume the space around us.

In mere minutes, the assault of the wind and dust against the tent escalated into a relentless barrage, the fabric of our makeshift shelter shuddering under the onslaught. I turned towards Paul, seeking some semblance of reassurance in his proximity. The darkness rendered his face invisible, but the steady rhythm of his breathing, rough yet uninterrupted, suggested he was oblivious to the chaos unfurling around us. The knowledge that he could remain so undisturbed, so deeply ensconced in sleep while a storm raged just beyond our thin refuge, was both baffling and enviable.

Faced with the impossibility of sleep under such conditions, I lay back, directing my gaze upwards towards the silent, unseen ceiling of our tent. The growing knot of anxiety in my stomach was a stark contrast to Paul's peaceful slumber, a reminder of the different ways we were navigating this ordeal. The storm's fury, as it battered against our temporary haven, was a relentless reminder of our vulnerability.

As Paul stirred beside me, his movements punctuated by a soft moan, concern laced my whisper into the dark, "Paul, are you okay?" The quiet of the night made every sound more profound, every shift more noticeable. His response, however, was far from verbal—a sharp twitch of his leg, his toenail catching my shin in a way that drew a sharp gasp from me.

The unexpected pain was a stark reminder of the cramped quarters we shared, of the intimacy forced upon us by circumstance.

Retracting my leg with a mix of surprise and irritation, I couldn't help but silently scowl at the reminder of Paul's poorly maintained nails—reminders of his brother's similar neglect. It was a small, mundane detail that, under normal circumstances, might have been overlooked. But here, in the tense atmosphere of our shelter, it felt like yet another test of patience.

With a sigh, I carefully extricated myself from under the blanket, the fabric whispering softly against the mattress as I moved. I then shoved the blanket towards Paul, creating a barrier between us, tucking his unintentional weapons away from my skin. It was a small act of self-preservation.

Paul's response was another moan, this one followed by a series of strong leg twitches that spoke volumes of his restless state. My concern for him mingled with my own discomfort, creating a complex tapestry of emotions. Straining my eyes in the futile attempt to discern his expression in the pitch black, I wished for the umpteenth time that our situation were different, that the darkness did not serve as such a complete barrier to understanding.

The sudden onslaught of the wind against our tent was like a physical blow, startling in its intensity. The fabric walls shuddered and strained with the storm's growing ferocity outside. The absence of natural sounds—no rustling leaves, no howling through unseen streets—made the experience all the more surreal. Surrounded by the vast emptiness, the only auditory companions were the relentless movement of dust particles and the unsettling cacophony of the tent's fabric battling the wind.

My reaction was instinctive, a jolt of surprise that coursed through me as the tent seemed to convulse under nature's assault. The sensation was unnerving, the lack of warning noises a stark reminder of our isolation. With each gust, the tent seemed to breathe—an inanimate object momentarily endowed with life by the force of the storm.

The hairs on my arms and the back of my neck stood on end, a visceral response to the eeriness enveloping us. It was as if the very atmosphere had shifted, charged with an invisible tension that left me feeling exposed and vulnerable.

Amidst the tumult, a distinct sound caught my attention—the clinking and rattling of a tent pole on the far side. The noise was alarmingly loud in the confined space, a sign of distress. My mind raced to diagnose the problem even as the storm raged on. The pole, vital to the structural integrity of our shelter, hadn't been secured properly. The locating spring, designed to lock the pole in place, must have failed to engage fully, leaving the tent vulnerable to the wind's merciless attacks.

"Shit," escaped my lips, a whisper that carried the weight of my sudden realisation. The tent's precarious situation demanded immediate action, yet the enveloping darkness rendered me virtually blind. The specific location of the compromised pole eluded me, hidden within the shadowy confines of our shelter. Despite the impossibility of visually identifying the problem, the urgency of the situation propelled me forward. The survival of our tent hung in the balance, threatened by the relentless assault of the wind.

"Ro... mmm," Paul's groan, laden with distress, pierced the tumultuous symphony of the storm. The sound, rich with agony, sent a chill through me. *Was he caught in the throes of a nightmare?* The instinct to comfort him, to awaken him from his torment, was strong. Yet, the escalating danger posed by the wind's fury left me torn. Another violent gust rattled the tent, the pole's clinking a dire reminder of the task at hand.

No, there's no time to wake him now, I realised with a sense of resignation. My priority had to be the tent; our immediate safety depended on it. Paul's nightmares, as harrowing as they might be, would have to wait.

Scrambling down the mattress with as much grace as the cramped space and urgency would allow, I made my way on all fours towards the disturbance. The floor beneath me felt cool and uneven, a stark contrast to the warmth of the bed I had just left. My hands, sweeping ahead in the darkness, sought out the familiar texture of the tent's fabric, the only guide I had in this blind endeavour.

"Finally," relief washed over me as my fingertips brushed against the cool, nylon wall of the tent. Guided by sound and instinct, I traced the perimeter towards the clamour, the cacophony growing louder with each inch I covered. The moment my hands found the pole, the source of our potential undoing, the rattling ceased as if acknowledging my presence. The silence that followed was almost as startling as the noise had been.

Gripping the pole firmly, I pulled myself to a stand, the fabric of the tent brushing against my face. The abrupt cessation of the noise, while a relief, was a stark reminder of how close we had come to a structural failure. Standing there in the dark, holding the pole steady, I felt a mix of relief and determination. The storm outside might rage on, but for now, our small bastion against the elements held firm.

"Rose!" The sound of Paul's scream cut through the air, a sharp, piercing cry that sent a jolt of fear straight through me. In an instant, my body reacted, head snapping towards the source of the distress with a mix of confusion and alarm. *What the hell!?* The raw edge of agony in his voice sent my mind racing. *Has he hurt himself?*

In the confusion of the moment, my grip on the tent pole faltered, my hands shooting up in a belated attempt to defend myself. It was futile; the pole struck me sharply on the side of the head, the impact disorienting, sending me reeling. The world tilted, and I found myself crashing down onto the tent's floor, the shock of the fall echoing through my body. My heart thundered against my ribcage, a rapid drumbeat fuelled by adrenaline and fear. The sense of impending danger, already looming large, intensified in that moment, a feeling of terror that I was powerless to see or prevent the unfolding catastrophe.

As I lay there, dazed and disoriented, the tent's structure gave way, the wing collapsing inwards with a whoosh of fabric and air. The weight of it pressed down on me. My body, already tense with fear, jolted at the collapse, then trembled uncontrollably, overwhelmed by the sudden encroachment of the material world into my small space of safety.

"Make it stop!" The desperation in Paul's voice was a sharp jolt to my system, snapping me out of the brief paralysis that fear had imposed. My body, previously locked in a moment of terror, found new purpose. I couldn't—wouldn't—succumb to the panic. With a determination borne of necessity, I began to extricate myself from the suffocating embrace of the collapsed tent fabric, dragging myself across the tent's floor in a bid for freedom.

"It's going to kill us," Paul's voice broke through again, each word punctuated by laboured breaths that spoke volumes of his fear. The raw edge of terror in his voice was chilling.

"Paul. What's wrong?" The question left my lips almost involuntarily as I continued my desperate search for stability, my fingertips grazing the ground in search of the mattress. But as soon as the words were out, I mentally chastised myself. *What a stupid question.* The reality of our situation was crashing down around us, both literally and metaphorically. Yet, as I hesitated, a deeper concern gnawed at me. *Is there more to Paul's fear?* The possibility that he might be injured—or worse, that we were not alone in this collapsing tent—sent a fresh wave of fear coursing through me.

"Clivilius is going to kill us," Paul's whisper cut through the dark, a sharp and chilling declaration. The name, a harbinger of our collective dread, brought a momentary relief. Paul wasn't physically hurt; his panic was rooted in the psychological torment Clivilius had inflicted upon us. It was fear, not physical injury, that had seized him so completely.

Exhaling quickly, I latched onto this sliver of relief, even as it did little to alleviate the immediate danger of our collapsing shelter.

Gathering my resolve, I continued to push through the darkness, my actions driven by a dual purpose: to secure our immediate safety and to reassure Paul. The knowledge that our adversary was not here, in the physical sense, offered a thin thread of hope to cling to.

"Rose, is that you?" Paul's voice, tinged with panic, sliced through the tumultuous noise of the storm raging around us.

"What the hell, Paul?" My frustration boiled over as I shouted back, struggling to make sense of his confusion over the relentless assault of dust battering our fragile shelter. Resuming my blind search for the mattress in desperation, my hand brushed against something unexpectedly warm, unmistakably human.

"Aargh!" Paul's scream, sharp and startled, jolted me as he instinctively pulled away, his reaction amplifying the tension that already thrummed through the air.

Then, a brief sensation of movement brushed my face—a fleeting whisper of air that was quickly followed by the sound of Paul's scuttled movements across the tent's floor.

"Shit," escaped my lips in a hiss, a mix of fear and urgent concern fuelling my voice. "Paul! Come back!" My plea, desperate and raw, sought to bridge the distance his panic had created between us.

"I'm coming, Rose!" he called back, his voice a blend of determination and distress. Paul's misperception, his hallucination fuelled by the nightmare and the overwhelming darkness, had propelled him into a frenzy of fear.

The realisation hit me hard—I needed to stop him, to prevent him from further endangering himself in his disoriented state. My heart raced, not just from the immediate adrenaline of the situation, but from a deeper, more profound sense of dread. I hated this place, this situation that had thrust us into such dire circumstances. The thought of being left alone, truly alone in this darkness, was unbearable.

The sharp sound of the tent's front flap unzipping cut through the darkness, amplifying the sense of urgency and fear that had taken hold. "Paul! Stop!" My voice, louder and more desperate than I intended, echoed my panic as I forced myself to stand, my movements unsteady, driven by a mix of determination and dread.

"Shit!" The word burst from me again as I stomped my foot in frustration. In that moment, I was convinced: Paul's actions, driven by panic or confusion, were going to be the death of me, of that I was certain.

Then, out of the corner of my eye, a small glow arrested my attention. My initial gasp of fright quickly gave way to annoyance as I recognised the source—the campfire embers. The flap of the tent, now a victim of the wind's whims, offered intermittent glimpses of the fire's dying light. *Paul hadn't managed to properly extinguish the embers properly.* A seemingly minor oversight, yet in our current situation, every small mistake felt magnified, every negligence a potential threat.

With a sense of urgency propelling me forward, I rushed to the tent's entrance, the biting dust assaulting my exposed skin. Instinctively, I shielded my eyes, peering through the gaps between my fingers into the darkness. The need to locate Paul was pressing; the risks of being separated in such conditions were too great to ignore. My gaze swept the campsite, searching for any sign of him, driven by the knowledge that failing to bring Paul back quickly could lead to consequences far graver than I was prepared to face.

"Paul, where are you? Talk to me," I called out into the darkness, my voice laced with urgency. The wind whipped around me, turning my words into faint whispers against the tumult of the dust storm.

"Jamie," Paul's voice came back, plaintive and lost. "Where are you?" The relief that flooded through me at the sound of his voice was palpable, a bright spot in the midst of our dark ordeal. *Thank fuck.* The thought that Paul was close, perhaps just a few feet away to my left, sparked a flicker of hope.

"I see you..." Paul's voice began, cutting through the night. My heart lifted slightly, relief starting to seep in. *Thank God Paul's senses are returning*, I thought, a momentary respite from the panic that had taken hold.

"I'm coming, Rose," he concluded, his words sending a jolt of fear through me once more. A faint shadow darted between me and the dim light of the campfire embers, a visual confirmation of my worst fears. Paul, still caught in his hallucination, was moving towards the fire. The frustration that coursed through me was almost palpable, a mixture of fear, irritation, and desperation.

"For fuck's sake, Paul! Stop!" I shouted, my demand slicing through the night, an attempt to halt his dangerous trajectory. The wind and dust created a cacophony around us, muffling his response into an indistinguishable mumble. Time was running out; the urgency of the situation demanded immediate action.

With no other choice, I propelled myself into the storm, the wind slamming against me with a force that seemed intent on pushing me back. Thousands of tiny dust particles assaulted my skin, each grain a tiny needle against my flesh. Every step was a battle, a fight against the invisible hands of the wind that sought to keep me from reaching Paul.

Paul cried out in pain.

An unknown object hit me hard in the chest. Caught by surprise, I gasped for air as a burning pain seared across my chest, my eyes stung from the tears that begged to escape.

Paul's scream, a sound that seemed to embody pure terror, pierced through the chaos of the storm, urging me into action despite the overwhelming conditions. The dust swirled around us like a living thing, stinging my eyes and reducing visibility to nearly nothing. Yet, when Paul's shadow flitted across my line of sight, a surge of adrenaline propelled me forward. I knew he was within reach.

Extending my hands into the dark, the unexpected warmth of Paul's skin under my fingertips acted as a beacon in the tumult. Grasping him firmly around the waist, I pulled with all the strength I had left, our bodies crashing together onto the ground in a tangle of limbs and desperation. The impact startled us both, but there was no time to dwell on the discomfort.

I wriggled free from the heap, my voice firm despite the wind's howl. "Keep your eyes shut," I commanded, trying to shield Paul from the relentless assault of dust.

Paul's initial reaction was to pull away, a reflex born of confusion and fear. "Give me your fucking hand!" My shout was almost lost to the wind, a desperate plea for cooperation in the face of danger. Finally, I felt his hand clasp mine tightly, a small victory.

Each step back to the tent was an exercise in endurance, pain lancing through my chest with every movement. The harsh conditions didn't discriminate, punishing us both as we fought our way back to the relative safety of our shelter. The sound of Paul's body colliding with the tent pole was a harsh reminder of the fragility of our refuge. The wind, ever our adversary, seized the opportunity to bring the canopy down around us just as we crossed the threshold into the tent.

"Shit," I muttered under my breath, each inhalation a sharp reminder of the night's tumultuous events. Paul's quiet sobs echoed in the cramped space of the tent, a stark contrast to the storm's fury outside. My chest heaved with each breath, the pain from where the hot coal had struck me flaring with every movement. In the darkness, the extent of my injury was a mystery, but the sharp, persistent pain suggested it wasn't minor. The grim realisation that medical help was beyond our reach in this desolate place settled heavily on me.

I manoeuvred myself closer to Paul, finding him rocking back and forth in distress. Gently, I slid behind him, wrapping my arms around his trembling form in an attempt to provide some semblance of comfort. The contact of Paul's bare skin against the raw burn on my chest sent a jolt of pain through me, sharp enough to draw a gasp. My eyes stung, not just from the physical pain but from the overwhelming situation we found ourselves in.

Eventually, Paul's movements stilled. "I'm sorry, Rose," he whispered into the darkness, his voice laden with sadness and a palpable sense of helplessness. The agony in his words, intertwined with my own physical pain from the coal's burn, created a maelstrom of emotion within me. I stared blindly ahead, whispering back in a tone laced with reassurance, "It'll be okay. You'll be okay." The words felt like a vow, a promise amidst the uncertainty enveloping us.

Tears streamed down my face, unbidden, as memories surfaced—memories of holding Luke during his own battles with nightmares. The echo of that past moment, now reflected in my embrace with Paul, underscored the deep bonds of care and empathy that ultimately tied us together. "We'll be okay," I whispered again, more firmly this time.

4338.206

(25 July 2018)

SILENT DUST

4338.206.1

As the first light of morning began to seep into the tent, illuminating the cramped space with a soft, diffused glow, my head involuntarily rolled to the side. There, in the middle of our makeshift shelter, lay Paul, still lost in slumber exactly where I had left him after the tumult of the previous night. A blanket, which I had draped over him in a moment of protective thoughtfulness, shielded his exposed skin from the chill of dawn. It struck me as peculiar, his decision to retire so vulnerably in such an unknown and unforgiving environment. Yet, my acquaintance with Paul was limited; perhaps I was yet to fully understand him. The realisation dawned on me that maybe, the two brothers were more alike than I had initially perceived. *Perhaps I already know him better than I think*, my thoughts echoed, a silent acknowledgment of the bond forming despite our circumstances.

Weary, I rubbed at my eyes, the remnants of fatigue clinging stubbornly. The previous night had seen me succumbing to sleep far quicker than I would have imagined, no doubt a testament to the sheer exhaustion that had enveloped me. How long I had actually slept remained unclear, but I had awoken to a world transformed; the dust storm had retreated, leaving behind a haunting silence that seemed almost as oppressive in its stillness.

After stirring, my first act was to ensure Paul's comfort, covering his naked form with our solitary blanket. Then, finding my way to the mattress, I had lain there, enveloped in the residual darkness, my gaze fixed on the void above me. The blackness seemed almost mocking in its depth, a stark canvas upon which my thoughts and fears danced freely.

Now, navigating through the disarray inside the tent, I reached for my suitcase, buried under the remnants of what had once been the right wing. Dressing quickly in a fresh t-shirt and shorts, I prepared to face the day, the fabric feeling oddly comforting against my skin after the tumultuous night. As I emerged from the confines of our battered shelter, crawling from beneath the collapsed canopy, the morning sun greeted me with a harsh brilliance, its rays illuminating the world around us with an unforgiving clarity.

The landscape that unfolded before me was familiar in its desolation, yet starkly altered by the night's events. The relentless sunlight traced a path across my face and down my body, highlighting the dust and debris that now defined our surroundings. The same barren, dusty expanse stretched out before me, its monotony leaving a bitter taste in my mouth. *But it's not really the same at all*, the thought echoed in my mind, a realisation that deepened the hollow feeling of abandonment that had begun to settle within me.

A glance at the ground confirmed my fears: no footprints disturbed the thick layer of dust that carpeted the earth. The campfire, once a focal point of our small existence here, was now buried under a foot of gold and brown dust, its embers hidden from view, as if to erase any evidence of our brief presence. Apart from the tattered remains of our tent, which now offered little in the way of protection or comfort, all traces of our time in this forsaken place seemed to have been obliterated by Clivilius's unforgiving environment.

The stark realisation that we were but fleeting visitors in this vast, indifferent landscape weighed heavily on me. The storm had not only challenged our physical resilience but had also stripped away the fragile markers of our existence, leaving us even more isolated in its aftermath. As I stood there, taking in the silent, dust-choked world around me, the sense of impermanence was overwhelming. Despite the sun's warmth, a chill settled over me, a poignant reminder of our vulnerability and the relentless passage of time in a land that seemed intent on reclaiming every trace of our passage.

Turning my gaze back to what remained of our tent, I couldn't help but let out a scoff. The sight was pitiful, yet there was a sort of relief in noting that most of the damage seemed to be our own doing. Or more specifically, a small voice in my head remarked, *the chaos that Paul had unwittingly unleashed in his panic.*

My attention was then drawn to a small corner of blue material peeking out from beneath a layer of dust. Crouching down, curiosity piqued, I scrutinised it. It was unfamiliar, not something I immediately recognised as ours. The possibility that it might have originated from another camp sparked a series of rapid thoughts. *Could there really be other people out here? And if so, what would that mean for us? Were they friendly, civilised, or perhaps struggling to survive just as we were?*

Shaking off the whirlwind of speculation, I decided to uncover the mystery of the strange material. Grasping the corner of the fabric, I pulled it from the thick dust and gave it a few vigorous shakes. A chuckle escaped me as I realised what I held: dirty underwear. *So, Paul hadn't been completely naked after all, at least initially.* The realisation brought a momentary lightness to the heavy atmosphere that had settled around me since the storm.

Without further ado, I tossed the soiled underwear onto what was once our campfire, now just a small mound of dust. *It really was a rough night*, I mused to myself, a night that neither of us needed to be reminded of in such a tangible way. The underwear, a trivial yet telling artefact of our ordeal, would be the first to be burned once we managed to get a fire going again. It was a small decision, but it felt like a step towards reclaiming some semblance of control over our situation, a way to start anew after the night's upheaval.

The moment my hands wrapped around the first tent pole, a sharp pang shot through my chest, the weight of the canopy adding to the physical strain. My brow creased in discomfort, and instinctively, my teeth found my lower lip, biting down hard to suppress a groan. The small, darkened lump nestled uncomfortably between my pectoral muscles throbbed with a persistent, nagging pain, a cruel reminder of last night's mayhem.

But now is not the time for pain, I sternly reminded myself, trying to push past the discomfort with sheer willpower. The dawn of a new day, despite its promise of a fresh start, held no magic cure for the aftermath of our ordeal. It wouldn't erase the events that had unfolded, nor would it soothe the injuries sustained. And yet, as I stood there, grappling with the physical reminder of our vulnerability, I knew I couldn't afford to dwell on my own discomfort. Paul would be waking soon, and the state of our shelter demanded immediate attention.

❖

Dabbing at the small tear that had managed to escape my tightly held composure, I turned my attention back to the tent. The canopy was sorted, but the wing, though partially corrected, still hung awkwardly. However, my efforts had stabilised the structure for now, a small victory that was overshadowed by the increasing pain in my chest. It was a clear signal from my body urging me to pause, to acknowledge my own limits.

With a resigned sigh, I made my way through the thick blanket of dust that covered the ground, my bare feet leaving shallow impressions with every step. The destination was the river behind our tent, a ribbon of coolness that contrasted sharply with the arid landscape that surrounded us. The river, in its quiet flow, seemed oblivious to last night's events.

As I sat down at the water's edge, the initial touch of the cool river against my skin sent a shiver of relief through my legs, an almost immediate balm to the physical and emotional exhaustion that clung to me. My toes tentatively explored the refreshing flow, each ripple a whisper of calm that gradually eased the tension from my body.

With my eyes closed, I allowed myself a moment of respite, my head tilting back as I surrendered to the serene sounds of the water. The vacant contemplation was a welcome reprieve from the constant vigilance and problem-solving that had defined our time here.

"Rose!" The sound of Paul's voice, laced with panic, shattered the brief tranquility I had found by the river. My eyes flew open, a surge of adrenaline coursing through me as the echoes of last night's trauma threatened to resurface. *What the fuck!* The internal exclamation was a reflex, a response to the sudden shift from peace to potential peril.

"Where are you?" Paul's voice carried a mix of fear and confusion, pulling me further from my momentary escape.

Realising the situation—daylight still enveloped us, and Paul was very much awake but disoriented—I turned my gaze back towards the camp. "You had a nightmare, Paul," I called out to him with as much steadiness as I could muster. "Rose isn't here." It was crucial to ground him back in reality, away from the grip of his dream-induced terror.

Paul appeared at the side of the tent, clutching the blanket around his waist, a visible shiver running through him despite the warmth. "I don't understand," he admitted, his bewilderment clear in his voice and on his face.

"Come sit," I suggested, gesturing to the space beside me, hoping to offer him a semblance of comfort and normalcy amidst his confusion.

He hesitated, his gaze darting around as if he might find answers in the landscape that surrounded us. My patience frayed slightly at the edges, an involuntary eye roll betraying my frustration. *Paul's going to have to figure it out for himself*, I resigned myself silently, turning my attention back to the river.

The water, with its gentle ebb and flow around my feet, became a focal point once again. Its coolness provided a sharp contrast to the sun's growing heat, a reminder of the day's inevitable climb towards sweltering temperatures. Absorbed in the simple pleasure of watching the water swirl and dance around my legs, I acknowledged the day's potential challenges. Yet, in that moment, the river offered a brief reprieve, a physical and mental oasis that seemed all the more precious for its transience. It was going to be another sweaty day, indeed, but for now, the cool embrace of the river was a balm to both body and spirit.

"The water will help soothe your foot," I reassured Paul as he hesitantly approached.

As Paul gingerly lifted the blanket, exposing his feet, the condition they were in caught my gaze. They mirrored the distress of my own—reddened and battered, a visible sign of our ordeal. Paul's foot, in particular, bore the unmistakable marks of burns from his inadvertent walk through the remnants of our campfire in the darkness. The contrast between the soft, yielding dust on the ground and its transformation into a relentless barrage of abrasive particles when lifted by the wind was stark. Clivilius had shown us both its deceptive calm and its violent tempest.

"Ooh," Paul's voice broke through my thoughts as he tentatively dipped his feet into the cool embrace of the river. "That feels good." The relief in his voice was palpable.

A smile tugged at the corners of my mouth, unseen by Paul. *If only we could stay in the river all day*, I mused silently. The thought was both wistful and laden with a heavy truth. In this harsh, unforgiving environment, the river offered a rare respite, a momentary escape from the relentless heat and the omnipresent dust. It seemed, in that moment, to be the sole benevolent feature in a landscape that otherwise tested us at every turn.

The idea of remaining in this tranquil spot, away from the threats and uncertainties that awaited us beyond its banks, was tempting. Yet, the reality of our situation allowed for no such indulgence. The river, for all its soothing properties, was but a temporary sanctuary.

"Last night was a fucking disaster," the words tumbled out of me, shattering the silence that had settled between us like a dense fog. The statement felt both necessary and inadequate, a feeble attempt to encapsulate what we had endured.

"I guess," Paul's response was terse, almost distant. It was clear that the events of the night had left a deep impression on him, perhaps deeper than I had initially realised. As I observed him gazing blankly across the river, the weight of his thoughts seemed almost discernible.

"What happened to my foot?" His question broke through his reverie, his voice tinged with genuine confusion.

My eyebrow arched in surprise. "You don't remember?" It was hard to believe that he could forget such a harrowing experience.

Paul's face contorted in concentration, searching for a memory that seemed just out of reach, but ultimately, he could only offer a shrug in response.

"You went running out of the tent in pitch blackness in the middle of a fucking dust storm and trod on hot coals from last night's campfire," I stated plainly, not mincing words. "And all for a voice that wasn't real." The harshness of the truth felt necessary, a grounding force in the face of Paul's confusion.

"How do you know it wasn't real?" Paul's demand was sharp, his belief in what he had heard unwavering. "I heard Rose as clear as water."

I sighed heavily. Part of me wished for Paul's sake that his experience had been real, yet I knew with certainty that we had been alone in our struggle. "Pure blackness can make the mind go crazy," I offered gently, trying to bridge the gap between his perception and the reality of our experience.

I noticed Paul's lips relax slightly, a subtle shift that spoke volumes. Yet, as concern for his well-being surged within me, I found myself turning away, unwilling to let him see the worry that creased my brow. The thought that Paul, the optimist among us, might lose his grip on that optimism—or worse, succumb to the madness that this place seemed intent on fostering—was a prospect too daunting to face head-on. In this godforsaken expanse, Paul's optimism was not just a trait; it was a beacon. The idea of that light dimming, of both of us losing our way in the dark, was a fate I couldn't bear to contemplate.

"I'm going to fix the tent," I declared, pushing aside the persistent ache that had settled in my chest. The morning sun was already asserting its presence, its warmth a stark contrast to the cool relief of the river. "And this sun is feeling very warm already. You'd better get some clothes on. I hate to say it, but we may be spending a lot of time in the tent until we can get more shelter."

Without lingering on the conversation, I turned and walked away, each step kicking up fine particles of Clivilius's omnipresent dust. The dust clung to my damp feet, a frustrating reminder of the environment's relentless nature.

"Fuck off!" My irritation with the dust burst forth, a harsh snap at the inanimate yet ever-present annoyance. As I attempted to brush it away, the action felt symbolic, as if I were trying to rid myself of the broader hardships we faced in this harsh landscape.

Approaching the tent, I bent down to tackle the task of reassembling the shelter, starting with the corner tent pole. The logic was simple: secure this one, and the rest should follow more smoothly.

As I was absorbed in these thoughts, Paul's slow approach broke my concentration. "Have you seen Luke yet this morning?" he inquired, his voice tinged with concern.

His question ignited a sudden flare of anger within me. "Nope," I spat out. "Luke seems to be working to his own fucking agenda." The words were a vent for my frustration, a release valve for the pressure building inside.

Paul's reaction was immediate, his frown deepening. "Do you really have to be so negative? And do you have to swear every second sentence?"

His questions, meant to check my attitude, only steeled my resolve. "Yes," I retorted, my defiance unyielding. "Yes, I fucking do."

Waiting for Paul to move away, I let out the pent-up sigh of frustration that had been gnawing at me. Then, with a mix of determination and resignation, I drove the tent pole into the ground, the Clivilius dust swallowing it up.

DROP ZONE

4338.206.2

The heat was more oppressive than I'd given it credit for, or perhaps the task of repairing the tent had demanded more from me than I'd anticipated. The evidence was unmistakable —a sweat-soaked shirt clinging uncomfortably to my skin as I made my way back into the tent's dubious shelter. Paul's passing figure caught my eye, his movement towards the suitcases sparking a flicker of curiosity within me. There was an oddness to him, a detachment that seemed to mirror his brother's in ways I was only beginning to understand.

As I watched him momentarily, lost in whatever thoughts or distractions held his gaze, I couldn't help but draw parallels between the brothers. *He really is just as odd as his brother*, the thought echoed in my mind, a mix of bemusement and intrigue colouring my perception.

Turning my attention away from Paul, I sought out the small comfort of a fresh t-shirt from my case. The act of changing shirts was momentarily grounding, pulling my focus from the complexities of our interactions to the simple, physical sensation of removing the damp fabric. Yet, the action was not without its discomfort; a sharp twinge of pain lanced through my chest, a reminder of the injury concealed beneath.

"Hey, Jamie?" Paul's voice cut through the moment, casual yet carrying an undercurrent of something I couldn't quite place. My response was almost automatic, a surge of panic tightening my chest. *Did Paul notice?* The question raced through my mind, the fear of my secret being exposed momentarily overwhelming.

A soft gasp of pain slipped out as I wrestled the fresh shirt over my head, the fabric brushing against the tender area a sharp contrast to the mental turmoil swirling within. I steadied myself, pushing past the pain and the fear, to answer him. "Yeah," my voice emerged, more controlled than I felt, a façade of calm belying the storm of emotions and physical discomfort that vied for dominance within me.

"What did you like least about life back on Earth?" Paul's inquiry, unexpected and laden with curiosity, momentarily transported me from the immediate concerns of our predicament. A mix of surprise and a faint sense of relief washed over me, his question offering a brief respite, a gateway to reflections on a life now far removed from our current reality. "Hmm," I mused aloud, taking a moment to gather my thoughts, the question prompting a deep dive into memories I hadn't sifted through in some time. I turned to face him, "Not sure. Life was pretty good."

Paul's reaction was immediate, his expression lighting up with a blend of surprise and perhaps a hint of intrigue. It seemed my response had caught him off guard, an indication of the preconceptions he might have harboured about me, possibly influenced by whatever narratives Luke had shared.

I watched Paul carefully, mulling over the dynamics at play. It wasn't entirely surprising that he might have expected a different answer. The bonds between siblings often included a shared repository of stories and impressions, and it was evident that Paul and Luke were no exception. Yet, everyone's story is layered, unique to their own experiences and perceptions, including mine. A subtle grin began to form as I contemplated his expectations. "Were you expecting something different?" I prodded gently, curious about the assumptions he might have made.

Paul's reaction was almost immediate, his face flushing with a mix of embarrassment and perhaps a touch of regret at the direction of the conversation. "I... uh... that's not what I meant," he managed to stammer out, revealing his discomfort.

"Really?" My tone was light, playful even. "Then what did you mean?" I pressed, not to embarrass him further but to encourage a deeper exchange, to perhaps peel back another layer of our burgeoning understanding of each other.

"I mean..." Paul began again, his hesitation a clear sign of his internal struggle to articulate his thoughts.

"Hmm," I interjected, drawing out the moment with a teasing lilt to my voice. I settled myself beside Paul on the mattress, a silent invitation for him to continue, to share more of his thoughts.

"We get to leave all of the dramas of Earth life behind and start fresh," Paul said, his voice carrying a note of excitement that seemed to illuminate his face. The sincerity in his expression struck me, revealing a depth of belief in the potential of our dire situation that I hadn't fully appreciated before. *He really believes it*, a realisation that piqued my interest and left me eager to delve deeper into his perspective. "Go on," I encouraged, genuinely intrigued by his line of thought.

Paul, animated by the encouragement, didn't miss a beat. "Think about it. We don't have to go to work. I mean, yeah, we may need to 'work' here so that we don't die, but it's not the same thing as having set hours working for someone else." His distinction between the survival efforts required in our current predicament and the structured, often monotonous nature of employment back on Earth resonated with a part of me that had long chafed under those very constraints.

"And?" I pressed, sensing there was more to his vision than just an escape from the nine-to-five grind. His earlier distraction now made sense to me as the outline of a dream rather than mere disengagement from our reality.

"And," he continued, each word thoughtful as if he were piecing together the vision in real-time, "we get to leave all the annoying, stupid people behind. All the politics. All the stupid rules." His critique of Earth's societal flaws was blunt, echoing sentiments I'd often heard, sometimes voiced, sometimes left unspoken, but always simmering beneath the surface of day-to-day frustrations.

Wow! The comparison to Luke was unavoidable in my mind at that moment. *I didn't realise Luke and Paul were twins!* The thought was both amusing and enlightening, offering a new layer of understanding to the brothers' dynamic.

"And family?" I queried, curious to see how he reconciled this utopian vision with the more personal, intricate ties that bound us to others.

"Not necessarily," he replied, the caveat hanging between us like an unspoken challenge.

"How so?" I asked, needing him to elucidate on this point that seemed both radical and fraught with ethical complexities.

"What if we created a new civilisation here? One where we could bring only the family we wanted? Only the people who would participate and contribute productively to the society?" His proposal was ambitious, a bold imagining of a community built not on the happenstance of birth or geography but on shared values and mutual effort.

Paul's words lingered in the air, a vision of a new world order that was as tantalising as it was troubling. *People are stupid, sure, but does that really warrant such drastic measures?* The gravity of what he was suggesting weighed heavily on me. *Is it really our responsibility to play God and decide who is a worthy citizen and who isn't?* The simplicity of his solution belied the complex web of moral and ethical questions it raised. *Life just isn't that simple,* a counterpoint to Paul's dream that echoed silently within me, a reminder of the inherent messiness of human existence and the danger of oversimplification.

"Don't you think that's even a little exciting?" Paul persisted, his enthusiasm undimmed by my skepticism. "Don't you get it? We can create our own rules. Our own culture. Our own society." His words, so full of hope and determination, struck a chord within me, albeit one that resonated with caution and doubt rather than excitement.

Yet I was caught off guard by the audacity of Paul's vision, a vision that challenged the very foundations of what society had taught us back on Earth. His ideas, though radical, sparked an undeniable curiosity within me. Yet, the reality of our current predicament cast a long shadow over his optimistic projections. I fixed my gaze on him, searching his eyes for any sign of doubt. "After last night, do you really believe all of that is true?" My voice was laced with challenge, seeking to probe the depth of his conviction.

"I do," Paul replied, his confidence unshaken, a stark contrast to the tumultuous night we had just endured. His belief in the potential of our situation, in the face of such adversity, was both baffling and, in some strange way, admirable.

"As soon as Luke returns, I'm going to try and leave Clivilius again," I declared scornfully, a mix of frustration and resignation in my tone. I let myself fall back onto the mattress, seeking solace in the brief escape that closing my eyes offered. My arms settled behind my head, a makeshift cushion against the hard reality that surrounded us. Paul's relentless optimism was grating on me, his voice a constant reminder of our dire situation. *Perhaps if I ignore him, he might just go away,* I mused silently, a desperate thought born of a desire for peace, however fleeting.

And then, after several minutes filled with sighs and Paul's contemplative 'aha's,' the tent fell silent. Paul had left, granting me the solitude I had yearned for. Yet, the quiet also left room for reflection on the conversation we'd just had. Despite my resistance to his ideas, Paul's perspective lingered in the back of my mind, a nagging reminder that perhaps there was more to our situation than mere survival. His departure left me alone with my thoughts, the silence a waiting canvas upon which the possibilities of what could be painted a complex and uncertain future.

❖

"There's nothing else to do," my words carried a note of resignation as I settled beside the river, adopting a cross-legged position in the dust next to Paul. The landscape before us, both barren and beautiful, offered little in the way of distraction or purpose.

"Well," Paul began, his tone deliberate and thoughtful, "We could do with a place near the Portal where Luke can deliver things. We can then work out what to do with them." His suggestion, seemingly out of the blue, caught me off guard.

I turned to him, my expression one of bewilderment. "Well, that seems a bit random," I remarked, the idea striking me as a sudden leap from our current state of aimlessness.

Paul chuckled, a sound that carried a lightness we'd been missing. "It does a bit, doesn't it?" His admission, coupled with the gentle humour in his voice, coaxed a smile from me. Despite everything, Paul's relentless drive to find purpose, to plan for a future uncertain as it was, reminded me of the resilience of the human spirit.

Lost in thought, I gazed at the river's gentle flow, the water moving with a purpose that seemed to mock our current predicament. The notion of being permanently marooned in Clivilius was a weight I wasn't ready to bear, yet the idea of engaging in some form of project, as Paul suggested, offered a distraction—a way to mark the time with something other than my own thoughts.

"I guess it would give us something to do," I conceded after a moment, careful to temper my response. I wanted to offer Paul neither false hope nor outright dismissal, navigating the fine line between encouragement and realism.

Paul's enthusiasm was undeterred, his voice gaining momentum as he elaborated on his idea. "And not just finding a good spot. Getting Luke to leave whatever he brings through the Portal in a single spot, will give us something to do to move it." His plan, while simple, had a certain appeal—a concrete task in a reality that often felt disconcertingly abstract.

"And," I found myself saying, drawn in by the infectious nature of his optimism, "Luke is very intelligent, but he can also be a bit of a scatterbrain."

"Totally!" Paul agreed, his voice laced with a mixture of affection and frustration at Luke's idiosyncrasies. "I don't think it's wise for us to trust Luke to establish a settlement properly." The shared understanding, a rare moment of alignment in our outlooks, felt like a small victory.

With a newfound sense of purpose, however temporary, I rose to my feet and offered Paul a hand up.

"You coming then?" I called back, already moving towards the task ahead, the possibility of action a welcome change from the inertia that had gripped me. "It was your idea after all."

Without waiting for Paul to catch up, I set off towards the Portal with a brisk pace, my steps fuelled by a mix of determination and a need to occupy my mind. The sight of the large, translucent screen of the Portal, as it gradually came into view, served as a stark reminder of the strange reality we found ourselves in. I couldn't help but liken our current endeavour to the childhood adventures of building dens—full of enthusiasm and imagination, yet tinged with the innocence of believing in temporary escapes. This exercise, I reminded myself, was merely a distraction, a way to pass the time. Despite the momentary engagement, my resolve remained unchanged: *When Luke returns, I'm going home.*

Encountering a hand-sized rock that nearly sent me tumbling, I seized it in a reflexive grasp. The rock, jagged and solid under my fingers, served an unexpected purpose as I used its pointed end to etch a boundary in the loose dust. The site I had selected for our task was ideally situated: it was close enough to the Portal screen to offer convenience, yet far enough to maintain a respectful distance from the mystical threshold that connected worlds.

As Paul's uneven steps heralded his arrival, my attention shifted from the ground to his figure. I watched him, noting the determination in his movements as he began to gather larger rocks, methodically arranging them into a neat pile at one end of the line I had drawn. A spark of admiration flickered within me as I observed his actions—*Hmm, not a bad idea*, I mused internally. It was a simple gesture, but in the context of our shared endeavour, it felt significant. Paul's initiative, albeit silent, spoke volumes, encouraging me to engage with the task with a renewed sense of purpose.

The dust around us stirred with our movements, creating a subtle dance of particles in the sunlight. I found myself drawn into the rhythm of our shared task, moving alongside Paul to mark out the boundaries more clearly. With each rock we placed, a silent camaraderie built between us, underscored by the soft thuds of stones settling against the earth.

Together, we worked in silent agreement, each action synchronised as if by an unspoken understanding. We placed rock piles at each corner of the outlined area and spaced them at regular intervals along its perimeter, forming a tangible marker of our efforts. The physicality of the work, the weight of the rocks in my hands, and the dust clinging to my skin grounded me in the moment.

Stepping back, I took a moment to assess what we had accomplished. The boundary we had marked out in the dust was now clearly defined, a testament to our combined efforts under the unforgiving Clivilius sun. The perimeter stood out against the backdrop of the barren landscape, a small patch of order amidst the vast unknown.

"There," Paul stated, a hint of satisfaction in his voice as he wiped away the sweat that had gathered on his brow from the exertion and heat.

"Looks alright," I acknowledged, my gaze still fixed on the boundary we had created. The pragmatic part of me appreciated the tangible result of our labour, even if part of me remained detached from the enthusiasm that Paul exuded. "You got a name for it?" I asked, curious despite myself about what Paul would come up with.

"Hmm," he hesitated, taking a brief pause to mull over his response. After a moment's thought, he seemed to reach a decision. "Yes. The Clivilius Delivery Drop Zone," he declared, a sense of achievement lighting up his face with an almost childlike pride.

The name, earnest yet undeniably grandiose, caught me off guard, and I couldn't suppress the laughter that bubbled up from within. It was a laugh not of mockery, but one born from the sheer unexpectedness and the peculiar charm of Paul's naming convention. His enthusiasm, so pure and unguarded, made the name 'The Clivilius Delivery Drop Zone' sound both utterly absurd and endearingly appropriate.

"What?" Paul looked at me, a blend of confusion and amusement on his face.

"Nothing. It's as good a name as any," I managed between chuckles, my laughter fading into a soft smile. Deep down, I was reminded of the fleeting nature of my presence here, the internal reminder that I was planning to leave Clivilius at the first opportunity. Yet, as I spoke, a knot of discomfort tightened in my stomach—a silent acknowledgment of the bond forming, however reluctantly, between Paul and me. "But I'll just call it the Drop Zone for short," I added, an attempt to bridge my practicality with Paul's vision.

"Drop Zone," Paul echoed, a grin spreading across his face. "I like it."

A small smile found its way to my lips as I watched Paul bask in the simple joy of the moment. *At least one of us seems to be happy here*, I thought, the observation carrying a mix of resignation and a begrudging appreciation for Paul's ability to find a sliver of contentment in our challenging circumstances.

ALIVE!

1338.206.3

"Do you hear that?" The question escaped me almost reflexively as I reached out, halting Paul's motion just as he was about to launch another stone across the dusty ground.

Paul's action froze mid-throw, his body language shifting to one of alert curiosity as he tilted his head, straining to catch the elusive sound. "I think so," he confirmed, his voice tinged with a mixture of surprise and cautious optimism. "Is that... it sounds like a reversing vehicle?"

"Sounds like it, doesn't it," I echoed, a flicker of hope igniting within me at the recognition of something so mundane yet so impossibly out of place in our current surroundings. "And it sounds like it's coming from the Portal's direction. It must be Luke!" The realisation struck me with a mix of excitement and a pang of embarrassment at the obviousness of the conclusion. After all, where else would it be coming from and who else could it be?

"Luke!" Paul's voice cut through the air, louder and filled with an anticipation that mirrored my own.

Compelled by a sudden surge of hope, a feeling I hadn't allowed myself to fully embrace in what felt like an eternity, I didn't linger to exchange further words with Paul. My legs carried me forward, propelled by the prospect of escape, of salvation. The steady jog towards the Portal felt both surreal and desperate, a race against an opportunity that might as swiftly vanish as it appeared.

Arriving at the Portal, the sight that greeted me was one that seemed to bridge the gap between the impossible and the mundane—a small truck, meticulously navigating its way backward through the shimmering veil of the Portal's colours. The juxtaposition of such an everyday occurrence against the backdrop of our extraordinary circumstances was jarring.

Acting on instinct, I found myself moving to guide the vehicle, my hands waving in an attempt to direct its slow, careful reversal. The sight was almost comical, a bizarre mimicry of normalcy in the most abnormal of contexts.

"For fuck's sake, Luke!" The exclamation burst from me as the truck lurched awkwardly, prompting me to leap aside to avoid being caught in its path. The vehicle came to a shuddering halt, its journey through the Portal complete, but leaving behind a trail of dust and a cloud of unanswered questions.

The moment the cab door swung open and Luke descended with that insufferably cheery grin, a mix of relief and irritation swirled within me. "What the fuck are you doing, Luke? You know you're a bad driver! You almost hit me!" My voice carried the weight of the frustration and fear from his near miss.

"You shouldn't have got so close to me then," Luke shot back, his chiding tone grating on my already frayed nerves. It was like him to deflect, to make light of situations that had others teetering on the edge of panic.

"What happened to you?" Luke's attention shifted to Paul, noting his uneven approach. The concern in his voice was genuine, if somewhat belated in its appearance.

"I burnt it," Paul responded, his tone stripped of any self-pity or drama, a stark contrast to the gravity of his injury.

"Burnt it? How?" Luke's curiosity piqued.

Paul glanced my way, silently seeking support in recounting the ordeal. The memory of the previous night's episode pressed heavily on me, the fear and confusion momentarily tightening its grip around my chest. "Hmm," I managed, my voice steadier than I felt. "Let me summarise for you. No light, hot coals and a fucking dust storm." The words came out clipped, a terse summation of a night that had tested our limits in every conceivable way.

Luke's gaze flickered between Paul and me, his expression unreadable. My irritation simmered just below the surface. *Since when have I ever exaggerated?*

"Yeah, that's a pretty accurate summary," Paul chimed in, lending his confirmation to my account.

"Oh," was all Luke offered in response, his nonchalance striking a nerve.

Throwing my hands up, my frustration found its voice. "Is that all you have to say? Oh?" The disbelief in my tone was palpable, a reflection of the disbelief I felt at his underwhelming reaction.

Luke's shrugged. "What do you want me to say?" His question, though simple, felt like a dismissal, a refusal to engage with the gravity of our situation.

"I don't know," I retorted, the aggravation bubbling over. "But surely you could do a little better than just, oh." The exchange, fraught with tension, laid bare the chasm between our experiences of the previous night and Luke's detached arrival. His inability—or unwillingness—to grasp the severity of what we had endured only served to amplify the sense of isolation that Clivilius seemed to foster, a reminder that understanding, much like rescue, might be harder to come by than I'd hoped.

"So, what's in the truck, Luke?" Paul's voice, infused with an eagerness to shift the focus from the tension, couldn't hide his transparent desire for a change in topic.

The truck's back door swung open with a metallic clang that resonated off the side of the vehicle, signalling Luke's readiness to reveal the contents. "It's all the stuff from your list," he announced, his grin stretching wide, reflecting a mix of pride and satisfaction at having fulfilled Paul's request.

Paul's face lit up with a joy reminiscent of a child discovering presents under a Christmas tree. "Oh, that's great," he exclaimed, his enthusiasm undiminished by the earlier awkwardness.

"I need the two of you to unpack the truck. I'll come and collect it in an hour or so once the other tents have arrived," Luke directed, assuming the role of coordinator with an ease that seemed at odds with our situation.

"There's a spot over there where you can leave all the things you bring through the Portal," Paul interjected, pointing towards the meticulously outlined area we had designated earlier. "Jamie and I can take care of it from there." His voice carried a note of pride, a testament to our small achievement in organising this desolate space.

"Oh, cool," Luke responded, his interest piqued but his tone remaining casual, almost indifferent to the significance of what Paul and I had attempted to create.

"It's the Clivilius Delivery Drop Zone," Paul declared, unable to conceal the wide smile that spread across his face, clearly delighted with the official title he had bestowed upon our makeshift logistics area.

"I love it!" Luke exclaimed, offering a thumbs up in approval, his enthusiasm momentarily aligning with Paul's.

"I just call it the Drop Zone," I found myself saying, an interjection that surprised even me. There was a part of me that questioned why I felt compelled to engage in what seemed like a trivial exchange, given the broader context of our predicament.

"Jamie helped," Paul added quickly, casting a glance in my direction, a nod towards my contribution to the plan.

I glared at Paul, irked by the implication that my involvement was somehow unexpected or noteworthy. "You say that like you both expected that I wouldn't."

"I... uh... umm," Paul faltered, caught off guard by my reaction, his earlier confidence dissolving into uncertainty.

With a roll of my eyes and a dismissive huff, I moved closer to the back of the truck, driven by a mix of curiosity and a need to distract myself from the irritation bubbling within. If Luke was so proud of what he'd brought, I figured I might as well take a look for myself. The action was less about interest in the materials themselves and more about seeking a momentary reprieve from the complexities of our interactions.

"You better drive the truck over there for me," Luke instructed, his tone brisk as he tossed the keys in Paul's direction with a casual flick of his wrist.

Paul, ever determined, took a cautious step forward to catch the keys. The grimace that briefly crossed his face as he shifted his weight onto his injured foot did not go unnoticed. The sight tugged at something within me, a mixture of concern and frustration at our situation.

"I can do it, if you like?" I found myself saying, reaching out instinctively towards the keys, ready to take on the task to spare Paul any further discomfort.

Paul glanced at me, a mix of gratitude and stubborn pride in his eyes. "Nah. It's all good, I'll manage. Thanks though." His voice carried that familiar resilience, an unwillingness to let his injury slow him down more than necessary.

"Sure," I replied, masking my concern with a nonchalant shrug. "Suit yourself." Watching Paul slowly manoeuvre himself into the driver's seat, I couldn't help but admire his determination, even as I questioned the wisdom of pushing through pain.

With Paul now occupied, I turned my attention to Luke, the urgency of our predicament pressing heavily on my mind. "I want to try and leave again," I stated, my resolve firm. There was no room for ambiguity in my intent, no doubt about the seriousness with which I viewed our situation.

Luke's response was a shrug, noncommittal and frustratingly indifferent. "You can try if you want," he offered, his skepticism clear. "But I'm not sure it's going to do you any good." The lack of support, the dismissal of my determination as futile, grated on me.

"Well, we've got to fucking try at least," the words burst from me, a raw expression of my frustration and refusal to accept our circumstances as permanent without exhausting every possible avenue for escape.

"Sure, go for it," Luke sighed, his resignation hanging in the air between us like a challenge. His apathy, in stark contrast to my desperation, underscored the isolation of our predicament—not just from the world we knew but sometimes, it seemed, from each other.

As Paul drove the truck away, leaving a swirling aftermath of dust in its wake, I found myself drawn towards the Portal with a mix of trepidation and desperate hope. My hands stretched out before me, I inched closer, the myriad colours of the Portal swirling hypnotically. Then, abruptly, two vibrant strands of colour—a fierce green and a deep red—shot towards me, sparking as they collided with my chest. The sensation was startling, as if the very essence of Clivilius sought to mark me, yet they vanished as quickly as they appeared, absorbed into me, igniting a fleeting hope. *Could this be it? The moment when I break free from this place?*

But that hope was quickly extinguished by the booming, emotionless decree of Clivilius itself. *I've already told you, Jamie Greyson. You can never leave!* The words reverberated through my mind, a cruel reminder of my seeming fate.

"Fucking piece of shit!" The words burst from me in a mixture of defiance and frustration as I lashed out, my foot connecting with the vibrant hues of the Portal. The backlash was immediate—a forceful repulsion that sent me stumbling backward to land heavily on the ground.

Do not approach me again, Jamie Greyson, the voice of Clivilius commanded, its tone leaving no room for negotiation. "Or what?" I retorted, defiance flaring as I faced the mass of swirling colours. "You'll fucking kill me?" My voice broke through the silence, each word punctuated by laboured breaths.

"Jamie!" Luke's voice, sharp with reprimand, cut through my tirade. "Just calm your farm, would you?"

"Still can't leave then?" Paul's question, though softly spoken, carried the weight of our shared predicament as he joined us.

My gaze remained fixed on the Portal, the object of our entrapment, and the focus of my growing resolve. *This isn't over yet, Clivilius,* I vowed silently, a fierce determination taking root. *I will find a way.* The conviction in my heart was clear, a silent promise to myself and to my companions. Despite Clivilius's warnings, despite the seeming futility of our situation, I was not ready to accept defeat. The journey was far from over, and I would continue to seek our freedom, whatever it took.

"Oh," Luke casually dropped the bombshell as if it were an afterthought. "I need your wallets."

Struggling to my feet, I dusted myself off, a mix of disbelief and irritation taking hold. "What for?" My skepticism was palpable, the request feeling absurdly out of place.

"Those tents are expensive," Luke stated matter-of-factly, as if that explained everything.

"How much did you spend?" I asked with a grimace, concern beginning to grow that even if I did find a way to return, Luke would have already destroyed everything we'd worked so hard to build by the time I did.

Luke's hesitation only served to heighten my anxiety. "How much?" I pressed, needing to understand the full extent of the damage.

"The credit card is almost maxed out," he admitted, his reluctance clear. The words hit me like a physical blow.

I kicked at the dust in frustration, the particles swirling into the air as I vented, "Shit, Luke." The implications of his actions, the potential ruin of our carefully constructed financial stability, were overwhelming.

"It's not like you can use any of it here anyway," Luke retorted defensively, his words doing little to quell the rising storm within me.

"Oh, fuck you! Just rub it in, why don't you! I get it, we're stuck forever in this fucking hole of a dustbowl and it's all thanks to... guess who!?" My anger boiled over, each word punctuated by another furious kick at the dust, sending clouds of it into the air—a futile gesture against the weight of our situation.

"Here," Paul interjected, his voice cutting through the tension as he extended his wallet to Luke, an act of compliance that seemed to me in that moment both defeatist and absurd.

"You can't be fucking serious!" My outrage was uncontrollable, the thought of capitulating to Luke's demands, of handing over what little link we had left to our lives back on Earth, was unbearable.

Paul merely shrugged, a gesture that felt like a surrender, a resignation to our fate that I was not yet prepared to accept. The complexity of emotions, the anger, the frustration, the sense of betrayal, swirled within me as potent as the dust clouds at my feet. The divide between us, between our perceptions of our situation and our responses to it, had never felt more pronounced.

"I'll need you to write down all your bank account details too," Luke's request cut through the air with a gravity that immediately set my nerves on edge. He stepped closer to Paul, taking the offered wallet with a sense of purpose that belied the seriousness of his intentions.

"What sort of details?" Paul's voice was tinged with caution, his instinct for self-preservation evident in the hesitancy of his question.

Luke met his gaze squarely, the intensity in his eyes leaving no room for ambiguity. "Everything," he stated flatly. "Online logins, pin codes. Over the next few days, I'm going to convert as many of your assets as possible into cash." The finality in his voice was chilling.

The fear that flashed across Paul's face was palpable, a visible manifestation of the realisation of what he was being asked to surrender. After a moment of stunned silence, Paul's resolve hardened. He took a deep breath, reclaiming his wallet from Luke's grasp with a snatch that spoke volumes of his decision.

Luke, taken aback by Paul's reaction, threw his hands up. "What's up?" he asked, his voice betraying a hint of frustration at the unexpected turn of events.

"I can't let you do that, Luke," Paul asserted, his voice firm despite the tremor of emotion that underpinned it. "I need to think of my children." His refusal was not just a rejection of Luke's plan but a declaration of his priorities. "Claire still has access to those accounts. She'll need the money to take care of the kids, especially now that I have no way of supporting them myself." Paul's words were a poignant reminder of the lives that extended beyond the confines of Clivilius, of responsibilities and bonds that remained unbroken despite the distance.

Luke's reaction was immediate, his previously determined demeanour softening as the implications of his request became clear. "Of course," he conceded, the earlier assertiveness in his voice replaced by a more sombre, tone. "I understand."

"Here, take mine," the words tumbled out, heavy with a sense of defeat. It felt like a surrender, not just of my wallet but of any semblance of control I had clung to. "It's just the two of us anyway. You may as well have it," I added, a mix of resignation and bitterness colouring my tone as I tossed my wallet towards Luke. It landed with a significant thud at his feet, a reflection to the weight of the decision.

Luke stooped to retrieve it, his movements slow, almost reverent. "Thanks," he murmured, offering me a soft smile that was both appreciative and tinged with sorrow. It was a small gesture, but in that moment, it felt like an acknowledgment of the sacrifices we were being forced to make.

"Shit, Luke. This is insane," I couldn't help but exclaim, the full weight of our actions crashing down upon me. It was a moment of clarity, bitter and sharp, the reality of our situation piercing through the fog of despair and resignation that had settled over me.

"I know," Luke's response was quiet, almost resigned. "But this is just how it is now." His acceptance of our fate, though pragmatic, did nothing to ease the growing turmoil within me.

Paul seemed to shrink under the weight of our conversation. "I'll go and get us some paper," he offered, his voice barely above a whisper as he turned to leave, his limp more pronounced with each step.

As he walked away, I was left facing Luke, the enormity of our predicament making me feel light-headed. My chest ached, each throb a painful reminder of the physical and emotional toll this place had exacted on me.

"Come here, Jamie," Luke's voice broke through my spiralling thoughts, his arms open in a gesture of comfort and solidarity. Hesitating, I took a few tentative steps towards him, each one heavier than the last.

"Everything will be okay," he tried to assure me, his voice carrying a warmth that I hadn't realised how much I needed to hear.

I stopped, a mere few feet away from him, struck by the sincerity in his voice. Despite everything—the anger, the frustration, the fear—it was clear that Luke really did care. And it dawned on me then, that my feelings for him hadn't waned; they had only deepened. The realisation brought tears to my eyes, tears that threatened to spill over not from the pain of my injuries, but from the pain of acknowledging how much damage I had allowed my fear and anger to inflict on our relationship. In that moment, it was evident that the financial strain, the maxed-out credit cards, paled in comparison to the thought of losing the relationship that Luke and I had built together.

"Really," Luke's assurance echoed in the air, his voice steady and filled with an optimism I found both comforting and bewildering in equal measure. "It's all going to be fine."

The weight of my guilt, a heavy shroud around my shoulders, compelled me to lower my gaze. "I'm so sorry, Luke," the words barely more than a whisper, a confession long held back.

"Sorry?" Luke's repetition of my apology carried a note of confusion, his brows knitting together in concern. "Sorry for what?"

The question hung between us, a chasm that seemed to widen with each passing second. "I... uh." My voice faltered, the truth I had concealed now a tangible presence, demanding to be acknowledged.

Luke's eyes, sharp and penetrating, searched mine for clarity, for understanding. The cautious distance in his stance was palpable.

"The other night," I started, the admission clawing its way up my throat. Each word felt heavier than the last, laden with the weight of my betrayal. "When you called me up and I told you that I was working late," another pause, a breath drawn in a silent plea for strength. "I was with Ben," the confession fell from my lips, the name a witness to my failure. "I'm really sorry," I added, the whisper barely audible, a feeble attempt to convey the depth of my remorse.

Luke's reaction was immediate and startling. In a swift movement that left no room for anticipation, he closed the distance between us. His hands, firm and warm, grasped my arms, pulling me towards him with a decisiveness that left me breathless. And then, his lips met mine in a kiss that was both a surprise and a balm, firm yet gentle against my dry lips.

Frozen, the unexpectedness of his response rendered me immobile, a storm of emotions whirling within me. *What should I do?* The question ricocheted through my mind, leaving a trail of uncertainty in its wake. Responding, engaging in this kiss, could it be construed as a signal, a message to Luke that there was hope for us yet? Would such a response only serve to weave a deeper web of deceit, offering a promise of reconciliation that my actions had already jeopardised?

In that moment, caught in Luke's embrace, the future of our relationship hung in the balance, a precarious thing of beauty and pain. The path forward was clouded, obscured by the complexity of our emotions and the consequences of my actions. Yet, in the midst of the turmoil, Luke's kiss whispered of forgiveness, of a possibility for healing, leaving me to wonder if, despite everything, there might still be a chance for us to mend what had been broken.

If there was any chance, any hope, for once I was going to take it. Embracing the moment, I returned Luke's kiss with all the passion I could muster. It felt like crossing a threshold, a decisive step away from the shadows of guilt and towards a sliver of redemption. It was as if the kiss had awakened us from a prolonged slumber, a period marked by the monotony of survival, devoid of the vibrant colours that paint the essence of life. The intensity of our embrace, the fervent exchange of apologies and silent promises conveyed through the dance of our tongues, was a testament to the raw, pulsating life that still coursed through our veins.

Feeling Luke's lips part in invitation was like the first breath of air after being submerged underwater for too long. It was exhilarating, a surge of life force that invigorated my soul, reminding me of what it means to feel truly alive. The passion that ignited between us, a blazing inferno after the smallest of sparks, served as a declaration—a declaration that despite the adversities we faced, the essence of who we were remained unextinguished.

Luke's hand slid automatically down my back and squeezed my firm ass. Fighting the ingrained instinct to pull away, I let him pull me in closer. My engorged dick pushed against Luke's crotch, almost eliciting a gasp. It had been months since I had felt any inclination towards arousal around Luke, and now, it felt so intoxicating that I didn't want it to stop.

Our renewed intimacy seemed to transcend the mere physicality of two people seeking comfort in one another; it was a profound reconnection, a rekindling of a flame that I feared had been lost to the cold, unforgiving void of life. It was a rebellion against the resignation that had threatened to consume me, a bold affirmation of life in the face of desolation.

"So, you've made up then?" Paul's words sliced through the air, jarring me back to reality from the cocoon of emotion Luke and I had enveloped ourselves in.

Startled, the connection between Luke and me was abruptly severed as I retreated, putting physical distance between our bodies while still grappling with the lingering warmth of his touch. My hands, acting of their own accord, found Luke's shoulders, pushing gently but firmly until we were an arm's length apart.

With my face burning, a visible sign of the intense emotions that had just been exchanged, I grabbed the paper Paul offered. The action was mechanical, a desperate attempt to anchor myself to something mundane, something normal in the midst of the emotional storm. Hastily scribbling down my bank details, I handed the paper to Luke. "That's it," I managed to say, my voice steadier than I felt.

Luke's hand found my shoulder, offering a reassuring squeeze that spoke volumes of promises and shared secrets. "I'll spend it carefully," he assured me, his voice carrying a weight of responsibility and a trace of something more, something unspoken that hung between us. Then, with a resolve that seemed to draw from our moment of connection, he turned and stepped through the Portal. The swirling, electric colours enveloped him before the light they cast abruptly vanished, leaving a striking reminder of the chasm that lay between our current reality and the world we longed for.

"I want to be alone," I declared, my voice laced with a mix of defiance and a need for solitude. Without a glance at Paul, I turned and walked away, each step carrying me further from the moment of vulnerability I had just experienced. As I distanced myself, the echo of Luke's promise lingered in my mind, a bittersweet reminder of the complexities of love, loyalty, and survival in an unforgiving landscape.

❖

The journey away from the Portal, away from Luke and Paul, felt interminable. Each step I took was a battle, fought under the scorching sun that seemed to amplify the turmoil swirling within me. The heat was oppressive, mirroring the intensity of the emotions that I grappled with. My chest ached with a pain that was far more than just the physical throbbing between my pecs; it was a manifestation of the guilt and the myriad of emotions that waged war within my heart.

That wasn't quite what I had expected, but Luke seems to have taken it well, I tried to reassure myself, a feeble attempt to find some solace in the aftermath of my confession. *Maybe he'll forgive me after all.* The thought offered a fleeting sense of hope, a possible light at the end of a tumultuous tunnel. Yet, as quickly as that hope appeared, it was dashed by a more sobering thought, a reminder from my gut telling me the harsher truth. *More likely, maybe Luke just wasn't surprised.*

I let out a heavy sigh, the sound lost in the vast emptiness that surrounded me. The truth was, the flirting with Ben hadn't been a sudden occurrence; it had been a slow-burning fire that had ignited several months ago. Despite Luke's attempts to fan the flames of our intimacy, the reality that our relationship had been teetering on the brink of collapse was undeniable. He had to know, just as well as I did, that what we had been desperately clinging to had likely disintegrated long before this moment. Our relationship, once strong and vibrant, had been reduced to ashes, leaving us grasping at the remnants of what used to be.

The realisation was a bitter pill to swallow. It was only the fear of confronting the truth—that our decade-long partnership might have reached its inevitable conclusion—that had allowed me to resist Ben's advances for as long as I did. The acknowledgment of this fact weighed heavily on me, a solemn confirmation of the fragility of relationships and the sometimes insurmountable distance that can grow between two people, no matter how much they once loved each other.

Removing my top and letting it fall carelessly to the dusty shore, I approached the lagoon's clear waters with a sense of resignation. Each step into the refreshing embrace of the water served as a reminder of my new reality. *And now*, I mused silently, the cool liquid enveloping me as I ventured deeper, with my eternal exile from Earth confirmed, the complexities of my past relationships seemed both infinitely distant and painfully close. I wouldn't have to navigate the turbulent waters between Ben and me again, that much was certain. And Luke—well, Luke would undoubtedly find ways to immerse himself in activities or projects, ensuring our paths intersected minimally, if at all.

"But that kiss," I found myself whispering to the stillness around me, the words floating away on the gentle breeze that skimmed the surface of the lagoon. The question that followed was more to myself than to the vast, uncaring expanse of Clivilius. "Why?" The kiss had been a moment of connection, a flash of something raw and real amidst the desolation of our surroundings. Yet, I struggled to comprehend its significance, to understand the hope it seemed to offer—a hope I was afraid to grasp, for fear of it dissolving like a mirage in the desert.

The lagoon's tranquil waters offered no answers, merely reflecting back my own confused visage as I sought clarity in its depths. The future, once a path we walked together, now branched into separate ways, leaving me to ponder the remnants of what was and the shadow of what might have been.

As the fabric of my shorts tightened against my body, the deeper waters of the lagoon embraced me, pulling me further into its enigmatic depths. The sensation, otherworldly and strangely compelling, seemed to permeate my very being, a reminder of the unnatural essence of this place. My forehead furrowed in a mix of frustration and resignation. "This fucking lagoon," I voiced aloud into the solitude, my hand slipping beneath my shorts in a desperate attempt to alleviate the mental and emotional strain that had become my constant companion.

With each determined pull of my cock, the water around me stirred, creating ripples that seemed to carry my tension away, dispersing it into the lagoon's mysterious expanse. A momentary escape, a fleeting release, allowed a soft moan to escape my lips, a sound of surrender to the moment's fleeting relief.

Surrender yourself, Jamie Greyson, the soft, insidious whisper of Clivilius filled my mind, startling in its intimacy. The voice, unexpected and unsettling, drew a sharp intake of breath from me. *What the hell was that?* The question echoed within, my eyes snapping open as the presence felt closer, more intense.

Give yourself to me and I will grant you new life, it persisted, the words weaving through my consciousness, sending a cascade of shivers down my spine, the promise both tempting and terrifying.

With a final surge of unrestrained emotion, I allowed myself to be carried away by my carnal sensations, releasing my hold on the lingering remnants of restraint. The lagoon's waters, pure and mysterious, received my explosive surrender without judgment.

"What the fuck..." I whispered, staring into the water as I bent over to get a closer look. *Surely my eyes are deceiving me?* I watched as the water separated the ejaculate, sending bright, glowing sperm in every direction.

As clarity began to seep back, whispering of a promise fulfilled, I stood, stretching my arms wide in a gesture of liberation, of acceptance. "I feel so alive!" The declaration, bold and unabashed, was a testament to the moment's raw intensity. But that proclamation was short-lived as I lost my balance, my back meeting the lagoon's surface with a resounding splash, enveloping me once more in its depths.

The fall, unexpected yet oddly invigorating, served as a poignant metaphor for my journey here in Clivilius—a constant oscillation between fighting for control and yielding to the unknown forces that shaped this existence. In that moment, submerged in the lagoon's embrace, the line between surrender and liberation blurred, leaving me to wonder if perhaps, in this strange new world, being truly alive meant embracing the entirety of the experience, the ecstasy and the agony, without reservation.

CONCRETE FOUNDATION

4338.206.4

The return to camp was marked by a sense of solitude that I hadn't realised I was craving. The sun, high and unrelenting, had done its work well, drying my clothes and warming my skin, a natural remedy to the chill of the lagoon's embrace. As I navigated through the tent's flap, the absence of Paul was a silent relief. It afforded me a moment of privacy, a chance to collect my thoughts and steel myself for whatever lay ahead.

Glancing down at my boardshorts, their vibrant hue seemed almost defiant against the backdrop of Clivilius's desolate landscape. They bore no trace of my earlier descent into the lagoon's depths—a small but significant victory in maintaining the façade of normalcy. Nevertheless, driven by a need for caution, I quickly changed into a fresh pair, erasing any lingering evidence of my moment of surrender to the lagoon's mysterious waters.

With Paul presumably still busy at the Drop Zone, I found myself alone under the shade of the canopy. It was a brief respite from the sun's scrutiny, a moment to gather my thoughts and brace for the afternoon's heat. Taking a deep breath, I steeled myself for the inevitable return to the sun's domain.

The walk to the Drop Zone was a meditative experience, each step kicking up small clouds of dust that caught the light in a dance of particles. There was a simplicity to it, a rhythm that felt almost therapeutic. My shoes, the architects of these miniature disturbances, seemed to connect me to the moment in a way that was both grounding and liberating.

As I journeyed, the weight of recent events seemed to lift slightly, allowing a childlike sense of wonder to take its place. My mind, usually a battleground of thoughts and worries, drifted aimlessly, touching on thoughts only to let them go as quickly as they came. It was an unusual state for me, this acceptance of mental drift, this lack of urgency to direct or control my thoughts.

For the first time in what felt like forever, I allowed myself to simply be—to exist in the moment without the constant pressure to analyse, plan, or resist. It was a freeing sensation, a release from the internal strife that had become my constant companion.

As I neared the Drop Zone, the glare of the sun forced me to narrow my eyes, scanning the horizon for any sign of activity. My gaze settled on a solitary figure seated in the dust, a small distance away from a conspicuously large, rectangular box. It was Paul, his attention so intensely fixed on the object that he seemed to be in another world entirely. *What is Paul doing?* The question formed in my mind as I observed his stillness, a curiosity bubbling within me. *Could he be in some sort of trance?* The thought seemed almost plausible given the unwavering focus he exhibited towards the box.

A chuckle escaped me as the scene before me became clearer, and I realised the truth of the situation. Paul wasn't caught in any mystical reverie; he was simply zoned out, lost in thought or perhaps overwhelmed by the vastness of our predicament. It was a sight I was familiar with, having seen Luke in similar states of detachment, where the world around him faded into the background, leaving him adrift in his own thoughts.

"Hey! You actually going to do anything with that besides stare at it all day?" I called out, a hint of amusement in my voice. My words, light and teasing, were designed to snap Paul back to the present. I couldn't help but let out another soft chuckle as Paul jolted at the sound of my voice, the sudden intrusion into his solitude making him jump.

Turning rapidly, Paul's body twisted to face me as his eyes widened in surprise. "Umm. I'm not really sure," he admitted, his response tinged with uncertainty.

I stepped closer, curiosity drawing me towards the contents of the Drop Zone that had captivated Paul. "It's a lot of stuff," I remarked, my voice laced with a calm surprise as my gaze drifted over the assortment before us. Large bags of cement, a variety of garden tools, and a conspicuous big red tool trolley painted a picture of ambitious plans. It was a tangible representation of Luke's, and now Paul's, efforts to carve out some semblance of settlement in this strange new place. The realisation that I was genuinely impressed by their initiative caught me off guard.

My attention finally settled on the box that had ensnared Paul's focus. The image on its side, depicting a large, green shed, made the reason for Paul's fascination immediately apparent. *No wonder Paul's perplexed,* the thought crossed my mind, understanding his reaction to the ambitious project symbolised by the box.

"What?" The question slipped out as I noticed Paul's gaze had shifted to me, his expression one of inquiry mixed with a hint of concern.

Paul's response was almost reflexive, his eyes blinking rapidly before he attempted to steer the conversation towards neutral ground. "So, how was your walk?" he inquired, trying to infuse a sense of casualness into the moment.

"Fine," I replied succinctly.

"Find anything interesting?" he prodded further.

"Mmm, not really," came my noncommittal answer. The lagoon, with its unnerving yet cathartic embrace, wasn't something I was going to discuss.

The silence that followed was familiar, neither uncomfortable nor pressing. "The lagoon is nice," I ventured after a moment, offering a piece of my experience without revealing the turmoil it had momentarily eased.

"It is," Paul agreed, his nod a simple acknowledgment of the lagoon's tranquil allure.

Our conversation tapered off into silence once again, a silence that had become a comfortable aspect of our interaction. My gaze returned to the box and then swept over the Drop Zone, now cluttered with boxes of varying sizes, each a promise of labour and adaptation. *It looks like a lot of work*, the realisation dawned on me, contemplating the effort required to transform these materials into something meaningful. The enormity of the task ahead was not lost on me, yet in this moment, surrounded by the tangible evidence of Luke and Paul's attempts to persevere, there was a sense of determination that felt almost invigorating.

"So..." Paul's voice trailed off, a hint of pride mixed with uncertainty as he gestured towards the array of materials and tools scattered around us. "This is pretty much everything from the first list that I gave Luke."

Hearing this, my initial surprise morphed into genuine admiration. My eyebrow raised, a silent acknowledgment of their efforts. "Really? You've both actually done a really good job." The words were out before I fully registered the depth of my own approval.

Paul chuckled, a sound that seemed to carry both relief and a bit of self-mockery. "You sound surprised."

"Well," I confessed, my gaze sweeping over the Drop Zone —a tangible manifestation of Luke and Paul's determination to make the best of our situation. "You've managed to get us all this stuff, but do you actually know what to do with any of it? Guessing from the way you've been staring at the picture on the box for so long, I'd guess you've got no clue."

Caught off guard, Paul's response was a mix of hesitation and reluctant acceptance of his limitations. "Umm... well..." he stammered, before finally conceding with a sheepish admission, "No, not really."

Figured, my mind commented dryly. *He's just as not-so-handy as his brother.* Yet, despite the realisation of our collective inexperience, there was something almost comical about our predicament.

"But really, how hard can it be to put a few sheds together?" Paul mused aloud, his optimism undeterred by the daunting task ahead.

His question prompted me to take a closer look at the shed's picture, considering my own skills—or lack thereof—in such projects. *I've cut and laid tiles, wallpapered several walls, and built some very rustic stone steps. But a shed?* The complexity of the task suddenly felt all too real.

"I think we're a bit fucked," I stated, the blunt honesty of the assessment hanging heavily between us. Paul's loud groan cut through my thoughts.

"But..." I continued, pausing to gather my thoughts and perhaps offer a glimmer of hope amidst our shared apprehension. "But I do know that before we can start working on the shed, we need to pour the concrete foundations." It was a small piece of knowledge, but in that moment, it felt like a crucial first step.

"Of course," Paul's response was quick, filled with a newfound determination as he pushed himself up to stand. His eyes sparkled with a mix of excitement and naivety. "Let's get this started then," he declared, a clear eagerness in his tone that was both endearing and slightly alarming.

"Hang on a sec," I interjected, my hand reaching out to grasp Paul's arm just as he made a move towards the first bag of cement. There was an urgency in my voice, a need to pause and reassess before diving headlong into what could potentially be a disastrous endeavour.

"What?" Paul's confusion was evident, his head tilting slightly as he awaited my next words.

"Have you ever actually laid concrete before?"

Paul's response was a shake of the head, an admission of inexperience that didn't bode well for our plans. "No."

With a sigh, I pushed past him, taking the initiative to grab the first bag of cement myself. Turning it over, I scrutinised the instructions on the back, a sinking feeling in my stomach. *We really are fucked*, I thought, the realisation hitting me hard. Yet, I was acutely aware of Paul's gaze on me, filled with expectation and trust. *Foolish?* Most likely. But for now, I accepted the role I had unwittingly assumed.

"What's it say?" Paul's impatience broke through my thoughts, his voice laced with a hope that I was desperately trying to keep alive.

"Not much," I admitted, the instructions offering little comfort. "It only explains how to mix the concrete. But I am pretty sure we need to prep the ground first." The words were spoken with a confidence I didn't feel, a façade of knowledge in the face of our glaring ignorance.

"Oh," Paul's reaction was subdued as he turned to survey the tools and materials scattered around us. Then, with a spark of optimism, he suggested, "We can use the pickaxe to dig the foundation hole." The suggestion was made with a hopeful tone, a clutch at straws in an attempt to find a starting point.

"Now you just sound like you're throwing words together," I couldn't help but laugh, the absurdity of our situation momentarily lightening the mood.

"Yeah. I kinda am," Paul conceded, his broad smile infectious. He moved to pick up the pickaxe, his movements lacking any real sense of purpose. "We may as well give it a try," he said, brandishing the pickaxe with an enthusiasm that was both reckless and heartening.

Standing there, watching Paul wave the pickaxe around with misplaced confidence, I couldn't help but feel a mix of trepidation and camaraderie. We were out of our depth, yet there was something about facing this challenge together, about attempting the impossible, that felt incredibly human. In the vast, unforgiving expanse of Clivilius, we were about to embark on a project that was likely doomed from the start. Yet, in that moment, it didn't matter. Paul was determined to try, to make this alien place a little more like home, one misguided step at a time.

"You'd better let me do the digging," I suggested to Paul, narrowly avoiding another of his enthusiastic but hazardous swings with the pickaxe. I managed to pry it from his grasp, half-joking about his current state. "You're already crippled," I pointed out, nodding towards his injured foot, trying to keep the mood light despite the circumstances.

As we stood on the edge of the Drop Zone, contemplating our next move, the vastness of our surroundings became even more apparent. "Where do you want it?" I asked, ready to get started but keen on ensuring Paul felt involved in the decision-making process.

Paul joined me, casting his gaze over the landscape, contemplating the possibilities. "We could put the sheds anywhere, really," he mused, the freedom of choice in such an expansive place seeming both liberating and daunting.

I pressed him for more practical considerations. "Think, Paul. It has to be practical," I urged, recognising the importance of planning but wanting to ensure Paul took ownership of our strategies. Deep down, I knew guiding us through the construction was my role, yet I was adamant that Paul's input lead our decisions on location.

Paul paused, weighing his options before finally speaking up. "Well... If they were near the Drop Zone, we wouldn't need to carry items too far." He paused, thinking through the logistics, then continued, "Oh, yes, but then we'd still need to carry stuff to the campsite, which is where it'd most likely be required." I could see the wheels turning in his head as he talked himself through the options. "... near the campsite, someone would need to move stuff there initially, but it would be closer and easier access for everyone else."

"Everyone else?" I couldn't help but interject, my thoughts momentarily breaking free from their frustrated loop. *There's only two of us here.* Paul's grand visions of building a new civilisation seemed both endearing and a little concerning in their ambition. *And I'm really not sure that I like it.*

Determined, Paul made his decision. "We're building the sheds near the campsite," he declared with a newfound confidence.

"Okay then," I acquiesced. I grabbed the shovel and began the trek back to camp, dragging the tools behind me, a tangible sign of my commitment to this new plan.

"I'll grab the cement," Paul's voice reached me from the Drop Zone, his tone eager and filled with purpose. Despite my reservations about the scale of Paul's vision, there was no denying the sense of partnership that these moments of collaboration fostered. As we set about laying the foundations for our future in Clivilius, I couldn't help but wonder what other challenges—and perhaps opportunities— lay ahead.

❖

Swinging the pickaxe with all the force I could muster, the tool easily cut through the layer of dust before striking the ground beneath with a resonant crack. The impact sent a jolt of searing pain across my chest, a stark reminder of the injury hidden beneath my clothes. Bracing myself for another swing, the sharp ache reminded me of my current physical limitations.

"Wait!" Paul's voice pierced through my focus, halting my motion.

Grateful for the interruption, though I wouldn't readily admit it, I paused and turned to face him, lowering the pickaxe slightly. "What?" I asked, a hint of irritation mixed with relief colouring my tone.

Paul approached, his gaze fixed on the crust of earth revealed by my initial strike. "That crust is really firm. Maybe we should just leave it and only move the few feet of dust?" he suggested, his voice carrying an unexpected note of practicality. "I reckon the concrete will set better on that solid ground."

Considering his words, I couldn't help but acknowledge the sense in his suggestion. "That's actually not a bad idea," I conceded, trying to mask the throbbing pain that each movement seemed to exacerbate. My primary concern wasn't the optimal conditions for setting concrete but rather avoiding any further agony from the relentless assault of the pickaxe against the unyielding ground. Paul's suggestion offered an appealing alternative – one that promised less physical strain on my part.

Paul's face brightened with a mix of relief and pride at having his idea accepted. "I'll go get us some water for the concrete mix," he said, eager to contribute further to our makeshift construction project.

"Sure," I responded, setting aside the pickaxe in favour of the shovel. The decision to switch tools was not just a strategic move to accommodate Paul's strategy but also a personal victory. I silently congratulated myself for the foresight of bringing the shovel, appreciating its lighter burden compared to the demanding heft of the pickaxe.

As Paul departed to fetch water, I was left alone with my thoughts, the shovel in hand. The task ahead seemed daunting, yet there was a certain satisfaction in finding ways to adapt to our challenges, to make do with what we had. The pain in my chest served as a constant reminder of our fragile existence, but in moments like this—working side by side, making decisions, and finding solutions—I felt a glimmer of hope that perhaps we could carve out a semblance of a life here, against all impossible odds.

❖

The sun bore down mercilessly, transforming the task at hand into a gruelling ordeal of heat, sweat, and relentless discomfort. Each shovel of dust lifted and each manoeuvre around the solid crust beneath was a testament to the physical toll this endeavour exacted on my body. The sharp, persistent pain in my chest served as a cruel reminder of my vulnerability, yet there was no option but to persevere. After all, in this vast, desolate expanse that Clivilius had marooned us in—this world, or land, or whatever it was—Paul and I could only rely on each other. There were no others to share the burden, no unseen allies to lighten the load.

As I worked, the thought of Clivilius' promise to me lingered in the back of my mind, a cryptic bargain that I hadn't fully understood, much less accepted in full consciousness. The entity had whispered of a new life, a concept that seemed both enticing and elusive under the current circumstances. Had my actions at the lagoon, my moment of unguarded surrender to the lagoon's waters, sealed this pact? The terms were vague, the outcomes uncertain.

Regardless of the ambiguity surrounding Clivilius' promise, I found within myself a resolve to hold this unseen, omnipresent force accountable. A new life... The words echoed hollowly against the backdrop of our immediate struggle for survival and adaptation. Yet, I clung to them, a flicker of hope—or perhaps defiance—in the face of our isolation and the daunting tasks ahead.

In this moment, as I laboured under the oppressive sun, the concept of a new life granted by Clivilius became a beacon. It didn't matter that the promise was shrouded in mystery, or that I couldn't fathom what shape this new existence might take. What mattered was the commitment to the notion that something beyond our current hardships awaited us, that our efforts here, amidst the dust and sweat and pain, were not in vain.

So, for now at least, I would continue to dig, to plan, to build—grinning and bearing the hardships—because the alternative was to succumb to despair. And if there was any truth to Clivilius' enigmatic offer, I was determined to see it through, to discover what lay beyond the struggle, what new life could possibly emerge from the ashes of our old lives left behind on Earth.

❖

Paul, with the bucket of water now secured beside him, seemed momentarily lost in contemplation as he scrutinised the instructions on the cement mix bag. Observing his prolonged focus, I realised that if I didn't intervene, we'd likely spend the rest of the day under the scorching sun achieving nothing. Motivated by a desire to see tangible progress, I decided to step in.

"I'll pour, you stir," I suggested, taking charge of the situation. Paul nodded, his actions syncing with mine as he carefully poured half of the cement mix into the wheelbarrow. The process felt like one of the few structured activities we had managed to coordinate.

"You finished clearing the dust already?" Paul's question came as he glanced over towards the area designated for the shed.

"Yeah. I think it's as good as it's going to get," I responded, trying to sound more confident in our preparations than I actually felt. My body was a testament to the physical toll of the work; muscles ached in protest, and my skin was coated with a fine layer of dust that seemed to find its way into every crevice. The thought of dealing with any more of that ubiquitous dust was enough to fray the last strands of my patience.

"Great," Paul replied, his attention now fully on the task at hand as he picked up the stirring stick. His response, simple and unassuming, marked the beginning of our next phase of work.

Exhaustion had fully set in by the time we finished with the first ten kilograms of concrete mix. I slumped into the dust, a makeshift seat at the edge of our nascent foundation, while Paul ventured back to the Drop Zone for the next bag. My gaze, heavy and blurred from the pain and fatigue, flitted over the work we had accomplished. It wasn't until Paul's figure reemerged into my field of vision, bag in tow, that I snapped to attention.

"Stop!" The word burst from me with an urgency that made Paul freeze mid-motion, his hands poised to tear into the new bag of concrete mix. "This isn't looking right," I declared, squinting at our handiwork.

"Really?" Paul's query was laced with doubt. To him, our efforts appeared adequate, perhaps even commendable given our lack of expertise.

But I was certain of the misstep. "Nah. It shouldn't be clumping like that. And see how it is seeping into the surrounding dirt," I pointed out, indicating the problematic area that had caught my eye.

"Hmm," Paul hummed, his optimism momentarily clouded by the potential flaw in our execution. Yet, his tone remained hopeful, a testament to his ever-present belief in our ability to overcome.

My own confidence, however, wavered. The mixture's behaviour wasn't aligning with my expectations, though admittedly based on scant knowledge of concrete laying. "We could probably fix it," Paul suggested, his voice buoyed by a resilience I found both admirable and unnerving.

"I dunno," I responded, the doubt in my voice mirroring the uncertainty of our situation. The notion of consulting a more knowledgeable source suddenly seemed the most logical step. "Maybe we should ask Luke to bring us a short how-to guide for laying concrete for a small shed?"

Paul's eyes, surveying the expanse of our endeavour, reflected a concession to reality. "You're probably right," he admitted.

Resigned yet unresolved, I could only offer a conclusion that felt as unsettled as the ground beneath us. "Well..." I started, my gaze drifting across the expansive desert. "I really don't know what else we can do," I admitted, the words heavy with the acknowledgment of our limitations and the vast, unknown challenges that still lay ahead.

Paul's stomach broke the silence between us with a loud gurgle that almost seemed to echo in the vast emptiness surrounding us. He rubbed his abdomen in a half-hearted attempt to quell the noise, then glanced over with a wry smile that didn't quite reach his eyes. "I'd suggest we get something to eat," he said, his voice laced with a hint of resignation. "But even that is a little challenging at the moment."

Feeling the grime caked on my skin and the aches in muscles I didn't know I had, I was all too aware of our grim situation. My chest was a thumping mass of pain, each heartbeat a reminder of the exertion and stress I'd been under. The uncertainty of our food situation loomed large, adding to the weight of our predicament. "Fuck it!" The words burst from me, a raw expression of the frustration that had begun to simmer beneath the surface. In a moment of overwhelming irritation, I threw my hands in the air, surrendering to the impulse to do something, anything, to change our dire circumstances.

"Where are you going?" Paul's voice reached me, tinged with concern and confusion as he came after me.

"To the Drop Zone," I called back, not pausing in my stride. The determination to find food propelled me forward, each step kicking up small clouds of dust that marked my path through the desolate landscape.

"What for?" His question floated to me over the short distance, his steps quickening as he struggled to catch up.

"To look for food," I replied, the words sharp with the edge of desperation. The idea of finding something edible at the Drop Zone was a slim hope, but it was a hope nonetheless. The thought of scavenging for whatever morsel might have been left behind in the heat was not appealing, but the gnawing hunger in my stomach pushed me forward.

Trudging toward the Drop Zone, the dust swirling around my boots, I couldn't help but reflect on the absurdity of our situation. Here we were, two figures in a vast, unforgiving landscape, driven by the basic need to eat. The simplicity of the task contrasted sharply with the complexity of our circumstances, and yet, in that moment, finding food felt like the most important mission in the world.

DEATH SENTENCE

4338.206.5

As we crested the final dusty hill, a large huff from Paul breezed past me, mingling with the dry air that seemed to carry every sound with crystal clarity. "But I just came from there and..." His words trailed off into the vast expanse that lay before us, unfinished and hanging in the balance.

Before us, the Portal erupted into life, a spectacle that, despite its now familiar presence, never failed to capture my full attention. Its colours, an ethereal mix of hues I could hardly find names for, swirled and danced in the air, creating a mesmerising display of light and energy. Sparks flew, igniting brief but brilliant fires whenever the larger streams of light collided, painting the sky with fleeting moments of intense beauty.

"Luke?" I found myself uttering the name, though I knew the answer even as I spoke. It was more a confirmation of my own thoughts than a question meant for Paul.

"I guess so," he responded, his tone reflecting a mixture of resignation and intrigue. It was clear that the Portal's activation was no longer an unusual event for us, yet it retained an element of surprise.

"Were you expecting anything else?" Paul turned to face me, his expression one of genuine curiosity. It was a fair question. The Portal, with its sudden activations and the mysterious arrivals it heralded, was fast becoming a constant source of speculation.

My face must have been a canvas of thought, wrinkles forming as I concentrated, piecing together the possibilities.

"Oh," the realisation struck me suddenly, like a missing piece of a puzzle snapping into place. "It could be the tents Luke said he had ordered." It was a mundane conclusion, yet it made sense given our needs and Luke's previous information.

Paul looked at me with a blend of skepticism and curiosity. "In a truck?" he asked, his voice laced with the incredulity of the situation. The idea of something as normal as a delivery truck appearing in proximity to the Portal with tents seemed almost laughable, yet here we were, contemplating just that.

"Who knows," I replied, my voice tinged with dry humour. "This is Luke we're talking about, remember." Luke's methods and decisions often bordered on the unconventional, if not outright bizarre. It was part of what made dealing with him both frustrating and oddly reassuring; you could never quite predict what he would do next.

"True," Paul conceded with a nod, the corners of his mouth turning up in a reluctant smile.

As if on cue, the truck, a solid mass of metal and intent, came to an abrupt stop ten meters from the Portal's reach. The sudden halt threw up a cloud of dust, enveloping the vehicle in a haze that seemed to blur the lines between the mundane and the mystical. There it was, a tangible link to the world we once knew, parked incongruously on the edge of the unknown. The sight of it, so ordinary yet so out of place, was a stark reminder of the duality of our existence: caught between the familiar and the unfathomable, always on the brink of the next discovery.

"You're not even going to drive it into the Drop Zone?" I couldn't help but huff out my disbelief as Luke made his agile descent from the cab.

Paul reached out to grab the keys still dangling from Luke's hand, perhaps thinking ahead to moving the truck ourselves.

"No!" Luke's voice snapped through the air, sharp and urgent, cutting off any further speculation. He turned on his heel, rushing to the back of the truck with a purpose that left no room for argument. Paul and I exchanged a quick, bemused glance before hurrying after him, drawn into the unfolding drama.

"But..." Paul started, obviously still trying to piece together a plan that made more sense than standing idly by.

"There's no time to move it. The delivery guy is in the toilet. We only have a matter of minutes to get all these boxes out!" Luke's voice was thick with urgency, his explanation tumbling out in a rush. The situation was far from ideal, teetering on the edge of absurdity.

"Shit!" The expletive slipped out, a reflexive acknowledgment of our predicament. Time was not our ally, and the unexpected complication of a temporarily absent delivery driver only added to the pressure.

"Tents?" Paul sought confirmation.

"Yeah," Luke confirmed, his actions betraying his haste. He threw the back door of the truck open with such force that the resulting clang resonated like a gong, the sound reverberating off the truck's metal confines and into the open air around us. The noise was so unexpectedly loud in the quiet that surrounded us, it felt like a physical blow.

"Shit, Luke," I couldn't help but cry out, my hands flying to my ears in a vain attempt to muffle the ringing that ensued. The world seemed to vibrate with the echo of metal on metal, a harsh reminder of our urgency.

"Oops," Luke's voice carried a hint of sheepishness as he reached up to grab the metal pole just inside the door, pulling himself up with ease.

"How many are there again?" Paul's voice was steady as he reached up, ready to take the first box from Luke.

"Three."

"At least that will give us something to do," Paul commented, throwing the statement in my direction, a wry acknowledgment of our sudden shift from searching for food to frantic activity.

I don't want something else to do, my tired brain wailed silently. The day's exertions had already taken their toll, and the thought of additional tasks was anything but welcome. *I just want to go home.* Yet, despite my internal protests, I reached out to take another box from Luke. "True," I found myself agreeing, albeit reluctantly. The admission was heavy with resignation, a tacit acceptance of our shared plight.

The urgency of our task lent an almost frantic pace to our movements as the three of us worked in tandem to unload all the tent boxes. We dumped them unceremoniously in the dust at our feet, a testament to the haste dictated by the circumstances. I had already formulated a plan in my mind, intending to leave Paul with the task of relocating the boxes to a more suitable spot once Luke had disappeared from the scene. It was a silent expectation, one born of necessity rather than desire.

"Thanks," Luke's voice cut through the thick air, a semblance of gratitude lacing his words as he jumped down from the back of the truck. His motion for Paul and me to close up the back was swift, a clear indication of his rush to return to the cab. The urgency was palpable, a tangible force that seemed to drive every action, every decision in those moments.

"You coming back soon?" I called after him, the words almost catching in the dryness of my throat. "I'm hungry." It was a half-hearted attempt to inject a semblance of normalcy into the situation, a reminder of mundane concerns amidst Luke's chaos. But Luke's silence in response was as telling as any words could have been.

I looked at Paul, seeking some semblance of understanding or perhaps solidarity in our shared predicament. And Paul looked back at me, his gaze reflecting the resignation that had settled over us. It was a silent exchange, one that spoke volumes of our expectations—or the lack thereof—when it came to Luke's promises and assurances. We were not surprised by the lack of response, it was a pattern we had come to expect.

The truck roared to life, a mechanical beast awakening, and vanished as quickly as it had appeared, leaving behind a cloud of dust and the echo of its departure. The abruptness of its exit left a palpable void.

"Odd," I said aloud, my voice breaking the silence that had settled over us. My brow creased in thought, a reflection of the puzzlement that nagged at the back of my mind.

Paul picked up the corner of one of the larger boxes, his actions pragmatic as always. "What is?" he asked.

"The Portal is still open," I replied, my words tinged with a sense of foreboding. I moved closer to it, drawn by an inexplicable curiosity and perhaps a hint of concern. The Portal's persistent openness was an anomaly, one that did not align with the usual patterns we had come to expect.

"Luke must be coming back then," Paul surmised, his statement more a reflection of hope than conviction. It was a possibility, of course, one that offered a semblance of reassurance in the face of the unknown. Yet, as I stood there, staring into the swirling colours and the infinite possibilities beyond, I couldn't shake the feeling of unease that settled over me. The open Portal was a doorway to untold stories, and Luke's silence hung between us like a heavy curtain, obscuring what lay ahead.

Standing there, barely an inch away from the swirling colours that obscured the Portal's usually translucent screen, a mix of dread and curiosity welled up inside me. The vibrant hues seemed almost alive, a mesmerising dance of light and shadow that beckoned and warned all at once. Daring to hope, yet aware of the potential consequences, I tentatively pushed my hand towards the vibrant wall of colour, my heart hammering in my chest with a mix of fear and anticipation.

Do not tempt me, Jamie Greyson! The voice of Clivilius, cold and stern, crashed into my thoughts like a wave against rocks, sending a shiver of fear down my spine. *Or the next time I will rescind the offer of new life. And you will need it.* The threat, laced with a chilling certainty, echoed in the recesses of my mind, turning the fear into a tangible force that gripped my heart.

"Fuck!" The word tore from my lips, a raw expression of frustration and anger, as I kicked at the ground, sending a large cloud of dust billowing into the air. The action was futile, a physical manifestation of my inner turmoil, yet it offered a brief, cathartic release.

"No luck then?" Paul's voice drifted to me, tinged with a note that sounded perilously close to sarcasm, though I knew it was more likely an attempt at levity in the face of our bizarre and tense situation.

Sardonically, I responded not with words but with a gesture, my middle finger raised in a silent reply. It was a crude but succinct expression of my current state of mind. Words felt inadequate, too constrained to convey the tumult of emotions roiling within me—anger, frustration, a gnawing sense of helplessness.

I wanted to lash out at Clivilius, to scream into the void that the threats had opened within me, but a sharp pain in my chest, a physical reminder of my vulnerability, made me reconsider. *Is this what Clivilius meant?* The question spun in my head, a dizzying reminder of the precariousness of my situation. *Is this wound going to kill me if I don't surrender?*

Shaking my head vigorously, I sought to dispel the dark thoughts, to reject the notion of surrender as an option. *No, I'm not going to die. Not like this.* The defiance, stubborn and fierce, surged within me, a beacon against the encroaching despair. I was determined, in that moment, to find another way, to defy the odds that seemed so insurmountably stacked against me. The resolve hardened within me, a silent vow that I would not let Clivilius's threats dictate the course of my fate.

Bringing myself back to the present, I turned my attention towards Paul, who was methodically moving boxes, his figure etched against the backdrop of chaos we had found ourselves in. "Where are you taking that?" I inquired, my voice breaking the heavy silence that had settled between us, just as Paul hoisted one of the smaller boxes into his arms.

"Why do you care?" His response came sharp, a bark really, laced with an edge of frustration. He didn't even bother to turn and face me, his body language closed off, a physical barrier to match the emotional one he had just erected.

"What the hell is that supposed to mean?" I couldn't hide the sting in my voice, a mix of surprise and irritation bubbling to the surface. I found myself jogging to catch up, eager, or perhaps desperate, to bridge the distance his words had created.

Paul stopped then, his movements halting as abruptly as his words had. "I'm sorry," he said, his voice softer now, the harsh lines of his figure relaxing as he shook his head, a gesture of regret. His gaze lowered, perhaps in shame, perhaps in exhaustion. "I'm just tired and my whole body is aching."

Hearing the genuine weariness in his voice, I couldn't hold onto my frustration. It melted away, replaced by a thread of empathy. "It's okay," I replied, my voice gentle, trying to offer solace in the sparse comfort we had at our disposal. "I get it." The truth was, I did. The physical toll of our situation was matched only by the mental and emotional strain we were both grappling with.

Paul's gaze then lifted, locking onto mine, and in that moment, I felt a wave of discomfort wash over me. It was an intense scrutiny, one that seemed to search for something I wasn't sure I wanted found.

Seeking to break the tension, I reached for a distraction. "That dust storm last night was pretty brutal," I said. I lifted my sweat-drenched t-shirt to reveal the evidence of the storm's brutality—a very red chest marred by a large welt sitting squarely between my pecs—the intention was to share in the mutual acknowledgment of our shared ordeal.

"What the fuck!" The exclamation burst from Paul, a mix of shock and concern colouring his tone. "What the hell is that?" His approach was swift, a step closer taken with the intent of inspecting the damage.

Quickly, almost reflexively, I let go of my top, allowing the fabric to fall back into place, concealing the angry mark on my chest. Despite knowing the severity of the injury, I hadn't mustered the courage to examine it closely since first pulling the shirt over my head earlier. Paul's reaction, a mix of shock and concern, was unsettling. It served as a stark reminder of the situation's gravity—a reality I was all too keen to downplay in my own mind. Yet, despite the unease that twisted in my gut, I managed to muster a façade of nonchalance.

"I think one of the hot coals struck me last night," I found myself saying, trying to sound matter-of-fact. It was a simple explanation, one that belied the actual pain and the sudden fear that came with the realisation of how close we were to real danger.

"Shit, Jamie! I'm so sorry!" Paul's exclamation was laden with immediate concern, his earlier frustration forgotten in the face of tangible harm.

"It wasn't you," I hastened to assure him, pushing back against the guilt that seemed to shadow his features. "I think it just got caught in a gust of wind." My words were chosen to alleviate blame, to frame the incident as an unfortunate act of nature rather than anyone's fault. The truth was, in the unpredictability of our current existence, such accidents were perhaps inevitable. Yet, admitting that felt like acknowledging our vulnerability more fully than I was prepared to do.

As I watched Paul struggle with his emotions, his eyes brimming with tears and his breaths coming in heavy gulps, a weight seemed to settle over us, tangible and oppressive. "But you wouldn't have been out there if it weren't for me," he managed to say, his voice choked with guilt. It was a confession, an acknowledgment of a shared burden we both bore, though he seemed inclined to shoulder it alone.

In response, I reached down, picking up the corner of the box that had slipped from Paul's grasp in his moment of distress. Seeking to redirect our focus away from the brewing storm of guilt and recrimination, I proposed a practical course of action. "If we're going to set these up down by the river with the other tent, we may as well take these boxes straight there rather than bother with the Drop Zone," I said, my voice steady, attempting to inject a sense of pragmatism into the situation. Without waiting for his response, I turned to walk away, signalling the need to keep moving, both physically and metaphorically.

"Jamie," Paul's voice called out, a note of desperation threading through my name.

I gestured for him to follow, unwilling to pause, to allow the conversation—and by extension, our fears and doubts—to catch up to me. But Paul was persistent.

"Jamie!" His voice, louder now, carried a note of urgency that forced me to stop. "You need a doctor!" he exclaimed, hobbling to catch up, his concern for my well-being overruling any discomfort between us.

Whipping around, I confronted him, and with him, the reality of our predicament. "We don't have a fucking doctor!" I yelled, the fear and frustration I had been battling all morning breaking free in a raw, unguarded outburst.

Paul stopped, the impact of my words hitting him as visibly as a physical blow. In that moment, the barriers between us seemed to crumble, leaving us exposed to the raw pain and vulnerability we each carried.

As the tears I had been staunchly fighting began to well in my eyes, betraying the fear and desperation I felt, I found myself unable to maintain the façade of strength I had clung to. A hard sniff was my futile attempt to hold back the floodgates.

Then, unexpectedly, Paul closed the distance between us, wrapping me in a bear hug that was both surprising and grounding. "I'm so sorry, Jamie," he whispered, his voice laden with remorse and empathy.

With my eyes closed, I allowed a single tear to break free, tracing a path down my cheek. My face grew rigid, not from the physical discomfort but from the emotional turmoil that swirled within. Paul's embrace, though comforting, served as a stark reminder that our battle was far from over.

In the privacy of my own mind, I reached out to Clivilius, the entity whose presence loomed over us, unseen yet palpable. *I accept your offer, Clivilius!* The declaration was bold, a silent scream against the darkness. *So, what the fuck do you want from me?*

Sharp, insistent barking cut through the tension like a knife, snapping my focus to the present and momentarily forgetting the heavy emotions that had enveloped me. Instinctively, I pushed Paul away, my movements abrupt but driven by an urgency that went beyond our current conversation.

"Henri!" The name burst from me in a surprise. My steps quickened into a run, eager to close the distance between myself and the small, barking figure that had somehow entered the madness.

As I reached him, I bent down, my arms scooping up the chubby brown and white Shih Tzu with an ease born of many such greetings. Henri, in his unbridled joy, wasted no time in covering my face with licks, each one a testament to the bond we shared. It was a moment of pure, unadulterated happiness, a stark contrast to the complex web of emotions I had been navigating just moments before.

However, the simplicity of the moment was short-lived. My elation cooled, turning into a complicated mix of emotions as Luke appeared through the Portal, a solid figure against the pulsating colours, carrying Duke in his arms. My face dropped, the fleeting happiness of reuniting with Henri now tinged with a sense of foreboding.

"Luke! What the fuck are you doing!? Why the hell did you bring them here!?" The words erupted from me, a visceral response to the sight before my eyes. I had already made an unspoken pact with Clivilius, a promise to tether myself to this uncertain existence in exchange for some semblance of protection for us all. Yet, standing there, confronted by Luke's actions, I couldn't help but wonder what more I would be asked to sacrifice to keep the encroaching nightmare at bay.

The tension that vibrated through the air seemed to unsettle Duke, and Luke, sensing the dog's discomfort, set him down in the dusty terrain. Freed from Luke's arms, Duke almost a mirror image of Henri, with little hesitation, he began to explore his new surroundings, his nose buried in the dust as he navigated through this unfamiliar landscape with an innocence that belied our grim reality.

"What the fuck, Luke!" My frustration boiled over once more, propelling me forward. With a surge of emotion-driven strength, I gave Luke a hard shove in the chest. It was an impulsive act, driven by a mix of fear, anger, and a desperate need for answers. The force of my push sent Luke stumbling backwards.

As Luke's face hardened into an expression of anger and defiance, his words came at me like a physical blow. "Fuck off, Jamie!" he retorted with a ferocity that matched the tension crackling between us. "They'll be fine," he continued to yell, and mirroring my aggression, he shoved me hard in the chest, a gesture that felt like both a rebuttal and a challenge.

The force of his push caught me off guard, sending a sharp pain through my chest as I stumbled backwards. An involuntary cry escaped my lips as my hands flew to my burning chest, a reflexive attempt to shield myself from further harm. For a moment, the world seemed to pause, the air around us growing deathly still, charged with the weight of the confrontation.

"Is that blood?" Luke's voice cut through the silence, his tone shifting from anger to concern as he took a cautious step towards me. The change in his demeanour, from confrontational to worried, only served to heighten the surreal nature of the moment.

Shaking my head, I tried to dismiss his concern. "It's nothing," I insisted, though the pain and the evident physical damage suggested otherwise. My attempt to downplay the injury was a reflex, born out of a desire to avoid further conflict and perhaps to protect myself from acknowledging the severity of my condition.

"Nothing?" Luke's repetition of my words was sharp, his skepticism evident as he moved closer, dismissing my attempts to conceal the injury. With a decisiveness that left no room for protest, he snatched my arm away from my chest and lifted my shirt, revealing the extent of the damage.

The gasps from Paul and Luke were simultaneous, a shared reaction of shock and dismay that echoed my own sense of dread. As my gaze drifted downwards, the sight that greeted me was grim—a rupture where Luke's shove had aggravated the existing welt, now oozing blood and pus in ugly trails down my body. The reality of my condition, was now laid bare for all to see.

Luke's wide eyes, filled with a dawning understanding of the consequences of his actions, held mine in a silent exchange filled with unspoken fears and accusations.

I didn't dare break my lock on Luke's eyes, the intensity of our gaze conveying more than words ever could. "You've sentenced us to death, Luke," I said softly, the words heavy with resignation and an underlying accusation. My statement was not just an expression of anger but a declaration of the grim reality we faced. "Welcome to the fucking nightmare," I added, the bitterness in my voice a reflection of the harsh truth we could no longer avoid.

❖

Before the camp's familiarity could offer any semblance of comfort, I veered northwest, following the river upstream with a single-minded determination. The wound on my chest, a relentless reminder of the confrontation and the raw vulnerability of my situation, continued to ooze. Each step sent a fresh trickle of blood weaving down my abs, but the physical discomfort paled in comparison to the turmoil within. The notion of escape, of finding a way out of this relentless nightmare, propelled me forward. I clung to the hope that beyond the horizon lay answers, or at the very least, a respite from the madness that had engulfed my life.

The camp, with its fragile sense of safety and companionship, faded into the distance as I pressed on.

Ahead, the landscape unfolded in a tapestry of reds, browns, and the occasional splash of orange—a stark, beautiful wilderness that seemed indifferent to human suffering. The sweat that beaded on my brow and soaked through my t-shirt was a testament to the effort of my trek, the fabric clinging to my skin with an uncomfortable persistence. My shorts, damp with sweat, chafed against my inner thighs, each step becoming a test of endurance. Yet, the discomfort, the pain—it all seemed a small price to pay if it meant finding a way out.

But as the desert stretched on, the initial rush of determination began to wane, replaced by the creeping realisation of my physical limits. My legs, once driven by a desperate need to escape, began to betray me, shaking with exhaustion until they wobbled uncontrollably. The landscape, once a blur of colours and possibilities, narrowed to the immediate struggle with each faltering step.

"Shit," I whispered to the empty expanse, the word barely a breath as my legs finally succumbed to the strain, folding beneath me. The ground came up to meet me, the soft, ochre dust a cold comfort as I groaned in agony. The fall, a harsh return to reality, was a reminder of my humanity. As I lay there, the fight to keep my eyes open became increasingly difficult, the world around me blurring at the edges until, finally, I could fight no more. My eyelids fluttered closed, surrendering to the exhaustion and pain that I had tried so hard to outrun.

REST

4338.206.6

Summoned from the depths of my fading consciousness by the distant echo of my name, I struggled against the pull of darkness that sought to claim me. The voice, familiar yet seemingly miles away, pierced through the fog of my exhaustion, urging me to respond. I mustered every ounce of strength to force my eyes open, yet they remained defiantly heavy, barely fluttering in acknowledgment of my effort.

Again, the voice called out, persistent and increasingly urgent, until it finally bridged the gap to my dulled senses. "Here," I managed to croak, my voice a mere whisper against the vast silence that enveloped me. My eyelids twitched, granting me the briefest glimpse of the world before my voice faltered, leaving my plea hanging in the air. Paul's voice, once a beacon of hope, receded once more into the distance, and with it went my resolve, my eyes closing under the weight of my weariness.

But then, unexpectedly, my world began to sway, a gentle rocking motion that stirred me from my resignation. Through the sliver of vision afforded by my stubborn eyelids, a blur of brown and orange danced before me. "Paul?" I attempted to call out, though my voice betrayed me, morphing the question into an unintelligible mumble.

Suddenly, an unmistakable scent cut through the haze of my confusion—garlic. It was a scent I associated with one person alone. "Luke," I whispered with a newfound clarity, recognition sparking within me.

The sensation of movement became more pronounced as Luke, with determined strides, carried me through the dust, my body slung over his shoulders in a manner that spoke both of urgency and care. The jarring motion of our progress, rather than unsettling me, served as a strange comfort. It was a tangible sign that I was not alone, that despite the direness of my situation, there were still those who would shoulder my burdens alongside their own.

As we neared the camp, Duke's sharp yips pierced the heavy silence that had settled around me, carried by Luke's determined strides. The sound triggered an almost involuntary surge of anger within me, a reminder of the bone of contention that had sparked the earlier confrontation. My frustration with Luke's decision to bring the dogs into our precarious situation lingered, a smouldering ember that refused to be extinguished. If only I could articulate my thoughts, express the turmoil churning inside me. But my physical state, weakened and barely coherent, rendered me mute, my voice as incapacitated as my body.

As Luke brought me into the tent, the sight of Henri scampering beneath my limited field of vision offered a brief distraction from my brooding thoughts. Luke's movements were gentle as he laid me down on the mattress, a stark contrast to the turbulence of emotions that raged within me. The care he exhibited, though comforting, did little to quell the storm inside.

Duke, ever the embodiment of unconditional affection, wasted no time in rushing to my side to offer his version of comfort—several enthusiastic kisses on my cheek. Despite the warmth of the gesture, a reminder of the innocent joy the dogs brought into our lives, my return to a semblance of lucidity brought with it a resurgence of my earlier frustrations. Almost reflexively, I moved to put a stop to Duke's affectionate assault, my actions not so much a rejection of his warmth but a manifestation of the complex web of emotions I was entangled in.

"Shit, you really scared me there, Jamie," Luke's voice was tinged with a relief that barely concealed his underlying worry.

"I'm fine," I retorted, more out of reflex than genuine reassurance. My response was brusque, an attempt to ward off his concern and perhaps to shield myself from the vulnerability of the moment. I pushed at Luke, both physically and metaphorically, creating a distance that I mistakenly thought would fortify my resolve.

"What the hell were you doing out there?" Luke pressed, his frustration evident. "We thought you had stormed off to the lagoon." His question, laden with confusion and concern, echoed the chaos of my own thoughts. I closed my eyes in a desperate attempt to sift through the fragments of my memory, to piece together the narrative of my actions before darkness had claimed me.

"And you've got no shirt on to protect your chest!" The accusation came suddenly.

I strained against the fog that clouded my memory, searching for any clue that might explain my actions, but found nothing but emptiness. A black void had settled over the events leading up to my collapse, erasing any trace of rationale or reason. The realisation that I could not account for my whereabouts or actions, nor explain the absence of my shirt, left me grappling with a sense of disorientation.

Finally, grasping at straws in an effort to offer some explanation, however feeble it might seem, I ventured, "I went to bathe in the river. I guess I got a bit too hot. I'm probably just a bit dehydrated." The words felt hollow even as they left my lips, a makeshift explanation that did little to illuminate the truth of the situation but served to fill the silence between us.

"I'll get you some water," Luke responded swiftly, his immediate acceptance of my explanation, whether out of concern or a willingness to overlook the holes in my story, I couldn't tell. Without another word, he rushed from the tent, leaving me alone with my thoughts and the unsettling gaps in my memory.

Duke's boundless energy was a stark contrast to the lethargy that weighed heavily on me. Watching him scamper to one of the small dog beds that had been strategically placed along the back wall of the tent's central room, he returned triumphantly with a long, skinny, brown toy horse in tow. Despite the turmoil of emotions and unanswered questions swirling within me, a genuine smile found its way to my face at the sight.

I reached out, taking the toy horse's head in my hand, and gave it several playful squeaks. The sound, comically high-pitched, sparked a light chuckle from me, a rare moment of levity in what had felt like an endless sea of grim reality. Duke, fully immersed in the game, growled playfully, his teeth securely around the toy's soft, fluffy foot, his entire body vibrating with anticipation.

Henri, ever the observer, seemed to decide that now was the perfect moment for a display of his own peculiar brand of theatrics. He spun in several tight circles, a ritual of comfort and contentment, before collapsing into the corner of the mattress. His final snort of contentment seemed to punctuate the moment, a reminder of the simple joys that still existed.

Duke, releasing his grip on the toy, sat back with his tail wagging expectantly, his eyes locked on mine, waiting for the next phase of our game. "I can't throw Horsey in here, Duke. Your claws will rip holes in the floor," I explained, my tone gentle yet firm. It was a practical concern, the reality of our living situation imposing limits on our play.

Luke's return to the tent was marked by an immediate sense of purpose. "Here," he announced, thrusting the water bottle under my nose. "Drink all of it." My body, still reeling from the exertion and dehydration, welcomed the command. I took the bottle, my hands shaky but grateful, and I drank deeply, the water a soothing balm to my parched throat. From the corner of my eye, I observed Luke rummaging through Duke's toy box, his actions momentarily mysterious until he retrieved what appeared to be an envelope.

After quenching my thirst, I handed Luke the now-empty bottle, exchanging it for the envelope he offered. "What's this?" Curiosity laced my voice, my gaze drawn to the envelope's plain surface, devoid of any postal markings or addresses.

"It's a letter from Gladys," Luke disclosed, a hint of something unreadable flickering in his expression.

"A letter? Why did she write me a letter?" The confusion was evident in my voice, the concept of receiving a letter in our current circumstances seeming almost anachronistic, a relic from a life that felt increasingly distant.

"Well," Luke began, his tone suggesting a blend of bemusement and resignation, "That's what I first said. But she's got a point. She can't talk to you, so she decided a letter was the next best option." His explanation, simple yet profound, touched on the essence of human connection—our need to communicate, to reach out, regardless of the barriers that stand between us.

The mention of Gladys and her letter brought to mind the small message I had scrawled on an empty spring water bottle, a desperate attempt to bridge the chasm that had opened between my world and hers. "So, she believed my message then?" I probed further, the implications of her belief in my extraordinary claim dawning on me. "Does she believe where I am?"

"Yeah," Luke replied, his shoulder shrug embodying a casual acceptance of the unbelievable. "They're sitting on the couch at home now, waiting for me to return without the dog's beds and toys." His words painted a surreal picture, a snapshot of a reality that seemed both incredibly ordinary and utterly fantastical.

"They?" My curiosity piqued further, eyebrows arching in surprise at the mention of another waiting at home with Gladys.

"Beatrix," Luke clarified, his tone carrying a hint of reluctant compliance. "Gladys didn't exactly leave me with much choice."

I scoffed loudly, the news of Gladys's actions not entirely catching me off guard. It was just like her—Gladys had an uncanny ability to find herself in precarious situations without any external provocation. Yet, she seemed to derive a peculiar kind of enjoyment from these escapades, especially when she managed to involve Beatrix. The dynamics of their relationship, always teetering on the edge of mischief and mayhem, momentarily distracted me from my own situation. The message I had sent, a desperate attempt to communicate across worlds, now seemed to have woven itself into their latest adventure. *Did Gladys show Beatrix my message? Was that the impetus behind this unexpected correspondence?*

"Have you read it?" I inquired, curiosity piqued despite my attempts to maintain a veneer of indifference. I held up the sealed envelope to Luke, searching his face for any telltale sign of knowledge withheld.

"No," Luke responded simply, his answer leaving no room for doubt. "It's for you."

I slid the envelope underneath the pillow behind me, a temporary reprieve from the questions that lingered. "I'll read it later," I declared, my voice carrying a hint of finality. The truth was, the prospect of uncovering the contents of Gladys's letter filled me with a mixture of anticipation and apprehension. Why would she feel compelled to write to me now, of all times? And more importantly, what could she possibly have to say that couldn't simply be passed on word of mouth via Luke?

"Sure," Luke's response was brief, his tone suggesting a mix of concern and haste. "I think Paul's out looking for you." The mention of Paul's name brought a flicker of guilt, a reminder of the worry I must have caused.

"I know," I shot back quicker than I intended, my voice carrying an edge of defensiveness. I was fully aware of the potential panic my absence might have sparked, yet admitting it out loud made it all the more real.

"He should be back soon," Luke continued, his voice softening slightly. "I have to go. Don't go doing anything stupid again. Stay in bed for the rest of the day." His instructions were clear, underscored by a note of loving admonition before he exited the tent, leaving me in the quiet company of the dogs.

I sighed softly, the weight of the day's events settling over me like a thick blanket. Turning my attention to Duke, I attempted to lighten the mood, even if just for my own sake. "Well, Duke," I said, engaging in the simple, comforting act of play by waving Horsey under his eager nose. "And Henri," I added, leaning over to stroke his fur, finding solace in the tactile connection with the animals. "Looks like you're both stuck with me now."

Duke, seizing the opportunity for play, snatched Horsey from my grip with a youthful exuberance that was both endearing and momentarily uplifting. He made his way onto the mattress, claiming a spot at the opposite corner to Henri, and settled down with his prize. As he stared up at me, his eyes seemed to convey an understanding beyond his canine comprehension, a silent acknowledgment of the shared moment.

Groaning softly, I allowed myself to sink back into the mattress, the simple interaction with Duke and Henri offering a brief respite from the swirling thoughts and concerns that had plagued me. In their company, I found a semblance of peace, a reminder of the uncomplicated joys and the comfort found in the presence of loyal companions. It was a small comfort, but in the isolation of the tent, with the complexities of our situation pressing in from all sides, it was a comfort I clung to fiercely.

With a sense of resolve, or perhaps resignation, I reached beneath the pillow for the envelope that held Gladys's message. "May as well see what Gladys has to say," I murmured to myself, a trace of curiosity threading through the weariness in my voice. The act of retrieving the letter felt almost ceremonial, a bridge to a world and a life that felt increasingly distant with each passing hour.

My fingers, clumsy with anticipation, slipped under the envelope's seal, breaking it open with less finesse than I might have mustered under different circumstances. I extracted the single sheet of paper, unfolding it carelessly, a stark contrast to the significance of the act. The moment of unveiling Gladys's words was tinged with a mixture of apprehension and a deep-seated need for connection, for a sign that the bonds that tied us to our previous lives remained unbroken despite the physical and metaphysical distances that separated us.

As the words on the page came into focus, I braced myself for what Gladys had felt compelled to communicate through such a traditional, tangible medium.

Jamie,
I really hope you get this!

Luke tells me that you have gone through a Portal into a new world. He is calling it Clivilius. I wasn't sure whether to believe him, but then he pulled out an odd-looking device and showed me the Portal to me. Its colours are simply stunning! Unless I choose to believe that I have finally gone mad, which we knew was always a possibility, I have no choice but to believe what he tells me.

As you know, Cody and I have been seeing each other for over three months now. I think I really like him. And I am pretty sure he likes me too. I know you said you thought he was trustworthy, but things have been getting just a little strange.

He snuck into my room last night. It was after midnight! I have no idea how he got into my house. I was terrified! But he told me to trust Luke. To help him. To do whatever he asks me to do. I didn't even know he knew Luke. This is all getting too weird for me.

And that message of yours on the bottle. Is that really true? Was Brody really murdered? Why didn't you tell me?

I wish you were here. I really miss talking to you already. You're my best friend.

I drank too much last night. I liked it. It's the only thing that keeps my head from spinning out of control. Brody's face haunts me. Almost. Every. Night.

I haven't told anyone else yet, but work fired me last week. I didn't mean for it to happen. They made me give a urine sample for a random alcohol test and I failed.

Jamie, I don't know what to do. Please just come home.

I need you.

Gladys

As I poured over Gladys's letter for the umpteenth time, my emotions churned with confusion and disbelief. Cody, whom I vaguely remembered with a kind of fondness, seemed to have ventured down a path that left a sour taste in my mouth. The notion of him becoming someone unrecognisable, perhaps even unsettling, was disheartening. Yet, what baffled me more was the connection between Cody and Luke. *How had their paths crossed in such a way that Cody felt compelled to seek Gladys's trust in Luke?* The layers of secrecy and implied knowledge that Gladys had burdened me with, coupled with this new revelation, knotted my thoughts into an impenetrable tangle.

The letter hinted at a complexity of relationships and secrets that felt beyond my grasp. The idea that Luke might be entangled in something as sordid as an affair with Cody struck me as ludicrous. Yet, the seed of doubt, once planted, had a way of festering. "There is definitely a different explanation," I found myself saying aloud, an attempt to dispel the absurdity of my thoughts. The paper crinkled under my grip as I refolded it, a physical manifestation of my frustration and confusion.

The notion of replying to Gladys flitted through my mind, teetering on the edge of action and inaction. *Should I draw her into this web of Clivilius's making, into a reality so far removed from the mundane intricacies of interpersonal dramas?* The very thought seemed as outlandish as it was desperate.

"So many ridiculous thoughts!" I muttered, a scolding to my overwrought imagination. Slipping the envelope into the pillowcase, I sought to bury the letter and its implications, at least for the moment. "Must be the heat stroke," I concluded, half-jokingly attributing my tumultuous thoughts to the physical strain I had endured.

Yet, even as I tried to dismiss the letter's impact, the undercurrents of mystery and unanswered questions lingered, a subtle reminder that our entanglements with others were not so easily set aside or solved. The complexities of human relationships, magnified by our extraordinary circumstances, seemed to weave an ever more intricate tapestry of intrigue and uncertainty.

❖

The sudden movement at the tent's entrance jolted my weary eyes open. "You look worse than I do," I managed to say, my voice raspy and strained from exhaustion and the remnants of pain.

Paul's reaction was immediate, his head snapping up in surprise, concern etched across his features. "Where the hell did you go? I've been searching for you," he blurted out, his voice a mix of relief and frustration.

"I know," I responded, a hint of guilt threading through my words. "I could hear you calling out, but every time I try to move, it starts to bleed again." The admission felt heavy, a tangible reminder of the fragility of my current state.

Paul's gaze fell to my bare chest, taking in the stark evidence of my ill-advised excursion. "The water didn't help then?" he inquired, his question laced with concern.

I shook my head slowly, the motion laboured. "I didn't make it to the river," I confessed, the words barely a whisper as I grappled with the influx of returning memories. "I went too far upstream and then I collapsed before I had the chance to get in the water." The admission was both a relief and a burden, acknowledging the limits of my endurance and the foolhardiness of my actions.

"Probably just as well," Paul mused, the hint of a grim smile touching his lips. "Or you could have collapsed in the water." His attempt at finding a silver lining did little to mask the gravity of the situation, the 'what ifs' that hung unspoken between us.

"I know," I agreed, the weight of the realisation settling heavily on my shoulders. "Thankfully Duke found me." The mention of Duke brought a small sense of comfort, a reminder of the unexpected ways in which we find salvation. In that moment, the presence of Duke and Henri in the tent felt like more than mere companionship; it was a testament to the unexpected guardianship they provided, a beacon of hope and resilience in the face of adversity.

"And how did you make it back here?" Paul's question was laced with genuine curiosity as he gave Duke a quick scratch behind the ear that seemed to bridge the gap between human concern and animal gratitude.

"Luke," I simply answered, the name carrying a weight of gratitude and a hint of surprise at the turn of events. "Duke fetched Luke, and he carried me back here." The admission felt like an acknowledgment of both Luke's unexpected role as my saviour and Duke's as the unanticipated hero of the hour.

"Luke was here?" Paul's asked with surprise.

"Yeah," I confirmed, a small gesture encompassing the tent's interior where Duke and Henri's beds lay alongside their box of toys.

"At least he gets some things right." Paul's words, light and teasing, managed to draw out a more genuine smile from me, one that spread freely across my face, softening the hard lines of stress and weariness.

Yes, I mused silently, my gaze drifting to Duke and Henri. *He does get some things right.*

"I'm going to start putting up another one of these tents," Paul announced, his statement pulling me back from my thoughts. "Do you need anything first?"

"No," I replied, a gentle shake of my head conveying my current state of near-exhaustion. "I think I might try and get some sleep." The prospect of rest, however fleeting, seemed like the most precious commodity at the moment.

"Good idea." Paul's agreement was simple, yet it carried an undercurrent of understanding and concern.

With that, my eyes closed, the act itself a surrender to the fatigue that enveloped me. I waited for the telltale signs of Paul's departure, the soft shuffle of his steps leaving the tent, a signal that I could let go completely and succumb to the desperate need for rest.

Yet, in the fragile space between consciousness and slumber, where reality blurs into dreams, the expected sound never registered in my awareness. It was as if the world around me had stilled, suspended in a moment of quiet anticipation. In truth, the exhaustion claimed me entirely, dragging me down into the depths of sleep with such swiftness that Paul's movements, should they have occurred in those brief moments, were lost to me.

❖

Duke's sudden burst of barking, loud and insistent, pulled me from the edges of sleep with a jolt. His sharp barks continued, a reaction to the rustling sounds of bags from outside that permeated the tent's fabric. "Shut up, Duke," I snapped, more out of the immediate discomfort his noise caused than any real anger towards him. My hands moved to rub the sleep from my eyes, an attempt to clear the grogginess that enveloped me.

As voices, muffled and indistinct, filtered through the tent walls, both Duke and Henri seemed to interpret them as a call to action, quickly scampering out with a haste that left me momentarily alone in the sudden quiet. I rubbed at my forehead—*or was it my temples?* No, the realisation dawned that my entire head was throbbing, as if a bomb had gone off inside it, leaving behind a pulsating pain that seemed to echo with each beat of my heart.

Shortly after their departure, Duke burst back into the tent, his tail wagging furiously, a blur of motion that resembled a feather duster in overdrive. In his mouth, he proudly carried a small packet of dog treats, the paper now glistening with saliva, making it evident he considered this a prize worth the intrusion.

As he approached, perhaps a little too confidently, I reached out and snatched the soggy packet from him. The action was reflexive, spurred by the absurdity of the situation and the slight amusement at Duke's evident pride in his find. Despite the pounding in my head and the irritation at being woken, the sight of Duke, so pleased with himself and his 'loot,' brought a reluctant smile to my face.

"Luke's brought us a heap of groceries," Paul announced as he made his way into the tent.

Relief washed over me like a much-needed rainfall in a parched desert. "Thank fuck," I managed to articulate, despite the discomfort that clung to me like a second skin. Hunger gnawed at my insides, a relentless reminder of the body's simple needs amidst the complexity of pain.

As I attempted to shift into a sitting position, every muscle and bone in my body seemed to protest. A soft moan escaped my lips, betraying the effort it took to simply move. The dilemma of my physical state presented itself as a cruel riddle: was it the incessant pounding in my head that was more unbearable, or the deep, throbbing ache that enveloped my chest? In that moment of physical agony, I felt trapped in my own body, a prisoner to my injuries. Yet, in the midst of this turmoil, I found a sliver of distraction by focusing on something, anything, other than myself. I reached for the bag of groceries, my fingers gingerly exploring its contents until they found the treats. I shared them with Duke and Henri, finding solace in their simple joy. It was a brief respite from the internal dialogue of despair that whispered relentlessly in the back of my mind.

"So, you're feeling better then?" Paul's inquiry pulled me back from the edge of my spiralling thoughts.

"I think so," came my reply, a lie wrapped in a thin veneer of hopefulness. I couldn't let him see the full extent of my struggle; it was a pride thing, perhaps, or maybe a feeble attempt at normalcy. "I think I actually fell asleep." A part of me wondered if admitting to sleep was akin to acknowledging a momentary defeat to my body's demands.

Paul's laughter, light and carefree, contrasted sharply with the weight I felt within. "Yeah. You did." His words, simple as they were, carried an undertone of relief that I wasn't keen to dissect in the moment.

I offered a smile, an expression that felt foreign and forced upon my face. It was a mask, one I hoped would conceal the turmoil brewing beneath the surface.

"Well, now that you're awake, I may as well bring these bags inside," Paul declared, practical as ever. "Better than leaving them outside in the heat."

The offer to help was out of my mouth before I could weigh the consequences, driven by a stubborn refusal to be rendered completely useless. "I'll help you," I said, the words laced with a determination that my body couldn't match. As I made a feeble attempt to rise, my body's rebellion was swift and unyielding. Gratitude mixed with frustration as Paul insisted I stay put, his firm "No" closing the door on any argument I might have mustered.

Resigning myself to my limitations, I eased back onto the mattress, a motion fraught with caution and an acute awareness of my body's fragility. The darkness at the edges of my consciousness threatened to engulf me once more, a reminder of the thin line I was walking between recovery and regression. "Maybe just for the rest of today," I conceded, my voice barely a whisper as I surrendered to the inevitable. In that moment, the tent felt like a sanctuary and a prison all at once, a place of healing bound by the chains of my own physical limitations.

SURRENDER - PART 1

4338.206.7

The moment was an assault on every sense, a brutal ambush that left me reeling. A shockwave of pain, so fierce and unexpected, erupted from the very core of my chest, sending violent ripples throughout my trembling body. My eyes, wide with fear and pain, flew open involuntarily, a scream tearing from my throat, raw and laden with agony.

In the haze of my torment, I felt strong hands press firmly against my shoulders, anchoring me to the mattress as my body instinctively tried to escape the source of my pain. A part of me, driven by a primal urge for relief, wanted to fight off the restraint, to flee from the invisible force that held me captive. But my head spun with such ferocity that reality blurred at the edges, leaving me disoriented and powerless.

Duke's barks pierced the air, a soundtrack to the turmoil unfolding within the confines of the tent.

"Jamie!" The sound of my name, bellowed with urgency, thundered through my already throbbing head, adding another layer to the cacophony that besieged me.

"Stay out!" The shrill scream of a woman cut through the commotion, her voice laced with panic and command. "Get them the fuck out!" The intensity of her words barely registered as my focus narrowed to the overwhelming sensation of constriction, a heavy pressure immobilising my waist, anchoring me to a reality I desperately wanted to escape from.

Paralysed! The thought screamed in my mind, a terrifying realisation that left me gasping for air, each breath a

Herculean effort against the invisible weight that pinned me down.

Then, without warning, another wave of excruciating pain tore through my chest, a merciless thief of breath and coherence. I screamed, a sound so fraught with suffering it seemed to belong to someone else. It was a scream that transcended physical pain, touching the very essence of fear and vulnerability.

"Hold him!" The command, sharp and desperate, cut through the haze of my agony. "Last time!" The promise, or threat, did little to soothe the storm of panic that raged within me. I wanted to writhe, to escape the invisible shackles that bound me, but my body betrayed me, remaining agonisingly still even as my mind willed it to move.

Panic took firm hold, a relentless tide that threatened to drown me in despair. It clamoured for the thunderous voices to cease, for the agony to end. Yet, amidst the tumult of pain and fear, a part of me clung to the voices, to the presence of others, as a lifeline in the overwhelming darkness that threatened to consume me.

As the pain began to recede like a storm passing, a softer voice cut through the fog of my agony, a beacon of calm in the tumultuous sea of my suffering. "I need some clean water," it said, its tone a stark contrast to the grating that had filled the tent moments before.

My mind, previously a battlefield of pain and panic, started to find its footing on more stable ground. "I'll get it," Paul's familiar voice responded, grounding me further to the reality of my surroundings.

The release of pressure around my waist felt like breaking free from iron chains. A deep, life-affirming gulp of air filled my lungs as the oppressive weight was lifted, and slowly, my eyes, blurred by tears of pain and fear, cracked open. For the first time in what felt like an eternity, my brain seemed to reconnect with the rest of my body, granting me the simple autonomy to wipe away the tears that stained my cheeks.

My gaze, still hazy and uncertain, locked onto a face framed by long, golden hair. Confusion and residual anger from the ordeal mingled, fuelling my harsh, defensive snap. "Who the fuck are you?" The words were more of a reflex, a defensive mechanism against the vulnerability I felt.

"I'm a doctor," came the reply, devoid of any emotion, as if stating a simple fact devoid of the drama that had unfolded.

It was Luke's entrance and his words that added a layer of context to the scene. "And she just saved your life. You should be grateful."

"Grateful!" I echoed back, the word laced with sarcasm, as I spat out the physical manifestation of my turmoil, a ball of built-up bile. It was a bitter, involuntary response, a testament to the rawness of my emotions. "You expect me to be fucking grateful?" The question hung in the air, charged with the complex interplay of gratitude for survival against the backdrop of pain, vulnerability, and the sheer indignity of my situation.

Duke let out a low, menacing growl, a sound that seemed to vibrate through the tense air of the tent. His instincts, finely tuned to detect threat or discomfort, had kicked in, his protective nature manifesting in the only way he knew how.

"Duke! Stop it!" Luke's voice, firm yet tinged with concern, broke through the thick atmosphere. Yet, despite his command, the tension didn't dissipate; it only morphed, taking on a new, more immediate form.

Attempting to navigate this fraught situation, I tried to leverage myself into a sitting position, driven by a mix of defiance and the desire to assert some control over my circumstances. However, the woman who had introduced herself as a doctor was quick to intervene. Her hand reached for my shoulder with a professional assertiveness, pressing me back down onto the mattress. The action, meant to be therapeutic, felt like another layer of restraint, adding to the sense of helplessness that had pervaded the tent.

In a flash of fur and teeth, Duke's protective instincts escalated. One short bark followed by a snap was all it took before the doctor, in a swift reaction, swatted Duke hard on the head. "Get off me!" she yelled, her voice sharp with adrenaline. The impact forced Duke to release his grip on her arm, a grip I hadn't even realised he had secured in his confusion and loyalty.

Luke sprang into action, scooping Duke into his arms with a speed that spoke of his desperation to quell the chaos. "Oh Glenda," he began, his voice laced with an apology that seemed to hang heavily in the air, unfinished and heavy with regret.

But Glenda was having none of it. Her glare was sharp, a clear warning for Luke to maintain his distance. "Back away, Luke," she demanded, her authority undisputed in that moment.

Luke's response was soft, a gentle concession in the face of Glenda's unwavering stance. "I'll lock him out," he said, retreating outside with Duke in tow.

As I lay there, the name 'Glenda' echoed within the confines of my mind, its syllables bouncing around with a mixture of irony and disdain. *That's the name for a witch. Or just a bitch*. The thought was uncharitable, perhaps, but in the moment, it felt fitting, a small, petty rebellion against the situation and the pain that shackled me to this makeshift bed.

My eyes followed Glenda's movements, noting the meticulous way she wiped at the droplets of saliva that drizzled down her forearm. Duke, in his protective fervour, had indeed given her a fair go. Yet, despite his best efforts, it didn't seem like he had managed to pierce her skin. There was a part of me that admired his loyalty, even as I recognised the mayhem it had wrought.

Driven by a blend of pain-fuelled irritation and a stubborn streak that refused to be subdued, I couldn't help but call out across the tent, my voice laced with an accusatory tone. "It's your own fault, you know." It was a declaration, a challenge even, tossed into the air between us like a gauntlet. I wanted a reaction, some acknowledgment of the turmoil that had unfolded, a sign that she understood the ripple effects of her actions, however well-intentioned they might have been.

The witch—or doctor, as she claimed to be—gave no reply. Her silence was a wall, impenetrable and unyielding, and it served only to stoke the flames of my frustration. In her silence, I read a dismissal, a refusal to engage with the accusation or the underlying tension that crackled like a live wire in the aftermath of the altercation.

Lying there, a mix of anger, pain, and a begrudging respect for Duke's loyalty swirling within me, I couldn't help but feel isolated in my own battle. The silence from Glenda, the absence of Duke, and the physical pain that enveloped me like a suffocating blanket—all of it compounded into a sense of solitary confinement within the canvas walls of the tent.

The tent felt smaller somehow, the atmosphere charged with a tension that seemed to amplify each sound and movement. "Luke," Glenda's voice cut through the silence, a sharp contrast to the muted exchanges that had preceded her call. As Luke re-entered the tent, her tone shifted into one of urgency, directing him with a clarity that left no room for misunderstanding. "Listen carefully. I need you to return to the Medical Centre and get me a few supplies."

Luke's response was prompt, a simple acknowledgment laced with a readiness to assist. "Sure. What do you need?"

Watching Glenda, I couldn't help but notice the theatricality with which she grabbed a t-shirt and began wrapping it tightly around the bite. *A little dramatic. And you call yourself a doctor?* The thought was a reflex, a defensive jab born from my own discomfort and the surreal nature of the situation. Despite her professional demeanour, there was something in her actions that seemed to straddle the line between necessity and performance.

"I need..." Glenda's voice trailed off as she paused, her request hanging in the air momentarily. "Do you have any paper and a pen?" The simplicity of her request, juxtaposed with the complexity of our circumstances, struck me as oddly grounding. It was a reminder of the mundane necessities that continued to tether us to the world outside this canvas enclosure.

Luke's smile, in response, was a small beacon of normalcy. "Actually, we do." His words, tinged with a hint of optimism, seemed to momentarily lift the weight of the situation, offering a brief respite from the gravity of our predicament.

As Glenda readjusted the makeshift bandage around her arm, Luke rummaged for the requested items.

"Here," Luke said, presenting the pen and paper to Glenda with a gesture that was both simple and significant.

"Thanks," Glenda's response, accompanied by a short smile, was a fleeting glimpse into the human behind the doctor. It was a reminder that beneath the professional exterior lay a person, navigating the same storm of uncertainty and challenge that had enveloped us all.

Turning my attention away from Luke and Glenda, whose quiet collaboration seemed to momentarily suspend the reality of our precarious situation, I found my gaze drifting downward, towards my own battered form. The sight that greeted me was unexpectedly reassuring. The swelling that had marred my chest, a vivid reminder of the trauma I had endured, had subsided significantly, leaving behind skin that looked surprisingly clean, almost untouched by the recent ordeal. It was a small victory, perhaps, but in the moment, it felt significant

Beside me, almost lost in the shuffle of survival, lay my shirt, crumpled and forgotten. As I reached for it, my fingers encountered an unexpected texture amid the fabric. There, embedded within the grey gunk that seemed to have claimed my shirt as its own, was a long, charcoal splinter. The sight of it was jarring, a stark reminder of the violence that had been visited upon my body. The urge to gag rose unbidden as I considered not just the visual affront but also the foul odour that emanated from the shirt. The realisation hit me hard: *Had all of that really come out of my chest?*

My eyes, drawn inexorably back to Glenda, viewed her in a new light. The skepticism and irritation that had clouded my judgment began to dissipate, replaced by a burgeoning sense of guilt. Here was a woman who, despite my initial resistance and suspicion, had navigated the treacherous waters of my injuries with a steady hand. *She really has just saved my life.* The thought resonated within me, its truth undeniable despite the whirlwind of emotions that had characterised our interactions thus far.

As Glenda spoke, her voice steady and authoritative, I couldn't help but notice the subtle shift in the atmosphere of the tent. "A lot of this you can actually find in my examination room," she said, her eyes meeting Luke's as she handed over the list. Luke, now squatting beside her, took the paper with a solemnity that seemed to weigh heavily between them. "The rest," Glenda continued, her gaze unwavering, "The ones with the asterisks, you'll have to take from the shared supply room."

At her words, Luke's reaction was immediate, his head snapping up as if the gravity of the situation had suddenly become clearer to him. There was a moment, brief yet charged, where the unsaid seemed to hang heavily in the air.

"I'm sorry, Luke, but we are going to need it all," Glenda's voice broke through the silence, her tone imbued with a mix of apology and resolve.

Luke's response was a silent nod, his acceptance mute but palpable. "I'll be quick. I promise," he said, his voice a blend of determination and an underlying current of anxiety.

Then, in a moment laden with unspoken fears and camaraderie, Glenda reached out, her hand grasping Luke's arm with a grip that spoke volumes. "Luke," she said, her voice a soft yet firm command, "Be careful."

Luke's reaction was immediate, his face a canvas of resolve as the lines etched into his expression deepened. The seriousness with which he took her words was unmistakable, a silent testament to the gravity of his task. With a final nod, an unspoken promise to heed her warning, he left the tent.

Left in the wake of his departure, I found myself staring at the empty space where Luke had been, a myriad of questions racing through my mind. *What the hell is going on?*

In the quiet that settled after Luke's hurried departure, Duke positioned himself as my unwavering sentinel, his loyalty manifesting in a silent, steadfast presence by my side. Glenda, for her part, seemed content to keep a respectful distance, a decision that, under normal circumstances, I would have appreciated. Yet, the tension that lingered in the air urged me to seek some semblance of harmony within the confines of our temporary shelter.

I suggested, perhaps naively, that Glenda might bridge the chasm of distrust with Duke by extending an olive branch in the form of a treat. It was a simple gesture, one that I hoped would serve as a metaphor for the forgiveness and understanding we were all in desperate need of. However, Duke, with his canine intuition and unwavering loyalty, was not so easily swayed. He remained unmoved by Glenda's hesitant offer, his refusal a clear sign that forgiveness was not to be granted lightly, not even for the price of a favoured snack.

This standoff, albeit silent and on a scale much smaller than the challenges we faced, mirrored my own concerns. Given my initial hostility and the barrage of accusations I had hurled at Glenda, the hope that she might extend to me the understanding Duke withheld from her was a thread of anxiety that wove itself through my thoughts. I had been abrasive, driven by pain and the disorientation of my circumstances, my words and actions a reflection of the turmoil that churned within. Now, in the aftermath of my outburst and witnessing Duke's steadfast refusal to acknowledge Glenda's attempt at reconciliation, I couldn't help but wonder about the dynamics of forgiveness and the possibility of second chances.

The tent flap announced Paul's arrival with a rustle that seemed louder than usual, cutting through the tense atmosphere that had settled within. As he ducked his head inside, his gasp was almost theatrical in its intensity, a sound that momentarily redirected all attention towards him. "Are you okay, Glenda? What happened?" His questions tumbled out in rapid succession, concern etched in every word, barely allowing a breath between inquiries.

Glenda's response was calm, almost too calm given the undercurrents of tension that had been running high. "I'm fine," she assured, her voice steady. "It's just a surface wound. This shirt is just a precaution until Luke gets back with some antiseptic." Her words were meant to downplay the situation, to bring a semblance of normalcy back to the chaos that had momentarily gripped us.

Yet, inside my head, skepticism reared its head with a vengeance. *Oh, fuck off!* The thought was involuntary, a silent retort to what I perceived as an understatement. *Surface wound my ass. There's not even any blood!* My mind, it seemed, was not ready to accept Glenda's nonchalance, not when the evidence before my eyes suggested not even a hint of the prior altercation.

Paul, still grappling with the scene before him, stuttered, "But, what..."

"Duke doesn't like her," I found myself saying, the words slipping out with a flatness that belied the turmoil underneath. There was a pause, heavy with unsaid things, before I added, "And neither do I." The admission was cold, a reflection of the bitterness that had taken root within me. It was a declaration, one that I could not, would not retract, despite the immediate reprimand it drew.

"Jamie!" Paul's voice carried a note of scolding, a reminder of the line I had just crossed.

"She shouldn't be here," I persisted stubbornly, unwilling to back down, to pretend that the complexities of our interactions could be smoothed over with polite lies.

Paul's retort was swift. "If she wasn't here, you'd be bloody dead within a few days!" His words were a chide, laced with the harsh truth of our situation, a truth I was loathe to acknowledge even as it stared me in the face.

Turning away, I moaned softly, an expression of both physical discomfort and the emotional turmoil that churned within. The attempt to roll onto my side was instinctive, a physical manifestation of my desire to escape, to turn away from the confrontations and the truths laid bare.

"You'd best stay on your back for now," Glenda's voice cut through my reverie, a command wrapped in the guise of advice. Her words, though spoken with a clinical detachment, carried an undercurrent of concern that I found both irksome and oddly comforting.

Reluctantly, I acquiesced, settling back onto my back, a position that felt like a surrender not just to my physical limitations but to the tangled web of emotions and alliances that had ensnared us all. In that moment, lying there, I was acutely aware of the fragile balance between need and resentment, between the life-saving interventions of those we may not like and the begrudging acceptance of our dependence on them.

Paul's approach towards Glenda carried an air of determined purpose, his movements deliberate as he navigated the tent. "Well, I've brought you some clean water," he announced, a statement that felt oddly ceremonial under the circumstances. His action of pushing Duke away with his foot, though gentle, seemed an unnecessary assertion of space as he placed the small bucket in front of Glenda. Without lingering for thanks or further conversation, Paul turned on his heel and exited the tent with a promptness that left a lingering sense of abruptness in his wake.

Well, that was a bit dramatic and odd, I mused silently, my gaze trailing after Paul's departing figure.

Glenda's actions brought me back to the present moment. She dipped a fresh t-shirt into the bucket, and I watched, almost mesmerised, as clear water droplets cascaded from the fabric. When she looked up at me, her question caught me off guard. "Do you want to hold him?" she asked, her eyes flicking toward Duke.

My response was instinctual, a gesture of inclusion and protection. Patting the bed beside me, I beckoned Duke, who, sensing the gravity of the moment, joined me without hesitation. "It's okay," I whispered, my voice a blend of reassurance and resolve, as I cradled him lovingly yet firmly.

As Glenda approached, her movements were precise, the silence that enveloped her actions not empty but filled with a professional focus. The sensation of cool water on my chest was startling in its intensity, the liquid seeping into the wound with a penetrating chill that seemed to reach deep into the core of my being. Each droplet felt like a harbinger of renewal, a promise of healing that was both physical and, perhaps, emotional.

I allowed myself the luxury of closing my eyes, surrendering to the moment as my body relaxed further into the mattress. A strange sense of peace enveloped me, a stark contrast to the tumultuous emotions and events that had led to this point. *New life, Jamie,* the voice of Clivilius echoed within the depths of my mind, emotionless yet imbued with an odd sense of wisdom. *And this is just the beginning.*

In that moment, with Duke by my side and the sensation of cleansing water seeping into my wounds, I couldn't help but wonder about the truth of that internal whisper. *Was this indeed a new beginning, a pivotal point from which things would start to change?* The thought was both daunting and filled with a cautious optimism, a recognition of the potential for transformation amidst the suffering and pain.

❖

The sound of Luke's voice, calling out to Glenda and Paul from outside, cut through the heavy air of the tent, a reminder of the world moving forward, even as I lay there caught in a moment of vulnerability. Hastily, I swiped at my cheeks, trying to erase the evidence of tears that pain and exhaustion had wrung from me. It was a futile gesture, perhaps, but one that spoke volumes of my desire to appear stronger than I felt.

Luke's entrance was marked by a sense of urgency, the bags he was carrying dropped unceremoniously as he made his way to my side. His question, "You okay?" was loaded with concern, his eyes searching mine for the truth that my hastily wiped face might have hidden.

"Yeah," I managed to sniff, the word barely a whisper, betraying the turmoil that lay beneath my attempt at stoicism. "Just in a lot of pain." It was an admission, a concession to the reality of my condition, spoken with a raw honesty that I could no longer disguise.

Luke's response was immediate, a balm to the open wound of my pride. "You'll be right now," he said, his voice carrying a conviction that felt like a lifeline. "I've got you some strong pain medication." The promise of relief was a beacon of hope, a tangible sign that the worst of the ordeal might soon be behind me.

As Glenda directed Paul to prepare a space with a spare blanket along the back wall of the tent, the dynamics of our small group shifted into a well-oiled machine, each of them playing a part in the dance of survival and healing. Paul's compliance and Glenda's swift organisation of the medical supplies on the newly laid blanket spoke of a practiced efficiency.

"I'm pretty sure I've got all the items on the list without an asterisk," Luke said, a note of pride in his accomplishment mingled with the acknowledgment of the job yet undone. "But I'll have to go back now and check the supply room for the rest."

"Yes," Glenda agreed, her voice firm. "I will need the antiseptic and antibiotics. I can't dress Jamie's wounds properly without them. Go," she insisted, her directive underscored by the seriousness of my condition.

Laying there, watching the flurry of activity around me, a strange sense of detachment settled over me. The pain, the fear, and the vulnerability that had defined my existence in the wake of the injury were momentarily pushed to the background by the concerted efforts of those around me. Their actions, their concern, and their unspoken solidarity were a lifeline in the turbulent sea of my recovery. In this moment of orchestration, I found an odd comfort, a glimmer of hope that perhaps, just perhaps, things might indeed be okay.

The involuntary moan that escaped me as I shifted my position was an echo of the relentless grip of pain. Every movement was a calculated risk, a balance between the need for slight comfort and the threat of exacerbating my already throbbing wounds.

"Just try and relax," Glenda's voice, firm yet not without a touch of empathy, floated to me. "Not much longer now and I'll have something to take the pain away and help you sleep." Her words were meant to offer solace, a promise of relief on the horizon. Yet, as I exhaled loudly, the concept of relaxation seemed like a distant, almost foreign concept. *Relax?* I huffed internally. *Well, that would be much easier said than done.*

Paul's voice broke through my inner turmoil, offering a brief distraction. "Well, if you don't need me, Glenda, I'll go and see if I can finish getting this other tent up." His offer, a gesture of continued support, reflected the ongoing efforts to maintain not just my well-being but our collective survival.

"That's fine," Glenda responded, her attention still partly on me. "I'll come and help you when I've sorted Jamie."

As Paul's footsteps receded, leaving the tent, I closed my eyes, embracing the solitude that his departure offered. *I'd rather not engage in further conversation if I can help it.* The thought was a silent plea for peace, for a moment of respite from the constant reminders of my vulnerability and the dependency on those around me.

Time seemed to warp, stretching out in a thick, uncomfortable silence that filled the tent once Paul had left. My mind wandered, restless and uneasy. *I wish Glenda would wait outside.* The thought was a silent echo of my yearning for solitude, for a brief escape from the constant scrutiny and the palpable tension that Glenda's presence brought. *Luke is taking long enough; she could have helped Paul after all.* The rational part of me understood the necessity of her presence, the importance of her preparing to tend to my wounds with the supplies Luke was fetching. Yet, irrationally, I found myself wishing for her to be elsewhere, anywhere but here, as I lay in wait, caught between pain and the promise of relief.

❖

"How did you go?" Glenda's question was directed at Luke as he re-entered the tent, his arms laden with more bags that promised relief and recovery. Her voice was a mix of hope and urgency, reflective of the critical nature of his mission.

Luke's response came with a grin, a sign of triumph. "I'm pretty sure I've got everything from your list," he announced, his confidence momentarily uplifting the heavy air that had settled around us. His grin, a rare commodity in these dire circumstances, was infectious, even to someone in my state.

Glenda eyed Luke with a hint of suspicion as she picked up two of the bags.

"Oh," Luke added, somewhat sheepishly, "And then I just grabbed a heap of random stuff for good measure. I'm not really sure what any of it is."

"Well, that's not surprising," I found myself croaking, my voice tinged with impatience as I rode waves of sharp pain. Each breath was a battle, and my comment, though meant to lighten the mood, was a stark reminder of the fine line we were walking between preparedness and desperation.

Glenda's acknowledgement of Luke's efforts, "Thank you, Luke," was followed by her reaching for some drugs, a movement that captured my full attention. The anticipation that swelled within me was palpable, my gaze fixated on her actions with the syringe. Her promise of a strong medication had kindled a flicker of hope in the dark expanse of my pain.

Morphine, or better, I mused, the thought more a prayer than a guess.

The clinical precision with which Glenda swabbed my arm with antiseptic, followed by the swift, decisive jab of the needle, was both a relief and a surrender. The injection of the painkiller, closely followed by a dose of sleeping medication, marked the beginning of my body's slow acquiescence to the chemicals designed to ease my suffering.

The transformation was almost immediate, a wave of relaxation sweeping over me, the warmth spreading through my veins like a gentle tide reaching for the shore. My eyes, betraying my struggle to remain anchored in wakefulness, fluttered several times, each blink a battle against the encroaching shadows of sleep.

In the end, the realisation that surrender was the only viable option settled over me like a soft blanket. The fight to stay awake, to maintain a grip on consciousness, faded into the background as the medication coursed through my system, promising respite from the pain and the tumultuous reality that awaited beyond the fragile sanctuary of sleep.

REDRESS ANTICS

4338.206.8

The sound of the tent flap being unzipped sliced through the quiet, Duke's low growl immediately filling the tense space as someone intruded upon our temporary sanctuary. *Must be Glenda*, I surmised, lazily cracking open an eye, the fog of sleep still clinging stubbornly to my consciousness. Duke hadn't budged from my side, his disdain for Glenda remained palpable despite her ongoing efforts to bridge the gap between them.

"It's okay, Duke," I murmured, offering a reassuring pat to his head, attempting to soothe the tension that vibrated through his frame.

"Sorry," Glenda's voice floated through the air, tinged with a genuine apology as she navigated the darkening space towards me. "I didn't mean to wake you."

"I was already awake," came my soft response, a yawn threatening to undermine my claim to alertness.

As Glenda crouched beside the collection of medical supplies, a small curse slipped from her lips, drawing my attention. "Ahh, shit," she muttered, her frustration barely contained.

"What is it?" Curiosity piqued, I propped myself up on one elbow, the action sending a ripple of discomfort through my body.

"Several of the gauze dressings have been torn to shreds. And one of the bandages is missing." Her announcement was a mix of disbelief and annoyance, a sentiment I quickly shared as my mind raced to identify the perpetrator.

My eyes rolled instinctively, the conclusion as clear as day. There could only be one culprit for such a crime. "Henri!" The name burst from me, a mix of exasperation and command, as I reached across Duke, my fingers racing to grab the stolen bandage nestled between Henri's front paws.

As Glenda crept closer to where I lay, the tension in the tent was palpable, a silent testament to the precarious balance between necessity and the comfort provided by our limited supplies. "I found your missing bandage," I announced, my voice tinged with a mix of frustration and resignation as I engaged in a futile tug-of-war with Henri over the contested item.

Glenda's response came with a huff, her patience evidently worn thin by the day's events. "You may as well let him keep it," she advised, her pragmatism slicing through my half-hearted attempt at salvage. "We can't use that now."

With a resigned eye roll, I conceded defeat, allowing Henri to claim his prize. The small victory brought a fleeting moment of satisfaction to the dog. It was a momentary distraction, a brief interlude in the ongoing struggle for survival.

"Take these," Glenda commanded, breaking through my reflections with a bottle of water and a handful of capsules thrust into my view.

"What are they?" I inquired, more out of a sense of due diligence than any real skepticism. Without waiting for her answer, I swallowed the first capsule, the water chasing it down my throat in a desperate bid for relief.

"There are a couple antibiotics and then some pain and sleeping medication," Glenda explained, her voice carrying the weight of her medical authority. Her clarification came as a reassurance, a promise of relief wrapped in the guise of pharmaceuticals.

I didn't hesitate to follow through with the rest, tossing the final capsules into my mouth and washing them down with a large gulp of water. The act of swallowing the medication was a small victory in itself, a defiance against the pain that had become my constant companion. Laying back down, a sense of accomplishment washed over me, marred only by a single wince.

"Watch the dog for me," Glenda's voice was firm, her focus squarely on the task at hand. Her directive, while practical, grated on me slightly. *No wonder Duke doesn't like you*, the thought flitted through my mind, a silent critique of her impersonal reference to Duke. Despite my discomfort, I reached out, draping my right arm around Duke, drawing him into the small sanctuary of warmth and safety beneath my armpit. It was a small gesture, but one that spoke volumes of the bond between us, a silent pact of mutual comfort and protection.

As Glenda began her work, her hands moved with a practiced ease that belied the complexity of her task. She carefully removed the soiled dressings, her actions meticulous, designed not to disturb the delicate process of healing that lay beneath. The cleanliness of the wound was her priority, and she attended to it with a dedication that was both clinical and, in its own way, compassionate. The quick redressing of the wound was a silent testament to her proficiency, a choreography of care in the unlikeliest of settings.

The exhaustion that had been lurking at the edges of my consciousness began to assert itself more forcefully, my eyelids heavy with the weight of fatigue and medication. My face slackened, a sign of the inevitable surrender to sleep, even as the world around me—Glenda, the tent, the very fabric of my immediate reality—began to blur into a hazy in-between. The clinking of medical supplies, a subtle but persistent reminder of the situation, tethered me to a fleeting awareness, a resistance against the pull of oblivion.

"I'm taking the supplies to the other tent," Glenda announced, her voice cutting through the fog of my drowsiness. "Away from Henri." Her decision, pragmatic as it was, carried an undertone of protectiveness, a safeguarding of the resources that were so vital to our continued survival.

My fingers stretched out instinctively, seeking the familiar warmth of Henri, who had become a focal point of our makeshift camp's dynamics. *Henri loves his new toy*, I mused, a thread of amusement weaving through the fatigue that pressed down on me. That Glenda had repurposed the bandage, turning a necessity into a source of joy for Henri, struck me as an unexpectedly thoughtful gesture.

"Glenda," I managed to call out, my voice barely above a whisper, a last-ditch effort to bridge the gap that had formed between us.

Her gaze met mine, those beady eyes locking onto my face with an intensity that felt almost tangible. "Thank you," I mumbled, the words a simple but sincere acknowledgment of her efforts, her care, and the complexities of our shared human experience.

After she left, the tent felt suddenly more expansive, more isolated. The battle to remain conscious, already a losing fight, came to an end.

4338.207

(26 July 2018)

DOGGY PADDLE

4338.207.1

"Henri!" My whisper cut through the stillness of the tent, sharp with the authority I scarcely felt, given my weakened state. "Get your head out of it!" The command, however, fell on deaf ears—or, more accurately, was ignored in favour of the intriguing scents that beckoned from within the large bag.

The small brown, furry head of Henri, undeterred by my words, continued its investigation, every sniff an exploration into the forbidden. Duke, ever the stoic observer, sat beside his brother, a silent guardian angel in canine form, his patience a stark contrast to Henri's impulsive curiosity.

Capturing Duke's gaze, I posed a question that seemed almost redundant given their current preoccupation. "Are you hungry?" The simplicity of the inquiry belied my growing understanding of their simple, yet profound, needs.

A quiet chuckle, born of amusement at the scene unfolding before me, filled the tent. Duke's reaction, a twirl of pure canine joy, was mirrored by Henri's sudden withdrawal from the bag, both dogs now united in their expectation of what was to come.

"Come on then," I conceded, the effort of moving from the mattress a demonstration to the depth of my affection for these two companions. Approaching the bag from which Henri had just extracted himself, I found myself faced with the task of providing for them. Pulling out a tin of dog food, I announced the contents with a mix of curiosity and revulsion. "Diced kangaroo and vegetables," the label read, a culinary adventure for the canine palate. "Delicious," I added sarcastically, my expression one of mock horror at the thought.

The response was instantaneous. The mere mention of food, regardless of my personal sentiments, sent Duke into an ecstatic dance, his hindlegs moving in a rhythm that spoke of pure, unadulterated happiness. Henri, lacking the same grace but matching the enthusiasm, bounced around his older brother, a chaotic ballet of anticipation and hunger.

Staring at the food bowls positioned next to the box of toys, a dilemma presented itself, prompting a silent debate within me. "Dust?" The question floated softly from my lips as my gaze drifted towards the tent's entrance, visualising Duke and Henri frolicking outside. "Or no dust?" My eyes shifted back to the vacant food bowls beside the playful distractions of their toys. The prospect of having them dine inside the tent was far from appealing, yet the thought of exposing them to the harsh outdoor elements while they ate was equally unattractive.

Resignation laced my next breath. "Oh well. No dust it is," I conceded aloud to my furry companions, though they were blissfully unaware of the internal conflict their mealtime had sparked. With a sigh, I proceeded to open the can of dog food, dividing its contents between the two bowls. I distributed roughly half into one bowl and the remainder into the other, fully aware that the concept of equality held little significance to them. True to their nature, I anticipated the inevitable game of musical bowls they would engage in, swapping places numerous times until every last morsel was consumed.

No sooner had the food been served than two eager, furry heads dove into their respective bowls. The sight was endearing for a mere moment before the reality of their manners—or lack thereof—struck me. They chewed with open mouths, the sloppy sounds of their eating sending a shiver down my spine. The aroma emanating from the bowls did nothing to ease my discomfort, adding a layer of olfactory offence to the auditory assault.

This makeshift dining arrangement within the tent confirmed one thing: the necessity of finding a more suitable spot for their meals. The urgency of the task was undeniable, not just for the sake of maintaining some semblance of cleanliness within our living space, but also for my own sanity. The boys, oblivious to my growing resolve, continued their messy feast, a reminder of the simple joys and sometimes tests of patience, that came with their companionship.

For the first time since waking up, my thoughts veered towards the physical reminder of the reason for my tent-bound state—the sore on my chest. With a tentative curiosity, I eased my fingers under the edge of the dressing, gently lifting it to steal a glance at the wound beneath. A spontaneous smile broke across my face at the sight; it was healing, looking significantly better than it had the day before. The realisation brought a sense of relief, a lightness I hadn't felt in days. The pain, now just a dull ache, was a vast improvement from the sharp, unyielding discomfort that had been my constant companion.

This small victory buoyed my spirits, setting a lighter tone for the day. I turned my attention to retrieving a fresh pair of undies from the depths of my suitcase. My supply was finite, a reminder of our remote location, far removed from the conveniences of modern life. *A splash in the river is no substitute for a proper wash*, I mused silently, *but I can at least wear fresh clothes*. This thought, a blend of resignation and appreciation, lingered as I prepared to slip into the day's attire.

The act was a careful ballet of balance and coordination, my body slightly bent, one foot suspended in air, aiming for the sanctuary of cleanliness. It was a moment of vulnerability, of simple human need, when the abrupt sound of the tent zipper cut through the morning's tranquility. The flap was pulled back with an unexpected swiftness.

"Oh, I'm so sorry," came Glenda's voice, drenched in surprise and immediate regret. She closed her eyes in a swift gesture of respect and embarrassment, her back turned to me as she retreated, leaving the flap to fall back into place with a gentle swish.

A chuckle erupted from me, loud and sincere, echoing off the tent walls. It was a sound of genuine amusement, born from the absurdity of the situation and the innocence of the mistake. My laughter was not at Glenda's expense but shared in the moment of human awkwardness we both found ourselves in. I felt a surge of empathy for her, far outweighing any flicker of embarrassment on my part.

"I didn't expect you to be up and moving," Glenda's voice, tinged with a mix of surprise and relief, floated towards me from outside the tent.

Her words coaxed another chuckle out of me, a sound that seemed to carry a lighter air with it. "It's okay," I reassured, as I navigated my way to the entrance, poking my head through the front flap to find her. The sudden appearance of my head must have caught Glenda off guard, as she gave a small, startled jump, her body tensing for a moment before relaxing once she realised it was just me.

It was then that Duke decided to make his presence known. With a determination that only a dog with a mission could possess, he bulldozed his way through the small opening, nearly tripping me in his haste. Ignoring our amused gazes, he dove nose-first into the myriad scents the dust had to offer, darting off with an energy that belied the early hour. His tail was a banner of excitement, waving as he embarked on his morning investigation.

Henri, on the other hand, was the embodiment of reluctance. Peering out from the shadows of the tent with a cautious gaze, he seemed to weigh his options. Crouching down, I extended a hand towards him, offering a gentle nudge of encouragement. "Come on, it's not so bad out here," I murmured, my voice a soft coaxing thread designed to ease his hesitation. With a tentative step, Henri finally acquiesced, stepping into the new day with a disinterested grace that contrasted sharply with Duke's reckless enthusiasm.

Once the canine duo had embarked on their morning explorations, I turned my attention back to the task of dressing. I opted for a clean t-shirt, the fabric feeling soft and comforting against my skin. The board shorts I slipped into were the same ones I had worn the day before. They bore the marks of yesterday's adventures, but in the absence of alternatives, they would have to suffice.

Finally ready to leave the confines of the tent behind me, I stepped out of the tent, fully embracing the day that lay ahead. The air was fresh, carrying with it the promise of new experiences and the lingering warmth of the rising sun. It was a moment of transition, from the private world within the tent to the vast, open expanse that surrounded us.

"How are you feeling this morning?" Glenda's voice cut through the crisp morning air, her concern as clear as the daylight beginning to spread across the sky.

"Much better. My chest doesn't feel nearly as sore," I replied, offering her a glimpse of optimism as I stretched my arms above my head. The motion was smooth, an acknowledgement of the healing that had taken place, a marked improvement that filled me with a quiet sense of relief.

"That's good news," she responded, her voice carrying a note of genuine happiness for my recovery.

The conversation shifted seamlessly as an idea sparked within me. "I was about to go and take Duke for a walk," I mused aloud, the thought blossoming fully formed yet unexpected. The realisation that it actually sounded quite appealing followed swiftly. "We've both been rather cooped up the last twenty-four hours. I think it'll do us both some good." The prospect of stretching my legs and allowing Duke the freedom to explore seemed increasingly like the right decision, a small step towards normalcy.

"I agree," Glenda chimed in. Her next offer, however, took me by surprise. "Can I change your dressing before you go?" she asked, her tone implying both a suggestion and a gentle insistence.

"Sure," I agreed without hesitation, the practicality of her suggestion overriding any initial reluctance. Pulling my shirt over my head, I exposed the wound to the morning light, and to Glenda's scrutinising gaze.

She carefully removed the soiled dressing, her focus intense as she examined the healing skin beneath. "It is looking much better," she observed, her professional assessment mingling with a hint of relief. A smile found its way to my lips, an unspoken thank you for her agreement.

"Why don't you go lay back down while I grab some fresh dressings from the supply tent," Glenda suggested next, although it sounded more like a mild directive.

"Really?" I asked, my voice laced with a mix of surprise and a hint of annoyance. The thought of returning to the confines of the tent, even briefly, was unappealing. The freedom of the outdoors beckoned, and the tent represented a return to limitation, a barrier to the morning's fresh promise.

"Just for five minutes," Glenda insisted, her tone brooking no argument. "If we had a chair, I'd say you could sit, but we don't."

Her words, meant to be practical, instead reminded me of our austere conditions. *Why does Glenda have to remind me just how much this place sucks?* The thought was a shadow over the morning's light, my frown a silent echo of my internal protest.

"Yet," Glenda quickly added, her voice carrying a hint of hope, a promise of improvement. "We don't have a chair, yet."

"Fine," I huffed, the word leaving my lips with a mixture of resignation and the faintest trace of annoyance. Retreating back into the tent, I lowered myself onto the mattress, a makeshift bed that had seen better days. As I settled in, the sensation of stale sweat clinging to my back was unmistakable, an unpleasant reminder of the harsh realities of our current living conditions. The air was thick with the scent of exertion and the great outdoors, a pungent cocktail that made me acutely aware of my own need for cleanliness. I staunchly refused to let my discomfort escalate to gagging, yet I couldn't deny the glaring truth in the privacy of my own thoughts: I was in dire need of a shower.

Glenda's return was swift, her presence bringing a sense of action and purpose. She began tending to my wound with a gentle efficiency, pouring fresh water over my chest to clean the area. "This really is looking much better already," she observed, her voice carrying an undercurrent of professional approval. "Your burns look superficial. Most of the damage appears to have been from the splinter."

Her assessment was a balm to my lingering concerns. "I really don't feel much pain now at all," I admitted, grateful for the significant improvement.

"And you've had no complaints with any upper body movements?" she inquired, her hands deftly securing the final gauze dressing over my wounds.

"None," I answered with a smile, my spirits lifting at the confirmation of my recovery. It felt as if Clivilius had indeed held up its end of the bargain, granting me a reprieve from pain and a swift healing process.

"Well, that's great news," Glenda responded, her light tap on my shoulder serving as a signal that her work was done.

Eager to leave the confines of the tent and breathe in the fresh air, I sat up quickly. The need for movement, for a change of scenery, was pressing. Duke would surely be in need of a shit by now, especially after his breakfast. The thought of him patiently waiting, or perhaps not so patiently, spurred my desire to get moving. The likelihood of him having already made his mark near the tent was not lost on me, a reminder of the practical aspects of pet ownership.

"But," Glenda interjected, her hand pressing gently against my chest in a halting motion, "I still need you to take another couple of antibiotic capsules."

Her words, meant for my well-being, momentarily bristled against my growing impatience to be free of medical concerns. *Is that really necessary?* The question echoed in my mind, a silent protest against further treatment.

"You'll need to take several daily for the next few days to make sure it doesn't get infected," Glenda's voice was firm, underscored by the seriousness of preventing infection in an environment far from the sterility of a hospital.

Without hesitation, I snatched the capsules from her outstretched hand, sending them on a swift journey down my throat accompanied by a gulp of water that seemed to echo in the quiet of the morning. "Thanks," I managed, my voice a blend of gratitude and eagerness to move past this moment. I wiped my mouth with the back of my hand, a rough, almost reflexive gesture, before hurriedly pulling my t-shirt back over my head, eager to reclaim some sense of freedom.

"You're good to go," Glenda announced, delivering a reassuring pat on my back that seemed to signal not just the end of the medical procedure but a sort of send-off into the day ahead. "But don't go too far, and the moment you start to feel tired or any dizziness, you need to stop and rest. Then as soon as you are able, make your way back to camp." Her instructions were clear, a reminder of the balance I needed to maintain between pushing forward and acknowledging the limits of my current physical state.

I nodded in acknowledgment, absorbing her words and the weight they carried. Internally, I was still wrestling with the frustration of our situation—Luke's decision to bring another person into our fold without consultation. Yet, as I stood there, feeling the effects of Glenda's care, I couldn't help but begin to see the necessity of her presence. Her expertise, suddenly indispensable, cast a new light on my initial irritation.

But why had she agreed to do this? The question lingered in my mind. *What drove someone like her to leave behind whatever life she had, to venture on a one-way ticket into the unknown with strangers?* It seemed a decision that spoke of courage, perhaps a sense of adventure, maybe a dedication to helping others regardless of the setting. *Or most likely, just plain ignorance or stupidity.*

"I'll go downstream," I declared to Glenda as we emerged from the tent, the fabric doorway fluttering shut behind us. "There's a lagoon just around the bend. I'll take Duke with me. He'll love it." The thought of the lagoon, with its serene waters and the tranquility it offered, seemed like the perfect escape. Duke, ever eager for exploration, would undoubtedly revel in the new sights and smells.

"And Henri?" Glenda's inquiry pulled my attention towards the other four-legged companion.

My gaze drifted to Henri, who was meandering by the campfire, his movements deliberate and unhurried through the fine dust that coated the ground. The contrast between his cautious approach to the world and Duke's boundless energy was stark. "I don't think Henri's going to make it too far," I said, a chuckle escaping me at the thought.

"I'll keep an eye on him," Glenda offered, her voice laced with a warmth that spoke of her genuine fondness.

"Thanks," I responded, grateful for her willingness to look after Henri. Turning my attention to Duke, who was still enthusiastically investigating every inch of ground with his nose, I raised my voice, "Come on, Duke." At the sound of my call, Duke's head snapped up, his expression one of immediate understanding. There was a brief moment of connection between us, a silent agreement that it was time for an adventure.

❖

The campsite quickly receded into a memory, a backdrop to our adventure, as Duke and I embraced the freedom of the open landscape, playing tag with the shadows and light that danced through the soft dust alongside the river. The world around us was a stark contrast to the familiar confines of our property back on Earth. Here, everything was uncharted, wild, and imbued with a sense of discovery. Duke, with his limitless curiosity, navigated this new terrain with an eagerness that was both heartwarming and slightly anxious. The river, a ribbon of life cutting through the landscape, drew his attention. Several times, I found myself cautioning him, a gentle but firm reminder to respect the unknown elements of our surroundings. The river was not a playground, and I was not about to let Duke's first potential swim be a test of survival.

As we journeyed on, the anticipation of reaching the lagoon grew within me, a beacon of natural beauty that promised a moment of peace and perhaps a bit of fun. The final dune before us stood as the last guardian to this hidden oasis. As we crested its peak, the lagoon revealed itself, a serene expanse nestled below. The sight of it sparked a lightness in my heart, but that lightness was quickly laced with surprise and a rush of fear as I watched Duke. His excitement overcame his caution, and as he clumsily descended the slope, my heart hitched in my chest. The edge of the lagoon loomed, a natural barrier I was sure he would respect. Yet, with a burst of unexpected grace, Duke launched himself into the air, his hind legs propelling him forward as his front legs reached out, slicing through the space between himself and the lagoon. He landed with a splash, a good meter from the shore, transforming my apprehension into awe.

Frozen in place, I watched, my breath caught in my throat, as Duke demonstrated an innate understanding of his abilities. His little head bobbed confidently above the water, his front legs paddling in a determined circle, propelling him through the lagoon with a skill that belied his earlier uncertainty. A laugh, born of relief and joy, escaped me as I realised the truth of the moment.

Duke was a natural at doggy paddling. The sight of him, so assured and joyful in the water, washed away my fears and replaced them with a profound sense of gratitude. Here, in this moment, away from the constraints of our past life, Duke was not just surviving; he was thriving. Watching him, a smile spread across my face, and a warmth filled my chest—a reminder of the resilience and surprises that life, especially this new life, held.

As Duke hauled his drenched form out of the lagoon and onto the shore, the transformation from water creature back to land dweller was instantaneous. He embarked on a vigorous shake, starting from his head and rippling down to the very tip of his tail, casting droplets of the lagoon's embrace into the air. It was a spectacle of shimmering beads suspended momentarily before they succumbed to gravity, the thirsty dust below eagerly claiming each one. The sight was a simple, pure moment of nature and dog merging into one.

I moved closer, my hand outstretched with the intention of giving Duke a well-earned pat on the head, a gesture of my approval and shared joy. However, my attempt was rendered futile as Duke, caught in a whirlwind of exhilaration, darted off. He wove a chaotic tapestry of wild circles, his paws kicking up a storm of water and dust. It was a dance of pure, unbridled joy, with Duke as the choreographer, zigzagging and looping with an energy that seemed to come from the very earth itself. With a precision that spoke of a plan known only to him, he returned to the same small rock that had been his launch pad and, without hesitation, catapulted himself back into the lagoon for another round.

Watching Duke's antics, I couldn't help but shake my head, a wide grin spreading across my face as a genuine belly laugh erupted from deep within. It was a laugh of surrender to the moment, to the joy and absurdity of life that Duke so perfectly embodied. Once the echo of the splash had faded, and Duke was once again navigating the calm waters of the lagoon with his expert doggy paddle, I found myself speaking aloud, my voice tinged with amusement and wonder. "Why is it that you treat the bath like it's trying to kill you, yet you'll happily drown yourself in a huge lagoon?"

It was a rhetorical question, one born of the countless times I'd witnessed Duke's dramatic aversion to baths—a stark contrast to the fearless abandon he now displayed. The question hung in the air, a testament to the mysteries and contradictions that make up the beings we love. Duke, in his simple, joyous pursuit of happiness, reminded me of the important lessons hidden in everyday moments—about fear, joy, and the unexpected places we find courage. Watching him, I suddenly felt a strange and unexpected deep connection to the present, to the beauty and comedy of life, and to the endless surprises it holds.

The tranquility of the moment shattered abruptly, much like the ground beneath me, betraying my trust with a suddenness that left me gasping. The soft earth, which had seemed so solid, gave way beneath my weight, plunging me into an unexpected descent. My legs buckled, my balance lost to the treacherous bank, and I found myself sliding, a clumsy, uncontrolled motion that ended with a jolt as my rear connected with the remnants of solid ground. The shock of the fall was quickly overtaken by an altogether different sensation—a zing of pleasure, so immediate and intense, it felt as though it was racing through my veins, starting from my toes and surging upwards with an electrifying speed.

My heart hammered against my ribcage, a rapid drumbeat in the quiet of the lagoon. The arousal, unbidden and unwelcome, sent a wave of panic through me. Duke's presence, innocent and unassuming, only compounded my discomfort. More than anything, I dreaded the voice of Clivilius intruding into this moment, a reminder of a connection I was still grappling to understand. Desperation lent me strength, and with a frantic effort, I pushed against the crumbling bank, retreating from the water's edge as if it were the source of my turmoil. My breaths came in long, deep gulps, each one a lifeline pulling me back to a semblance of calm as I stared at the lagoon, its waters now an object of my wary contemplation.

"That was too close, Duke," I muttered, more to myself than to Duke, who seemed blissfully unaware of the inner panic the incident had sparked in me. As if on cue, Duke shook himself, a full-body gesture that sent droplets flying in a halo around him. I shielded my eyes instinctively, a small laugh escaping me despite the recent scare.

When the moment passed and I dared to look again, Duke had found solace atop a large rock, basking in the warmth of the sun. His contentment in such simple pleasures was a balm to my frayed nerves. "You're a smart one," I conceded, a smile tugging at my lips despite the recent adrenaline surge. Compelled by a desire for companionship and a momentary escape from my thoughts, I joined him on the rock.

Side by side, we lay there, two creatures seeking comfort in the presence of the other. The hard surface of the rock prompted me to shift, seeking a more comfortable position, and as I rolled onto my back, Duke moved closer, his head finding a resting place on my abdomen. It was a gesture of trust and familiarity that eased the last remnants of tension from my body.

With Duke's steady breathing as a backdrop, my eyes drifted shut, and I allowed myself to be carried away into a realm of pleasant daydreams. The warmth of the sun, the gentle lull of the water, and the weight of Duke's head anchored me to the moment—a peaceful interlude amidst the unpredictability of our lives.

THE BODY

4338.207.2

"Duke! Jamie!" The sudden call from Luke shattered the tranquility of our serene moment by the lagoon. Duke's response was immediate; his excited barking pierced the calm, propelling me from the comfort of daydreams back into reality. My eyes snapped open, and I found myself instinctively sitting up, turning towards the source of the disturbance. There was Luke, a figure of frantic energy, his hands waving wildly as he made his way across the hilltop that framed our secluded spot. A mix of confusion and irritation swirled within me. *What the heck is Luke running about like a lunatic for?* I couldn't help but wonder, my mind struggling to piece together the urgency of his actions.

"Duke," Luke's voice carried a note of happiness as he finally came to a halt, his presence a stark contrast to the calm we had been enjoying.

Duke didn't hesitate. He scrambled up the hill, his small body navigating through the thick dust, a testament to his unwavering loyalty and perhaps, curiosity. My own reaction was less enthusiastic. The interruption, especially by Luke, pricked at my sense of peace. With a sigh, I grabbed my shirt, throwing it over my shoulder in a gesture of reluctant readiness, and followed after Duke, my mind still tethered to the tranquility of the lagoon.

"Good to see you're feeling better," Luke greeted me as I arrived, his attention briefly shifting to offer Duke a welcoming pat. The simple act, meant as a gesture of camaraderie, did little to ease the annoyance of being pulled from my rest.

Reaching the summit, I found myself panting, my breaths echoing Duke's laboured ones. "Yeah," I managed to say between breaths, a line of frustration creasing my forehead. The hill, not particularly steep, had somehow become a challenge, a fact that didn't sit well with me. *Come on, Jamie, it wasn't that steep.* "Duke and I had a nap in the sun. I seem to be feeling much better for it," I admitted, trying to brush off the irritation and focus on the positive outcome of our brief respite.

"A nap in the sun?" Luke repeated, amusement clear in his voice. "Duke looks like he is soaked."

I cast a glance down at Duke, realising that Luke's observation was spot on. Duke, far from being the dry, sunbathing companion I had left on the rock, appeared as though he'd indulged in another aquatic adventure. "You're a funny boy," I told Duke, a smile breaking through my earlier annoyance.

Luke's gaze lingered on my bare chest, a silent observation that felt as invasive as the sun's rays. "You really should keep your shirt on though," he advised, his voice carrying a hint of concern masked by practicality. "It's warm out."

The comment nudged me towards a realisation I hadn't fully embraced until that moment. "I've only had it off since it got wet by the lagoon," I explained, my voice trailing off as I drew a deep breath, feeling the warmth of the sun on my skin. It was a warmth that felt different, lacking the harsh bite I had come to associate with prolonged exposure. "It's odd though," I ventured further, allowing my thoughts to find their voice.

"What is?" Luke's inquiry, genuine and tinged with curiosity, prompted me to delve deeper into the peculiarity of the situation.

"I don't feel like my skin is burning at all." The words hung between us, an acknowledgment of an anomaly that defied our expectations of the sun's effect on the skin.

"Hmm," Luke murmured, his response laced with interest. "I guess that would be a good thing." His casual acceptance of the situation sparked a blend of relief and curiosity within me.

"Perhaps the sun is different here," I pondered aloud, the theory forming as the words left my lips. The idea that we were dealing with a celestial body that behaved differently than what we were accustomed to on Earth seemed both fantastical and increasingly plausible.

"Perhaps," Luke echoed, his agreement serving as a tacit acknowledgment of the myriad mysteries that surrounded us. The conversation, brief as it was, left me contemplating the adaptability of the human body and the endless possibilities of this new environment. Could it be that we were slowly becoming attuned to this place, its sun gentler on our skin, or perhaps our bodies were adjusting in ways we had yet to understand? The thought was comforting and unsettling in equal measure, a reminder of the vast unknowns that lay ahead.

The tranquility of our conversation shattered instantly, replaced by a jolt of terror that coursed through me as a scream sliced through the air. It was a sound that froze my blood, a harbinger of dread that no one is ever truly prepared for. The fear mirrored in Luke's eyes amplified the chill that seized me, a silent acknowledgment of the gravity of what that scream signified. Without hesitation, I turned, my body acting on a primal instinct to confront the source of our alarm.

"Luke," the words fell from my lips, icy and sharp, a stark contrast to the warmth that had just moments ago bathed us. My gaze locked onto Paul, who stood by the lagoon, a figure of shock and confusion, looming over what was an unmistakably human form sprawled on the sandbank. The sight ignited a fire of accusation within me. "What the hell have you done?" The question was a dagger thrown in desperation and disbelief.

"Oh fuck," Luke's response was a whisper of despair, a confession of utter bewilderment that mirrored my own turmoil. "I have no idea."

Driven by a mixture of fear and urgency, I found myself navigating the treacherous descent towards the unfolding nightmare. The ground beneath my feet offered little resistance as I slid and stumbled down the slope, each step a battle against the pull of gravity and the dread that clawed at my chest.

"Jamie! Wait!" Luke's voice reached out, a futile attempt to slow my reckless advance. But the plea fell on deaf ears, my focus narrowed to the grim tableau unfolding at the water's edge.

"Shit, Luke! Who the fuck is that?" The question erupted from me, a desperate plea for some semblance of understanding. My breath came in laboured gasps, each one a testament to the shock that thundered through my veins.

Across the lagoon, Paul's movements were frantic. He scrambled towards the opposite of the lagoon, his actions a chaotic dance of panic and urgency.

"Holy fuck!" My scream tore through the silence that had once again settled over the lagoon, a silence that now felt ominous. "What the fuck is Joel doing here?" The name slipped from my lips, a realisation that deepened the mystery and horror of the moment.

Luke was rendered speechless, his struggle for words a visible representation of our collective disbelief. The situation unfolded like a nightmarish tableau, each of us caught in the grip of a reality that was as incomprehensible as it was terrifying.

As I rushed forward, every fibre of my being was taut with urgency, the reality of the situation unfolding before me slicing through any lingering disbelief. Kneeling beside the young man, whose body lay eerily still on the sandbar, a wave of emotion crashed over me. Tears began to form, stinging my eyes with a salty burn, a physical manifestation of the shock and denial swirling within me. It was a moment suspended in time, where hope and despair mingled in the harsh light of day.

Leaning in closer, desperate for any sign of life, I found it. "He's still breathing!" The words burst from me, a lifeline thrown into the abyss of fear that had momentarily engulfed me. Relief, sharp and potent, cut through the fog of panic as I prepared to act.

Positioning myself behind Joel's head, I reached forward, my hands finding the solid, unresponsive mass of his shoulders. The intention was clear: to drag him from the perilous grasp of the water, to bring him back to the safety of solid ground.

But then, unexpectedly, firm hands clasped around me, pulling with a force that spoke of urgency and fear. The suddenness of the action caught me off guard, my grip slipping as I lost my balance, the ground rising to meet me with a jarring thud. Dust billowed around me, a gritty cloud marking my fall.

Fury ignited within me as I scrambled to my knees, confusion and anger intertwining into a volatile mix. My hand, clenched into a fist, flew towards Luke's face, full of my bewildered rage. He dodged, his movements reflexive, a dance of survival honed by instinct.

"What the fuck did you do that for?" The words tore from my throat, a raw expression of betrayal and hurt. My voice was a weapon, sharpened by fear and frustration, spitting out the question like a challenge.

"Take a look at his throat," Luke's response cut through the tension, a directive that carried with it the weight of unseen truths.

Turning back to Joel, the world seemed to narrow to the horrific sight before me. Each blink was a futile attempt to clear the tears that scorched my eyes, each one a testament to the disbelief and despair gripping my heart. Crouching over him, time seemed to stand still as I confronted the reality of the deep gash across his throat—a wound so severe, so final, that my mind rebelled against its implications. *Surely the arteries have been severed. This isn't real. It just can't be.* Desperation clawed at the edges of my consciousness, a frantic wish for escape from this nightmare that refused to release its hold. Rage surged from the depths of my being, a tidal wave of emotion that threatened to overwhelm my senses.

"What the fuck!" The outcry was a raw explosion of grief and confusion, my hands acting on instinct as I attempted to pull Joel away from the mocking serenity of the lagoon's waters. His body, so familiar and yet rendered so alien by this brutal act, seemed an anchor dragging me further into despair.

"Jamie, stop!" Luke's voice was a distant call, attempting to pierce the fog of my fury.

"Jamie!" Another voice, young and familiar, cut across the lagoon, momentarily halting the chaos within me.

"What the fuck have you done, Luke?" The accusation tore from me, a desperate attempt to find a target for the maelstrom of emotions that battered my psyche. My footing lost, I tumbled to the ground, the impact a cruel reminder of the physical reality of our situation. Tears blurred my vision, each one a tribute to the incomprehensible loss laid bare beside me—the lifeless body of my son, a truth too cruel to bear.

"Help me take him back to camp," I croaked, the plea a ragged whisper of hopelessness. The impossibility of acceptance, of understanding, clawed at me, even as I sought the assistance of those around me to carry Joel back to the semblance of civilisation we had in our camp. It was a task born of necessity, a final act of care in the face of an unspeakable tragedy.

"Wait," Glenda's voice cut through. "Let me check him first." Her intervention, authoritative yet gentle, brought a momentary pause to the nightmare unfolding around me.

I watched, my heart caught in my throat, as Glenda squatted beside Joel with the precision and care of a seasoned professional. She took her time, her examination thorough, her demeanour calm amidst the storm of emotions raging around her. When she let out a surprised gasp, my heart skipped a beat, hope flaring in the darkness. Her hand moved with a tenderness that belied the gravity of the situation, sliding under Joel's shirt to rest on his stomach. It was a gesture of discovery, of connection, a bridge between despair and the faintest whisper of hope.

"He's breathing," she announced, her words slicing through the thick air like a lifeline thrown into tumultuous waters.

"Joel," I whispered, my voice barely audible, as I placed my palm lightly on my son's forehead. The reality of her words, the fact that Joel was breathing, ignited a flicker of hope within me, fragile and desperate.

"But barely," Glenda continued, grounding us in the harsh reality of Joel's condition. "I think he may actually be alive. But I don't understand how that is possible." Her professional analysis, stark and bewildering, laid bare the miracle and mystery of his survival. "His colour suggests he has lost so much blood that his circulatory system has collapsed." Her gaze met mine, a silent affirmation of the criticality of the situation, yet her next words offered a sliver of hope, a course of action amidst the helplessness. "You're right. I agree we should bring him back to camp."

The agonised tension that had contorted my face eased slightly at Glenda's words.

"What? Seriously?" Luke's incredulity echoed the surreal nature of our predicament.

"Help us," I pleaded, desperation lending strength to my voice as I slid my hands underneath Joel, ready to do whatever it took to save him.

Luke, after a moment of hesitation, joined us, his actions speaking louder than any words could. Positioned across from Glenda, he too slid his arms beneath Joel's limp form, ready to assist in the delicate task ahead.

"Ready. Lift," Glenda's voice was firm, guiding us through the motions with the assurance of her expertise.

As we lifted Joel together, a sharp pain lanced across my chest, a physical reminder of my own ongoing healing. I suppressed a grimace, pushing aside the discomfort. Joel's life hung in the balance. The weight of his body in our arms was a weight I would carry a thousand times over if it meant bringing him back from the brink. In that moment, as we moved together towards hope, Joel was all that mattered.

As we navigated the edge of the lagoon, the presence of my nephew, Kain, barely penetrated the turmoil of my thoughts. His sudden appearance, stepping in to assist us, should have brought relief, but instead, it only added to the confusion and frustration swirling inside me. There he was, thrust into the middle of this nightmare, his vibrant youth a stark contrast to the gravity of our situation. The camp's latest arrival, now part of this harrowing journey back, seemed both surreal and desperately needed.

Ignoring the glances from Luke, my emotions teetered on the edge of a precipice. The anger, a fierce and relentless force, threatened to consume me once more. The reality of carrying Joel, my son whose existence had only recently come to light, was overwhelming. And now, with Kain involved, the situation felt even more personal, more dire. *What the fuck is going on inside Luke's head!?* The thought was a venomous whisper in my mind. *If Clivilius doesn't kill Luke, I'll bloody do it myself.*

"You coming, Paul?" Glenda's voice, calling across the lagoon to where Paul sat in a daze, barely registered as a distant echo. The urgency of our mission to get Joel back to camp, to safety, was paramount.

"I'll meet you there soon," came Paul's distant reply, his voice a thread of sound carried on the wind.

With a deep, impatient breath, I steeled myself against the whirlwind of my emotions. *We have to keep moving.* The imperative to continue, to lead the way through the uncertainty, lent me a semblance of purpose amidst the despair.

Encouraging the others with a decisive step, I led our small, burdened procession forward. The journey back to camp, through thick dust and over undulating hills, felt endless—a trek across a landscape that mirrored the desolation in my heart. The wide expanse of nothingness that stretched out before me was a physical manifestation of the void within, a path that I trudged with a singular goal: to bring Joel to a place where hope, however fragile, might still exist.

SURRENDER - PART 2

4338.207.3

"Put him on the mattress," I commanded, the urgency clear in my voice as the campfire came into view. The weight of Joel in our arms grew heavier with each step.

"I don't think that's a good idea. We only have one. He could be infected," Glenda countered, her voice laced with concern. Her objection, pragmatic as it was, struck a nerve.

I halted in my tracks, the frustration boiling over. "Bit late to say that now," I retorted sharply. "If Joel's infected then it's likely we are too." The words hung between us, a grim acknowledgment of our shared vulnerability.

Glenda's expression tightened, the muscles in her face betraying the internal conflict she felt between her medical instincts and the reality of our predicament.

"Jamie's right," Luke chimed in, siding with the decision to proceed despite the risks. "We may as well."

With a tense nod, Glenda conceded, stepping forward to hold the tent flap open.

Inside the tent, Kain sprang into action, stripping the blankets from the mattress with a haste born of necessity. Together, Luke and I gently placed Joel down.

Luke stepped back, a silent observer to the unfolding scene. I, too, found myself moving aside, making space for Glenda to take over. She knelt beside the mattress, her posture one of focused attention as she leaned over Joel. I watched silently, as she examined him, her eyes and fingers moving with practiced care.

Her gaze lingered on Joel's eyes, those bright, blue orbs that seemed to defy the pallor of his skin, shining with a vitality that belied his condition. For a moment, time seemed to stand still, the connection between them a bridge of silent communication.

A sense of pride welled up within me, an emotion fierce and tender in its intensity. *Joel definitely has my eyes.* The realisation was a beacon of light in the darkness, a link between father and son that no circumstance could sever. A smile, weary yet genuine, found its way to my face, a silent tribute to the resilience and hope that Joel represented.

As Glenda inhaled deeply, her subsequent words seemed to hang in the air, heavy with implications that defied logic. "Both Carotid arteries seem to have healed, assuming they were ever severed." Her analysis was clinical, yet her voice carried an undercurrent of disbelief. "Aside from the obvious slice across his throat and what I'd assume are bumps and bruises from his time in the river, he doesn't appear to have any other major physical wounds." Her brows furrowed in concentration as she grappled with the incongruity of Joel's condition. "I'm not sure how he could have lost all this blood if not through major artery damage."

Luke's input only served to solidify the mystery, his confirmation blunt. "His throat was definitely slit. There was a lot of blood."

His words acted as a spark to the powder keg of emotions within me. My body tensed, a mixture of anger and disbelief coursing through me with the force of a tempest.

Glenda's response to Luke's assertion was a casual shrug, an outward sign of her internal struggle to make sense of the situation. "It's not making much sense," she admitted, her professional calm at odds with the confusion that clouded her features.

My patience shattered. "What do you mean you know his throat was slit?" The question burst from me, a demand for clarity in the swirling maelanage of half-truths and mysteries. "And how the fuck would you know how much blood there was?" The accusation flew from my lips, aimed squarely at Luke, a pointed challenge that left no room for ambiguity. My words were a manifestation of the turmoil within, a demand for answers that seemed as elusive as the shadows that danced across the tent's canvas walls.

Luke's question, seemingly an attempt to navigate the tension, did little to quell the storm within me. His inquiry about defensive wounds felt like a diversion, a sidestep around the core of my anger. Glenda's confirmation, "No, none," only deepened the mystery. "Were you expecting any?" her subsequent question to Luke hinting at her own search for understanding.

Luke's response, that the lack of defensive wounds suggested a quick, surprising attack, did nothing to soothe my frayed nerves. My glare remained fixed, my hands involuntarily forming fists, the physical manifestation of my inner turmoil. "Well? You haven't answered my question," I demanded, my voice a tight coil of anger, seeking not just answers but accountability.

Luke took a deep breath. "Joel was the driver that delivered the tents back home. I was surprised to see him; I didn't recognise him at first. Not until I saw his name sewn into his shirt," he explained.

The collective gasp that rippled through the tent was a shared reaction to the revelation, a unison of shock and disbelief.

As Glenda carefully revealed the small rip in Joel's shirt, the evidence of his identity laid bare, the name "Joel" served as a stark reminder of the person at the heart of this enigma.

"Henri and Duke coming here was all an accident," Luke continued to defend himself. "Joel accidentally let Henri outside and he ran through the Portal when we tried to catch him. I forgot I was still carrying Duke when I followed after Henri." His words, a confession of sorts, painted a picture of unintended consequences, of actions and reactions spiralling beyond control.

"And Joel saw all of this?" Glenda's question, cautious yet probing, sought clarification, a need to understand the extent of Joel's involvement.

"Yes," Luke confirmed. "And when I returned, I found him lying in a pool of blood in the back of the truck."

Kain's soft exclamation, "Holy shit," mirrored the disbelief and shock that rippled through me, a sentiment that seemed to echo off the tent's fabric walls.

"But that was yesterday," I found myself saying, the timeline gnawing at me, a glaring gap in our shared understanding of events. "Why didn't you tell me?" The question, heavy with accusation and betrayal, hung between us, a chasm that seemed to widen with each passing second.

Luke's response, a dry gulp followed by the admission, "I thought you'd blame me for it," was like a spark to kindling. His words, meant to explain, only served to ignite the anger that had been smouldering within me. "I do fucking blame you for it!" The cry was torn from the depths of my being, a raw outburst of frustration and pain.

Glenda's attempt to intervene, her voice firm and authoritative, briefly cut through the tension. Yet, my accusations continued, a torrent of blame and incredulity directed at Luke. "And then you brought him here and dumped his body in the fucking river! That's some seriously fucked up shit!"

Luke's denial, a shout laden with desperation and horror, "It wasn't me! I would never do something so terrible!" was a plea for understanding, a defence against the unthinkable.

Glenda's second intervention, louder and more forceful, "Boys! Stop it!" demanded attention, her voice a command that brooked no dissent.

The tent, in the wake of her demand, succumbed to an eerie silence, a heavy quiet that seemed to press in from all sides. The weight of the revelations, the accusations, and the denials hung in the air, a palpable tension that no one dared to break. In that silence, the gravity of our situation settled over us, a sombre cloak that offered no warmth, only the cold realisation of the complexity and heartache that lay ahead.

Breaking the silence, I found my voice, albeit quieter, more controlled than before. "Well, what did you do with the body?" The question, while direct, was asked with a restraint born from a deep-seated need to understand, to piece together the fragmented reality we were now navigating.

"We buried him," Luke's admission was simple, yet it carried the weight of actions taken in desperation, decisions made in the shadow of unimaginable circumstances.

My skepticism must have been evident, but before I could articulate the flood of questions swirling in my mind, Glenda voiced the query that loomed the largest. "We?" Her single word, sharp and incisive, cut to the heart of the matter.

Luke's response, a hesitant admission, "Beatrix, Gladys and I," unveiled yet another layer to this complex tapestry of events.

"This is insane," Kain muttered, an echo of the confusion and incredulity that gripped us all.

Glenda's professional assessment brought us back to the immediate concern—Joel's inexplicable condition. "I really don't understand any of this at all," she said. "But I can do some basic surgery and stitch his throat back up. I can't guarantee anything. He might be breathing and have his eyes open, but that doesn't mean that he is actually alive. He hasn't spoken and isn't responding to any of my stimuli," she explained.

"So, what does that mean? What's happening to him?" My question, voiced amidst the tumult of my thoughts, sought clarity in the face of overwhelming ambiguity.

Glenda's admission of uncertainty, "I really don't know," was a testament to the complexity of Joel's condition, a puzzle that defied easy answers.

Luke's retreat marked a turning point in our conversation.

"Alright," I found myself saying, a resolve settling over me despite the uncertainty. "What do you need?" My offer of support to Glenda, a commitment to do whatever was necessary, was a small act of defiance against the distress that threatened to consume me.

Glenda's hesitant start, "Well... I need..." trailed off, a moment of vulnerability that laid bare the enormity of the task before us.

Crouching beside her, I placed my hand on her shoulder, an attempt to offer comfort, to bridge the gap between despair and determination.

Glenda looked over at me. "I'm going to do a horizontal mattress suture. I need a medium saline solution with... gloves... needle..." Her words melded into a blur of medical jargon that left me feeling utterly out of my depth. My gaze locked with hers, but my mind was adrift, grappling with the reality of the situation. *What the hell did Glenda just say?* The thought echoed in my head, a mix of confusion and concern. The term "basic surgery" seemed a gross understatement for what was about to happen.

"You stay here and watch him," Glenda told me, and giving me a firm pat on the shoulder, she got to her feet. "I won't be long," she said. "I'll just get what I need from the medical tent and be straight back," she promised.

"You stay here and watch him," Glenda instructed, her hand on my shoulder grounding me momentarily to the present. Her assurance that she would return promptly did little to ease the swirling thoughts. *When did Luke and Kain leave?* The realisation that I was now alone with Joel, save for his unconscious presence, dawned on me slowly. Luke's rapid departure, likely spurred by guilt and confusion, left me to face the unfolding drama with only my thoughts for company.

Turning back to Joel, the weight of recent discoveries pressed heavily on me. "I only found out you existed a few months ago," I found myself whispering, a confession to both Joel and myself. The absurdity of our situation, the mystery surrounding his condition, lay between us, unspoken yet palpable. I halted mid-sentence, the reality that Joel's condition defied logical explanation hanging heavily in the air.

Yet, as I gazed into his eyes—those wide, blue eyes that mirrored my own yet revealed nothing of his condition—I felt a resolve harden within me. Despite the bewildering circumstances, the lack of answers, and the myriad of questions that remained, hope stubbornly took root. Joel's life, however precarious it might seem, was not something I could easily resign to fate. The determination to cling to hope, to believe in the possibility of his survival, became a beacon in the storm, a steadfast resolve that no matter how bizarre or inexplicable the situation, I would not give up on my son.

❖

Within two minutes, which felt more like an eternity in the thick tension of the tent, Glenda returned to our makeshift operation scene. She moved with a purpose, her steps quick and determined as she knelt beside Joel's prone form. With a brisk motion, she donned a pair of blue medical gloves, the material snapping against her wrists. She then handed another pair to me, her eyes meeting mine with a seriousness that cemented the gravity of the situation. "You'd better wear these," she directed, her voice carrying the weight of her medical authority.

I donned the gloves quickly, the blue fabric stretching over my large hands, which felt clumsy and oversized in the moment. The latex hugged my skin tightly, a tangible reminder of the severity of the situation we found ourselves in.

"Now, hold this tray for me," she instructed, handing over a sterile metal tray filled with medical instruments. Nodding quickly, I took the tray from Glenda, my hands shaking as if they were betraying my attempt to appear composed.

"And try not to tremble too much," said Glenda, her voice sharp but not unkind. "I don't need any other distractions." I nodded again, more quickly this time, feeling the weight of her expectation and the responsibility on my shoulders. My hands steadied slightly, motivated by the need to be useful, to not let Joel—or Glenda—down in this critical moment.

Glenda began to prepare Joel's neck wound for suturing with a focus that was both impressive and intimidating. The room felt charged with a silent urgency, every move she made was precise and calculated. The air felt heavier, charged with the palpable tension of life hanging in the balance.

"Why a mattress suture?" I found myself asking, my curiosity getting the better of me despite the situation. I was trying hard to show Glenda that I could keep a level head, that I was more than just a pair of trembling hands holding a tray.

"No unnecessary talking during surgery," she said flatly, her focus unwavering from the task at hand. Her reprimand was a clear reminder of the seriousness of our makeshift operation, a slap back to reality that this was no time for a medical inquisition.

I gulped dryly, the lump in my throat growing. Despite her strong exterior, I could sense a flicker of uncertainty in Glenda's eyes, a shared human moment that revealed she might be almost as scared as I was. Yet, her hands were steady, her movements sure. I really hoped she knew what she was doing. In the silence that followed, filled only with the sound of our breathing I found a moment of internal solace. *She's a doctor*, I told myself silently, clinging to this fact like a lifeline. *Of course she knows what she's doing.*

As Glenda finally began the surgery, the cold light of the tent seemed to sharpen, focusing intently on the small, critical space of Joel's neck wound. She grasped the edge with forceps, and I couldn't help but flinch as she drove the needle through his skin with a precision that belied the gruesomeness of the act. The medical instruments rattled ominously on the tray, a jarring soundtrack to my uncontrollable shaking hands. This moment was a stark, harrowing departure from the relatively benign emergencies I'd encountered before, far worse than the time I had to assist Luke in carefully extracting a long splinter lodged deep within Henri's paw, where the worst outcome was a whimper and a lick.

Glenda paused in her meticulous work, her gaze shifting to me, piercing through the tension. "You okay there, Jamie?" she asked, her voice a mix of concern and focus. "You're not about to pass out?" Her question, though straightforward, carried an undercurrent of support, a recognition of the strain of our unconventional operation room.

"No, I'm fine. Sorry," I managed to reply, my voice betraying the whirlwind of emotions inside me. "You're doing a great job," I added, attempting to mask my unease with encouragement. It felt necessary to acknowledge her skill, even if just to break the heavy silence with words of support.

"We've got a long way to go yet," she replied, her voice steady, grounding us both in the moment. Her determination was a beacon in the fog of my fear, a reminder of the gravity of Joel's situation and the need for steadfastness.

With a renewed sense of purpose, I forced myself to focus on the surgery, to watch as Glenda confidently drove the needle through the other side of Joel's sliced neck. The needle pierced the skin, re-emerging on the opposite side with a precision that was both awe-inspiring and terrifying. My hands, however, betrayed my attempt at composure, trembling anew with the visceral reality of the situation.

I closed my eyes briefly, seeking solace in the darkness behind my lids. I inhaled deeply, trying to steady the storm within. *It's only for a moment.* The words echoed in my mind, a mantra to anchor me to the present, to the necessity of the task at hand. "Just for a moment," I whispered under my breath, a silent pledge to myself and to Joel. I opened my eyes, resolved to bear witness, to support Glenda's skilled hands with my own, however unsteady they might be. This moment, as harrowing as it was, was about survival, about doing whatever it took to save my son.

The passage of time seemed to defy all natural laws. Seconds stretched into minutes, each minute dilating into what felt like an endless hour. My role, largely that of a spectator armed with a tray of surgical instruments, forced me into a state of hyper-awareness. Every so often, I had to close my eyes, if only to escape the sight of Joel's open wound, to give myself a momentary reprieve from the tension that clung to the air like a thick fog.

It was during one of these brief retreats into darkness that I heard Glenda's voice cut through the heavy silence, her tone vibrant with triumph. "We did it!" she exclaimed loudly, her words acting as a beacon, pulling me back to the present. My eyes snapped open, the moment of relief lasting longer than I had initially anticipated. The surge of hope that followed her announcement was palpable, washing over me like a wave, offering a brief respite from the relentless anxiety that had taken residence in my chest.

I looked down at Joel, my son, lying still on the mattress. Glenda had closed the slice on his neck with perfect precision, her skilled hands transforming what once was a gaping wound into a neatly sutured line. The sight of it, so clinical yet so profoundly personal, stirred a complex mixture of emotions within me.

"So, he'll be okay now?" I found myself asking, my voice laced with a cautious optimism. The question hung in the air between us, fragile and laden with the weight of a father's hope.

For a fleeting moment, Glenda's smile had been a reassuring beacon. But as quickly as it appeared, it vanished, replaced by a sombre expression that seemed to draw the warmth from the room. The shift was jarring, like a sudden plunge into cold water, and a lump formed in my throat as my heart sank, heavy with dread.

The absence of her smile, that sudden withdrawal of reassurance, spoke volumes, conveying a complexity of outcomes that words could not. It was a stark reminder that the path to recovery was fraught with uncertainty, that the closing of a physical wound did not immediately translate to a guarantee of well-being.

The moment Joel gasped for air, it shattered the fragile calm that had settled over us. His desperate attempts to breathe, so reminiscent of a fish out of water gasping for life, sent a jolt of fear straight through my heart. The stark, haunting image of my son struggling for each breath was something I could have never prepared for, an ordeal that seemed to wrench the very soul from my chest.

Caught utterly off guard by the sudden turn of events, my grip faltered, and the tray I had been holding, along with its meticulously arranged medical instruments, crashed to the floor of the tent. The loud clang echoed off the canvas walls, a grim soundtrack to the chaos unfurling before my eyes.

Glenda, too, was taken by surprise. She fell backwards with a startled exclamation, "Shit," a rare slip that underscored the abruptness of the situation.

"Help him," I insisted, my voice tinged with panic, as if my words could somehow bridge the gap between our desperation and the solution we so urgently needed. But the rushing panic was not just in my head; it was a tidal wave threatening to engulf me.

"I don't understand," Glenda replied, her voice laced with confusion and a hint of fear. "This is out of my scope. I'm not trained for this." Her admission was a cold splash of reality, a stark reminder of our isolation and the limitations we faced. My eyes widened in fear at her words. *What does she mean, not trained? She had just stitched his throat back together with such confidence and skill. How could this be beyond her?*

In a frantic effort to regain control, Glenda grabbed hold of Joel's arms, pinning them down as his body began to convulse, a terrifying testament to his struggle. The sight of my son in such a state, fighting against his own body, was a sight so devastating that it threatened to break me.

And then, as abruptly as it had begun, Joel went still. His eyelids fluttered closed, the storm of convulsions ceasing as a haunting silence filled the tent. The absence of movement, the sudden stillness, was as shocking as the convulsions had been. My heart, which had been racing moments before, now felt as if it had stopped entirely, caught in the horrifying limbo of waiting for what would come next.

As I stared, wide-eyed, at my son's motionless form, a chilling wave of disbelief washed over me. *What's happening?* The question ricocheted through my mind, a desperate plea for some semblance of understanding. *Why did Joel's eyes close?*

Slowly, with a heaviness that seemed to pull at her very soul, Glenda released her grip on Joel and backed away. Her movements were those of someone carrying a burden far too heavy, her next words even heavier. "I'm so sorry, Jamie. He really isn't alive," she told me, her voice barely above a whisper, her eyes unable to meet mine. The distance she put between us felt like a chasm.

My head began to swirl with emotion, a maelstrom of confusion, denial, and burgeoning grief. *I don't understand.* The thought was a mantra, a feeble attempt to shield myself from the truth. *Glenda's a doctor. She's supposed to save him.* The role of a healer, a saviour, was one I had unconsciously bestowed upon her, and the realisation that even she had limits was a bitter pill that I wasn't yet prepared to swallow. I gave a big sniff, struggling to navigate through the fog of my emotions. "Can't you resuscitate him?" I asked, my voice breaking between light sobs, clinging to the hope that perhaps, just perhaps, there was something more that could be done.

"He has no blood for his heart to pump around his body," Glenda explained slowly, the weight of each word seemingly crushing her. "I'm sorry, Jamie," she whispered, a solitary tear tracing its way down her cheek—a testament to the depth of her empathy, to the pain of bearing witness to such a loss.

It was then, in the depths of my despair, that the soft voice of Clivilius spoke inside my mind, offering a stark contrast to the tangible grief that enveloped me. *Surrender to me, Jamie.* The words, imbued with an eerie calm, promised an escape, a way out. *New life, remember?*

But, I replied silently, my mind grappling with the offer, the temptation. *But I don't understand.* The confusion was overwhelming, a tumultuous sea in which I was drowning. *I thought you'd already given me new life?* The question was a plea for clarity, for some sign that the bargain struck was not in vain, that there was still hope amidst the despair.

Surrender, Jamie Greyson, the voice whispered again, a siren's call beckoning me towards an unknown fate.

In that moment, a primal, instinctual understanding surged within me, guiding my actions with a clarity that seemed to cut through the fog of despair. I reached out, my hand firmly grasping Glenda's arm, compelling her attention towards the desperate plan forming in my mind. "We have to take him back to the lagoon," I declared, my voice imbued with a determination that brooked no argument, even as it masked the tempest of fear and hope wrestling within me.

"But why?" Glenda countered, her confusion evident in the shake of her head, her brow furrowed in a mixture of skepticism and concern. "What good will that do him now?" Her question, logical and laden with the weight of reality, sought to anchor me back to the harshness of our present circumstances.

"We have to try," I insisted, my resolve undeterred. I quickly crouched above Joel's head, my hands positioning themselves under his shoulders in preparation to lift him. The action, so simple yet so charged with urgency, was a physical manifestation of my refusal to succumb to despair.

"It's no use, Jamie. He's gone," Glenda said softly, her voice a gentle, sorrowful attempt to cushion the blow, to bring me back to the cruel finality we faced. Her words, meant to be kind, instead felt like another brick of grief added to my burden.

Tears streamed down my face without restraint, the dam of my emotions breached by the overwhelming tide of loss and desperation. "Please, Glenda," I begged, my voice breaking, my plea a raw, exposed nerve. "Help me." The vulnerability in my request laid bare the depth of my anguish, a father's plea for his child's life.

Another silent tear traced its way down Glenda's cheeks, a mirror to my own sorrow. She closed her eyes, perhaps in a moment of prayer, of resignation, or of gathering strength. "Please," I croaked through the pain, the word barely more than a whisper torn from the depths of my despair.

Surrender! Clivilius roared within my mind, the voice demanding, unyielding.

Driven by desperation, I lifted Joel with a soft grunt, the effort burning my chest, every muscle strained under the weight of my son and the weight of our shared ordeal. Joel's feet fell from the mattress with a soft thud, a poignant reminder of the gravity of my actions as I dragged him around the still kneeling Glenda and across the tent, a macabre procession fuelled by a father's love and a sliver of hope.

Glenda, witnessing the depth of my determination, rose to her feet and helped me lift Joel's shoulders, her actions a silent concession to my plea, a joining of forces in the face of the incomprehensible. Knowing Glenda's sense of helplessness, recognising the sacrifice of her professional judgment in this moment of shared humanity, I gave her a silent nod of appreciation. It was a small gesture, but within it lay the entirety of my gratitude and the unspoken understanding between us: in the face of the unfathomable, we choose to act, to try, despite the odds.

As we emerged from the tent, the stark contrast between the inside's sombre atmosphere and the outside's harsh, unyielding daylight struck me with force. Glenda's voice, strained yet clear, cut through the heavy air as she called out, "Paul! Kain!" Her words were a beacon, summoning aid in our moment of desperate need as we navigated the uneven ground with Joel's heavy, lifeless body between us.

The toll of the emotional and physical strain became abruptly visible when Glenda's legs gave way. Her knees hit the dust with a dull thud, stirring up a cloud that momentarily enveloped her in a fine, gritty haze. The sight of her collapsing, even as she clung to her professionalism, was a vivid reminder of the day's harrowing reality.

Paul and Kain, responding with the urgency Glenda's call demanded, rushed toward us. Their approach was swift, their faces etched with concern and confusion, mirroring the tumultuous swirl of emotions churning within me. I wished I could help her, extend a hand to lift her from the ground, but my arms were bound in duty to Joel.

With a resilience that seemed to define her, Glenda brushed herself off, the dust clinging to her clothes serving as a stark symbol of our ordeal. She rose to her feet, her movements quick but shaky.

"I'll take him," Paul announced, his voice firm, offering a semblance of stability. He reached across Glenda, his hands finding purchase on Joel's shoulder, an act of solidarity and support.

"Where are we taking him?" Kain's voice, laden with a mix of uncertainty and readiness to act, broke through the thick air as he relieved me of Joel's other shoulder.

"To the lagoon," Glenda instructed, her voice carrying the weight of command yet underscored by a tremor of vulnerability. Her directive, concise and clear, propelled us forward, a small procession united in a singular, desperate purpose. The lagoon, a place of natural beauty and tranquility, now beckoned us with the promise of miracles, of salvation found in the embrace of its serene waters.

NEW LIFE

4338.207.4

As we navigated the terrain toward the lagoon, the weight of Joel's limp body shifted between us, a tangible manifestation of the burden we carried in our hearts. The solemn procession, marked by the heavy silence and the softness of the dust beneath our feet, seemed to stretch on indefinitely, each step a testament to the gravity of our shared purpose.

Upon reaching the lagoon, a place that had once offered escape, I found myself propelled forward by a sense of urgency that eclipsed everything else. I rushed ahead of the group, driven by a desperate hope that the lagoon's waters could somehow reverse the irreversible. The immediate zing of sexual exhilaration that shot through me as my exposed legs made contact with the cool water was a stark, almost jarring contrast to the solemnity of our arrival. Yet, even this fleeting sensation was quickly subdued by the gravity of the moment.

I held Joel's head with a gentleness born of both love and fear, steadying him as Kain and Paul carefully lowered his body into the water. The cool embrace of the lagoon seemed to hold us in a moment suspended in time, a fragile bubble of hope amidst the crushing reality of our situation.

"Make sure he is on his back," Glenda's voice cut through the tense air, her directive sharp amid the flurry of our actions.

My eyes widened as I watched Kain splash into the lagoon without hesitation, his actions marked by a resolve that mirrored my own. The sight of him, so fully committed to our shared cause, bolstered my resolve, reminding me that we were not alone in this— that in our darkest hour, we had each other.

"No!" I called out to Paul, noticing his intention to untie his shoes, a move that seemed incongruent with the urgency of our task. "Kain and I have got him covered," I insisted, my voice laced with a determination that left no room for delay. In that moment, my focus was singular: to protect Kain, to preserve his dignity from the lagoon's intense urges that he would undoubtedly quickly feel. It was a testament to the depth of my love for my nephew, a love that demanded acknowledgement, even in the face of overwhelming despair.

As Kain and I waded deeper into the lagoon, the cool water enveloping us with a surreal calm, we carefully assisted Joel's body, ensuring it maintained a stable floating position. The act, so deliberate and filled with intent, seemed to bridge the gap between the realms of hope and despair, a silent prayer offered to the serene waters.

"You sure?" Paul's voice, tinged with concern and uncertainty, carried over the water, breaking the solemn stillness that surrounded us.

"Certain," I replied, my voice stronger than I felt, echoing my resolve back to him. There was no room for doubt, not here, not in these moments that felt suspended between the world we knew and something else, something beyond comprehension.

I motioned to Kain, signalling him to follow my lead further into the depths of the lagoon. It was crucial to keep our backs to Paul and Glenda, a silent agreement between us to shield them from the raw intensity of our endeavour. As the water reached our upper bodies, the reality of our actions settled around us like a cloak, heavy with significance.

The decision to move deeper into the water, away from the prying eyes of our companions, was more than a strategic manoeuvre; it was a gesture of protection, a way to maintain a semblance of privacy and dignity in this most vulnerable of moments. The cool embrace of the lagoon seemed to understand, its waters whispering around us, carrying our burdens with a gentleness that belied the strength of its currents.

"Just ignore it," I whispered quickly, watching Kain's face contort uncomfortably. "It'll pass," I lied, knowing full well that overwhelming sexual desire was unavoidable.

Paul's voice, carrying a note of frustration mixed with concern, echoed across the water, breaking the spell of concentrated silence that had enveloped Kain and me. "It would be nice if they didn't keep their backs to us. I can't see much at all," he said, his words slicing through the heavy air with an edge of helplessness. From the corner of my eye, I saw Kain glance across at me, a silent query in the brief connection, wondering if we should reconsider our stance, to offer Paul and Glenda a semblance of inclusion in this uncertain vigil.

I shook my head, the motion almost imperceptible, a silent command born of a desperate need to maintain a private circle of hope around Joel, to protect this last vestige of belief from the piercing eyes of skepticism. Kain understood, his nod subtle as he stayed his course, our shared resolve solidifying in the unspoken agreement.

Then, as if in response to our collective yearning for a miracle, speckles of tiny, faint glow began to emerge in the water, drawing closer to the surface. This ethereal display, unexpected and otherworldly, ignited a fresh spark of hope within my heart, a beacon in the overwhelming darkness of despair. Unblinking, I watched, entranced by the spectacle. Although I didn't understand the mechanics of what was unfolding before us, I was willing to trust Clivilius, to surrender to the possibility of the miraculous, at least for now.

The glow intensified, its acceleration mesmerising, a visual symphony of light that seemed to defy the very laws of nature. My gaze remained fixed on this luminescent display, a part of me unable to reconcile the sight with what I thought was possible. How it had survived for this long, how it had come to be here, at this moment of our greatest need, was beyond my comprehension. Yet, despite my lack of understanding, I watched in awe as the small glow of my sperm penetrated Joel's exposed flesh, disappearing within him as if called to a purpose far greater than I could fathom.

The air around us seemed to hold its breath, the world pausing in reverence to the mystery unfolding within the lagoon's embrace. In that moment, as the glow found its way into Joel, it felt as though we were standing on the precipice of something profound, a thin veil between despair and hope, between the known and the unknowable. My heart, heavy with grief and fear, dared to beat with a renewed intensity, buoyed by the sight of the impossible made possible, a testament to the power of faith, of belief in something greater than ourselves. Of the formidable power of true surrender.

❖

The moment Joel gasped loudly for air, it was as though time itself had paused, the sound slicing through the silence and marking the beginning of something miraculous. His bright blue eyes flew open, vibrant and full of life, a stark contrast to the stillness that had claimed him just moments before. The sight of him, so suddenly animated, filled me with a tumult of emotions, joy and disbelief warring within me.

"What's happening?" Glenda's voice, sharp with shock and disbelief, echoed across the lagoon, her professional demeanour momentarily overtaken by the sheer unexpectedness of the moment.

A broad smile uncontrollably spread across my face, an instinctive reaction to the sight of my son's revival. "He's breathing again," I yelled back, my voice carrying a mixture of triumph and relief, a beacon of hope in the face of the impossible.

Beside me, Kain stood frozen, his body rigid as if he were unable to process the turn of events. It was a sight so surreal, witnessing Joel's sudden return to the land of the living, that it momentarily suspended belief.

As Joel's arms began to twitch involuntarily, a sign of his body's reflexive struggle to adjust, a new urgency took hold. "Steady him," I instructed firmly, my focus narrowing to ensuring Joel's safety. The last thing we needed was for him to swallow water in his vulnerable state.

Kain's expression shifted, the surprise morphing into a stern concentration as he understood the gravity of the situation. He pressed Joel's left arm against his belly and moved in closer, his actions deliberate, ensuring Joel remained stable in the water.

"Just breathe gently. It's okay. You're okay," I found myself saying, my voice a calm, soothing presence for Joel. It was more than just words; it was a lifeline, a promise that he was not alone in this bewildering transition back to consciousness.

Gradually, Joel's breathing evened out, becoming a steady, rhythmic routine that was music to my ears. The panic and fear that had clenched my heart began to ebb away, replaced by a profound relief and a sense of awe at the resilience of life.

"He has blood now?" Kain's question, laden with surprise and a hint of incredulity, pulled me back from my reverie. He looked up at me, searching for confirmation, for some explanation that could make sense of what we'd just witnessed.

"Of course he does," I responded flatly, the answer leaving no room for doubt. Despite the surreal nature of the situation, in that moment, my belief didn't waver. The impossible had become possible, and I clung to that certainty with a fierce determination.

When Joel's twitching finally ceased, a sign that his body had calmed from its initial shock, Kain cautiously released Joel's arm. The gesture was a silent acknowledgment of stability, of a crisis averted and a miracle embraced. In the cool waters of the lagoon, we bore witness to a moment of rebirth, a testament to the unfathomable mysteries that lay just beyond the veil of our understanding.

As I held Joel gently in the lagoon, a warm smile spread across my face, a reflection of the burgeoning hope and relief that filled me. Joel's bright blue eyes, clear and alert, followed my every move.

"What's going on out there?" Glenda's voice, tinged with a mix of concern and professional duty, cut through the tranquil moment. I could hear the rustle of her movements as she started to remove her shoes and socks, her readiness to wade into the unknown with us evident in her actions.

"It's okay," I called back, my voice steady and reassuring. "We've got it under control," I told her, opting for a veil of simplicity over the complex, inexplicable truth of Joel's revival. The decision to withhold the full extent of what had transpired was born out of a protective instinct, a desire to shield this delicate moment from the harsh light of scrutiny and disbelief.

"But I really should examine him," Glenda insisted, her dedication to her role as a healer making her reluctant to stand by without offering her expertise. Her voice carried the weight of responsibility, a reminder of the world beyond the lagoon's waters that awaited us.

Ignoring Glenda's persistence, I continued to move Joel through the water, focusing on the here and now, on the gentle, rhythmic motions that seemed to soothe both him and me. The water around us, cool and calming, felt like a sanctuary, a haven from the storm of emotions and events that had led us to this point.

As the minutes passed, I caught sight of Paul and Glenda turning their backs on us from the corner of my eye. With a mixture of resignation and relief, they headed back to camp, their departure unmarked by so much as a simple wave. A part of me understood their decision, the need to retreat and process the day's events in their own way.

I breathed a sigh of relief as they disappeared from view. *They don't need to stay*, I thought, the realisation settling in with a sense of finality.

"I should probably leave too," Kain murmured, his voice carrying a hint of reluctance as he turned toward the shore, signalling the end of our shared vigil by the lagoon. His words, simple yet heavy with the implication of solitude, struck a chord of panic within me.

"Kain, wait!" I found myself rushing out the words, a surge of desperation to not be left alone colouring my plea. The prospect of facing the aftermath of today's events without the comfort of another's presence was suddenly more than I could bear.

Kain paused, turning back to look at me. His eyes, filled with a complex mix of understanding and a longing for release, begged silently for my permission to leave. It was a look that conveyed the weight of the day's events, a silent plea for respite.

"Please stay with me. Just for a while," I asked, my voice softening, imploring. In that moment, my request was more than a plea for companionship; it was an admission of my own vulnerability, of the need for support in the face of overwhelming emotions.

After a moment's hesitation, Kain slowly nodded his acceptance. Relief washed over me as I whispered, "Thank you," my gratitude sincere and profound.

Suddenly, Kain gasped, his body tensing as his eyes closed tightly. The abruptness of his reaction caught me off guard, confusion and concern flooding my mind in equal measure. *Is he okay? Is something wrong?* The questions tumbled through my thoughts, unvoiced but palpable.

Then, without warning, Kain's entire body shuddered, a visible manifestation of an internal struggle or realisation dawning upon him. My heart raced, anxiety spiking as I tried to decipher the cause of his distress.

As the realisation of what was about to happen dawned on me, a sense of urgency overtook my earlier concern. "Get out of the fucking water!" I yelled, the command tearing from my throat as fear and protection surged within me.

Kain's eyes flew open, wide with alarm, as he scrambled onto the shore. His movements were hurried, almost frantic, as his legs threatened to buckle beneath him, his knees sinking into the soft dust of the shoreline.

Despite my concern and the lingering fascination with the unfolding situation, I turned my gaze away from Kain, offering him a semblance of privacy in what appeared to be a profoundly personal moment. But I couldn't help grinning as the air was filled with Kain's loud, pleasurable moan, the kind of sound that reverberated with an overwhelming sense of ecstasy. The thud of Kain's body into the dust was distinct, followed by another soft moan, the epitome of intoxicating bliss.

When the heavy blanket of silence finally descended again, my curiosity overcame the hesitation, prompting me to glance towards Kain. Lying on his back, my nephew seemed to have succumbed to unconsciousness, overwhelmed by the sheer intensity of his experience. An unexpected laugh bubbled up from within me, a release of tension in the face of the surreal. "This lagoon is insane," I remarked, half to myself, half to Joel, whose presence beside me felt like an anchor.

As if summoned by my voice, Kain stirred, his hand coming up to shield his eyes from the relentless glare of the sun. Propping himself into a sitting position, his voice carried a mixture of confusion and awe. "What the hell just happened?" he called out, struggling to piece together the fragments of his experience.

"I'd say you've just had your first true orgasm," I replied with another loud chuckle.

Kain looked away, presumably embarrassed.

"You passed out," I explained, gently guiding Joel closer to the shore with a care that belied the casual nature of our conversation. "But don't worry. It was no more than a minute." My words were meant to reassure, to minimise the concern that shadowed his features.

Kain's cheeks flushed a deep shade of red, a visible sign of his embarrassment, or perhaps, the lingering effects of his experience. He averted his gaze once more, as if seeking solace in the lagoon's mysterious expanse.

The water splashed gently as I sat on the rocky bank of the lagoon, my feet dangled in the water, balancing Joel delicately from underneath his back as he continued to float calmly.

"Consider yourself lucky the others had left already," I offered with a light-hearted smile, attempting to inject a bit of humour into the situation, to ease the tension that still lingered in the air.

Kain's hesitation was palpable as he ventured a question, his curiosity piqued. "Is... Is this why you didn't let them come in?" he asked, his voice tinged with a newfound understanding of the lagoon's unpredictable nature.

"Mostly," I admitted, acknowledging the partial truth in his assumption. The lagoon, with its mysterious properties, was a place of both healing and transformation, its effects as unpredictable as they were profound.

"Only mostly?" Kain pressed, seeking clarity amidst the whirlwind of emotions and revelations.

My brows knitted together as I considered his question, the complexity of the lagoon's influence on us a puzzle yet to be fully understood. "I think it happens to all of us," I began, choosing my words with care. "But perhaps a little differently," I mused, hinting at the individual experiences that tied us to this place, each encounter with the lagoon's waters a personal journey of discovery and change.

"How differently?" Kain asked.

"Well, sure, I've felt aroused in the lagoon. But nothing like you experienced," I found myself confessing to my innocent nephew.

Kain's eyebrow arched in surprise, a silent question mark written across his face as he digested the information. His reaction, a mixture of curiosity and skepticism, prompted me to elaborate further, despite the complexities and uncertainties that surrounded the lagoon's mysterious properties.

"Parts of the river seem to have a similar effect. Although very minor," I added, trying to paint a broader picture of the natural wonders that seemed to envelop our surroundings.

The comparison was meant to provide some context, to somehow normalise the extraordinary events we had just experienced.

Kain's expression shifted to one of quizzical intrigue, his eyes searching mine for further explanation. "So," he began hesitantly, his voice laced with a cautious curiosity, "How do you think this affects Joel?" His question, direct and loaded with concern, pierced the protective veil I had unconsciously wrapped around the details of Joel's revival.

"Hmm," I murmured, buying myself a moment to think deeply about the implications of what had happened. "I uh..." My voice trailed off as I grappled with the enormity of the question. *Just how much should I be telling Kain?* I wondered internally, weighing the benefits of openness against the potential burden of knowledge. The responsibility of deciding what to share felt heavy, a balancing act between honesty and the need to protect.

Before I could formulate a response, Kain interjected, his voice cutting through my hesitation with an understanding that surprised me. "It's okay," he said, his tone gentle yet firm. "You don't have to explain, really." His words, offered as a reprieve, carried a warmth and acceptance that eased the tension knotting my shoulders.

Well, I thought, *if Kain is going to share personal moments with me, even if unwillingly, it's only fair that I return the favour. Besides, it feels good to have someone to talk to about it.*

"You saw that glow in the water, didn't you?" I asked.

"Yeah," Kain replied. "What was that? Looked like some sort of algae or something."

"It was sperm," I said, laughing lightly. "My sperm."

Kain's reaction was immediate, his mouth dropping open in a mix of shock and disbelief. "What the fuck," he whispered, the words barely escaping his lips. His astonishment was palpable, a raw response to the surreal events we'd just witnessed. "But I saw it enter Joel's body. Through his skin!" His voice carried a mixture of wonder and confusion, grappling with the reality of what his eyes had confirmed but his mind struggled to accept.

"Yeah," I acknowledged, my own voice tinged with a sense of wonder and confusion. The mysteries of the lagoon, its inexplicable effects on us, were as baffling to me as they were to him. "I don't really understand it at all. But I think the water might have healing properties. See this scab on my chest?" I queried, lifting my shirt to reveal the evidence of the lagoon's miraculous touch.

Kain's gasp was loud, a sharp intake of breath that echoed my earlier astonishment. The sight of the healed wound, which had once threatened my life, now reduced to a mere scab, was a testament to the lagoon's mysterious power.

"Just yesterday this was a life-threatening welt. I probably would have died if not for this lagoon," I explained, feeling a profound sense of gratitude wash over me. The reality of my survival, so closely linked to the lagoon's intervention, felt both humbling and surreal. "And Glenda," I quickly added, acknowledging her role in my recovery. Her medical expertise, combined with the lagoon's unexplainable healing properties, had snatched me back from the brink of death.

"Oh," Kain murmured softly, his voice a whisper in the silence that followed. The revelation seemed to settle over him, a heavy cloak of realisation that we were dealing with forces beyond our understanding.

"And what you saw today wasn't the first time," I continued, the weight of my next words hanging in the air between us.

"It wasn't?" Kain repeated, his surprise evident. The notion that what had occurred with Joel was part of a pattern, rather than an isolated incident, added another layer of complexity to the mystery enveloping the lagoon.

"No," I said. "I uh... I had a wank in the lagoon yesterday. As soon as I ejaculated, I noticed the glow immediately, so I assumed that's what it was."

Kain swallowed nervously. "So, that glow was still from yesterday?" he asked.

"I think so," I said quickly, and then my face screwed up with an odd sense of reflection. *I had come down here with Duke earlier.*

"What?" Kain prodded.

My nose scrunched as I thought how to reply. "Unless it was from someone else," I said. "But I'm pretty sure it was mine," I said confidently. It was what I needed to believe. Besides, now that I thought about it, I hadn't noticed Duke appearing the least bit affected or stimulated by the lagoon. Not that I had been paying that much attention. *But surely*, I told myself, *it would have been obvious if it had.*

"I should probably clean myself up," Kain announced, breaking the contemplative silence that had settled between us. With that, he pushed himself to his feet, his movements still slightly unsteady from the ordeal he'd just undergone.

"Make sure you take the river," I advised him, concern edging my voice. The river, with its deceptive calmness, could be unforgiving to the unwary. "But stay close to the edge. It gets deep quickly and has a strong current." My warning was borne of an intimate knowledge of the landscape we found ourselves in, a mixture of beauty and danger.

"Sure thing," Kain responded, his nod an acknowledgment of my caution.

"Hey, Kain?" I couldn't let him leave without expressing what weighed on my heart. As he paused, turning with a swivel that kicked up short bursts of dust, I found the courage to voice my thoughts.

"I'm sorry you ended up here," I told him, my sincerity flowing with the words. The regret for the circumstances that had pulled Kain into this surreal nightmare was genuine, a sentiment that tugged at me with the complexity of our situation. "But I'm glad we've got your help." It was important for him to know that despite the unforeseen and perhaps unwelcome challenges, his presence, his contributions, were deeply valued.

Kain's response was a simple shrug, an understated gesture that belied the depth of our shared experiences. Without another word, he turned and made his way toward the river, his figure gradually blending with the landscape until he disappeared around the bend and behind the hill.

❖

"Looks like it's just the two of us now," I murmured to Joel, the words a soft declaration in the quiet that surrounded us. As my feet began to cramp from the awkward position on the rocky bank, I allowed myself to slide back into the soothing embrace of the lagoon's water, seeking relief from the discomfort.

Joel's response was subtle yet unmistakable. His eyes blinked rapidly three times, a simple action that, in the context of our recent ordeal, felt monumental. My heart skipped a beat at the sight, a mix of hope and disbelief coursing through me.

I gasped, caught in a moment of pure astonishment. "Did you just...?" The words trailed off, my voice a whisper of awe, as the reality of Joel's awakening began to set in. It was a moment so fragile, so filled with emotion, that I found myself at a loss for words.

Then, as if to erase any doubt of his return to us, Joel's wet arm rose above the water, each droplet that fell from his skin back to the lagoon sparkling like a testament to the miracle I was witnessing. The sight of his movement, deliberate and filled with purpose, was a visual confirmation of his revival.

The warmth of Joel's hand on my bare flesh sent a jolt of emotion through me, a tangible connection that spoke volumes. His grip on my arm was tight, a silent communication of his presence, his return to the world of the living. It was a touch that conveyed so much more than words ever could, a lifeline that bridged the gap between despair and hope.

"Dad," Joel whispered, his voice croaky yet unmistakable. The sound of his voice, a sound I had feared I might never hear, was like a balm to my soul. In that single word, spoken with such effort and yet with such clarity, the world beyond seemed to fade into insignificance.

SON

4338.207.5

"Son," I whispered softly, my voice a mixture of wonder and relief as I gazed at Joel. "You're alive. You're really alive." The words felt surreal, echoing around us, affirming the impossible that had become our reality.

"I think so," Joel managed to croak out, his voice raspy and strained, barely above a whisper. The sound of his voice, though weak, was the most beautiful melody to my ears, a sign of life against all odds.

"Don't talk. Save your voice," I cautioned him gently. Reflecting on Luke's timeline, it dawned on me that Joel hadn't spoken for more than twenty-four hours. Considering the ordeal he had been through, including the lack of blood or moisture, it was inevitable that his throat would be sore and his voice raspy for a while. The priority was his recovery, his comfort.

"I'm going to try and bring you back out of the water now," I announced, preparing both him and myself for the next step. "We'll see what happens. The first sign of you slipping away again and we'll be straight back in here." The plan was clear in my mind, a delicate balance between hope and caution, ready to react at the slightest hint of distress.

Joel's response was a slow blink, leaving me to interpret his agreement or understanding. My brow furrowed in concentration. *Did that mean Joel agreed?* The need for clear communication pressed on me, urging me to find a simple yet effective way to ensure we understood each other.

Taking a deep breath, I ventured, "I know this sounds very cliché, but it seems to be effective in the movies. Blink once for no and twice for yes," I explained, hoping this method would bridge the gap between us, allowing Joel to express his needs without straining his voice.

"Do you understand me?" I asked, watching him closely for his response.

Joel blinked twice quickly, his action a clear affirmation that he understood my makeshift system of communication. A sigh of relief escaped me, my heart lighter, a grin spreading across my weary face at this small but significant sign. *Progress*, I reminded myself silently. *We're making progress.*

Gently, I navigated Joel's buoyant form towards the more rugged part of the lagoon's bank, aiming for an area where the rocks offered a semblance of stability. I found the largest, smoothest rock as a makeshift platform and, with care, climbed onto it. Gripping Joel under his shoulder blades, I hoisted him from the water's embrace, ensuring his head was delicately positioned upon the rock, a precarious but necessary measure for his comfort.

As I began to pull my t-shirt over my head, a moment of hesitation gripped me. The scar that marred my chest – a vivid reminded of our first night in Clivilius – was something I was instinctively protective of. *Do I really want Joel to see my injury?* The vulnerability of exposing my wound to my son weighed on me, a silent battle between concealment and the need to provide for him. Yet, the decision was made. I removed my t-shirt, rolling it up to create a makeshift pillow. Despite parts of it being damp, it offered a softer alternative to the unforgiving hardness of the rock.

"Are you comfortable?" I asked, the words slipping out before I could gauge their appropriateness. The question seemed almost absurd in the context of what Joel had endured. The last few days had been nothing short of a tumultuous journey between life and death. *Or perhaps maybe heaven?* The thought briefly crossed my mind, a fleeting consideration of the metaphysical journey Joel might have experienced. I quickly dismissed the speculation, focusing instead on the present reality. The philosophical musings on where Joel had been were secondary to ensuring his current well-being.

Joel's eyes fluttered closed, a brief movement that sent a sharp pang of panic slicing through me. The fear, irrational yet gripping, was a visceral reminder of how precarious our situation remained. But then, just as quickly, his eyes opened again, followed by a deliberate blink. The relief that washed over me was immediate, though it did little to ease the undercurrent of anxiety that had taken root.

"Shit," I muttered, a nervous chuckle escaping me as I tried to mask the depth of my concern. "You gave me a bit of a fright there." My attempt at light-heartedness felt clumsy.

The corners of Joel's mouth twitched into what could only be described as a wisp of a smile. It was a small gesture, but in that moment, it was everything – a sign of resilience, a glimmer of a man returning from death.

As we settled into a calm silence, my mind became a whirlwind of thoughts and emotions, a tumultuous sea of questions and things I desperately wanted Joel to know. There was so much to say, so much he had missed. *Where should I start?* The mention of Kate, Luke, and the myriad of life events that had unfolded in my absence of his life loomed large in my mind.

"I still can't believe you are here with me," I confessed to Joel, the words heavy with emotion. The sentiment was true; despite the joy of having him back, a part of me wished fervently that the circumstances of our reunion were different.

As I began to spill the stories of my early adult years, a flood of words poured from me unbidden. But abruptly, I halted, my gaze returning to Joel. He lay there, so still, so quiet, a silent witness to my outpouring. A twinge of pain knitted my brow as I considered the fairness of my actions. It struck me then, the unfairness of unloading all my pent-up thoughts and emotions onto him, especially when he was in no position to ask for respite.

The silence enveloped us once more, a thick blanket that seemed to stretch infinitely. My gaze drifted out across the lagoon, its waters still and clear. In that vast, tranquil expanse, I found a mirror for my own turbulent thoughts, a quiet reminder of the complexity of our situation. Here, in this serene yet charged atmosphere, the weight of everything unsaid hung heavily between us.

Taking a deep breath, I braced myself for the revelation that had weighed heavily on my heart. "I didn't know about you until a couple of months ago, you know," I confessed, turning to face Joel, who lay motionless beside me on the rugged embrace of the shore. The admission hung in the air between us, a truth that had reshaped the very foundation of my existence.

As the words settled, a small tear escaped the corner of Joel's eye, tracing a path down his cheek. The sight of it, glimmering against his beautiful blue eye, struck a chord deep within me. It was a silent, poignant reflection of the emotions that the revelation stirred - a mixture of pain, wonder, and perhaps a hint of relief at the unburdening.

I bit my lip, a physical reminder to rein in the flood of explanations and emotions threatening to spill forth. Now was not the time; Joel's fragile state couldn't bear the weight of our complicated history. "We'll talk about it later," I stated, a promise of a future conversation, one that we both needed but were not yet ready for.

As the minutes stretched into an uneasy calm, I sensed a shift in Joel's presence beside me. It was as if the turmoil that the revelation had stirred was beginning to settle, giving way to a tentative peace. The decision of where to start unravelling our tangled story had loomed large over me, but as I watched Joel, a resolve crystallised within me. *I'll start with Kate*, I finally decided.

The choice felt right, a starting point that offered a bridge between past and present, a thread that could weave together the fragmented pieces of our shared story. Kate's role in our lives, her impact, would serve as the foundation for the many conversations that lay ahead. In deciding to begin with Kate, I was choosing a path of honesty and openness, a commitment to building a relationship with Joel grounded in truth, no matter how complex or painful that truth might be.

As the gentle breeze swept across the desolate landscape, carrying with it small clouds of fine dust, a stark reminder of our isolation, I became acutely aware of the harshness of our surroundings. The sun bore down on us, relentless and unforgiving, its heat unmitigated by the barren sky above. My skin felt dry, almost parched, a sensation that only heightened my concern for Joel.

Touching the back of my hand to his face, the heat radiating from him was unmistakable. He felt alarmingly hot and dry, symptoms of overexposure that couldn't be ignored. "We need to get you out of the sun," I announced with a sense of urgency, the realisation dawning on me that the harsh elements could only compound his recovery. "Too much exposure can't be good for you. I'll get some water to dampen your skin. It'll help your healing." The words were as much for me as they were for him, a plan of action in a situation where feeling helpless was all too easy.

Perched precariously on the edge of the large rock that had become Joel's makeshift recuperation bed, I leaned over to scoop water from the lagoon. My hands, cupped together, seemed woefully inadequate for the task, but it was all I had. By the time I brought them back to Joel, most of the water had slipped through the gaps between my fingers, leaving only a few precious drops to offer. I watched the droplets fall onto his forehead, each one a small mercy in the oppressive heat.

Then, with what moisture remained on my hands, I gently rubbed across Joel's face, trying to provide some semblance of relief. The action, though simple, felt deeply personal, a small act of care in the face of adversity. It was a reminder of our precarious situation, of the delicate balance between life and the harsh elements surrounding us.

After my second futile attempt to carry water in my hands, the dry reality of our situation became painfully clear. My efforts, though well-intentioned, were proving to be ineffectual against the relentless sun. I scanned our immediate surroundings, desperation creeping into my thoughts. *There has to be something I can use to scoop the water*, I thought anxiously. Yet, all that met my gaze were the unforgiving rocks and the pervasive dust, silent witnesses to our plight.

The idea that came to me next was one born out of necessity rather than preference. *I shouldn't, should I?* The internal debate was brief, my situation leaving little room for the luxury of choice. With a resigned shrug, answering my own silent query, I slipped off one of my shoes and dipped it into the water. It was an unconventional solution, to say the least, but desperation had stripped away the veneer of convention.

"I know it's not exactly the nicest way. But it's all we've got," I explained to Joel, hoping for his understanding, if not his forgiveness, for the unorthodox method. With that, I tipped a shoeful of water over Joel's chest, the liquid spreading across his skin, a makeshift baptism in our desert sanctuary.

I hurried back to the face the lagoon for another load, the urgency of the situation lending speed to my actions. Joel's soft grunts reached my ears, a sound that sent my heart racing with a mixture of hope and anxiety. *I must hurry, I urged myself. Joel is drying out.* The realisation that time was of the essence, that each moment and each action could tip the scales, propelled my actions.

As I turned around, ready to douse Joel's parched body with another shoe of water, my breath caught in my throat. The sight that greeted me was nothing short of miraculous. Joel hadn't been grunting from the discomfort of dryness; he had managed to sit himself up! The resilience and strength he displayed in that simple act filled me with a mix of awe and relief.

"Home," Joel uttered in a soft, raspy voice, the word hanging between us, laden with longing and vulnerability. My heart twisted at his words, the simplicity of his request clashing with the complexity of our reality.

I felt a surge of anger rise within me, a tempest of frustration directed at the circumstances that had brought us to this point, and at Luke, for reasons that seemed both justified and yet futile to dwell on in the moment. For the sake of my son, I had to quell that storm, to maintain the calm and assurance he needed from me. There would be time later to confront Luke, to unleash the turmoil that churned inside me. *But how could I tell my son that his concept of home, as he knew it, was no longer within reach? This desolate, alien place was our reality now.*

"Okay," I responded, my voice steady despite the tumult inside. I couldn't offer him a return to Earth, to the home he remembered, but I could provide him with the next best thing: safety and care at our camp. It was a promise, a commitment to his well-being, no matter the circumstances.

Taking a moment to assess Joel's physical condition, I noted that he didn't look much taller than myself, his frame slight. The realisation that I could physically carry him, that I could offer him the support he needed in this moment, fortified my resolve.

"Let's get you back to camp," I declared, determination firming my words. "I'll carry you." It was a declaration of my dedication to him, of my role as his protector, his guide in this uncertain new world.

"Okay," Joel replied softly, his acquiescence a demonstration to his trust in me.

Crouching down, the coarse, dry earth pressed hard against my knees. I scooped my arms beneath Joel, feeling the unexpected weight of his body as a soft grunt escaped my lips. It wasn't just his physical weight; it was the weight of responsibility, of fear, of love. Joel, seemingly understanding the strain of the moment, wrapped an arm around my neck, pulling himself closer, seeking comfort in the warmth of my chest. His trust was a heavy mantle, but one I bore willingly.

The ground beneath us was thick with dust, a fine, grittiness that clung to my feet and legs, hampering every breath. Each step became a battle, a fight against the invisible hands of the desert trying to pull us back, to bury us in its desolate embrace. The top of the first hill loomed ahead, a minor victory in our arduous journey. Setting Joel down felt like relinquishing a part of myself, a temporary severing of our shared resolve.

The smoke from the campfire was a beacon in the bright afternoon sky, curling upwards in a lazy dance, taunting us with its promise of safety. The barren landscape stretched endlessly around us, a vast emptiness that made the camp seem like a mirage, an oasis too far to reach. "See that smoke?" I asked Joel, pointing towards our distant haven. "That's where we're going. That's home." The word 'home' felt strange on my tongue, a concept too fragile for this harsh wilderness.

I looked down at Joel, his face a mirror of my own determination, tinged with the innocence of youth. Then, back at the sky, where the sun's journey painted the horizon in shades of orange and pink. A frown carved deep lines of worry across my forehead, each line a reflection of the fears that haunted me. Dusk would soon be approaching.

The memory of our first night, the cold, the sounds, the fear, snapped at my heels like a persistent wolf. The terror was a tangible thing, a monster that lurked in the darkness, waiting for the sun to flee. I could not, would not, let that darkness engulf us again. With a renewed sense of urgency, I lifted Joel back into my arms. "We need to keep moving," I whispered, more to myself than to him. The weight of my son felt lighter now, buoyed by the determination that surged through my veins. *I have to get Joel back to camp before nightfall*, I vowed silently. For him, for me, for the promise of another dawn after the darkness.

I crouched low, the muscles in my thighs tensing as I prepared to scoop Joel up into my arms once more. But this time, Joel's voice, croaky and weak yet laced with a determination that took me by surprise, cut through the silence.

"Stand," he said.

My eyes widened in disbelief. "You want to stand?" I echoed, needing clarification, hoping I hadn't misheard him. It was a simple request, yet it carried the weight of a thousand hopes.

"Yeah," Joel replied, his voice a whisper of resolve.

A wave of caution washed over me. "Actually, I'm not sure you're ready yet," I admitted, my gaze shifting back to the distant camp. The landscape between us and safety was marred with several more hills, each a daunting barrier in its own right. Doubt gnawed at me, gnarled fingers of worry tugging at my mind. The thought of not being able to carry Joel all the way, should he need it, sent a shiver down my spine.

But there was something in Joel's eyes, a flicker of something unbroken, that made me reconsider. "Okay," I relented, my voice a mixture of apprehension and hope. Carefully, I placed my arm behind him, offering the support I feared he might need too soon.

As Joel wobbled to his feet, his body swaying like a sapling in the wind, my heart hung suspended between hope and fear. He stepped forward, an awkward, clunky motion that was nevertheless a step. It was a moment of pure, unadulterated triumph. A glimmer of hope ignited in my heart, a beacon in the twilight of our ordeal – a testament to the fact that my son, despite everything, was very much alive.

With each step, supported yet increasingly confident, Joel's strength seemed to grow, as if drawing from the earth itself. It was a slow, painstaking process, each movement a victory over the circumstances that sought to keep us down. I could feel the shift in the air, the subtle strengthening of his resolve. It was palpable, this growth, not just in physical strength but in spirit too.

As we embarked on the descent down the small, yet deceptively steep hill, a sense of caution hung heavily in the air. The ground beneath us was a treacherous carpet of soft dust, unforgiving and eager to betray. It was then, in a heartbeat, that the earth seemed to conspire against us. Joel's foot, so cautiously placed, found no purchase. Instead, it gave way, initiating a chain reaction that neither of us were prepared for. My reflexes kicked in, my hand shooting out to grasp Joel's arm as his body began to slip, an ephemeral cloud of dust marking the spot where stability failed him.

The weight of Joel's body, suddenly a force unbound by gravity's whim, pulled at me with a desperation I couldn't ignore. My face contorted in terror, a silent scream etched into my features as I felt the ground betray me too. We were no longer masters of our descent but captives of the hill's whim.

Like tumbleweeds subjected to the desert's indifferent gusts, we found ourselves tumbling uncontrollably down the hill. The world around us became a blur of dust and sky, an indistinct canvas of chaos. Clouds of dust rose like spectres in our wake, witnesses to our involuntary surrender to gravity's embrace.

The sudden stop at the bottom left me gasping, the breath knocked out of me, a sharp pang in my chest competing with the throbbing ache in my ankle. For a moment, I was caught in a whirlwind of panic, unsure which pain demanded my attention first.

"Joel!" My voice tore through the silence, laced with fear and concern. "Are you okay?" The urgency in my call was a mirror to my racing heart, each beat a question mark hanging in the air.

Dragging myself through the dust, a landscape now painted with the evidence of our fall, I reached Joel's side. His whispered apology, "Sorry," was a fragile sound in the vastness of our surroundings.

"It's not your fault," I assured him, my voice a blend of warmth and an attempt at reassurance. "This place isn't exactly friendly." The words tumbled out, a truth I couldn't mask. But as quickly as they came, I bit my tongue, a physical stopper to my thoughts. I had ventured too close to the edge of despair, a line I had promised myself I wouldn't cross. Positivity, in this unforgiving environment, was a choice I had made, a debt I owed to my son. The weight of that promise, much like the dust we were covered in, clung to me, a constant reminder of the strength required to forge ahead.

As I cast my gaze over Joel, assessing him for any additional signs of harm, he appeared remarkably intact. Given the tumble we'd just endured, this was no small feat. Yet, considering the fragility of his condition prior to our fall, my relief was tinged with uncertainty. The truth was, in the dust and adrenaline of the moment, discerning any subtle changes in his well-being was a challenge I wasn't confident I could meet.

"Can you stand?" The question left my lips, buoyed by hope yet weighted with concern.

"I think so," Joel replied in his raspy voice.

As I aided Joel to his feet, my own body protested. My foot, an unwitting casualty of our descent, throbbed mercilessly. Each pulse of pain shot up my calf like lightning, a cruel reminder of our vulnerability. I clenched my jaw, swallowing the pain, determined to keep my discomfort hidden. At that moment, there was something far greater at stake than my own suffering.

The urge to vocalise my agony was overwhelming, a primal scream hovering at the edge of my consciousness. Yet, it remained unvoiced. The well-being of my son, standing bravely beside me, eclipsed every personal affliction. He was my priority, the one concern that overshadowed every sharp stab of pain.

Leaning on each other, Joel and I resumed our trek. Our pace was painstakingly slow, each step a laborious effort. The solidarity between us was palpable, a mutual dependency born of necessity. Yet, as we made our way, a heavy sigh escaped me. The journey ahead loomed large, a daunting expanse that stretched out before us. The realisation of how much distance we still had to cover settled in, a heavy cloak of reality draped over my shoulders.

As Paul's voice cut through the dimming light of the afternoon, a surprising wave of relief washed over me. "Jamie!" he called out, his concern unmistakable even from a distance. "Is that Joel?" The urgency in his voice bridged the gap between us, pulling him closer with every word.

With my free arm, I gestured frantically, the movement a beacon in the waning daylight. "Come and help us," I managed to say, my voice a mix of desperation and gratitude. It was a strange feeling, this relief at seeing Luke's brother.

Paul moved with a purpose, his steps careful yet swift as he navigated the dusty terrain that had been our adversary just moments before. Sliding under Joel's free arm, he took on the weight of my son with a steadiness that belied the uncertainty of our situation. "Thought I'd better get him back to camp before dark," I said, the words more a plea than a statement, urging us into motion.

"Good idea," Paul responded, his voice a solid, grounding force.

Even with Paul's added strength, the journey back to camp proved arduous. Every step was a battle, not just against the physical terrain, but against the accumulated weariness of the past days. It wasn't just the physical toll; a relentless headache hammered at my temples, a cruel symphony to the mental and emotional duress we'd been subjected to.

"Hurt your foot?" Paul's inquiry broke through my grimace of pain as I navigated another step.

"Yeah," I grunted in acknowledgment, the simplicity of my response masking the complexity of our ordeal. "The hill where you found us was a bit tough," I added.

Paul's attention shifted to Joel. "Has he spoken yet?" His question was gentle.

"Not really," I admitted, my eyes flickering to my son. Despite the silence, Joel's presence, his continued fight, was a testament to progress, however silent it might be.

Paul then turned his gaze to Joel, offering a semblance of comfort in the midst of our desolation. "You've got your father's eyes," he said, a statement meant to bridge the gap between the past and our present struggles. "Let's get you home."

At his words, a quiet scoff escaped me, a sound muffled by the dust and despair that seemed to cling to us. Despite Paul's intentions, the concept of 'home' felt alien, a distant memory that no longer held any truth in our current existence. No matter how much I wished to believe otherwise, the stark reality remained—this place, this situation, could never be 'home.' It was a harsh truth, a reminder of everything I had lost and everything that a part of me was still wanted to fight to regain.

❖

As the minutes stretched into what felt like an eternity, each step we took was a testament to resilience in the face of unrelenting pain and exhaustion. The endless tapestry of reds and oranges beneath our feet seemed to mock our slow progress, but the sight of the camp finally breaking through the horizon offered a glimmer of hope. "We're nearly there," I silently urged my trembling, aching legs, commanding them to carry me just a bit further.

"Glenda!" Paul called out.

The moment Paul's voice broke the silence, calling out for Glenda with a sense of urgency, my heart skipped a beat. *Luke's here*, I realised, the surprise lifting the fog of exhaustion momentarily. As Glenda and Luke hurried over, the sight of familiar faces in this desolate place felt like a rare blessing.

"He's bleeding!" Glenda's cry jolted me from my daze, her alarm slicing through the haze of fatigue that clouded my senses. Luke's reaction, a stunned silence as he stared at Joel, mirrored my own shock. Before Luke could snap out of it, Kain sprung into action, his responsiveness a stark contrast to our collective paralysis. "I got it!" he declared, rushing over with tissues in hand, a small but critical act of kindness in our moment of need.

"Ta," Glenda acknowledged with a simple word as she took the tissues from Kain, pressing them against Joel's nose in an attempt to stem the flow of blood. Her directive to get Joel seated was met with immediate compliance, Paul and I guiding my son to a large log by the campfire. The log, rough and unyielding, was a far cry from proper seating, but it was the best we could offer in a place that had long forgotten comfort.

"Not too close," Glenda warned as we settled Joel near the fire, her concern for his wellbeing evident in her voice. "Is it just his nose?" she inquired, her gaze sharp and assessing.

"I think so," I answered, the guilt gnawing at my insides. The realisation that I hadn't noticed Joel's bleeding sooner was a blow to my already fragile sense of competence as a father. *Had the blood been a silent witness to our harrowing descent down the hill?* The question haunted me, casting a shadow over the small relief of having reached the camp. *What a lousy father I'm turning out to be already,* I chastised myself internally, the weight of my perceived failures adding to the burden of our physical and emotional ordeal.

Glenda's actions, as she knelt before Joel, struck me as a blend of concern and perplexity. Joel, drooping yet supported by Paul and me, seemed almost too fragile in that moment. "I don't understand how he can be bleeding. I'm certain there was no blood in him earlier," Glenda mused aloud, her brows knitted in confusion.

I found myself shaking my head, an involuntary reaction to the surreal situation unfolding before us. "I didn't give him any. But he seems to have plenty of it now," I responded, my voice laced with a mix of amazement and disbelief as I glanced at the bloodied tissues in my hand. The sight was both reassuring and unnerving; blood meant life, but the sudden appearance was a puzzle.

Glenda's agreement only deepened the mystery. Her examination of Joel, the gentle prodding along his arms and legs, was methodical, almost ritualistic. "There is definitely blood in his veins now. It's a medical anomaly!" she declared with a kind of clinical fascination that seemed out of place in the dusty camp.

Then, with a fluid motion that broke the gravity of our discussion, Glenda stood and accepted the whiskey bottle from Luke. "You better lie him down again once the bleeding stops," she advised before taking a swig from the bottle. I stared, dumbfounded. The incongruity of her actions, the casual sip of whiskey while my son sat bleeding, ignited a flare of indignation within me. My initial reservations about Glenda, briefly assuaged by her medical intervention, surged back with renewed vigour. Duke's instinctual wariness of her echoed in my mind, a reminder that perhaps the dog's judgment was more reliable than I had wanted to admit.

As Paul shifted his gaze to the sky, "Nightfall can't be far away now," he observed, his voice cutting through the tension like a knife. "I'll prepare some dinner for us."

Kain's eagerness to assist, a quick, "I'll help you," suggested an undercurrent of discomfort, perhaps a need to find his place among us or to make amends, or *Perhaps Kain's still feeling a little self-conscious*, I mused with a silent chuckle.

❖

As the campfire flickered, casting elongated shadows that danced across the dust-laden ground, Joel and I lingered in its warmth. The meal I consumed was small, barely enough to sate the hunger that gnawed at me, but it was the fresh air that seemed to breathe a bit of life back into both of us. The sky, once painted with the last strokes of twilight, had deepened into an inky blackness that threatened to pull me into sleep. Fighting the weight of fatigue that pressed down on my eyelids, I ushered Joel towards the tent, our steps slow and measured. The need for rest was undeniable, a silent plea from our bodies for a reprieve from the day's trials.

"You take the mattress," I instructed Joel, my voice soft in the enveloping darkness of the tent. Squinting to make out his form in the scant light, I guided him down, ensuring his comfort was paramount.

"Clothes," Joel's whisper cut through the silence, a simple request yet laden with vulnerability.

"Oh," I responded, the realisation sparking a sudden alertness within me. "Do you want help taking them off?" My offer was tentative, born of concern yet mindful of his dignity.

"Yes," Joel's voice was a croak, laden with exhaustion.

"Okay."

As I helped Joel, a feeling of awkwardness enveloped me, a sensation foreign and yet intimate. I had never found myself in such a caretaker role, especially under circumstances as unique as these. Joel, a son suddenly thrust into my life, represented a new chapter, one that required a level of care and attention I had never anticipated providing. The situation was uncharted territory for me, a mix of duty and tenderness that I navigated with cautious reverence.

Reflecting on the moment, a surprising revelation washed over me. Despite the initial awkwardness, there was an underlying sense of fulfilment, a connection forming in the act of caring for Joel that I had not expected to find. It made me question my long-held stance against having children, a stance I had defended vehemently against Luke. The reasons for my resistance seemed to blur, overshadowed by the tangible bond forming between Joel and me. In the quiet of the tent, I found myself reconsidering the possibilities that lay in the paths not taken, the choices made in the certainty of adulthood now questioned under the beckoning sky of fatherhood.

The weight of my newfound responsibilities as a father momentarily lifted as I addressed the practical matter at hand. "You should be able to fit into some of my clothes," I suggested, trying to navigate the unfamiliar territory of caring for Joel with something resembling normalcy. Yet, his refusal, a simple "No. No clothes," to my offer brought me back to the reality of our situation. It wasn't just about clothes; it was about respecting his current state, his needs, and preferences in a moment when normalcy seemed like a distant memory.

"Okay." Accepting his decision without protest, I pulled the blanket up to Joel's shoulders, ensuring he was comfortable and warm. His quiet "Thanks" was a small reassurance.

Watching Joel's bright blue eyes close, a sign of trust in my care, filled me with a profound sense of responsibility. It was a reminder that, despite the challenges we faced, there were moments of peace, however fleeting. Satisfied that he was settled for the night, I moved across the tent's floor to the opposite wing. This space, however minimal, was a gesture of respect for his privacy and independence, a balance I was determined to learn to navigate.

Spreading one of the new sleeping bags beneath me, I lay down, not seeking the solace of sleep but rather a moment to reflect. The distance from the campfire and its communal warmth was intentional. I needed this solitude, a quiet space to process the day's events and the enormity of the journey ahead. The crackling of the fire and the muted conversations of the others felt like they belonged to another world, one where the simplicity of gathering around a fire didn't come with the weight of survival and newfound parenthood pressing down on my shoulders.

IMPASSE

4338.207.6

The night's silence was shattered by Paul's loud cackle, a sound so jarring it seemed to penetrate the fabric of the tent, encroaching on the fragile peace I'd carved out within its confines. Glenda's voice followed, her words laced with humour yet cutting like a knife. "Shh. The zombie is sleeping," she quipped, her laughter mingling with Paul's in a chorus of mockery.

A wave of heat surged through me, a visceral response to their callousness. *What a rude bitch.*

Kain's chuckle added insult to injury, his justification for their cruelty - "Well, I didn't know how else to describe him" - only deepening the wound. The pain that shot through my chest was more than physical; it was the pain of betrayal, of having those I considered allies mock my son in his most vulnerable state.

The anger that boiled within me was a tempest, fierce and blinding. *How dare they make fun of my son!?* My mind raced with indignation, my heart ached with the injustice of their words. Tears, unbidden and hot, blurred my vision, a tangible sign of the hurt that words could inflict. In a desperate attempt to shield myself from their cruelty, I covered my ears, but the damage was done. The laughter, the mocking tone, had already etched a deep scar.

Startled by the sudden presence of another in the tent, my body tensed, ready to confront yet another intruder into our small sanctuary. The realisation that it was Luke, moving quietly across the floor towards me, did little to ease the tight knot of anxiety in my stomach.

As Luke continued his silent approach, stopping at my waist, I hastily wiped away the tears that betrayed my emotional turmoil. Even in the dim light, the outline of his silhouette was familiar, yet it did nothing to dispel the shadow that their laughter had cast over the night. The darkness around us felt heavier, laden with words unsaid and comfort yet to be offered. Luke's presence was a question in itself, a silent inquiry into the depth of hurt their words had inflicted.

Carefully, Luke raised his leg and slid it across my body. The rest of him followed with smooth motion.

I glared at Luke straddling my waist, and felt my face turn hot with unbridled anger. *How the fuck can Luke be horny now?*

Luke leaned in and kissed me gently on the neck.

Feeling paralysed, I didn't stir. Like scared prey avoiding a predator, I'd learnt over the years that if I didn't respond, Luke would bore quickly.

Luke's tongue slithered to the tip of my ear; his left hand reached behind and enclosed itself firmly around my crotch.

I tried to ignore it. I tried my best to stop my dick from responding. *But fuck Luke is good with his hands!*

My reaction was instinctual, a firm push against Luke's chest, propelled by a mix of confusion and indignation. "What the fuck are you doing, Luke?" The words slipped out in a venomous hiss, a defence mechanism against the unexpected and unwelcome advance.

Luke's response, a whisper meant to convey desire, only served to heighten the absurdity of the situation. "I want you so badly." The words, meant to bridge the distance between us, felt hollow, his intentions clouded by the unmistakable aroma of whiskey that hung heavy on his breath.

"You're drunk," I accused, the realisation doing nothing to quell the rising tide of frustration within me. Luke's retreat, both physical and emotional, was a small victory, but his words that followed felt like a low blow. "Oh, come on, Jamie. It's been at least six months since we've been intimate," he lamented, a mixture of accusation and desperation lacing his tone.

My rebuttal was swift, "I'm not in the mood," a simple statement that carried the weight of unspoken grievances and buried resentments. Luke's accusation, "That's always your excuse," was a jab at our fragile connection, his words unveiling the depth of his frustration and hurt. "You're never in the mood, are you! Oh, wait. I'm not Ben. Is that it?"

"That's not fair, Luke!" My voice broke, the volume a testament to the raw emotion that Luke's words had stirred within me. His bitter retort, "I know it's not fair!" was the breaking point, a verbal acknowledgment of the chasm that had grown between us.

As Luke stormed toward the tent flap, the finality of his exit left a void filled only by the oppressive darkness of the night. My sharply whispered, "Luke!" was a desperate attempt to salvage what remained of our conversation, our relationship, but it went unheeded.

Alone with my thoughts, the darkness seemed to close in around me, a suffocating blanket of regret and realisation. The bitter acknowledgment of our mutual destruction, "I may have fucked up our relationship. But Luke has fucked up our lives!" was an unheard confession to the empty air.

"I guess that makes us fucking even," I told the cool air, a hollow attempt at justifying the impasse we had reached. Taking a deep, stubborn breath, I rolled onto my side. The night's silence, once a comfort, now echoed with the remnants of our shattered connection, each breath a reminder of the distance between what was and what could no longer be.

4338.208

(27 July 2018)

INTERRUPTIONS

4338.208.1

The chill of the night had seeped into every corner of the tent, a stark contrast to the warmth Duke provided as he snuggled closer, seeking comfort beneath my arm. His paws, cold and intrusive against my bare chest, prompted a harsh whisper from me, "Duke! Do you really have to do that!?" Yet, even as I chided him, I couldn't help but brush his paws away with tenderness. The night's embrace had grown unexpectedly cold, and in a moment of need for warmth, I had surrendered to the sleeping bag's promise of comfort, inadvertently inviting Duke to seek refuge in its confines.

Across the tent, the faint stirrings of Joel and the familiar, soft snores of Henri painted a picture of tranquility amidst our otherwise tumultuous reality. Henri, ever faithful to his chosen spot at the bottom of the mattress, elicited a small smile from me. It was a simple joy, a reminder of the consistency his presence brought to my life, unaffected by the chaos that lay beyond the tent's fragile sanctuary.

Embracing Duke briefly, a silent thank you for his companionship, I carefully extricated myself from the sleeping bag's warmth. The ritual of sniffing yesterday's t-shirt before slipping it over my head was a testament to our current living conditions, carrying the scent of smoke and dried sweat.

As I made my way to Joel, his efforts to sit up caught my attention. The sight of him, struggling yet determined, supported by a makeshift fortress of pillows, stirred a complex mix of pride and concern within me.

"How are you feeling?" I asked, tamping down the swirling mix of emotions that threatened to surface. The shock of discovering I had a son only recently still felt unreal, a twist in my life's narrative I hadn't anticipated. I had Kate to thank for this ignorance, this gap in my life where knowledge of my son should have been. She must have known, must have made the choice to keep this truth from me, severing ties completely rather than sharing such a crucial piece of my own story.

"Water," Joel's request snapped me back to the present, his voice hoarse and weak. My frustration with the past momentarily faded, replaced by concern for his immediate needs.

"Of course," I responded, momentarily shaking off the weight of my thoughts to tend to Joel. I grabbed an unopened bottle of spring water. "Do you want to try opening it?" I held the bottle out to him, an offer meant to empower, yet prepared to assist.

Joel's attempt was heart-wrenching. The trembling of his hand as he reached for the bottle, his sharp cry of pain when his fingers failed to grasp it properly, and the subsequent fall of the bottle to the bed painted a vivid picture of his current vulnerability. My heart clenched at the sight, a mixture of empathy and a fierce desire to protect him from further pain washing over me.

"What's wrong?" My voice was steady, calm, despite the storm of worry within. I reached for Joel's arm, a gesture of support, while Duke's incessant barking at the rogue water bottle added a layer of annoyance to the moment. Ignoring Duke's reaction, my focus narrowed to Joel, to understanding the source of his pain.

"May I enter?" Glenda's voice, tinged with both formality and concern, cut through the quiet of the early morning, her head appearing through the tent's entrance as if on cue.

"Yeah," I responded, my attention shifting from Joel to her. Under different circumstances, the sudden intrusion might have sparked irritation within me, but given the context — Joel's apparent injury and our collective worry — her timing felt almost providential. "Come take a look at this." My voice, an invitation laced with urgency, beckoned her closer.

As Glenda approached, her eyes wide with a mix of professional curiosity and personal concern, I couldn't help but notice Duke's guarded stance. His gaze, unwavering and alert, followed her every step, a silent protector. A brief smile touched my lips despite the tension. *At least I can always count on you to have my back,* I thought, a silent nod of appreciation to my ever-vigilant companion.

"His hand is hurt," I explained, gently lifting Joel's arm towards Glenda, who had now knelt beside me on the tent floor.

Glenda wasted no time, her hands moving with the precision of experience as she assessed Joel's wrist and fingers. "Wrist movement seems fine," she noted, her focus narrowing as she delicately manipulated his hand, checking for mobility and signs of distress.

The moment she touched Joel's index finger, his reaction was immediate and sharp — a croaky yelp of pain that cut through the silence, startling even Duke. Glenda's response was swift, her diagnosis ready within seconds. Her quick judgment, ready to be shared, held the weight of our collective anxieties.

"I believe he has a broken finger," Glenda's pronouncement was both clinical and weighted, her gaze lifting from Joel's injured hand to lock eyes with his, conveying a mix of professional assessment and empathetic concern.

"How bad is it?" The question burst from me, my voice tight with sudden fear. The possibility of Joel's injury being more severe than anticipated sent a jolt of adrenaline coursing through me, igniting a flurry of worst-case scenarios in my mind. Glenda's expression, marked by a furrowed brow and the grim set of her mouth, did little to quell the rising tide of worry for my son's wellbeing.

"Impossible to say without an x-ray, but with our limited resources, I doubt it would make any difference even if we could x-ray his finger," she responded, her voice tinged with a resignation that only served to deepen my sense of dread. The slow shake of her head, a silent testament to our dire circumstances, felt like a blow, rendering me momentarily helpless.

Glenda's stark assessment felt like a cold hand gripping my heart, dragging it down into a chasm of despair. The thought that she might already be feeling defeated gnawed at me, a silent scream echoing in the confines of my skull. *Fuck you, Luke!* The accusation, aimed at the absent party responsible for the spiral of events leading us here, welled up with venomous clarity. Yet, the words remained unspoken, trapped by a sudden swell of emotions that threatened to overwhelm me. The frustration, fear, and anger at our situation, at Luke's part in this tangled web of consequences, simmered beneath the surface, a turbulent storm I struggled to contain.

"I'll go and check what supplies we have. I should be able to take care of it. I can always ask Luke for additional supplies if I need them," Glenda's voice was a blend of determination and practicality, offering a sliver of hope in the midst of our constrained circumstances.

"You've spoken to Luke?" The question leaped out, tinged with a hint of irritation. The thought that Luke might be out of touch with our immediate needs, that my well-being, our well-being, seemed to hover on the periphery of his concerns, stirred a familiar frustration within me.

"Not this morning. But I've given him my access card for the Royal. As long as he is careful, he will have access to all the supplies we'll likely ever need." Glenda's explanation, meant to reassure, instead highlighted a dependency on Luke's reliability—a gamble that felt increasingly risky.

"I'm glad you have that much faith in him," I sighed, the words escaping me in a breath of resigned skepticism. The likelihood of Luke having made his way to us this early, or at all, seemed slim, exacerbating my anxiety rather than alleviating it. *Luke can be so easily distracted. There's no way he can keep up with our survival needs,* I thought, the worry gnawing at me.

"You don't?" Glenda's inquiry, her eyebrow arched in silent challenge, sought to peel back layers of doubt I wasn't ready to openly confront.

My response was non-verbal, a tight press of my lips and a shrug that served as a barrier against further probing. Turning my attention back to Joel, I unscrewed the water bottle lid, focusing on the task at hand as a diversion from the uncomfortable truths lingering just beneath the surface.

As Joel took slow, careful sips, Glenda gently dabbed at the water that escaped down his chin. "Mind if I look the rest of him over?" Her request, directed to me but respectful of Joel's autonomy, prompted me to seek his silent consent.

Joel's nod, a soft but clear assent, granted Glenda the go-ahead. "Go for it. I have two hungry dogs to feed anyway," I said, diverting my worry into action.

At the mere hint of food, Henri's reaction was instantaneous, his body springing to life as he leapt from the mattress and darted towards the bags. I assumed his target: the tinned dog food we had managed to scrounge up. Watching him, a laugh escaped me, the sound a brief respite from the earlier tension. I reached out, giving Henri a playful scratch on the head as I retrieved a tin from the bag. It suddenly struck me how adaptable both dogs had been to our drastically changed environment.

Reflecting on our time back on Earth, Henri's preferences came to mind. Back then, his world had revolved around either the comfort of his cushion on the couch, or dictated by the leisurely pursuit of following sunlight across the living room floor. The outdoors had never been his domain, save for the deck. *Ah, the deck. That was the exception.* Even though he rarely showed interest in the world beyond its confines, there was a certain peace he found in simply lounging there, basking in the sun's warmth.

The thought brought a momentary pang of nostalgia, a longing for the simplicity of those days when our biggest concern was whether Henri had moved to catch the afternoon sun. Yet, observing him now, navigating the dust and unfamiliarity without a hint of complaint, I couldn't help but admire his resilience. Perhaps there was a lesson in Henri's easy acceptance of our new reality, a reminder to focus on the present and find comfort in the small, unchanged routines like feeding time, even when everything else around us had transformed so completely.

"Everything else seems to be okay. Your bruises will heal," Glenda's voice carried a note of reassurance, breaking through the temporary distraction of feeding the dogs.

"And his neck?" My voice echoed from across the tent, over the sound of Duke and Henri eagerly consuming their unexpected feast of lamb and vegetables with gravy.

"No sign of infection," Glenda called back, her response offering a momentary sigh of relief. "Don't do anything strenuous and with plenty of rest it looks like your throat will heal fine." Her advice, though directed at Joel, felt like a directive to me as well, a reminder of the cautious approach we needed to maintain.

The pungent aroma of the tinned dog food quickly overwhelmed me, a testament to my sensitive nose. Hastily, I retreated from the feeding frenzy, eager to escape the smell that clung to the air with an almost tangible presence.

Returning to Joel's side, I was met with Glenda's next suggestion. "I think it might be worth keeping a bucket of lagoon water here and dabbing some on his neck every few hours. I suspect that might help," she mused, introducing an unexpected element into our care regimen.

"Really?" The surprise in my question was genuine, sparked by the unconventional nature of her proposal. The idea that lagoon water might contribute to Joel's recovery was out of the ordinary, yet Glenda's seriousness reminded me that given the lagoon was the source of his current vitality, it actually made absolute sense.

"He really shouldn't be alive," Glenda's observation, stark and unfiltered, struck me with the force of a physical blow. The implication behind her words, the sheer improbability of Joel's survival, ignited a defensive fury within me. *Who the fuck does this woman think she is, telling me my son should be dead!?* My inner turmoil raged, fists clenching as I fought to contain the visceral reaction to her blunt assessment.

"But he is," Glenda continued, perhaps sensing the rising tension, her words a swift attempt to bridge the gap her previous statement had created. "I'd like to set up a lab to study the properties of the lagoon water. I'll talk with Paul and Luke about it this morning." Her proposal, a blend of scientific curiosity and proactive planning, hinted at a path forward, a possible exploration into the miraculous resilience that had kept Joel with us.

"Why Paul?" The question emerged from me, a mix of confusion and a slight easing of tension as my fists unclenched, releasing the pent-up frustration.

"With you being preoccupied with Joel, it would make sense for Paul to take responsibility for leading the camp's development." Glenda's rationale, though logical, didn't fully appease the simmering skepticism within me.

"Hmph," escaped me in a scoff. "Why not Kain? Why not you?" I pressed, unable to mask the challenge in my tone.

"I'm a medical professional. Medical matters are all that I have any interest in leading," Glenda responded, her tone matter-of-fact, leaving no room for argument. A silence followed, thoughtful, as she seemed to weigh her next words carefully.

"And Kain?" I couldn't let it go, the question hanging between us, demanding an explanation for the apparent oversight of my nephew's potential.

"Kain is a strong, young man. Luke was wise to choose him, but he lacks the experience we're going to need for our settlement to thrive." Her answer, delivered with a straightforward candour, made it difficult to continue my line of questioning. Glenda's assessment, though blunt, was rooted in a pragmatic view of our situation.

I found myself looking away, unable to hold her gaze as the reality of her words settled in. The acknowledgment of Kain's limitations in the context of our current predicament was a bitter pill to swallow, yet impossible to deny.

"Do you want me to get that bucket of water for you?" Glenda's voice softened, her offer breaking through my introspection.

"No," I found myself saying, my gaze shifting to Joel, who had managed to find a semblance of comfort in lying down again. The thought of stepping away, even momentarily, tugged at me with a mix of reluctance and necessity. "I don't ever want to leave your side, but it'll probably do me good to get a short walk and some fresh air." The admission was as much for myself as it was for her, a concession to the need for a brief respite from the weight of constant vigilance.

"Very well then. I'll be back shortly, and we'll get that finger of yours all sorted," Glenda assured Joel, her touch gentle as she patted his leg, a gesture of comfort before she rose to her feet and exited the tent.

Left alone with my thoughts, the brief exchange with Glenda lingered, a reminder of the complexities and challenges we faced. Her departure, though temporary, left a palpable void.

"You... you don't... like her... do... you?" Joel's words, fragmented by the effort it took to voice them, broke through the silence, carrying with them a weight of concern. As he struggled back into a sitting position, his eyes sought mine, looking for an answer or perhaps reassurance.

"I'm not..." The words caught in my throat as I watched him, the complexity of my feelings towards Glenda struggling to find expression. "She'll take good care of you," I finally managed, steering the conversation away from my personal reservations. The last thing Joel needed was to sense my unease, especially not when he was in such a vulnerable state. Handing him the water bottle, I hoped to divert his attention towards his immediate needs rather than our interpersonal dynamics.

"You two look well," Paul's voice, unexpected and somewhat jarring, pulled me from the moment of quiet understanding with Joel. His entrance into the tent was abrupt, his presence an intrusion into the fragile calm we had managed to establish.

"Well enough," I responded tersely, my tone reflecting my current state of mind more than I intended. The truth was, interaction was the last thing I desired, especially with the undercurrents of tension that seemed to follow overheard conversations as of late.

"I'm just collecting my things to take to the other tent," Paul announced, moving with a purpose that suggested he was keen to avoid prolonging our exchange. Watching him gather his belongings, a sense of curiosity overcame my initial irritation.

"Why?" The question was out before I could weigh its necessity, driven by a mix of surprise and a need to understand his motivations.

"Oh, Kain and I thought it would be a good idea if we took the third tent and left you and Joel to have this one," Paul explained, his actions brisk as he packed his things. "And Luke, if he ever stays with us."

"Hmph," was all I could muster in response. The mention of Luke staying with us sparked a cynical reaction, a scoff born of skepticism. "I'm not sure Luke will be spending many nights with us." My words were bitter, a reflection of the strained relationship and the complex web of feelings that surrounded Luke's presence—or absence—in our lives.

Paul's reaction, a furrowed brow followed by a silent departure, left a lingering sense of unease. Watching him leave, bag in tow, I was struck by the isolation of our circumstances, the shifting dynamics within our small group, and the unspoken tensions that seemed to dictate our interactions.

"Is there anyone… here… that you like?" Joel's question was unexpected.

I turned towards him, attempting to lighten the mood with a shrug. "I like you, don't I?" The words, meant to jest, perhaps fell a bit flat in the air between us.

"Hardly reassuring," Joel retorted, a flicker of disappointment in his eyes before he closed them, signalling a retreat from the conversation.

"What's that supposed…" My words trailed off, cut short by another intrusion.

"Hey, Uncle Jamie," Kain's entrance was abrupt, his timing impeccably poor. *For fuck's sake!* The irritation was instant, my patience worn thin by the constant barrage of interruptions. "Anyone else want to interrupt us this morning!?" The snap in my voice was sharper than intended, a raw edge of frustration breaking through.

"Sorry. I didn't mean to interrupt," Kain's reaction was immediate, his apology quick as he moved to leave, a clear attempt to escape the tension he'd unwittingly stepped into.

"Kain, wait," I found myself calling after him, the impulsive irritation giving way to regret. He paused, turning back with a hesitance that made me internally wince at my earlier outburst.

"I'm... it's okay if you stay." The invitation was a small attempt at amends, a bridge to mend the momentary rift my words had caused.

"I... I just wanted to see how Joel was doing," Kain admitted, his nervousness evident in the shuffle of his feet, a dance of uncertainty that I hadn't intended to provoke.

I gulped dryly, the discomfort of making Kain feel unwelcome gnawing at me. *I don't mean to make Kain feel uncomfortable.*

"I'm fine," Joel's whisper cut through the tension, a quiet assertion of his presence.

"Oh... you can talk now?" Kain's surprise was genuine, his approach cautious yet filled with a newfound curiosity.

"Getting there," Joel's response, though brief, was a testament to his resilience, a small victory in our current sea of challenges.

"You'd better give your voice a rest and have some more water. Keep your throat hydrated," I found myself saying, the protective instinct taking over as I gently pressed the water bottle against Joel's lips, assisting him in a simple act of care before helping him settle back down.

"You ready?" Glenda's voice cut through the tension that seemed to hang in the air like a thick fog, her entrance marked by the bag of medical supplies she carried with a sense of purpose.

"You don't need me, do you?" Kain's asked, his gaze flickering between Glenda and me, seemingly in search for an excuse to stay or leave.

"No, Jamie and I can manage," Glenda responded, her tone firm yet dismissive, as if to underscore my newfound role in this precarious balance of care. "He's getting good practice." Her words, perhaps meant as encouragement, felt like a double-edged sword, highlighting my forced participation in this unwanted crash course in field medicine.

"I'm not your fucking lap-dog," I snapped.

Kain's reaction, his face flushing with embarrassment or perhaps anger, was immediate. "I'm going to give myself a quick wash," he muttered, a quiet retreat from the growing discomfort within the tent.

Glenda knelt beside Joel, positioning the bag of supplies against her thigh. "Can you sit?" she inquired, her arms outstretched towards him in a gesture of support.

Fuck! I just laid him back down! The thought screamed in my head, a silent protest against the perpetual cycle of progress and setback. My body moved instinctively to help, only to be stopped by Glenda's sharp glare, a silent command to let Joel try on his own.

With my arms crossed defensively over my chest, I watched as Joel struggled to comply, his determination a flicker of light in the dimness of our reality. Beneath the surface of my simmering frustration, a swell of admiration for my son's resilience grew, softening the edges of my irritation.

"I'm going to get the fucking bucket of water," I announced, the words half growl, half resignation, as I turned to leave the tent, the flap closing with a whisper behind me.

The outside world greeted me with a breath of fresh air, a brief escape from the claustrophobic confines of our shelter. Duke quickly appeared at my side, his presence a silent comfort. "Come on, Duke," I found myself saying, the beginnings of a smile finding its way through the turmoil. "At least we like each other." The words, light and half-hearted, carried with them a truth that, for a moment, lifted the weight from my shoulders, a reminder of the uncomplicated loyalty and companionship Duke offered in a world where little else seemed certain.

FEEDING

4338.208.2

Relieved barely scratches the surface of how I felt, discovering Glenda had transitioned from her earlier task to a new endeavour—cooking breakfast—by the time Duke and I made it back with the water. The morning had stretched on with me holed up in the tent, offering Joel company, and consciously steering clear of the others. The tent's confines offered a sanctuary, a place where the complexities of our group dynamics could be momentarily forgotten, and where I could focus on the simple act of being there for Joel.

"Smells good," Joel's voice broke through the silence, a croak that betrayed the discomfort he was still feeling.

His words pulled me out of my reflections, and I glanced at him, noticing how the simple statement seemed like an effort. "Do you think you could eat?" I found myself asking. There was hope in my voice, a silent plea that maybe, just maybe, he was feeling a bit better.

"I could try." His response was weak but determined

As if on cue, the unmistakable aroma of bacon filled the air, a rich, savoury scent that immediately made my mouth water. *It's true, it does smell good*, I admitted to myself, my stomach chiming in with its agreement. There was something about the smell of bacon that felt like a warm embrace, a comfort that seemed to cut through the chill of the morning.

"I'll go and get you some," I said to Joel, pushing myself to my feet.

As I stepped out of the tent's shelter, Duke brushed past me with an urgency that brought a small smile to my face. His excitement was palpable, a blur of fur as he darted towards Glenda, positioning himself beside her with his tail whipping back and forth in a frenzy of anticipation. It was a simple joy, watching him so full of life and expectation.

Glenda, caught up in the moment, broke off a small piece of bacon and offered it to Duke. He accepted it with a dignified grace that seemed almost out of place in the wilderness, his mannerisms gentle, a testament to his character. Duke always had this refined approach to life, embodying a level of sophistication that belied his canine nature.

As this quiet scene unfolded, Henri, with his unmistakable foxy tail signalling his arrival, joined the assembly, his movements driven by a singular focus on the food. His presence was sudden, a stark contrast to Duke's measured approach, and his tail moved with a wild enthusiasm that seemed to capture his entire being's excitement for the prospect of a treat.

"Careful, he's a little..." My warning trailed off as Glenda extended a piece of bacon towards Henri. In an instant, his mouth expanded, a surprising display of eagerness and lack of restraint that caught Glenda off guard.

"Shit!" Glenda's reaction was swift, her hand retreating from Henri's less-than-gentle grasp on the treat. The moment was startling, yet it carried an undercurrent of humour that was hard to ignore.

"Shark," I finished with a laugh, the comparison between the two dogs becoming even more apparent in that moment. Duke, with his graceful acceptance of treats, and Henri, whose enthusiasm for food knew no bounds, were a study in contrasts. Henri, typically so calm and unassuming, transformed into a creature of sheer impulse at the sight of food, a transformation that was both amusing and slightly alarming.

"But he's always so placid," Glenda remarked, her gaze fixed on Henri as he devoured the bacon with only a token effort at chewing. Her surprise was genuine, a reflection of how Henri's demeanour shifted so dramatically in the presence of food.

"Unless there's food involved," I echoed, my own observations of Henri's behaviour coming to the forefront. "And he always seems to know when and where." It was a trait that fascinated and bewildered me, Henri's uncanny ability to appear precisely at the moment food was present, as if guided by an internal compass.

"Hmph," Glenda's response was a mix of resignation and amusement, her hands now safely tucked away from Henri's eager sniffs.

"No more, Henri. You've already had your breakfast," I stated firmly, addressing the young dog with a tone that brooked no argument. Henri, for all his eagerness, seemed to understand, even if his disappointment was palpable.

"You need to make sure you eat some breakfast too," Glenda said, as with a practiced hand, she assembled a breakfast plate that seemed to promise a momentary reprieve from the tensions that had woven themselves into the fabric of our days. She placed several rashes of bacon and a generous spoonful of scrambled eggs onto a plate, extending it towards me with a care that felt both comforting and necessary.

"Thank you," I responded, my gratitude genuine as I accepted the plate, the warmth from the food seeping into my hands. "Is there some for Joel too?" My concern for Joel was ever-present, a constant hum in the background of my thoughts, influencing my every action.

"Of course," Glenda affirmed. She reached for a second plate, her movements deliberate. "Have some beans too," she added, indicating for me to lower my plate again.

"Thanks, smells good," I commented, allowing the aroma of the meal to wash over me. The smell was comforting, familiar, and for a moment, it felt as though we could be anywhere else in the world—a momentary escape. My stomach responded with a loud, unmistakable growl, a testament to the hunger that gnawed at me, not just for food but for a sense of peace.

"Paul! Kain!" Glenda's call, robust and carrying, broke the momentary calm, her voice echoing through the campsite as she summoned the others for breakfast. She placed the frying pan on a nearby log, her posture shifting as she prepared to distribute the meal.

"Where are they?" I found myself asking, even as I bit into a piece of bacon, the savoury taste a sharp contrast to the bitterness of our situation. My thoughts briefly flickered back to a similar morning, the routine shattered by Luke's unforeseen demand to collect Paul from the airport. The memory served a sharp reminder of how quickly things had spiralled.

"Drop Zone. I'm surprised they're not back by now," Glenda mused, her tone casual but underlined with concern.

"Hmph," was all I could muster in response, my interest in dissecting Luke's decisions or contemplating the wider implications of our predicament waning. My priority was clear, crystallised in the concern for my son. "Thanks," I repeated to Glenda.

Turning towards the tent, Joel's plate in hand, I felt the weight of responsibility settle over me. The mess Luke had left us in, the uncertainty of our situation, it all paled in comparison to the simple, undeniable truth that I had a son to take care of.

Glenda's words trailed after me, her intention clear but her phrasing striking a nerve. "I'd like to be present when you feed him," she said, her steps echoing softly on the ground as she followed.

"Feed him!? He's not a dog!" The irritation bubbled up inside me, quick and fierce. The comparison, even if unintended, grated against my already frayed nerves. The situation was tense enough without reducing Joel's dignity to that of an animal's feeding time.

"Speaking of dogs, I wouldn't leave any of the food unattended while the little shark is circling." My attempt to lighten the mood, to bridge the gap her previous comment had widened, did little to soothe my annoyance.

"Hmm," Glenda mused, a practical note in her voice as she returned to her vigil by the fire, ready to defend the meal from Henri's opportunistic advances. "Let me know how you get on then."

"Sure," I managed, the word leaving me with a mix of resignation and a renewed focus on the task at hand. With Duke at my heels, a silent, comforting presence, I made my way back to the tent, the fabric flaps offering a semblance of privacy in the vast openness of our surroundings.

Entering the tent, the muted light casting long shadows, I presented the plate to Joel. "Here, see how you go," I said, trying to keep my voice steady, encouraging. "You might need to leave the bacon if it's too hard to chew or scratchy on your throat."

Joel's response was nonverbal, a silent nod as he carefully selected a bean, his movements deliberate as he placed it into his mouth.

Then, without warning, a scream shattered the calm, a sharp, terrifying intrusion. It propelled me out of the tent in an instant, every sense heightened, every nerve on edge.

"I'll go," Glenda's voice reached me, steady and decisive as she rose to her feet. "You watch the food."

Our agreement was silent, a mutual understanding in the midst of crisis. I hurried toward the campfire, the scream still echoing in my mind, a harbinger of turmoil. The air seemed to thicken around me, heavy with anticipation and dread as I watched Glenda disappear over the dune's crest.

The scream, so unexpected, so filled with terror, left a cold trail down my spine. And as I stood there, the grimace on my face reflecting the turmoil within, a single thought pierced the confusion. *Luke is here!* The implications of that realisation, the myriad ways it could unfold, weighed heavily on me, a storm cloud threatening to burst.

NEWCOMERS

1338.208.3

The morning's tranquility shattered in an instant, replaced by a sequence of events that would have been comical under any other circumstances. "For fuck's sake, Henri!" The words burst from me in a mix of frustration and disbelief as I lunged to intercept the dog, whose only concern was the tantalising smell of bacon. My movements, far from graceful, felt like a clumsy dance with disaster.

In a moment that felt scripted for maximum chaos, my right leg, seemingly with a mind of its own, found the frying pan handle. The pan, a silent participant until now, was suddenly catapulted into the spotlight as I nudged it, sending scrambled eggs soaring through the air like a flock of golden birds set free. It was a surreal, almost slow-motion spectacle, the eggs catching the light as they embarked on their brief flight.

Henri, ever the opportunist, seized the moment with a speed that belied his usual lazy demeanour. In the blink of an eye, he was in the midst of the mayhem, a canine lightning bolt seizing his target with a precision that was almost admirable. The last rasher of bacon, a prize beyond measure, dangled momentarily from his mouth before disappearing, forever.

With the breakfast now irretrievably lost to Henri's insatiable appetite, I was left with nothing but the sound of my own stomach, protesting loudly against the morning's turn of events. I brushed off the remnants of the skirmish, bits of egg that now adorned my leg as unwanted souvenirs of the debacle.

Stalking back to the tent, a mixture of resignation and irritation brewing within me, I couldn't help but mutter to myself, "At least my plate should be safe with Joel." The words were a small comfort, a silver lining in the cloud of disappointment Henri had brought. My glare at Henri, as I passed by him, was laden with the frustration of the moment, yet devoid of real malice.

The moment I pushed through the tent flap, my frustration from the latest antics still simmering, the sight that greeted me caused my frustration to momentarily spike. "Fuck me!" The words came out more as a scoff than anything else, my voice tinged with disbelief and resignation. There was Joel, seemingly oblivious to the drama outside, fully engrossed in breakfast, pushing the final morsel of scrambled eggs into his mouth. Duke, ever the opportunist like his brother, was happily cleaning up any remnants that fell from Joel's meal.

Watching Joel, I noticed the struggle in his movements, a reminder of the delicate balance we were trying to maintain between normalcy and the reality of our situation. His attempt to reach for the plate of bacon, hindered by his own body's limitations, was a stark illustration of the challenges he was facing. The grimace that flashed across his face, however brief, was enough to twist something inside me.

"I'll get it," I offered quickly, my tone softening as I knelt beside him. The simple act of moving the plate closer to him, only for him to push it away and rub his throat, spoke volumes. It was a silent communication we were becoming accustomed to, one that required no words but understood all the same.

"Eating the bacon makes it sore?" My guess was met with a nod and a half-smile from Joel, a small gesture that carried a weight of gratitude and understanding.

"Suppose I can eat it then," I said, a grin finding its way onto my face, trying to inject a bit of lightness into the moment. Yet, before the moment could fully blossom, Henri, driven by his insatiable appetite, made his move.

"Henri! No more!" The words were sharp, a reflexive response as I yanked the plate away, my growl at him mirroring the canine chastisement I hoped it would convey. Henri's retreat, tail tucked between his legs as he slunk off to his bed, was a small victory in the ongoing battle of wills. His scowl, though, was almost human in its misery, eliciting a momentary chuckle from me.

"I suppose I'd better check on Glenda," I said, shoving the last rasher of bacon into my mouth.

❖

As I emerged from the tent, the scene that unfolded before me felt like another chapter in our ever-evolving Clivilius saga. Glenda, with her usual purposeful stride, was returning to the camp, but this time, she wasn't alone. Two figures, older and unfamiliar, accompanied her, their presence another anomaly in our isolated existence.

The interaction that followed was as intriguing as it was unexpected. "Duke?" the tall, lanky woman inquired, her voice carrying a note of recognition as she bent down in the dust, welcoming Duke's enthusiastic greeting with open hands. Her familiarity with Duke, despite her admission of not truly knowing him, sparked a wave of curiosity and suspicion within me. *How the hell would she know Duke?* The question echoed my thoughts precisely.

Her next question only deepened the mystery. "Is Henri here too?" she asked, her gaze lifting to meet Glenda's. The mention of Henri, coupled with her prior knowledge of Duke, led me to a quick deduction: *she must be connected to Luke's work.*

Glenda's response, a heavy sigh followed by a pointed gesture towards the aftermath of Henri's breakfast escapade, offered a moment of levity amidst the confusion. "I'm assuming he had something to do with that mess?" she asked, her gaze shifting to me, implicating Henri in the disaster that had unfolded.

"That assumption would be correct," I admitted, a mix of resignation and a flicker of amusement in my voice. There was a strange comfort in knowing Glenda had witnessed firsthand the tempestuous nature of Henri's relationship with food before the situation had all turned to shit. "He's sulking in his bed now."

"Not quite." Glenda's laughter, bright and unguarded, cut through the tension as she pointed towards the tent, where Henri, true to form, had attempted to follow Duke but had given up, opting instead to linger near the entrance.

I sent Henri one last look of mild reproof before turning my attention to the strangers. "Hi, I'm Jamie," I offered, the greeting one of obligation rather than desire.

"Ahh, Luke's partner," the woman responded, her voice tinged with a recognition that felt too informed for comfort. "Yep," I confirmed, my mind racing with questions about how much she knew about me and why. It was unsettling, the idea that my life had become an open book to strangers through Luke's narratives.

"This is Karen and her husband, Chris," Glenda interjected, providing names to the faces. *Karen...* the name flickered through my memory, brushing against a conversation or mention in the past. "Bus friend, Karen?" I ventured, seeking clarity amidst the fog of surprise encounters.

"Yes," Karen replied, her chuckle soft but carrying a warmth that belied the awkwardness of our meeting location.

"That'd be me." There was an ease in her admission, a shared joke between us that momentarily bridged the gap of unfamiliarity.

"I'd normally say nice to meet you, but this is hardly a fun place to meet in," I said, my words blunt, stripped of the usual pleasantries. It wasn't the time for niceties, not with the backdrop of our current situation painting every interaction in shades of survival and tension.

"Do you mind if Chris and I take a moment for a quick chat, just us?" Karen's request, though polite, sent a ripple of discomfort through me. The way her gaze shifted, seeking an unspoken agreement from Glenda and me, only heightened the sense of intrusion into our already strained existence.

"Sure," Glenda agreed, her suggestion of the river behind the tents as a setting for their conversation carrying a hint of encouragement for them to take their leave. "Thanks, Glenda," Karen acknowledged, quickly taking the lead as she guided Chris away, leaving Glenda and me to ponder the brief interaction.

As they disappeared, I shared a look with Glenda, a mutual understanding that required no words. With a nonchalant shrug, I signalled my readiness to move past this interruption. *I've better things to be doing than deal with these weird new people.* The sentiment, though unsaid, hung heavily in the air between us.

The sudden interruption from Glenda halted me mid-step, a sharp contrast to the direction my thoughts had been taking me. Her voice, tinged with urgency, cut through the air, "Wait! Do you hear that?" Instinctively, I stopped, my body going still as I strained my ears, the atmosphere around us suddenly charged with anticipation.

Slowly, I turned, my movements deliberate, as I tried to pinpoint the origin of the sound that had caught Glenda's attention. My face contorted in concentration, I listened, the faint but unmistakable hum of an engine floating through the air. "Engine?" I voiced the question more to myself than anyone else, stepping forward as if being drawn by the sound itself.

"It definitely sounds like a vehicle," Glenda confirmed, her voice carrying a mix of disbelief and concern.

"That's impossible... Isn't it?" The words barely left my lips before a wave of incredulity washed over me. The notion that anyone else could be out here, in this vast and unforgiving wilderness, seemed as absurd as it was alarming.

"Shit," Glenda whispered, her eyes scanning our surroundings with a newfound wariness. "We should arm ourselves." The seriousness with which she spoke, the suggestion so sharp and unexpected, left me momentarily dumbfounded.

"Huh?" My disbelief was evident, my gaze fixed on Glenda as if trying to discern if the stress had finally gotten to her. The thought of us, armed and bracing for an unknown threat, seemed like a scene plucked from a far-fetched survival drama.

"Quickly," she urged, her grip on my arm pulling me back to the present, her insistence brooking no argument.

As I stood, somewhat dazed by the turn of events, I watched Glenda assess our impromptu arsenal with a seriousness that bordered on comical. She dismissed the log she initially picked up with a mutter of "No, too heavy," a decision that only added to my growing belief that the situation had veered into the realms of the absurd.

My bemusement grew as I watched her, the doctor, the rational one among us, seemingly embracing the moment's madness. When she triumphantly picked up the upturned frying pan, presenting it as her weapon of choice, I couldn't contain the grin that spread across my face. "It's only Paul and Kain!" I declared, recognising Kain's ute as it breached the hill.

"Oh, it is?" Glenda's response, a mix of relief and embarrassment, was almost drowned out by the sound of the ute making its final approach, its arrival kicking up clouds of sandy dust as it struggled towards us. The vehicle's dramatic entrance, culminating in a screech that seemed to announce the end of the ordeal, was a fitting conclusion to the brief, albeit intense, moment of panic.

As Glenda stood, brushing herself off and peering into the distance at the now stationary ute, the absurdity of her brief foray into survivalist tactics hung in the air, a reminder of the fine line between caution and paranoia. The sight of familiar faces emerging from the vehicle, safe and sound, was a welcome return to our new normalcy.

The air was thick with dust and the aftermath of adrenaline as Kain's jubilant proclamation cut through the stillness. Their high-five, a symbol of their shared thrill, felt jarringly out of sync with the apprehensive mood that had settled over Glenda and me. Watching the dust settle on the ute, a testament to their recent escapade, I couldn't help but feel a disconnect from their excitement.

"Apart from clogging up the engine!" Paul's carefree laughter rang out.

"Where the hell did that come from?" My question, laced with incredulity, seemed to float unheard over the heads of the two adventurers. Their ability to find amusement in the situation was bewildering, a stark contrast to the constant vigilance that had consumed my thoughts.

"Come on," Kain responded, his dismissal of my concern—or perhaps his failure to even register it—echoing oddly in the open air. "You have to admit even that was fun."

"Guys!" Glenda's voice, sharp and commanding, sliced through the conversation, redirecting their attention. "We have two new guests."

As Karen stepped into view, her presence seemed to solidify the surreal nature of our current predicament. "I wouldn't call them guests. They're not going anywhere," I remarked, my voice carrying a flatness that reflected my reluctance to fully accept the situation. The term 'guests' implied a choice, a temporary arrangement, neither of which felt accurate under the circumstances.

The silence that followed was palpable, a collective holding of breath as the group processed the introduction of Karen and her companion into our midst. It was a moment of uncomfortable realisation, the acknowledgement of how quickly our circumstances could shift, introducing new variables into an already unpredictable equation.

"I'm Paul," said Paul, breaking the silence with a straightforward introduction. His voice, clear and devoid of the earlier mirth, seemed to signal a return to the necessity of the moment: to adapt, to accommodate, and to navigate the complexities of our ever-evolving situation.

As Chris Owen introduced himself, his handshake with Paul seemed like a formal ritual, an attempt to graft normalcy onto our far-from-normal situation. His thin hair and slight frame marked him as unassuming, yet there was a quiet strength in his demeanour that hinted at more beneath the surface. "And this is my wife, Karen," he added, paving the way for further introductions that felt overly ceremonious given the context.

Paul's courteous greeting to Karen, his hand outstretched, elicited an internal eye roll from me. *Oh, get on with it already would you, Mr Politeness. Your shit is boring me here!* My patience for pleasantries was wearing thin, a silent craving for straightforwardness over formality gnawing at me.

Kain, ever the follower in social niceties, introduced himself next, claiming his relation to me as Jamie's nephew. Karen's reaction, a spark of recognition at Kain's words, hinted at further pre-existing narrative shaped by Luke. It was a reminder of the interconnected web of relationships and histories that had drawn us all here, willingly or otherwise.

As the conversation unfolded, I found myself an involuntary spectator from under the tent's canopy, Henri's unexpected loyalty grounding me in the moment. Karen's admission that Luke had spoken of me over the years piqued my interest, despite my attempts to remain detached. The distinction she made between 'us' and Chris's subsequent confusion only added layers to the already complex dynamics at play.

"Not you, darling. Jane," Karen's clarification to Chris introduced yet another name into the conversation, expanding the circle of Luke's acquaintances and leaving us with more questions than answers. *Who's Jane?* The query hung in the air, unanswered, as Paul, as I had done moments earlier, labelled Karen dismissively as one of Luke's 'bus friends,' a term that now seemed to sit uncomfortably with her.

The absence of Luke, now highlighted by Kain's direct question, loomed large over us. Karen's succinct "He's not here" felt like the closing of a door, a finality that none of us were prepared to face. Glenda's reaction, her shoulders dropping in resignation, mirrored my own feelings of frustration and disappointment. The revelation that our gathering was the result of another of Luke's 'accidents' was hardly surprising, yet it did nothing to ease the sense of betrayal that flickered beneath my frustration.

Kain's muttered "Figures," though barely audible, resonated with a shared sentiment of disillusionment. It was a moment that crystallised the precariousness of our situation, the realisation that we were all, in some way, casualties of Luke's actions or inactions. The weight of this understanding, coupled with the introductions and revelations, painted a complex portrait of our group, bound together by circumstances none of us could have predicted or desired.

"Not to be rude, but what do you actually do?" Paul asked.

The question from Paul, seemingly simple, sparked an exchange that felt both enlightening and, to me, slightly irritating. My internal response to his inquiry was a sarcastic thought about bugs—Karen's apparent area of expertise. However, when Karen declared herself an entomologist with an unmistakable burst of pride, my stomach churned with a mix of disbelief and disdain. The pride in her voice, the way her face lit up, it all felt so out of place in our current predicament.

"A what?" Paul's confusion mirrored my own feelings, though for different reasons. His genuine lack of understanding seemed almost comical against Karen's enthusiasm.

"She studies bugs," Kain chimed in, a simplistic explanation that even he, my nephew, understood well enough. My quiet scoff at the exchange was lost amidst the unfolding conversation, a small rebellion against the absurdity of discussing academic distinctions in our situation.

"Insects," Karen corrected with a pointed glare towards Kain, emphasising the difference between bugs and insects as if it mattered here, in the vast barren nothingness, where survival seemed to hinge on far more primal concerns. Her insistence on the distinction irked me, a pointless pedantry in the face of our broader challenges.

Karen's explanation of her work, delivered with an air of self-importance, was a torrent of words that left me baffled. The mention of the University of Tasmania, ecosystems, and environmental protections felt like a distant reality, worlds away from the immediacy of our situation. Her talk of petitions and community work, while undoubtedly important in another context, seemed irrelevant and pretentious.

The disparity between Karen's world of insects and the raw, unfiltered reality of our survival here underscored the vast differences among us. It highlighted the absurdity of trying to maintain our former identities and professions in a place that cared little for such distinctions. As she spoke, I couldn't help but wonder at the utility of her expertise in our immediate circumstances, my mind grappling with the juxtaposition of her academic passion against the backdrop of our more pressing concerns for safety and cohesion.

Paul's enthusiasm in response to Karen's detailed explanation about her work with insects was infectious, even if I couldn't quite share in the excitement. But it was Chris's turn that really piqued my interest. His answer, simple and unadorned, cut through the academic jargon and lofty ideals. "I do yard work," he said, a statement so refreshingly straightforward it felt like a breath of fresh air.

"Yard work?" Kain echoed, the question hanging in the air like an invitation for further explanation. Chris's response, though silent, spoke volumes. Crouching down, he scooped up a handful of the ochre dust that had become a constant in our lives, its presence a gritty reminder of the environment that now surrounded us.

"It's everywhere!" Paul exclaimed, a statement of the obvious that somehow needed to be voiced. My own agreement came out as a muttered affirmation, "Fucking oath, it is." The dust, omnipresent and relentless, was a tangible symbol of the challenges we faced in adapting to this new reality.

Chris's calm acceptance of our situation, as he let the dust run through his fingers, struck a chord in me. His words, acknowledging the possibility of this place becoming 'our home', were met with a mix of admiration and incredulity from my side. The thought was unnerving, the idea of settling into a life here, far from everything familiar, seemed a concession I still wasn't ready to make.

In the midst of the dust and uncertainty, Karen's optimism struck a chord, albeit a discordant one for me. "Call me crazy. But I trust Luke," she said, her smile a testament to her unwavering faith in Luke, a faith that seemed both misplaced and naïve given our circumstances.

"You're definitely crazy then," I retorted, the words slipping out louder and more sneeringly than I intended for anybody else to hear. My patience, worn thin by the trials of our situation, had reached its limit. The idea of trusting Luke, after everything, seemed to me not just foolish but dangerously delusional.

Karen's reaction was immediate and visceral. Her posture stiffened, her gaze sharpening into a glare that cut through the tension between us. "A beautiful masterpiece starts with a single brushstroke. This is our blank canvas. Let's create a masterpiece together," she declared, her words heavy with challenge and conviction. Her belief in the potential for transformation, for something good to emerge from our chaos, was clear, yet it clashed violently with my own skepticism.

The silence that followed her proclamation was palpable, heavy with the weight of unspoken thoughts and judgments. I felt the eyes of the group on me, their scrutiny more oppressive than the desert heat. The silence hung in the air, thick and uncomfortable, a tangible barrier that seemed impossible to breach.

"I better check in with Joel," I found myself saying, the words a lifeline, an excuse to escape the intensity of the moment. My farewell, "Nice to meet you both," was delivered with a half-wave, a gesture that felt inadequate to bridge the chasm that had opened up between us.

Retreating into the tent, I sought refuge in the familiar, away from the complex web of relationships and expectations that had ensnared us all. The simple act of checking on Joel, of returning to a task that required no debate or persuasion, was a balm to the turmoil churning inside me.

❖

The weight of our situation hung heavily in the air as I stepped back into the tent, the gaze of Joel, searching my face for answers or perhaps reassurance that I couldn't fully provide. "Luke's latest fuck-up," I muttered, the words tasting bitter in my mouth, a summary of our predicament distilled into a moment of raw honesty between us.

Joel frowned, a small crease forming between his brows. It was a look that tugged at my heartstrings, a silent testament to the confusion and upheaval he'd been forced to endure. I sighed heavily. Settling down on the edge of the mattress, I noticed the plate of beans, and began to pick at the last few remaining, my appetite as lost as my sense of sanity. "I'm sorry," I told Joel, my voice laced with a mixture of regret and frustration. Several deep sighs followed, each one a feeble attempt to release the tension that had built up inside me. "We shouldn't be here. We should be…" My voice trailed off, the words too painful, too laden with the weight of unfulfilled promises.

The flap of the tent rustled, and Paul entered, breaking the fragile moment. "Sorry. Need to get some paper," he announced, disturbing the tentative peace. His presence felt like an intrusion, an unwanted reminder of the reality we were trying to escape, even if just for a moment. I eyed him suspiciously as he rummaged through a small bag of supplies, the frustration bubbling up inside me again. "Oh, and I need Joel's address too," he added, as if it were the most natural request in the world.

"What for?" I barked, unable to contain my irritation. The question came out harsher than I intended, fuelled by the helplessness that gnawed at my insides. Paul's interruption had thwarted my attempt to find solace in the quiet company of my son.

Paul turned to face me, his eyes narrowing slightly in a challenge. "So Luke can bring him some fresh clothes," he said flatly. Despite my initial resistance, the logic of his request seeped through my frustration. It was a reasonable ask, one born out of necessity rather than intrusion.

With a reluctant nod, I motioned for Paul to hand over the pen and paper. Turning to Joel, I asked, "Do you want to try writing?" There was a part of me that hoped this small task might offer him a sense of involvement.

"Yeah," Joel croaked, his voice raspy. I watched as he struggled to grip the pen, his fingers trembling slightly. I placed the paper before him, steadying it with one hand while I gently guided his with the other. There was something profoundly heart-wrenching about this simple act, a poignant reminder of the resilience and vulnerability wrapped up in his battered frame.

"Thanks," Paul said, collecting the paper once Joel had finished, his voice carrying a note of gratitude that felt genuine. "Should have it by the end of the day."

"Thanks," Joel echoed, lifting his gaze to meet Paul's. There was a flicker of something in his eyes, perhaps gratitude or maybe just the relief of having contributed in some small way.

"No worries," Paul replied, his demeanour softening as he turned to leave the tent. The flap closed behind him, leaving us enveloped in the quiet once more.

As the silence settled around us, I found myself reflecting on the exchange. There was a certain solace in the small act. It was a poignant reminder that, despite everything, we were still here, still fighting, still holding on.

DIRTY OPTIMISM

1338.208.1

"Glenda, grab the pole!" The urgency in my voice sliced through the air as I watched the far corner of the tent wobble precariously, threatening to collapse for the third time today. The stakes were set too loosely, the ropes too slack, and my patience was wearing thinner by the second.

"Yeah!" Glenda's response came back, tinged with a casualness that only deepened the frustration etching itself deeper into my features. Over the last half hour, my face had become a canvas of irritation, each minute adding a stroke of vexation.

After extricating myself from the awkwardness of greeting the unwelcome newcomers, Joel's droopy eyes and his gentle prodding had managed to draw me back out of the tent. I found myself wanting to do something productive, something that might momentarily distract me from the brewing storm of emotions inside. That's how I ended up outside, attempting to help Glenda and the Owens with the pitching of another tent. Yet, the task at hand was proving to be anything but a welcome distraction. The enjoyment I had hoped to find in the activity was non-existent, replaced by a growing sense of futility.

My frustration peaked as, with Glenda's absence, the neglected corner finally gave way. The tent's fabric billowed like a sail caught in a gust, the pole slipping from my grasp as if it had a will of its own. The weight of the canvas, now unmoored, dragged my section down too, the structure succumbing to gravity and collapsing in a heap. The sound of the fabric whispering its surrender to the earth was drowned out by my own huff of exasperation.

Marching around to the other side of the tent, where I presumed I'd find the distracted trio, my steps were heavy, each footfall a punctuation mark of my growing ire. The scene that greeted me did little to quell the storm brewing within. "What the fuck are you three doing?" The question burst from me.

"Come take a look at this," Glenda's voice cut through my brewing storm of irritation, her enthusiasm seemingly unmarred by the annoyance that I was quite sure was evident in my own tone. She beckoned me over with a gesture that spoke of discovery, of something worth abandoning my post at the failed tent for. With a heavy sigh, masking the remnants of my frustration, I trudged over, the dust kicking up around my boots with each step.

As I approached, the scene before me was an odd one: Glenda and Karen, huddled together in the dust, their attention fixed on the ground. It was a striking contrast to the abysmal failure of our camping setup. Bending slightly, I peered over their shoulders, my height giving me a clear view of the small green leaves that seemed almost alien against the barren, dusty backdrop of our surroundings. Despite the visual evidence, my brain was sluggish to accept what my eyes were seeing. The sight was so out of place, so unexpected, that for a moment, it refused to register. "What is that?" I found myself asking, my voice tinged with a mixture of curiosity and residual annoyance.

"They're coriander plants," Karen's response came, laced with a tone that felt like a cold draft in an already chilly room. Her voice carried an edge, a clear indicator of the mutual distaste that had somehow sprouted between us as unexpectedly as the coriander plants before us. *The feeling is mutual, bug lady,* I thought, the unvoiced nickname a testament to the strained dynamics that had taken root among us.

The revelation did little to quell the simmering heat of my frustration. "Did you bring those here?" The question escaped my lips before I could reel it in, its obviousness striking me a moment too late. It was clear that Karen must have been the one to introduce these seedlings into this dusty, lifeless world. Aside from the lagoon, we hadn't stumbled upon any sign of life since our arrival, making the presence of these plants all the more remarkable—and suspicious.

"In a manner of speaking, yes I did," Karen's reply was shrouded in ambiguity, her words leaving more questions than answers hanging in the air.

"In a manner of speaking?" I echoed, my frustration finding a new focus in her vagueness. The phrase irked me, her reluctance to provide a straightforward answer grating on my already frayed nerves. *Either you did, or you didn't, is all you have to say,* I thought, struggling to keep the irritation from seeping into my voice.

Karen's explanation unfolded before I could unleash the torrent of frustration brewing within me, her words painting a picture that seemed both implausible and fascinating. "We found soil below the hard crust that's hidden beneath all the dust and sand. A few seeds accidentally fell out of my pocket and landed in the soil." Her voice, calm and matter-of-fact, clashed with the turmoil in my mind.

"And look what happens," Glenda chimed in, her enthusiasm cutting through my skepticism. She plucked a seed from the zip-lock bag in Karen's grasp, demonstrating their discovery with a flourish that felt both hopeful and naïve. She pressed the seed into the dirt cradled in Chris's hands, a makeshift planter that seemed as likely to foster life as the barren landscape that surrounded us.

"My hands are getting a little tired," Chris complained, his voice carrying a hint of weariness. The tremble in his hands became visible, a silent testament to the strain of holding the fragile hope of new growth in his palms.

"Last time," Glenda reassured, her tone gentle yet insistent. Karen's hands slid beneath her husband's, providing a steadying support that seemed symbolic of their collective effort. Despite their actions, my skepticism refused to wane. I watched their display, a mix of disbelief and impatience simmering within me. My eyes rolled involuntarily, their earnestness bordering on folly in my eyes. *What fucking idiots,* I thought, unable to comprehend their faith in such a barren place. "Just because you've planted something, doesn't mean it's going to grow," I snapped, my voice laced with the sharp edge of my dwindling patience.

"Just watch. It's incredible," whispered Glenda, her voice a mixture of awe and conviction that I found both irritating and, against my better judgment, slightly infectious.

As my gaze shifted back to the scene unfolding in Chris's hands, my skepticism was met with a sight that defied logic. My eyes widened, disbelief coursing through me. The seed, under the watchful eyes of hope and desperation, began to crack open. Tiny roots, with a life force of their own, burrowed into the soil, anchoring themselves with a voracity that seemed impossible under the circumstances. A short stem pierced the air, reaching upward with an urgency that left me dumbfounded. The first tiny, delicate leaves unfurled with a swiftness that bordered on the miraculous.

Are my eyes deceiving me? Am I hallucinating? Questions swarmed my mind, each one more incredulous than the last. The reality before me was undeniable, yet it challenged every expectation of this lifeless world. *What the fuck just happened? It's a fucking seedling!* The sight was a blatant contradiction to the desolation that enveloped us, a beacon of life in a place I had resigned to be a tomb of hope. In that moment, the impossible became possible, and my world, once defined by dust and despair, was punctuated by the green of new growth.

"This is great news," Chris's voice broke through the awe-struck silence that had fallen over us, his eyes sweeping across the empty expanse of land that stretched out, seemingly endless and barren, around us. His optimism, in the face of our desolate surroundings, struck a new chord of hope, however faint.

"Perhaps this might help to explain Joel's condition," Glenda mused, her gaze lifting to meet mine. The suggestion hung in the air, a potential link between the miraculous growth we'd witnessed and the mysteries surrounding Joel's condition. It was a thought that had crossed my mind, the possibility that this strange, new world held more secrets than we'd imagined.

"I'm not sure that Joel was buried in the dirt," I blurted out, the words escaping my lips before I could clamp down on the skepticism that still gnawed at me. Despite the evidence of life from the soil, the leap to conclusions about Joel felt premature, a jump across a chasm of unknowns without a safety net.

"Maybe not. First it was the lagoon's water and now it's the soil. There is definitely something different about this place," Karen added, her voice tinged with a mixture of wonder and scientific curiosity. The acknowledgment of the lagoon's water, followed by the soil's unexpected fertility, painted a picture of a land teeming with hidden potential, a remarkable contrast to the desolation that met the eye.

"Chris and I will make the study of the soil our priority. It may be possible to get a controlled ecosystem up and running," Karen declared, her determination clear. The prospect of harnessing this newfound source of life, of turning the desolate into the bountiful, sparked a flicker of excitement within me, despite my best efforts to remain guarded.

"Hold up. Don't get too ahead of yourselves," Chris cautioned, his voice grounding. "We should still apply a great deal of caution. Sure, these plants are a great sign, but we still don't know what the conditions here are really like. You and I have been here for less than a day and the others not much longer. We have no idea what dangers we might be yet to face. Cracking the surface could release more than we realise." His words were a sobering reminder of our vulnerability, of the countless unknowns that lay in wait. The delicate balance between hope and caution felt more precarious than ever.

"With miracle soil like this, it can surely only get better from here," Glenda said, her excitement palpable. Her enthusiasm, while infectious, also served as a mirror to my own internal conflict.

My expression was a battleground of emotions, my mouth twisting into shapes that couldn't decide whether to convey skepticism or forced optimism. There was a part of me, perhaps the part still clinging to hope, that wanted to see these seedlings as a beacon of change, a sign that maybe, just maybe, we could carve out a semblance of life in this empty place. Yet, the cynic in me, the part that had seen too much suffering, felt the tightening of a knot in my gut, a silent herald warning me not to get carried away.

"I'm ready to paint that masterpiece with you, Karen," Glenda's voice broke through my reverie, her laugh brimming with an energetic enthusiasm that felt so alien to me at that moment. It was like a splash of cold water, or perhaps more accurately, a jolt that sent a ripple of discomfort through me. Her optimism, so raw and unguarded, clashed violently with the caution that had taken root in my psyche. The very sound of it made something inside me recoil, a visceral reaction to what my brain screamed was naivety.

As if on cue, the moment of dissonance was shattered by the sound of an engine roaring to life, a sound that was becoming familiar yet always served as a reminder of our tenuous connection to the world we'd left behind. All heads, previously locked in discussion, turned in unison towards the source of the interruption. Kain's ute had become a symbol of our survival, carting supplies from the Drop Zone back to camp, though not without its own set of challenges – the dust was a constant nemesis, threatening to clog its workings and leave us stranded.

"I'll go," I found myself saying, the words escaping me almost as a reflex. It was an excuse, a way to extricate myself from the suffocating optimism that seemed to permeate the air around Karen, Glenda, and Chris. My feet moved before I fully registered my decision, carrying me away from the trio whose visions of the future seemed painted in hues far too bright for my current state of mind.

BOGGED

1338.208.5

The monotonous scrape of my trowel against the freshly poured concrete, smoothing it into what I hoped would be a solid foundation for one of the sheds, was abruptly interrupted by a loud bark. It was a sound that instantly pulled my attention away from the grey expanse beneath my hands, a stark reminder that life, in all its unpredictable forms, was determined to make its presence felt in our makeshift settlement.

"Lois!" Glenda's voice, tinged with excitement, cut through the air as she jogged to greet the golden retriever making a dramatic entrance over the crest of the nearest hill. The dog bounded into camp with an energy and enthusiasm that seemed to light up the dusty landscape, a stark contrast to the grim task I was engaged in.

"Not another fucking dog," I mumbled under my breath, the frustration evident in my tone. The last thing we needed was another mouth to feed, another variable in the already complex equation of our survival. Reluctantly, I turned my focus back to the concrete, trying to lose myself in the physicality of the task, to block out the distractions that threatened to undermine the precarious sense of control I clung to.

"Lois, down!" Glenda's command snapped me out of my reverie. The firmness in her voice prompted me to lift my gaze, curiosity overriding my initial irritation. My body reacted before my mind fully processed the situation, propelling me towards Joel who stood outside the tent, an observer to the unfolding scene. I halted, my stride breaking as the scene before me unfolded into something unexpectedly tender.

Joel, with a cautiousness that spoke volumes of his gentle nature, crouched down and enveloped the golden fur in his arms, his fingers stroking the dog with a gentleness that seemed at odds with our harsh surroundings. "Seems she likes you," Glenda observed, her smile broad and filled with a warmth that momentarily pierced the veneer of my frustration.

Duke approached the pair with a curiosity that was both cautious and calculated. He circled around, his nose working overtime as he tried to make sense of this new addition to our camp. Lois, startled by Duke's sniffing, leapt backwards, her tail a blur of excited motion. It was a dance of introduction, of tentative steps towards understanding and acceptance.

Henri, ever the introvert, made a fleeting appearance, his curiosity piqued but quickly overshadowed by his preference for the familiar confines of his bed inside the tent. His brief venture into the fray was a reminder of the diverse personalities that made up our little community, each reacting in their own way to the newcomer.

As Lois jumped around, a bundle of playful energy, and Duke continued his cautious assessment, I found myself caught up in the moment. The frustration and skepticism that had clouded my thoughts gave way, if only briefly, to an appreciation for the simple joys that these animals brought into our lives.

"We need a road," Paul's voice boomed, slicing the tranquility as he trudged down the final slope into camp, his boots leaving deep impressions in the soft earth. The fatigue in his steps couldn't mask the determination in his voice

Lois dashed towards Paul with a zeal that belied her size. Her paws, a blur of motion, kicked up little clouds of dust as she closed the distance, nudging him in greeting, her tail wagging like a metronome set to the rhythm of pure joy. Paul crouched down, indulging Lois with the affection she sought.

Showing her quick reflexes, Glenda caught the keys Paul tossed in her direction with a graceful ease that made it seem as though time had momentarily slowed down. Paul, in response, crouched down to scratch Lois behind the ears, his actions softening the rugged lines of his face. "Ooh, you're a beautiful girl," he murmured affectionately, a generous smile playing on his lips as he massaged her ears.

"My car's here?" Glenda's voice, tinged with both surprise and a hint of skepticism, broke the brief silence that had fallen over us. She held up the keys, her gaze shifting from Paul to the direction from when he had arrived.

"Yeah," Paul replied, his attention still partly on Lois, who seemed more demanding of his affection by the second. "It's got bogged just over the hill."

Laughter bubbled up from Kain, a sound that seemed to momentarily lift the day's fatigue. "We definitely need a road," he chuckled, the humour in his voice sparking a flicker of amusement in my own chest.

Paul's eyes, however, flashed a warning as they met Kain's, his mirth quickly fading. "I wouldn't be laughing if I were you," he said, the glare sharp. "You wanna be the one to collect the stuff in it or dig it out of the dust?"

Glenda huffed, her frustration laced with a begrudging fondness for the chaos that was our camp life. "Honestly," she exclaimed, "this camp is like living with a bunch of children sometimes." With Lois and Duke now her willing followers, she began walking in the direction Paul had indicated, her determination clear in the set of her shoulders.

Paul and Kain exchanged looks, their expressions a mix of guilt and amusement, reminiscent of children caught in a mischievous act.

"I don't think she's got any children," I joked, unable to resist the urge to lighten the mood further.

"I heard that!" Glenda's voice, stern yet laced with the unspoken laughter, echoed back to us.

"Come on," Kain said, a nod towards Glenda's retreating figure urging us into action. "Let's get this car."

Taking a deep breath, I joined the pair as they followed Glenda.

"Hey, where are the new people?" Paul asked as the three of us walked.

"Karen and Chris?" Kain clarified.

"Yeah."

I found myself shrugging in response, an involuntary gesture that belied a mixture of indifference and frustration. After the struggle with the tent and the concerted effort on the concrete slabs, the absence of Karen and Chris from these tasks hadn't gone unnoticed. Their lack of participation had left a sour note, one that I wasn't keen to dwell on. "They've gone for a walk," Kain offered, his voice filling the space my shrug had left open.

"Oh, to the lagoon?" Paul's question, laced with a smile, seemed to aim at lightening the mood, yet it only served to underscore the divisions among us.

"Pretty sure..." Kain's voice faded as we reached the dust-covered charcoal BMW, an unusual symbol of our isolation and the challenges it presented. The car, under its layer of grime, hinted at a life far removed from our current reality. *Bet it's a nice car underneath all that shit,* I mused, my thoughts briefly veering away from the immediate concerns as I circled to inspect the bogged wheel.

"Fuck! You've done a good job, Paul," the words escaped me as I crouched beside the wheel, now buried beneath the earth. It was a statement tinged with irony.

"It all happened so quickly," Paul's defence came swiftly, a mix of embarrassment and justification in his tone.

"I bet it did," my reply was skeptical, an unspoken critique of Paul's capabilities, or perhaps more accurately, a reflection of my growing frustration with the situation as a whole. It wasn't just about the car or Paul's driving; it was the cumulative weight of our challenges, each small setback a reminder of the precariousness of our existence.

Kain's soft chuckle cut through the tension, a light-hearted interjection that momentarily lifted the heavy atmosphere. Glenda, ever practical, opened the passenger door, her actions shifting our focus from the problem at hand to the task of rectification.

The futile swipes at the dust encapsulating the wheel felt like a metaphor for our current predicament—every effort to advance seemed countered by the environment's relentless pushback. As I scrapped at the ground, the dust seemed almost sentient, immediately refilling any space I cleared. "Shit," I muttered, a mix of frustration and resignation lacing my voice, the word dissolving into the dusty air as quickly as my efforts to clear it.

"Think we can dig it out?" Kain's question, filled with a hopeful undertone, pulled me from my reverie of defeat. He crouched beside me, his presence a reminder of the solidarity that had become our most valuable resource in this challenging landscape.

"Not with our hands," I responded, casting a sidelong glance at him as I demonstrated the futility of our actions—a handful of dust slipping through my fingers, instantly replaced by more.

"Shovels then?" Kain's suggestion was a pivot to practicality, a move towards a solution rather than a surrender to the problem.

Inhaling deeply, I took a moment to weigh our limited options, the dust swirling around us as if mocking our deliberations. "Shovel might work. Probably the best we can do," I conceded, the prospect of using proper tools offering a sliver of hope in the midst of our sandy quagmire.

"I'll go grab them."

"Hang on," I interjected, my hand reaching out to grasp his arm, halting his departure. "Go check the Drop Zone first. The shovels we've been using are all covered in cement. Might make it a little more challenging for us." My words were a reminder of our situation's complexity, where even the tools we relied on could become obstacles in themselves due to the conditions we were working under.

"Sure," Kain replied, his nod quick and decisive as he rose, the determination in his movement indicative of his resolve. I watched him navigate the small rise that separated us from the Drop Zone, his figure momentarily silhouetted against the harsh backdrop of our environment.

As he disappeared from view, I brought myself to my feet, dusting off my hands, though the action did little to remove the fine layer of grit that clung to my skin. There wasn't much point in making further attempts to free the wheel until we had the right tools.

"Do you want to carry anything back now? Or wait to see if we can dig this car out?" I found myself asking Glenda, trying to plan our next steps. Her head was halfway through the passenger door, rummaging through the contents as if searching for a lifeline in the clutter.

"Hmm," she hummed thoughtfully, her voice a soft murmur that seemed almost too gentle for the harshness of our surroundings. "I'll take this one for now…" Her words trailed off, leaving her decision hanging in the air like the dust that surrounded us.

"Joel?" My attention snapped away from Glenda and towards the figure making his way towards us, his steps uncertain and his posture that of someone carrying more than just physical weight. My voice barely rose above a whisper, a mix of concern and disbelief colouring my tone.

"I'll check on him when I get back to camp," Glenda responded, her attention still partially on the items within the car.

Ignoring Glenda's comment, which seemed to miss the urgency of the moment, I found myself moving towards Joel with a haste born of concern. "Joel! What the hell are you doing here?" My voice carried a mix of worry and frustration, the sight of him so far from where I thought he should be—safe in camp—setting my nerves on edge.

"Help," Joel's voice was a croak. His plea was simple, yet it sent a jolt of panic through me.

Shit! My pulse raced, the immediate fear that Joel needed help threatening to overwhelm my senses. "You need help?" I asked, my voice rising in pitch as I gestured frantically for Glenda to come over.

Joel shook his head quickly, his response not what I expected. "Help," he repeated, softer this time, his hand pointing towards the bogged car. The realisation that he was offering help, not needing it, washed over me in a wave of relief mingled with apprehension.

"I don't think that's a good idea. You should be resting," I found myself saying, my hands instinctively moving to his shoulders in an attempt to guide him back towards the safety and comfort of camp. The protective urge was strong, wanting to shield him from any further strain.

"Here, take this," Glenda interjected, her voice cutting through my internal debate. She brushed past me, dismissing my concerns with a determined gesture as she handed Joel a pillow. "As long as you are careful, I think some movement will be beneficial." Her words were confident, a reassurance that perhaps I was being overly cautious.

With a pout marking my face, a silent protest to the unfolding situation, I turned back to Joel. "Are you sure you can manage?" The doubt in my voice was palpable, a reflection of my torn feelings. On one hand, I wanted to wrap him in cotton wool, to protect him from further harm. On the other, Glenda's confidence and Joel's silent nod stirred a reluctant acceptance within me.

I still harboured deep reservations about him being out of bed, the instinct to protect him clashing with the realisation that he needed to feel useful, to contribute in whatever way he could. *But if he feels like he is ready to move, why should I be the one to stop him?* This internal debate underscored a broader struggle we all faced in this new world—balancing the need for safety with the desire for autonomy, each of us navigating our own paths through the constant uncertainty.

The revelation of Glenda's violin nestled safely within its case on the car's bonnet struck a chord within me, a brief interlude amidst our bogged dilemma. "This must mean that Luke has spoken with Pierre!" Glenda's exclamation, filled with a mixture of hope and longing, momentarily shifted the atmosphere. The instrument, a tangible piece of her past life, seemed out of place against the backdrop of our makeshift existence.

"Your husband?" My question, while intuitive, was more an attempt to bridge the gap between the present and the memories that Glenda's violin had conjured.

"Yes," she confirmed, her voice carrying a blend of affection and sorrow. "I miss him terribly already."

"How does your violin imply that?" I found myself asking, genuinely puzzled at the leap from the presence of the violin to the conclusion that Pierre had been in contact.

"I highly doubt that Luke would have known to bring me my violin." Glenda's explanation hinted at connections and communications beyond my comprehension, a web of relationships that had persisted despite the distance and disruptions.

"You'd be surprised," I responded, half-jokingly. Luke's actions had long since defied any attempts at prediction. *Nothing Luke brings us would surprise me at this point,* I mused silently, a thought kept to myself as I contemplated the unpredictability that had come to define Luke.

The conversation shifted as Glenda secured her violin, her actions methodical, a brief respite from the uncertainty that loomed over us. "Where is Kain?" Her inquiry, seemingly mundane, was a pivot back to the immediate challenge we faced.

"He went to the Drop Zone to see if there are any more shovels so we can dig this fucking wheel out," I explained, the frustration of our situation briefly surfacing.

Glenda's practical mind quickly turned to logistics. "Aren't there shovels near the shed site?"

I couldn't help but grimace. "They're covered in cement." The admission felt like an indictment of our current state of disarray.

"How the hell did they get... never mind." Glenda's frustration mirrored my own, a shared sentiment that needed no further discussion. She shook her head, a gesture of resignation, and slung the strap of the violin case over her shoulder, ready to tackle the next obstacle.

Then Joel's voice, weak yet determined, cut through the tension. "Help," he croaked, his intention clear, waving the pillow to get my attention.

"Right. Of course," I agreed, my resolve firming. As I reached into the backseat, a small smile crept across my face, a reflection of the pride I felt for Joel. *Kate's raised a great lad.* The thought was a testament to the strength and character of Joel's mother, qualities that Joel himself had inherited in abundance.

Pulling a large suitcase from the car, I looked up at Joel, who waited patiently on the hill. In that moment, I found myself pondering the broader tapestry of our lives, the connections and relationships that had been altered or severed throughout life. *I wonder if she ever found someone else... Does Joel have someone else he calls Dad?*

VIBRATIONS

1338.208.6

The campfire's crackle became the evening's soundtrack, each log Kain tossed into the flames punctuating the night with bursts of light and warmth. Sparks danced upwards, as the gentle breeze wove smoke around us, encircling the small assembly of settlers like a shawl. The afternoon's efforts, spent wrestling Glenda's car from the stubborn grip of the earth, had drained me more than I was willing to admit. The growing collection of eclectic personalities around the camp hadn't helped, each new face adding complexity to an already challenging situation. Despite my weariness and growing aversion to the social intricacies of our little community, Joel's eagerness to be part of the evening's gathering had pulled me into the fold. Seeing him there, my son, settled on his log with an expectant look, reminded me that some things were more important than my own reluctance. His presence here, among friends and makeshift family, was a small but significant triumph.

"Chicken tikka?" The question came from Luke, who navigated the circle with an ease that seemed at odds with the precious cargo he carried—an assortment of Indian dishes, a rare takeaway treat. The convenience of takeaway, a luxury so distant from our current reality, somehow made these moments of shared meals even more poignant. It was a reminder of life beyond our camp, a connection to a world we were all struggling to remember and preserve. Luke's procurement of these dishes, a break from our usual self-prepared meals, had a special way of drawing us together, underlining the importance of shared experiences and the simple pleasures that could unite us, even here in the barren wilderness.

"Lois, sit!" The command from Glenda, aimed at the ever-enthusiastic retriever, momentarily pulled my attention away from the ongoing distribution of food. Lois's excitement, mirroring the energy of the group, was a bright spot in the evening. I missed Karen's reply to Luke's offer, but found that the specifics of who ate what mattered little to me. My thoughts were singular in focus: *As long as I get butter chicken.*

The disruption drew my attention downward to Duke, sprawled between my boots, a picture of complete exhaustion. The day had been an adventure for him, filled with the highs of making a new friend in Lois and the lows of realising he couldn't quite match her boundless energy. Initially, Duke's enthusiasm was palpable, his tail wagging a testament to the joy of newfound companionship. However, as the hours wore on, Lois's relentless vigour proved too much, and Duke, despite his valiant attempts, simply couldn't keep up. Now, he lay there, a furry testament to the day's endeavours, breathing softly in the warmth of the campfire's glow.

Henri, in contrast, seemed to have navigated the day's challenges with a different strategy. From a distance, his satisfied snort reached my ears, a sound that spoke volumes of his disposition towards the day's events. Unlike Duke, Henri had opted for seclusion, steering clear of Lois's enthusiastic overtures and the increasing bustle of camp life. His choice to remain aloof had paid off when, after moving his bed outside near the campfire, he located it with precision, settling into its familiar comfort with an almost audible sigh of relief. Henri's ability to find tranquility amidst the camp's liveliness, as long as his personal space remained inviolate, was a small victory in the constant flux of our shared space.

"And butter chicken for you," Luke's voice snapped me back to the present, the warmth of the plastic container in my hand bringing a smile to my face despite the day's fatigue. The sauce, rich and vibrant, escaped its confines, a streak of culinary comfort against the backdrop of our makeshift camp. My gratitude was a simple nod, the taste of the spiced tomato sauce a brief escape to a world less complicated than our own.

However, my brief moment of contentment was interrupted as I noticed Luke bypassing Joel. "Hey, what about Joel?" I found myself saying, sharper than intended, my protective instincts flaring as Luke paused, his expression one of genuine surprise.

"I'm sorry, I didn't realise he could eat," Luke's admission, though apologetic, struck a nerve. The thought that Joel's needs might be overlooked in such a basic way ignited a frustration in me that was hard to contain. "Of course, he can fucking eat!" My response, perhaps more forceful than necessary, was driven by a mix of concern for Joel and irritation at the oversight.

Luke's subsequent interaction with Joel, offering a choice of beef madras, did little to quell my irritation. Joel's hoarse acceptance of the offer was a small comfort, but the exchange left a bitter taste, one not even the butter chicken could dispel. As Luke moved on, my glare lingered, a silent challenge to the casual disregard that had momentarily threatened the sense of community that was developing. In this new world of ours, every gesture, every word, carried weight, and I found myself more vigilant than ever in ensuring that Joel was not left feeling marginalised.

❖

"Ahem," Paul's throat clearing sliced through the ambient sounds of the evening, his voice carrying that unmistakable tone of self-importance that set my teeth on edge. He plowed ahead, not bothering to wait for the murmured conversations around the fire to quieten, "I need everyone to check in at the Drop Zone regularly to see whether Luke has brought any of your belongings. Or perhaps there might be something there that you find you need." The suggestion, while practical on the surface, reeked of Paul's thinly veiled attempt to dodge the more physically demanding tasks around the camp. *Typical Paul*, I thought, my eyes rolling so hard I worried they might get stuck that way. The man seemed to have a talent for crafting policies that conveniently lightened his own load.

"That sounds reasonable enough," Chris's response was diplomatic, his willingness to see logic in Paul's proposal was a testament to his patient nature, but Karen's immediate retort was a spark ready to ignite.

"Reasonable?" Karen's voice was sharp, her glare at Chris almost palpable in the firelight. "It's a long way to walk just to check. I'm too busy to wander over to simply check." Her frustration mirrored my own sentiments exactly. The idea of trekking to the Drop Zone on the off chance that something of ours had arrived seemed like an unnecessary expenditure of energy we could ill afford.

"I'm with Karen on this one," I found myself saying, jumping into the fray with a sense of solidarity. The moment was ripe for opposition, and I was all too happy to lend my voice to the chorus of dissent. "Too busy." The words were out before I could weigh them, a knee-jerk reaction to Paul's suggestion and a reflection of my growing irritation with his attitude.

"Busy!" Paul's exclamation was incredulous, his tone bordering on scornful. "All you've done is sit in the tent for the past two days!" His accusation, aimed squarely at me, was a low blow, ignoring the myriad ways each of us contributed to the camp's survival, visible or not.

"Fuck off, Paul!" The words left my mouth with a venom I hadn't intended to unleash, but the frustration had been brewing for too long. The piece of chicken on my fork chose that moment to make its dramatic exit, tumbling into my lap as if to punctuate my anger. I growled, a guttural sound of annoyance, and with a flick of my wrist, sent the offending piece of food into the flames of the campfire. It was a small, petulant act, but it felt satisfying in the moment.

"Didn't you want to be responsible for managing the Drop Zone anyway?" Luke's question, laced with a subtle challenge, was directed at Paul, his sideways glance cutting through the tension like a knife.

"I'm happy to wander over. It'll be a nice break and good to see what's there," Chris chimed in, his voice carrying a hint of diplomatic neutrality.

My eyes couldn't help but roll again, a silent commentary on the situation. This time, however, I opted for silence, my thoughts loud enough in my own head without adding to the verbal fray.

"You make a good Drop Zone manager, Paul," Glenda's endorsement came with a genuine tone, her support for Paul casting a positive light on the proposed solution.

"Well, he is shit at building things," Kain's muttered observation, though barely above a whisper, didn't escape my ears. The candidness of his comment, a stark contrast to the more diplomatic exchanges, forced a smirk onto my face—an involuntary reaction to the blunt honesty that Kain brought to the table.

"I think our settlement has more chance of thriving if we each focus on our own strengths," Glenda continued, her gaze briefly meeting Kain's before he looked away, a silent acknowledgment of the truth in her words. Her suggestion was a call for specialisation, a reminder that our survival depended not just on effort, but on the effective allocation of skills and talents.

Glenda's attention turned back to Paul. "With Luke bringing supplies through so quickly now, perhaps it would be best if the Drop Zone had a dedicated Manager." Her proposal was logical, a structured approach to managing the lifeline that the Drop Zone represented for us all.

"Fine," Paul's agreement, though reluctant, was a concession to the collective will. "I'll be responsible for notifying people when things arrive for them and for keeping the Drop Zone in some sort of order."

"Marvellous," Karen's approval, succinct and without further comment, seemed to draw a line under the discussion. It was a begrudging acceptance of a new status quo, one that might just bring a semblance of order.

Paul's declaration cut through the lingering silence, his voice firm with resolve, "But... if I am going to be going back and forth so often, we need to do something about this bloody dust! We need to build a road." The suggestion, practical as it was, underscored the endless battle we faced against the elements. The dust was more than just a nuisance; it was a constant reminder of the harshness of our environment, a barrier to efficiency and comfort alike.

"Fair enough," Glenda's agreement came quickly, her pragmatic nature recognising the necessity of Paul's proposal. It was a rare moment of consensus, one that highlighted our collective desire for improvement, however incremental it might be.

"I can help with that," Chris chimed in, his hand shooting up with an eagerness that felt oddly out of place in the ruggedness of our surroundings. His gesture, reminiscent of a keen student in a classroom, elicited an involuntary scoff from me. *His weakness will get us all killed,* the thought echoed in my mind, a harsh judgment perhaps, but one born of the relentless pressure to survive.

"Yeah, I guess we could all pitch in," Kain added, his voice carrying a note of solidarity as he scanned the group, seeking agreement. His suggestion was a rallying call, an attempt to unify us in the face of yet another challenge.

My gaze, drifting away from the circle, found Joel just as he spoke three raspy words: "I'll help too." The readiness in his voice, fragile yet determined, almost propelled me into objection. The instinct to protect him, to shield him from the rigours of our reality, was nearly overwhelming. Yet, the glint of resolve in his eyes, illuminated by the campfire's dance, stayed my words. *This time.* The silent concession was a testament to my conflicting emotions—pride in Joel's courage mingled with an ever-present fear for his well-being.

In that moment, as the group began to coalesce around the idea of building a road, I was reminded of the delicate balance we navigated daily. Each decision, each task, bore weight beyond its immediate impact, shaping not just our physical surroundings but the very fabric of our community. And as we each grappled with our roles within this fledgling society, it was the unspoken bonds, the shared glances, and the moments of restraint that often spoke loudest, painting a portrait of resilience in the face of uncertainty.

❖

The swift descent of twilight brought a crisp chill to the air, transforming the campfire into a beacon of warmth and light for us, the new settlers in this unfamiliar land. The usual cacophony of post-dinner conversation, lively and unstructured, had been a constant backdrop to the evening. It was abruptly pierced by the haunting melody of a raspy voice, drifting towards us on the breeze. My eyes instinctively sought out Joel, the source of this unexpected serenade. Knowing the hurdles he had faced with his speech, the sound of him humming was both astonishing and deeply moving, sending an involuntary shiver through me.

The melody was elusive, a tune that felt both ancient and intimate, as if it were woven from the very fabric of our shared experiences. My mind raced to identify it, but the familiarity was just out of reach, like a memory dancing on the edge of consciousness. Then, as seamlessly as the hum had begun, it evolved into words—a simple verse that seemed to encapsulate our collective journey:

"Let us celebrate our story
The words we've yet to write."

The transformation of Joel's humming into song was a revelation. The lyrics, simple yet profound, resonated with a truth that touched something deep within me. Here we were, gathered around the fire, each of us bearing our own scars and stories, yet united by a common purpose. Joel's song, his voice finding strength and clarity in the moment, was a reminder of our resilience, of the hope that continued to drive us forward against all odds.

Glenda's sudden movement, a graceful rise from her seated position, momentarily halted Joel's song, drawing a hush over our small assembly. Yet, his attention never wavered from the mesmerising dance of the flames before him, as if the fire itself was a conduit for his newfound voice.

"Please, don't stop. You have a beautiful voice," Glenda encouraged, her words soft yet filled with a sincere admiration that seemed to bridge the distance between them. Joel's response was not through words but in action; without missing a beat, or even offering a sign that he'd acknowledged her praise, he began anew. His voice, once silenced by circumstance, now filled the night air with a hauntingly beautiful melody.

The interlude, while Glenda retrieved her violin, stretched long, filled with anticipation. Upon her return, the violin in her hands seemed less an instrument and more an extension of herself, a bridge between her soul and the rest of us. The initial notes she played, a bit hesitant and searching, quickly found their place beside Joel's humming, weaving together in a spontaneous duet that felt as old as time and as fresh as the moment it was created.

"You know this song?" Karen's question, born of curiosity and wonder, broke the spell momentarily. Her inquiry reflected the thoughts of us all, marvelling at the seamless unity of voice and string before us.

"Not until now," Glenda's response, delivered without cessation of her playing, hinted at the magic of the moment. Her ability to join Joel's tune so effortlessly spoke volumes of her talent and the universal language of music that knows no barriers. It was as if the melody had always existed, waiting for the right moment to be brought to life by their combined talents.

The musical exchange had ignited a spark of curiosity within me. *Was this melody a newfound creation from Joel's own mind?* The thought lingered as Luke, ever the attentive host, wove through our gathering, ensuring each of us had a drink in hand. My focus, however, remained intently on Joel as he wove his spell with the same haunting refrain, the words and melody echoing into the night:

"*Let us celebrate our story*
The words we've yet to write.
How we all wound up with glory
In the world we fought to right."

The song, with its poignant lyrics and melody, was a mystery; it resonated with a sense of familiarity yet was entirely unknown to me. Compelled by a surge of pride and affection for Joel, I reached out, placing my hand gently on his knee in a silent gesture of support and admiration. But the sensation that greeted me was unexpected—a palpable vibration that startled me into withdrawing my hand as if burned by the fire itself.

After a moment's hesitation, driven by a mix of concern and curiosity, I allowed my hand to drift back to Joel's knee. The vibration was undeniable, stronger than before, pulsating with an energy that seemed to defy explanation. It wasn't merely physical; it felt charged with something more, an unseen force that buzzed with the intensity of a hidden current. The sensation was bewildering, leaving me grappling with questions that had no immediate answers. *What the fuck could it be?*

"To Joel!" Luke's voice, robust and filled with warmth, cut through the haze of my contemplation like a beacon, prompting an instinctive reaction from those gathered around the fire. The chorus of voices that followed, a unified "To Joel!" resonated with a heartfelt fervour, their cheers scattering into the night, mingling with the void above.

My glance swept across the faces illuminated by the campfire's glow. Each member of our makeshift family appeared caught up in the moment, their attention fixed on the simple joy of celebrating one of our own. Yet, beneath the surface of my own cheer, a thread of perplexity wove through my thoughts, tethered to the strange sensation I'd encountered just moments before.

"To Joel," my voice added to the chorus, my attempt at enthusiasm tinged with an undercurrent of concern. Despite my efforts to immerse myself in the camaraderie, I couldn't shake the niggling suspicion that something extraordinary was at play. The vibration I had felt in Joel's leg, so distinct and yet inexplicable, had ceased as abruptly as it began, leaving a trail of questions in its wake.

4338.209

(28 July 2018)

GHOSTS OF DARKNESS

1338.209.1

"Duke, stop it," I hissed, my voice barely above a whisper as the dog's head, previously a comforting weight on my forearm, lifted. His ears perked, and a low growl rumbled from deep within his chest. The sound sent a shiver down my spine, not out of fear of Duke, but because of the uncharacteristic edge to his demeanour.

Beneath the makeshift blanket at my feet, Henri, ever the embodiment of routine, initiated his nightly dance. Turning in precise circles, pawing at the fabric with a meticulousness that bordered on ritualistic, he finally settled into a compact curl. His contented snorts filled the space between us, a sound that, under other circumstances, might have coaxed a smile from me.

"At least you're settled tonight, Henri," I murmured with a hint of envy. My fingers found Duke's soft head, stroking gently in an attempt to soothe his nerves—and perhaps my own. The gentle touch seemed to calm him momentarily, his body relaxing as he settled back down with a sigh.

I lay there in the darkness, the silence of the night punctuated by the occasional sound from Duke or Henri. I couldn't help but reflect on Duke's behaviour. He was normally the epitome of tranquility, a steadfast presence that only erupted into action when a possum dared to taunt him from the safety of the back fence. His sudden restlessness was out of character, and it echoed my own unease. I found myself listening intently for any sound that might have disturbed him, my mind racing with possibilities.

The tent felt charged, the air thick with anticipation. Duke's unease had become my own, a shared tension that seemed to hover just beneath the surface of the night's quiet. I tried to reassure myself that it was nothing, that the shadows didn't hide anything sinister, that Duke's instincts were just momentarily misfired. Yet, the seed of unease had been planted, growing roots that twined uncomfortably around my thoughts.

❖

Lois's bark pierced the stillness of the night, a sharp, urgent sound that cut through the silence outside the tent. Duke reacted instantly, his body tensing as he prepared to leap into action. I felt his muscles coil beneath his fur, a spring loaded with energy and readiness.

Thankfully, years of having to react quickly to his exuberant nature had honed my reflexes. My hands shot out, gripping him firmly before he could bolt and potentially wreak havoc. It was a testament to our bond that he paused, even if just for a moment, allowing me to maintain a tenuous control over the situation.

"What's going on?" The concern in Glenda's voice was evident, even through the fabric of the tent. Her question seemed to hang in the air.

"We don't know," came Paul's response from somewhere outside. His voice, usually so sure and steady, carried a hint of uncertainty this time.

"What's happening?" Joel's inquiry, tinged with sleepiness, drifted from the opposite side of the tent. It underscored the disruption to our night, pulling us all back from the edge of sleep into alertness.

My heart responded to the commotion, its rhythm picking up speed. It wasn't just the cold night air or the sudden activity that caused my pulse to race but the uncertainty of what lay beyond our canvas shelter. "I'm not sure," I admitted, the words barely masking the adrenaline beginning to course through my veins. Duke and I moved as one, a scramble of limbs and determination, as we rolled off the sleeping bag. The urgency of the situation lent speed to our movements, propelling us across the tent's confines toward Joel.

"Hold Duke. I'll go and find out," I directed, the command more of a plea as I entrusted Duke into Joel's arms. It was a moment of trust, a silent acknowledgment of the need for cooperation in the face of the unknown. Joel's hands, though hesitant from the abrupt awakening, wrapped securely around Duke, a physical barrier against the commotion that threatened to unfold.

As I made my way to the front flap, the coolness of the night air brushed against my skin, a noticeable contrast to the warmth that had enveloped us inside the tent. Pressing my face against the mesh, I peered into the near darkness, the outside world a blur of shadows and mystery. My eyes strained to adjust, seeking clarity in the dim light.

"It's getting stronger. We'd better get inside the tents," I overheard Luke's voice, tinged with urgency, cutting through the whistle of the wind that had begun to pick up pace. His words were like a cold splash of reality, bringing with them a sense of impending change.

A gust of wind shook the tent, its force a reminder of nature's untamed power. I turned back toward Joel, my heart rate picking up as I considered our situation. "I think it's just an approaching dust storm," I said, trying to keep my voice steady. The words barely masked the fear that clutched at my chest—a fear rooted in a memory so vivid, it felt like it was happening all over again. The disastrous dust storm that had struck Paul and me our first night in Clivilius flashed through my mind, a chaotic swirl of fear and helplessness.

"Come, Lois," Glenda's voice, both calm and authoritative, cut through my spiralling thoughts. Her command to the dog, whose deep growls had been a constant undercurrent of tension, added a layer of immediacy to the situation.

Suddenly, a gasp pierced the stillness of the night, snapping me back to the present. It was followed by the sound of scampering paws, a familiar sensation as Duke's soft fur brushed against my leg in his haste. The bond we shared, typically a source of comfort, now fuelled my panic as he darted away.

"Duke! Get back here!" I yelled, the fear for his safety propelling me through the tent's flap in a desperate attempt to catch him. My bare feet sank into the fine Clivilius dust, adrenaline pumping through my veins. The dust, a reminder of this place's ability to shift from beauty to menace, swirled around my ankles as I scrambled after Duke.

The abruptness of Luke's shout, "Shit!" had everyone's nerves jangling like alarm bells in the night. The word cut through the tension with an edge sharp enough to slice the thick air. I found myself instantly on high alert, my heart hammering against my ribcage as I hovered protectively over Duke at the front edge of the tent canopy. My hands were poised, ready to act, as I declared my hold over him, "I got him!"

But then Kain's voice, laced with an unmistakable edge of alarm, escalated the situation. "Shit! We're surrounded!" he yelled. Those words sent a chilling wave of fear coursing through my veins. *Surrounded?* The very thought sent a spiral of panic through my mind. *What the hell could we be surrounded by in this desolate landscape?*

A sudden fear gripped me, a visceral reaction that clenched my chest tight as if a bolt of lightning had struck me from within. My mind raced, trying to decipher the unseen threat lurking in the darkness around us.

"What's going on?" The panic in Karen's voice was palpable as she and Chris emerged from their tent, their forms shadowy figures against the backdrop of the night. Their appearance, marked by confusion and concern, mirrored the collective apprehension that had taken hold of our group.

"I think it's just a dust—" Paul started, his voice trailing off mid-sentence. The reason for his abrupt halt became glaringly apparent to all of us in that moment. It wasn't just the encroaching peril we had assumed. The faint glow of the Portal's bright, rainbow colours briefly illuminating the dunes in the distance before disappearing cast a new layer of mystery and dread over our predicament. The Portal's presence, with its kaleidoscope of colours dancing across the desert, transformed our understanding of the situation in an instant.

"Is that Luke?" Karen's question, filled with a mix of hope and confusion, cut through the tension.

"I'm right here," Luke's response, close and clear, sent another shudder through me. His voice, though meant to reassure, only heightened the surreal nature of our circumstances. The realisation that we were potentially facing something far beyond a mere dust storm or the natural dangers of the desert was unsettling. The brief appearance of the Portal's colours in the distance, a phenomenon both beautiful and ominous, suggested that we were on the cusp of something unknown.

In that moment, a mix of fear, curiosity, and a profound sense of vulnerability washed over me. The night, once a canvas of predictable risks, had morphed into a scene of unpredictable possibilities. The darkness around us seemed to pulsate with unseen energies, and the silence was filled with the weight of our collective anticipation.

"Duke, stop barking!" The words tumbled from my lips more as a plea than a command, my voice barely rising over the cacophony of the night. Duke, with his body a bundle of nervous energy, seemed to vibrate with urgency, his writhing intensifying as if he was trying to communicate the depth of the danger we were in.

Then, cutting through the tumult, Lois's low growl was abruptly overshadowed by a chilling scream—a sound so harrowing it seemed to freeze the very air around us. The terror it instilled was instantaneous, a visceral shockwave that reverberated through the camp, igniting a pandemonium that sent bodies scattering in every direction. It was as if the scream had not only shattered the night's false calm but had also signalled the unravelling of our collective sense of security.

In the ensuing chaos, my attention was momentarily captured by the sight of my companions scattering, their forms shadows against the night, driven by primal instinct to flee. It was in this moment of distracted horror that Duke seized his chance, slipping from my grasp with a desperation that matched the intensity of the night.

"Duke!" My voice was a mixture of desperation and command, a futile attempt to reclaim control as I swiped at the air where he had just been. But it was too late; he was already melding into the darkness that enveloped us.

With determination fuelling my steps, I plunged into the night after him, the wind rising around me as if to challenge my pursuit. The fine dust kicked up by the storm stung my face, each particle a tiny needle against my skin, blurring my vision and threatening to overwhelm my resolve. Yet, the faint sensation of Duke's fur brushing against my fingertips reignited my hope, a brief contact that was as frustrating as it was encouraging. He was close, tantalisingly so, yet as elusive as a shadow in the tumultuous night.

My heart pounded in my chest, each beat a drum driving me forward through the darkness. The fear for Duke's safety mingled with the adrenaline of the chase, creating a cocktail of emotions that sharpened my focus. The world had narrowed to this singular purpose—retrieving Duke, my loyal companion, from the clutches of the night and whatever horrors it might hold.

The realisation that I was alone, save for the fleeting presence of Duke, in this vast, tumultuous darkness, pressed in on me from all sides. The storm, with its howling winds and biting dust, seemed a living entity, an adversary that I had to navigate in my desperate search. And above all, the eerie scream that had set this perilous dance into motion lingered in my mind, a haunting melody that underscored the urgency of my quest.

Moments later, Duke let out a yelp that cut through the tumult of the night, freezing me in my tracks. The sound was so raw, so filled with terror, that it sent a deathly cold shiver down my spine. It was a sound that dredged up a memory I had hoped to never relive—the only other time I had heard Duke cry out in such agony.

He had been just a puppy, full of life and oblivious to the dangers around him. One evening, caught up in the excitement of being underfoot in the kitchen, he found himself in the most unfortunate of spots at the worst possible time. The incident with the roasting bag, a mundane moment turned traumatic, flashed before my eyes. The bag, containing the freshly cooked chicken, had burst as it made its journey from the baking tray to the serving dish. Several drops of scalding fat and juices had rained down on Duke's back, a momentary lapse that led to immediate panic.

The memory of Luke and I, united in our frantic dash to the laundry sink, was as vivid as if it were happening all over again. It was perhaps the most unified effort of our relationship, a moment where nothing else mattered but the wellbeing of our beloved Duke. Plunging him into the cold water, we desperately tried to soothe the burn, to reverse the damage of those scorching droplets. We had been quick, but even the briefest contact of that heat with Duke's sensitive skin was too much. The memory of his cry, a sound of pure distress, had etched itself into my heart, a haunting reminder of how quickly joy can turn to despair.

Now, here in the darkness, Duke's yelp reignited those feelings of dread and helplessness. My mind raced, conjuring up the worst scenarios as I pressed on through the blinding dust storm. The fear for his safety was overwhelming, a tangible force that propelled me forward despite the stinging sand and raging wind.

The cold shiver that ran down my spine was more than a reaction to the chilling night air; it was the realisation of how vulnerable Duke was in this moment, and how desperate I was to reach him. The bond we shared, forged through moments of joy and pain, was a beacon in the tumultuous night, guiding me towards him. The thought of him in distress, possibly hurt and scared, fuelled my determination to find him, to protect him from whatever danger had elicited such a terrifying sound.

"Duke!" The scream tore from my lips with such intensity that it felt like it was scraping the back of my throat raw. The urgency of the situation, the sheer desperation to find Duke, lent a power to my voice that I scarcely recognised as my own.

In my frantic dash through the storm, I stumbled, the uneven ground betraying me. Falling to my hands and knees, I was engulfed by the dust, a gritty, choking cloud that invaded my mouth as I gasped for air. The fine particles seemed to fill my lungs, each cough a futile attempt to expel the invasive dust.

On all fours, I scrambled forward, my movements more instinctual than guided. My vision was obscured by the swirling sand, rendering my surroundings into a blur of indistinct shapes and shadows. The dim flickering of the campfire, once a beacon of warmth and safety, receded into the distance, growing smaller until it was little more than a pinprick of light in a sea of darkness.

"Duke!" I called out again, desperation lacing my voice, which now caught in my dry, dust-filled throat. The name of my lost companion was a plea cast into the void, a hope against hope that he would hear me and respond.

Suddenly, a cold hand gripped my wrist, halting my blind crawl through the darkness. Startled, I tried to pull away, but the grip was firm, unyielding. "Karen?" I asked, hopeful yet confused, feeling the brush of long hair against my bare chest—a familiar sensation, yet something was off.

"No," came the dry, unfamiliar voice of a woman, her tone devoid of any warmth I might have expected in such a dire situation. The realisation that I was face to face with a stranger in the midst of this mayhem sent a surge of fear through me, my heart pounding against my ribcage as if trying to escape the uncertainty that now gripped me.

Despite my attempts to pull away, to reclaim my autonomy in this bewildering encounter, the woman's grasp only tightened. It was clear she had a purpose, a reason for stopping me, though what that could be in the midst of a dust storm was beyond my comprehension.

"Take him," she said, her voice carrying a command that brooked no argument.

As the woman's firm grip on my wrist relaxed, I ceased my futile attempts to escape her hold and took the small, trembling form of the dog from her arms. "Duke?" The word was a whisper, laden with hope and fear as I stroked his head, desperately seeking the familiarity of his gaze in the oppressive darkness. My fingers trembled as they brushed against his fur, seeking any sign that the dog in my arms was indeed my Duke.

His breathing was shallow, each breath a struggle that tightened the grip of dread around my heart. "Duke, what's wrong?" I implored, my voice cracking under the weight of my growing fear. Then, a sensation I hadn't anticipated—warm liquid trailing down my forearm. My heart sank as the reality of the situation began to dawn on me. *Blood.* The realisation hit me with the force of a physical blow, sending my mind reeling as I grappled with the implications.

"We can't stay here," the woman's voice cut through my shock, her tone urgent yet composed, as she gripped my shoulder.

Rooted to the spot, my eyes blurred with tears, I could only stare down at Duke, my vision distorted by the pain and confusion that threatened to overwhelm me. Each blink was a battle against the stinging in my eyes, both from the dust and the tears that I fought to hold back.

"It's not safe," the woman reiterated, her voice cutting through the howling wind that seemed to protest our every moment. She tugged at my arm, her grip both reassuring and insistent, guiding me through the tempestuous night.

Half-walking, half-staggering under the burden of my emotions and the physical weight of Duke in my arms, I found myself alternating between navigating the uneven ground and casting frantic, worried glances at him. The feel of his shallow breaths against my arm was a constant reminder of the urgency of our situation.

As we approached the campfire, the reality I had been dreading began to materialise before my eyes. The warm, flickering glow of the fire, meant to be a source of comfort and safety, instead cast a harsh light on the grim reality. The blood that I had felt warm and sticky on my skin was now visibly painting my arms red, a stark contrast against the night, staining my chest with a vivid reminder of Duke's suffering.

"Help me!" The plea tore from my throat, raw and laden with desperation. It was more than a call for physical assistance; it was a cry that carried with it the weight of my fear, the depth of my concern for Duke, and the overwhelming sense of helplessness that had engulfed me since the moment I realised he was injured.

"Jamie! What's happened?" Karen's voice pierced the panic swirling within me, her words pulling me back to the present, to the dire reality we were facing.

My legs, once steadfast pillars of strength, suddenly felt as if they were made of nothing more substantial than jelly. The enormity of Duke's plight, the fear, the uncertainty, it all converged in a single moment, buckling my knees under the weight of our predicament. The ground seemed to rush up to meet me, a fall that felt both inevitable and symbolic of the collapse of hope.

"I've got you," Chris's voice was steady, a solid presence as his arms wrapped around me, preventing the fall. His quick reflexes and the warmth of his grasp provided a fleeting sense of stability.

As Karen gently took Duke from my trembling arms, the mysterious woman who had guided us back began to deliver a grim prognosis. "The creature's wounds are serious. He has lost a lot of blood," she said, her tone clinical. Karen's gasp was a sharp echo of my own heart sinking, a physical manifestation of the despair that clenched my chest.

The woman then turned to me, her gaze piercing through the fog of my despair. "There's nothing you can do for him now." Her words, meant to be a form of release, instead felt like a shackle, binding me to a reality I was desperate to escape from.

"Duke," I cried, the sound tearing from my throat as tears blazed hot trails down my cheeks. The physical act of breaking free from Chris's supportive embrace to retrieve Duke was both a defiance and a surrender. Wrapping him tightly in my arms, I whispered, "The lagoon," clinging to the thread of hope that perhaps, against all odds, salvation could be found there.

"It's too dangerous. What's out there will smell the blood and most certainly attack again," the woman cautioned, her words painting a vivid picture of the danger that lay in wait. "I can't protect you out there." Her refusal, while rooted in pragmatism, felt like another door slamming shut, leaving us cornered by fate.

The sudden commotion from the direction of the Portal ripped through the tension, a stark reminder that our ordeal was far from over. "Your friends need help," the woman stated, a call to action that seemed to galvanise her. In an instant, she was off, her movements fluid and determined, an arrow in one hand, a bow in the other, with the quiver bouncing on her back as she ran towards the new threat.

As the chaos of the moment swirled around us, a singular focus took hold of me. The river, with its whispered promises of healing, seemed like the only beacon of hope in a night shrouded in despair. Seizing this moment of distraction, I began my careful trek toward the river, each step a mixture of determination and dread.

"Jamie," Karen's voice, laced with urgency, broke through my resolve as her firm hand clasped my shoulder, compelling me to halt and face her. Her eyes, filled with fear, mirrored the turmoil churning within me. "There's no time," she implored.

"The river has healed before. It can heal again," I countered, my voice a blend of hope and defiance. The memory of past miracles, of the river's mysterious power, ignited a flicker of hope within me. Turning away from Karen's piercing gaze, I continued my journey to the riverbank behind the tents, driven by a desperate belief in the possibility of salvation.

"Then I'm coming with you," Chris declared, his presence suddenly at my side, a large makeshift fire torch in his hand casting light and shadows on our path.

In that moment, my mind was not on who accompanied me. The urgency of Duke's condition, the gaping wound that marred his belly, eclipsed all else. It was a wound so severe, so life-threatening, that only a miracle could mend it. Karen was right; there was nothing anyone could do for Duke now —not in the conventional sense.

The reminder that cut through the despair like a beacon of light: *Joel had no blood*. This recollection, this proof of the impossible made real, fortified my resolve. It was a reminder of the extraordinary, of the unexplainable healing powers that this alien landscape held. With each step toward the river, this memory became my mantra, giving me the strength to believe in the possibility of another Clivilius miracle.

The weight of Duke in my arms, the softness of his fur against my skin, and the steady beat of my heart mingling with the distant sound of the river all merged into a single, focused determination. The journey to the riverbank, though short in distance, felt like a passage through a threshold of hope and fear, where the possibility of healing lay just beyond reach, waiting to be summoned once more.

As we reached the riverbank, the night air heavy with an impending sense of both dread and hope, Karen's steady presence by my side was a silent pillar of strength. With her support, I carefully made my way into the river, the cool water a sharp contrast to the warmth of my skin, a physical manifestation of the crossing from despair into a fragile hope.

"It's okay, Duke," I whispered tenderly, lowering his injured body into the healing embrace of the river. "You'll be okay." The words were a prayer, a plea to the unseen forces of Clivilius that had offered miracles before. *Could they grant one more?*

The fire torch, held steadfast by Chris, cast a flickering light that danced in Duke's eyes, lending a momentary sparkle to his gaze that mirrored the tumult of emotions within me. "I'm so sorry I couldn't protect you, Duke," I sobbed, my voice breaking under the weight of my guilt and sorrow. My hand, moving beneath his head to rub his ear gently, was a gesture of comfort, a silent apology for the pain he endured. The tears that fell from my eyes, mingling with his blood-soaked fur, were the physical embodiment of my heartache.

Then, a small movement against my palm—a glimmer of hope, a sign that perhaps, just perhaps, the river's magic was stirring once more. A silent prayer of thanks whispered through my mind to Clivilius, a moment of gratitude for the grace I believed was about to unfold.

A rough tongue against my wrist, a simple act of affection from Duke, brought a soft smile through my tears. I looked into his eyes, seeing there a reflection of all the love and trust that had defined our bond. Leaning in, I placed a gentle kiss on his head, a gesture of love and a silent promise that I was here, with him, no matter what.

But then, the unthinkable. Duke's shallow breath halted, his eyes slowly closed, and with them, a part of me shuttered. "No, Duke! No!" My cry was a raw expression of agony, a refusal to accept what my heart already knew. I shook his head gently, desperately willing him to wake, to come back from the brink.

The water around us erupted into chaos as Chris's firm hands wrapped around my shoulders, a futile attempt to offer solace. Karen's presence, her form blurred through my tears, became the bearer of the unbearable truth. Her words, though spoken in a frenzy, carried a finality that split my world in two. "I'm sorry, Jamie. Duke's gone."

In that moment, the profound grief that gripped me seemed to open the gates to a realm where the river itself whispered of solace, its waters gently beckoning me away from the piercing reality of Duke's loss. The darkness of my sorrow, thick and all-encompassing, wrapped around me like a shroud, pulling me deeper into its embrace. I allowed myself to sink beneath the surface, surrendering to the river's cold caress, where the cacophony of the world above was silenced, and the sharp edges of my pain were dulled.

Here, in the depths of this aqueous sanctuary, I found myself adrift with the ghosts of darkness, where the echoes of Duke's presence haunted the murky waters, a poignant reminder of the bond we shared, now severed by fate's cruel hand. The river, in its endless flow, became a refuge from the unbearable weight of a world without Duke.

VENGEANCE

1338.209.2

As the first rays of dawn began to breach the horizon, painting the sky in hues of gold and pink, I found myself locked in a silent battle to keep my eyelids from surrendering to the weight of exhaustion. My head, heavy with grief and weariness, bobbed perilously close to the realm of sleep, only to jerk back into the harsh light of reality. For hours, I had remained a sentinel by the riverbank, my legs submerged in the cool embrace of the water, while I held Duke close to my chest.

Henri, ever the faithful brother, sat quietly beside us. His occasional nudges against Duke's lifeless form and the tender kisses he placed on his older brother's head were acts of mourning that should have twisted my heart with sorrow. Yet, I found myself ensnared in a cocoon of numbness, a void where pain should have dwelled but didn't. My emotions were a turbulent sea, yet in the eye of this storm was an unnerving calm, punctuated only by a deep-seated anger. Anger that the mystical forces of Clivilius, which I had so desperately believed in, had forsaken us in our hour of need.

The river, with its enigmatic powers that once stirred the waters of desire within me, now felt distant, its charms rendered ineffective against the fortress of apathy that grief had constructed around my soul. I was angry, not just at the cruel twist of fate that had claimed Duke, but at Clivilius itself for its silence, for its refusal to grant the miracle I so fiercely wanted. My pleas, my cries for healing, had dissipated into the night, unanswered, leaving me with nothing but the cold reality that Duke was truly gone.

The concept of his death was a jagged pill to swallow, its edges cutting deep as my mind rebelled against the notion, and my heart outright rejected it. Duke's absence was a chasm in my world, an emptiness that echoed with the remnants of our shared memories, each one a sharp reminder of what had been snatched away.

As I sat there, the dawn unfolding before me, a resolve began to crystallise amidst the shards of my broken heart. *Vengeance.* The word was a whisper in my mind, a vow that took root in the barren soil of my despair. If Clivilius had indeed turned its back on us, then I would not let this injustice stand unchallenged. For Duke, for the unbreakable bond we shared, I would find a way to make this right. The path forward was shrouded in uncertainty, the logistics of such a vow yet to be determined, but the conviction was as clear as the rising sun. There would be retribution for the pain, for the loss, for the betrayal. That much I knew with a certainty.

TORN ASUNDER

1338.209.3

As the camp slowly awakened, murmurs of life began to weave through the air, an incongruous backdrop to the tableau of grief that held me captive by the riverbank. People passed by, their footsteps hesitant, their glances filled with a mixture of curiosity and respect for the mourning that enshrouded me and Henri. We must have presented a picture of such desolation that it rendered them speechless, unwilling to breach the perimeter of our sorrow.

A new wave of anger, dark and potent, began to simmer within me as I sensed a familiar presence approaching. My body tensed instinctively, a physical manifestation of the storm of emotions that I was barely keeping at bay.

"Go away, Luke," I said, my voice a low growl, laden with warning. I didn't need to look up to know it was him; his presence, once a source of comfort, now a source of unwelcome intrusion.

Luke halted, a silent acknowledgment of the barrier I had erected with my words. The air hung heavy between us, charged with unspoken grief and regret, until Luke finally broke the silence. His voice, usually so steady, now cracked under the weight of emotions he struggled to contain.

"Jamie... I'm so..." His attempt at an apology was a spark to the powder keg of my rage.

"I said go away, Luke," I cut him off, my voice sharp, a clear edge of warning slicing through the morning air. The mere suggestion of his remorse was an insult, a mockery of the depth of my loss.

Yet, Luke dared to move closer, his actions defying my explicit command. As he crouched beside us, reaching out towards Duke, a visceral reaction surged through me.

"Fuck off, Luke!" The words exploded from me, a raw burst of anguish and accusation as I turned to confront him. My tears, a scalding testament to my pain, blurred my vision but not my anger. "This is all your fault. You don't fucking deserve to touch him. Ever!" My outburst was a detonation, sending Luke reeling backwards, a physical recoil from the force of my grief-stricken condemnation.

As Luke stumbled, the vulnerability on his face was laid bare, tears carving paths through the grime of a sleepless night. "I didn't mean for any of this to happen," he whispered, a plea for understanding in his eyes, seeking mine in a desperate bid for connection.

"It's too fucking late for sorry," I retorted, the bitterness in my voice a sharp lance, piercing any remnants of our shared past. I turned away, dismissing him with a finality as cold as the river that had refused to grant Duke salvation.

"Just fuck off, Luke. Please." The words left me deflated, my defiance crumbling into weary resignation. My voice cracked, a testament to the depth of my broken soul, as I bowed my head lower, surrendering once more to the solitary act of mourning. The silence that followed was a chasm, Luke's lingering gaze a weight I could feel even as I refused to meet it, a silent witness to the irrevocable rift that had formed between us.

❖

Why the fuck can't these people just leave us alone? The thought roared through my mind like a storm, as the sound of hesitant, approaching footsteps grated against my already frayed nerves. I yearned to unleash my fury upon the unwelcome visitor, to command them to vanish into the ether from whence they came. Yet, the sheer weight of my exhaustion anchored me in place, rendering me incapable of even lifting my head in defiance.

The footsteps decelerated, halting ominously close, accompanied by a loud, unmistakable gasp—a sound that pierced the heavy air with its resonance. *Beatrix?* The name flashed through my mind, igniting a fresh blaze of anger. *What the fuck are you doing, Luke? Wasn't the torment of losing Duke sufficient that you needed to drag Beatrix into this abyss as well?*

"Is he—" The whisper barely left Beatrix's lips, her voice fracturing under the weight of the question she couldn't bear to finish, as she collapsed to her knees beside me.

My gaze, blurred by tears that had turned my eyes red and swollen, shifted silently towards her. Despite the tumultuous sea of emotions raging within me, my hand persisted in its gentle journey across Duke's matted fur, a solitary act of devotion in the face of despair.

Then, without warning, Beatrix enveloped me in an embrace, her arms clamping around me with a desperation that seemed to draw from a well of sorrow as deep as my own. Her body trembled, her shoulders heaving with sobs that shattered her usually impenetrable façade, allowing her tears to flow freely.

In that moment, the barriers I had meticulously erected, brick by brick, crumbled under the weight of shared grief. Beatrix's embrace, unexpected yet unmistakably genuine, served as a poignant reminder that I was not alone in my mourning. The warmth of her grip, the dampness of her tears, bridged the chasm of isolation I had consigned myself to. Her sorrow, mingled with mine, wove a tapestry of shared loss, a silent acknowledgment of the depth of love we all bore for Duke.

For what felt like an eternity, I remained enveloped in Beatrix's embrace. As I noticed the jagged cuts marring her arm, evidence of her own nocturnal ordeal, a silent acknowledgment passed between us. Here we were, united not just by our grief for Duke but by our own scars, both visible and invisible.

When Beatrix finally released me, she did so with a measured reluctance, as if the physical distance would somehow sever the fragile connection we had forged in our moment of shared vulnerability. She shifted, her posture a blend of determination and sorrow, and reached out tentatively towards Duke. Her fingers brushed his fur with a gentleness that belied the ferocity of the emotions I knew churned within her.

With eyes that felt scalded by tears and the harsh light of reality, I fixed my gaze on Beatrix. "I'm going to get whatever did this," I declared, my voice a mix of raw grief and unyielding resolve. The promise was more than a vow of retribution; it was a pledge to Duke, to myself, to all of us who had loved him.

"Do you think it was a shadow panther?" Beatrix's inquiry broke through my thoughts, her voice carrying a mixture of fear and curiosity.

"A what?" Confusion furrowed my brow, the term foreign and yet laden with a sense of ominous significance.

"A shadow panther," she repeated, her hand absently rubbing the wounds on her arm, a grim souvenir from her encounter. "It's the creature that attacked me last night."

Before I could digest this new piece of the puzzle, another voice chimed in, its tone carrying an authority that demanded attention. "It wasn't a shadow panther," the voice asserted confidently.

Beatrix and I turned in unison towards the source, finding ourselves facing a new figure. "I'm Charity," the woman introduced herself.

"How do you know that it wasn't a shadow panther?" My question was laced with skepticism and a desperate need for answers.

Charity gestured towards Duke, seeking permission with a respectful, "May I?" Her cautious step forward was an intrusion into our circle of grief, yet something in her demeanour suggested she might hold the key to understanding the tragedy that had befallen us.

After a moment's hesitation, where every fibre of my being screamed against allowing anyone near Duke, I gave a reluctant nod. It was a concession driven by the hope that she might shed light on the darkness that had claimed my beloved friend.

Henri let out a low growl as Charity approached, but the loud clattering of pots near the campfire distracted his attention and his short, chubby legs took off. He stopped near the tent and looked back at us, as though he were checking for his brother or some sort of permission. And then he was gone.

I could feel my heart breaking all over again. Henri had never been the brightest of the two dogs. *Or of any dog I knew, really.* I couldn't help but let a half-smile crease my face, despite the heaviness in my heart. Henri, with his uncomplicated view of the world, had always been a source of unwitting comedy. He knew something was amiss with Duke, yet his instincts were overridden by the prospect of food—a testament to his singular priorities.

This bittersweet amusement brought back a memory, a lighter time when the most significant crisis was the overcooked roast that had filled our home with smoke and set off the smoke detector. Duke, ever the sensible one, had made a swift retreat to the safety of the back deck. Henri, true to form, had charged towards the source of his curiosity; a chicken in the oven, undeterred by the billowing smoke or the shrill alarm.

At least we know who would survive, Luke and I had laughed then, marvelling at Henri's unfailing ability to prioritise his stomach over his safety. The memory, so full of life and laughter, now felt like a relic from another era, its warmth overshadowed by the cold, harsh reality that lay before me.

Glancing down at Duke, motionless and forever silent, the weight of his absence pressed down on me with a gravity that threatened to crush the remnants of my spirit. The irony of those lighthearted jests about survival struck me with a cruel sharpness. Survival was no longer a laughing matter; it was a gaping, bleeding wound in my world that no amount of time or tears could ever hope to heal. The stark contrast between the vibrancy of life and the stillness of death lay heavily in my arms, a brutal reminder of the fragility of existence and the indiscriminate nature of fate. In this moment, surrounded by the remnants of our shattered normalcy, survival felt like an elusive, mocking ghost, haunting the edges of my grief-stricken consciousness.

As Charity squatted beside me, her proximity felt invasive. Yet, as she reached for Duke, a part of me understood the necessity of her actions. Reluctantly, I allowed her to move his body, exposing the underside where the fatal wound lay hidden beneath his fur. Her hands were gentle, yet purposeful, as she brushed aside the fur to reveal the truth I wasn't sure I was ready to face.

"See the edges around the wound?" Her voice was clinical, detached in a way that grated on my already frayed nerves. She didn't wait for my acknowledgment before continuing, "It's too clean to have been caused by any claw or tooth."

"Then what was it?" Beatrix's voice broke through the heavy air.

Charity's response was matter-of-fact, yet the implications of her words sent a chill down my spine. "Looking at the discolouration of the skin, my best guess is that it was an Okaledian dagger that killed the creature."

"Creature?" I couldn't hide the disgust in my voice, my heart recoiling at her callous phrasing. "His name is Duke." The need to defend Duke's memory, to assert his identity and importance, surged through me with a force that bordered on desperation. He was not just any creature; he was my companion, my friend, my family.

"You do know he is a dog, don't you?" Beatrix's interjection carried a hint of incredulity, a challenge to Charity's apparent ignorance. Her tone suggested disbelief that someone could be so disconnected, so unaware of what Duke represented to us.

Charity's response was a revelation in itself, her eyes narrowing as she continued her examination. "I've seen similar creatures... dogs, like yours, but nothing quite like it. Creatures like this aren't so common in Chewbathia." The name 'Chewbathia' was foreign, alien, hinting at a reality far removed from our own.

My head throbbed, each pulse amplifying the confusion and disbelief swirling within me. The revelation about Duke's death had unearthed a myriad of questions, leaving me grappling for answers in a situation that felt increasingly surreal.

"I feel like my brain suddenly has another dozen questions after that," Beatrix admitted, her voice laced with exhaustion as she rose to her feet, encapsulating the bewildering complexity of our predicament.

"So do I," I concurred, feeling the weight of our shared uncertainty. Duke's blood left a grim reminder on my forehead as I rubbed it absentmindedly. The most pressing question forced its way out, directed towards the newfound reality we faced. I looked between Beatrix and Charity, the tension palpable in the air. "But, if Duke was killed by a dagger," I paused, the gravity of the implications sinking in, "then who the fuck was wielding it?"

Beatrix gasped. "Do you think somebody in the camp killed Duke?" Her question, though whispered, echoed the enormity of our fears.

"Nobody that you know," Charity's cryptic answer added layers to the mystery, prompting a simultaneous demand for clarity from Beatrix and me.

"There's someone here that we don't know?" The realisation that we might not be alone, that an unknown threat could be lurking amongst us, sent a shiver down my spine.

"A Portal pirate," Paul's interjection announcing the arrival of his presence with an air of confidence.

"What the actual fuck?" The incredulity of the situation was overwhelming, my reaction a mirror of the disbelief that flickered in Beatrix's eyes.

Charity took it upon herself to elaborate on Paul's startling revelation, her explanation painting a vivid picture of our unseen adversary. "He's likely lost and been separated from his partner. Some danger must have befallen one of them before they could execute the location registration. They're always in pairs. Never work alone. Cunning and violent bastards when they're together. But alone, they can be brute savages. Their instinct for hunting and survival runs deep."

Each word from Charity's mouth added weight to the dread settling in my stomach. The idea of a Portal pirate, cunning and savage, as the architect of Duke's demise was a horror I hadn't anticipated. The reality that we were now entangled in a conflict far beyond our understanding, against foes whose very nature was predicated on violence and survival, was a concept too difficult to grasp.

Paul's words, tinged with a mix of excitement and gravity, cut through the dense air of grief surrounding us. "Charity managed to kill one of the beasts last night. It's at the camp if you want to see it." The enthusiasm in his voice seemed almost out of place, a formidable opposition to the sombre mood that had enveloped me.

I couldn't muster any desire to see the creature, my mind too entrenched in sorrow and the complexities of our current situation. "She wounded another and it appears, somehow, that a third shadow panther managed to follow Beatrix through the Portal to Earth." Paul's revelation spun my head around, igniting a fleeting spark of hope. The thought of leaving Clivilius, this place of loss and dangers untold, surged through me with a renewed intensity.

But Charity's words quenched that spark as quickly as it had flared. "It doesn't change anything for you," she said, her hand on my shoulder grounding me back to the harsh reality. "You'll never leave Clivilius alive." The finality in her statement felt like a physical blow.

"But I think Duke can," Paul suggested. "You could have Luke take him to be buried on Earth?" The mere thought of it —Duke being taken away, buried in a place I could not follow, and by Luke, no less—ignited a fierce anger within me. "Fuck no!" The words burst from me, raw and vehement. "It's not fair on Henri. Duke belongs here now. We'll find a suitable place to bury him here, today." My declaration was as much about preserving Duke's memory as it was about maintaining a semblance of control in a situation that felt increasingly beyond my grasp.

Paul, silenced by my outburst, nodded in acknowledgment, though I could sense the unease that lingered in the air.

Charity's blunt interjection shattered any illusions I might have harboured about laying Duke to rest in peace. "That's not possible to bury him," she stated. "You have no walls, no protection, burying him will only attract creatures much worse than shadow panthers and Portal pirates." Her words painted a grim picture, one where even in death, Duke could not find sanctuary.

"What do we do then?" Paul's tentative question hung in the air. Charity's answer, though practical, felt like a violation, an affront to Duke's memory and the life he had lived. "You'll need to cremate his body," she said, her voice carrying an unwelcome finality.

"Like fuck we will!" My response was visceral, a raw surge of defiance that propelled me to my feet, Duke cradled protectively in my arms. "Don't worry, Duke," I whispered, leaning in close to him. In that moment, my promise was not just words; it was a vow, a pledge that I would guard his memory, his legacy, with everything I had. "I won't let them destroy any trace that you ever existed."

Paul's voice broke through my resolve, his approach cautious yet determined. "Jamie," he said, his proximity a challenge to my stance, "we don't have a lot of options here." His gesture, inviting me to take in our surroundings, was meant to ground me in the reality of our predicament. But I couldn't, wouldn't, accept it. The acceptance of our vulnerability, of the unknown dangers that lay in wait, was a concession I was not ready to make. The very thought of it—of not knowing what a shadow panther even looked like—underscored the alienness of this world we were stranded in.

"No," my refusal was as much to Paul as it was to the situation, to the very idea of cremating Duke. "We're not burning Duke." My statement was final, a line drawn in the sand.

Glenda's voice, laced with panic, shattered the fragile calm. "Has anyone seen Joel this morning?" The crack in her sentence was like a mirror to my soul, fractured and splintering under the weight of continuous blows.

Beatrix's response, stating her presence with me, and Paul's assumption that Joel might still be resting, did nothing to quell the rising tide of anxiety. When Glenda confirmed the worst with a simple "No," it felt as though the ground beneath me had given way.

The physical toll of holding Duke, combined with this fresh wave of worry for Joel, overwhelmed me. My knees gave out, sending me crashing to the ground, a desperate attempt to maintain my grip on Duke the only thing preserving some semblance of control.

The collective cry of "Jamie!" as the others rushed to my aid was a distant echo, my focus narrowing to the pain that seemed to consume me from the inside out.

Squatting beside me, Glenda's quick directive for Paul to gather everyone at the campfire, barely registered as my world crumbled further.

Beatrix's introduction to Glenda, and the ensuing exchange, played out as if from another time and place. Glenda's determination to find something to wrap Duke in, her instruction for Beatrix to help me get cleaned up, felt like the motions of life continuing around me while I was stuck, frozen in grief and shock.

As Glenda and Charity departed, Beatrix's close proximity and her gentle encouragement, "Come on, let's get you clean," offered a sliver of warmth in the cold desolation that enveloped me. Her departure to fetch fresh clothes, leaving me with the instruction for Paul or Glenda to guide her, barely registered.

Turning my gaze back to the water, reflecting nothing of the turmoil within, I was acutely aware of the isolation that grief had woven around me. Despite the physical closeness of those around me, the chasm between my pain and their attempts to bridge it felt insurmountable. In that moment, the reality of our situation in Clivilius—the death of Duke and Joel missing—felt like a weight too heavy to bear.

❖

Emerging from the haze of grief, cleansed of Duke's blood and clad in the comfort of warm, clean clothes, I found myself kneeling beside him once more. The large bedsheet Beatrix had thoughtfully included with my clothes lay folded beside me, a final shroud for my fallen companion. With meticulous care, I spread the sheet on the ground, vigilant against the ever-present dust that sought to mar its pristine surface.

Lifting Duke, a task that felt both monumental and sacred, I placed him gently on the sheet. Each movement was a testament to the weight of the moment, the gravity of the act of laying someone to rest, even here, on alien soil. My hands, steady with purpose yet trembling with emotion, worked to wrap Duke, ensuring each fold of the sheet was both a caress and a guard against the world.

Tears, hot and relentless, threatened to breach the walls I had erected to contain them. The sting in my eyes was a reflection of the pain that clawed at my insides, a pain that seemed to grow with each fold of the fabric around Duke. I fought against their release, summoning every ounce of strength to keep them at bay. This moment demanded my composure, my respect for Duke, and my acknowledgment of his significance in my life.

Fold by slow fold, I swathed Duke in the sheet, each layer a tangible expression of my love, my loss, and my unwillingness to let go. With each tuck of the fabric, I whispered silent farewells, apologies, and promises of remembrance. This act, though solitary, felt laden with the weight of ceremony, a quiet defiance against the cruelty of fate that had claimed Duke's life.

As I completed the task, the finality of the act settled over me like a shroud. Duke, now enfolded within the sheet, seemed at peace. In that moment, wrapped tightly in my care, Duke was afforded a dignity in death that the harshness of Clivilius had denied him in life. Fighting back tears became a battle I was no longer sure I wanted to win, a battle that, perhaps, deserved to be lost in honour of the companion who had been so much more than just a pet. He was family, a part of my soul forever intertwined with his memory.

❖

As I made my way to the campfire, the lively conversation among the settlers dwindled to a hushed silence, their attention shifting towards me and the precious burden I carried. Wrapped snugly in my arms, Duke's presence was a sombre reminder of the loss we had all felt, yet my heart waged a relentless battle against the acceptance of his departure. The idea of leaving him behind was unbearable. My resolve to keep him close was a testament to the depth of our bond, unyielding even in the face of death.

"Jamie," Paul's voice, tinged with hesitance, cut through the quiet. "I know things are a bit painful right now, but we need to know when you last saw Joel." His question, a jarring reminder of another growing tragedy, momentarily anchored me back to a reality I had been drifting away from. The sharp pang of guilt for momentarily forgetting about Joel stung bitterly. "It was just before the attack last night," I found myself responding, the words heavy with regret. The realisation of my preoccupation with Duke, to the neglect of

Joel, was a self-rebuke that tasted of negligence. "He was in his bed in the tent when I took off after Duke."

Paul's next question was delivered with a delicacy that belied the weight of its implications. "And when you returned?" he probed, his inquiry a gentle nudge towards a truth I was reluctant to face. The guilt of not having been there for Joel, of not having ensured his safety, was a burden that rendered me speechless. My response was a silent, defeated shrug, the lifeless form of Duke in my arms a testament to the overwhelming loss that had consumed my attention.

Glenda's words, though spoken with a nervous tension that wrapped tight around her frame, resonated with a finality that brooked no argument. "Then it's settled," she declared, her crossed arms a barrier against the unsettling truth. "Joel is missing." Her statement, stark and devoid of ambiguity, laid bare the grim reality we were now forced to confront. Joel was missing—a fact that intertwined with the grief of losing Duke, compounding the agony of one loss with the frantic worry of another.

Charity's assertion of control was a beacon in the chaos that enveloped us, her declaration cutting through the fog of uncertainty with a sharp clarity. "I am certain Joel has been taken by the Portal pirate. I will hunt him down and bring Joel back." Her words were a lifeline, a promise of action in a moment plagued by fear and loss.

Compelled by a surge of determination, or perhaps desperation, I found my voice before I could weigh the implications of my decision. "I'm coming with you," I blurted out, the urgency of the situation rendering any hesitation irrelevant.

Charity's nod was an acknowledgment, a silent command to ready myself for what lay ahead. "Prepare your things. We leave immediately." Her directive left no room for doubt, propelling me towards a decision that felt both inevitable and impossible.

As I looked down at Duke, cradled in the bedsheet, a new wave of terror crashed over me. The realisation of the choice I faced—leaving Duke behind to save Joel—was a torment all its own. My heart raced as I grappled with the decision, every instinct in me rebelling against the notion of abandoning one for the other.

Charity's approach, her hand guiding my chin to meet her gaze, was a physical manifestation of the crossroads at which I stood. "If you want any chance of finding Joel alive, we must leave immediately." Her words, though spoken with resolve, felt like a vice around my heart.

The conflict within me was palpable, a storm of emotions that threatened to tear me apart. "I need to say farewell to Duke first," I managed to say, clinging to a sliver of hope that there might be a way to honour Duke's memory without forsaking Joel.

"Life is full of decisions and consequences, Jamie," Charity said, her gaze unwavering. "You need to make a choice: Joel or Duke." Her words, stark and unyielding, laid bare the brutal truth of our existence in Clivilius—a world where the luxury of mourning was a casualty of survival.

In that moment, the weight of the decision pressed down on me with an unbearable intensity. The choice between staying to mourn Duke, my loyal companion, and setting out to rescue Joel, my son, was a torment unlike any I had ever known. Charity's unrelenting stare was a silent challenge, a demand to confront the reality of our situation and make a choice that would define the path ahead.

Frozen by the gravity of the decision before me, every pair of eyes at the campfire seemed to bore into my very soul, awaiting my verdict. It was a moment that stretched into eternity, the weight of their gazes almost tangible in the air.

Finally, with a heavy heart, I gave Beatrix a nod, a silent signal that I had made my choice, though it felt more like a surrender than a decision.

Beatrix's approach was measured, her respect for the moment palpable. As she gently took Duke from my arms, a single tear traced its way down her cheek. "Duke knows you love him, Jamie. He won't ever forget that."

My lips quivered as tears breached the dams of my resolve, marking my cheeks with their warmth. Lowering my head, I bestowed upon Duke a final kiss, my voice barely a whisper as I bid him farewell. "I'm so sorry, Duke."

Gathering the shards of my resolve, I forced myself to face the path laid out before me. "I'll grab my things," I declared to Charity, meeting her gaze with a semblance of determination. My stride toward the tent was heavy, each step echoing the internal struggle I waged. A backward glance revealed the group, now drawn together in a tight cluster of shared sorrow and solidarity. Even Lois and Henri, sensing the shift in the air, had sought the comfort of the collective.

Pausing, I addressed the group, my voice carrying a blend of request and command. "Take good care of Henri for me." It was a plea for them to protect what remained of my heart in my absence.

Paul's response, "We'll keep him safe, Jamie. You have my word," was a beacon of hope in the dimming light of my spirit. His assurance, coupled with the action of embracing Henri, provided a momentary balm to my aching soul.

Inside the tent, my actions were mechanical, driven by necessity rather than thought. I packed swiftly, each item a reminder of the life I was momentarily leaving behind. The emotional tumult that threatened to overwhelm me was forcibly suppressed, pushed down to a place where it could not impede the task at hand. *Emotions,* I reminded myself with a harsh internal admonition, *were a luxury I could ill afford*. In Clivilius, they were a vulnerability that could prove fatal, not just to me, but to those I was striving to protect. With my belongings secured, I steeled myself for the journey ahead, the resolve to find Joel fortifying my step as I prepared to venture back into the unknown.

TO BE CONTINUED...

JAMIE GREYSON

Haunted by shadows of his past, Jamie Greyson navigates life with a guarded heart, his complex bond with Luke Smith teetering on the brink of collapse. When Jamie is thrust into a strange new world, every moment is a test, pushing him to confront not only the dangers that lurk in the unknown but also the demons of his own making. Jamie's quest for survival becomes a journey of redemption, where the chance for a new beginning is earned through courage, trust, and the willingness to face the truth of his own heart.

Dive into the captivating universe of Clivilius, and experience the vibrancy of a new civilisation. Embark on a mind-bending journey filled with mystery, drama, action, and romance.
Welcome to Clivilius—where creation meets infinity, and your new reality awaits.

CLIVILIUS
WHERE CREATION MEETS INFINITY

ISBN 978-1-4461-1352-3